Deep Blue Silence

Also by Pamela Johnson

Under Construction

'Irresistibly readable, with a striking storyline. Pamela Johnson writes with great feeling and wit' Helen Dunmore

'The slow, dizzying slide into love makes for compelling reading' James Friel

'Very well written, sensual, tactile first novel of more than usual promise' The Good Book Guide

Deep Blue Silence

PAMELA JOHNSON

SCEPTRE

First published in 2000 by Hodder and Stoughton
A division of Hodder Headline
A Sceptre book

10 9 8 7 6 5 4 3 2 1

This is a work of fiction. All characters in this publication are fictitious and any resemblance to real persons, living or dead, is purely coincidental.

A CIP catalogue record for this title is available from the British Library.

ISBN 0 340 71799 8

Typeset by Palimpsest Book Production Limited,
Polmont, Stirlingshire
Printed and bound in Great Britain by
Mackays of Chatham PLC, Chatham, Kent

Hodder and Stoughton
A division of Hodder Headline
338 Euston Road
London NW1 3BH

. . . art is described as being illuminating, and the rest of life as being dark . . . if there were a part of life dark enough to keep out of it a light from art, I would want to be in that darkness,
fumbling around if necessary, but alive . . .

Silence, John Cage

Family Album

Two little girls standing with their backs against a door.

It's sunny. The taller one squints, leans her head to one side, almost smiles. The smaller child stares hard, directly at the camera, despite the bright sunlight. No smile, mouth tightly shut and her arms stiff down either side of her tense little body. Her back is braced against the door. It's as if she's trying to push it open, escape, leave the picture; or, maybe she's trying to keep the door shut, hold back whatever lies behind. Is she going with gravity or resisting it?

I'd love to know what she sees. What's going on in the space behind her staring eyes? What memories are tucked tight beneath her woollen hat?

Both girls are wearing winter coats which they have outgrown; rough herringbone cloth tight across their chests, double-breasted, buttoned to the neck. Worn for more than one winter; two inches of skirt hangs below the hem of the taller girl's coat. The tightness of their coats makes them seem chubby, particularly the smaller child, yet each has skinny legs in knee-high socks, feet in the same round-toed shoes with a strap across the ankle. I imagine the layers of cloth held in beneath their too-small coats: vest, liberty bodice, dress, cardigan. Perhaps this is why the girls seem plump, because Faith has always been skinny as a bird.

I can't imagine Faith as a plump child.

The taller girl has a dark, straight fringe, but the hair of the smaller child is hidden beneath her hat. She has a deep, bare forehead. Both girls wear woollen hats which look like helmets, a strap fastens under the chin. Hand knitted. Perhaps Stella made these before she left, or after she went away. She might have sent them by post, carefully wrapped in brown paper, tied up with string, fastened with rust-red sealing wax. Maybe the smaller child looks cross because the hat makes her itch. See how potent even a child's knitted hat can be; the shape and texture of a story gathers around it. A story can also shape itself around what's left out. A story so closely guarded, never told, makes you wonder why. It grows, has many versions. Faith doesn't seem to understand this. I can't help it, the speculation creeps in even when I'm trying simply to describe what is in the photograph.

Two little girls standing with their backs against a door, in thick coats. It could be winter or early spring. This could be the front door of a house. The girls cover much of it; it's hard to say what kind of door. It might be a gate in the wall of a back yard.

On the brick wall, next to the smaller child, there is a cast shadow. I want to say, the shadow of a man. Man or woman, the shadow person is wearing trousers. Two distinct legs. He's not the photographer because his hands hang by his sides.

A shadow can't exist on its own.

This shadow is attached to someone. It has a positive; a real person, solid, three-dimensional, textured. Someone you could touch.

Frank.

I believe the shadow is Frank.

If so, it's the only image of him that I have, made because he blocked the light. The only evidence that he lived, apart from his name written on a marriage certificate and, of course, the glass.

I made a series of paintings from the evidence of this photograph, my first exhibition: *Family Album*. I know every grain of light and non-light, fixed by chemicals on to this paper. Grains of truth. I had copies of the picture made, square by square blown up: a shoe, a hand, a hat, two staring eyes, the shadow. I studied each detail for a time, leaving the prints pinned up in my studio. But the blow-ups only took me so far. If you look too much at the surface all you see is black and white dots. Once I started to paint I put the photographs away. I wanted to make the paintings from my memory of the image. The photograph recorded exactly what was in the frame at that split second. Painting gave me the freedom to explore what was not there.

Curiosity, memory, imagination made the paintings.

I worked on the series for three years but this photograph can still claim my attention. It's one of my few primary sources, evidence of Faith's history, of who she was before my living memory of her as my mother. A flat piece of paper, but to me it's three-dimensional. A dark place, momentarily exposed to the light. These are real people. The smaller child is recognisably Faith; saved, frozen at the click of a shutter. I know so little about this child. She stirs me, pulls me in deep, yet holds me away; both at the same time. In the turbulence the stories begin to tell themselves. I come back to the photograph, to remind myself that these are *stories*.

This happened: two little girls stood in front of a door to have their photographs taken, watched by another person.

One girl tried to smile. One girl scowled.

Click.

A cross little girl, a shadow and later, some broken glass. In between: silence. Silence so thick I can take it in my hands, paint it, mould it, piece it, trying to say in the work what hasn't been said in words.

Probably never will be said.

The whole story, the truth? No, that's not what I'm after. I've given up on the truth. A myth would do; a plausible myth based on the fragments, the grains of truth. I need this to hand on to my child. If there is to be a child. It's more than wanting to know where I come from; where am I going?

It's not the facts I'm after. The events, of which we must not speak, have almost become irrelevant. I've often thought that whatever led Faith and Irene to pose for this photograph might be nothing extraordinary at all.

Something and nothing.

It's the effects of not knowing, of living in the force-field of silence; this is what concerns me now. Faith's silence at the heart of the family was powerful. It held us apart, kept us together; companion stars trapped in orbit around a black hole.

Silence.

We came to depend upon it, an extra element. Vital as air.

Perhaps Faith really can't remember her past. Unlikely. How do you forget half a lifetime? No, there is a shadow across her memory.

From the grains of truth, the bits we do know, I need to conjure something I can depend upon; something more than a shadow, a black hole, a place where light can't reach.

One more thing. Turn the photograph over. The writing says: November 1930, Faith 6 years 11 months, Irene 8 years 9 months. The f, t, h and capital I with their long, loopy forms; I know this handwriting. Christmas and birthday cards throughout my childhood, until I was nineteen. Always a postal order tucked inside the card: *To my dear Madeleine with love from your Grandma Lilley*. She always signed herself: your Grandma Lilley. Letting me know, that whatever conspired to keep us apart, she was my Grandma. *Your Grandma Lilley*. A few words in faded ink. Vital marks, a trace of Stella.

Later, I learned that Grandma Lilley was Stella.

I met Stella three times.

Strictly speaking I met her twice, because the third time I met her she was dead.

Part One

In The Dark

'Don't you feel kinda spooky all alone here at night?' Hal asks.

'What's the matter with you? I was only gone five minutes,' I laugh and have to catch my breath, having run up from the cellar to the first floor. I can see that Hal's attention has wandered while I've been gone. He's stopped looking at the slides on our makeshift light-box. He's over by the window, pacing.

I don't use this room much, it's Annie and Jack's study, but it seemed a good place to lay out the slides; somewhere I can leave them over the next week without falling over them. I need to think carefully about the selection of images, move them around, make new configurations.

'Found them,' I say, waving the plastic wallet. These are slides of the paintings from my *Family Album* series, the ones Hal doesn't have. Now we have the full set. I lay them out with the others. The real light-box wasn't big enough, so we've rigged up a pane of glass which I found down below. One end of it rests on Annie's desk, the other on Jack's. One of Jack's books, *Tracking The Universe*, makes up the shortfall in height between the two. I've covered the glass with tracing paper to diffuse the light; two anglepoise lamps, their heads turned upwards, craning like a pair of herons, give us a wide enough beam to see my career at a glance. Twenty years.

'I'm not sure about a chronological arrangement,' I say. 'I mean, it's all around the same obsession. What goes around comes around. I'd say the new work I'm planning takes me right back to the ideas in *Family Album*. Even though it's twenty years apart, and isn't painting. I thought . . .'

'It's like you weren't here. Spooky.'

'Hal, come on. I was in the cellar.' He's restless now, his thoughts are elsewhere. It has been a long day.

'I mean it, Maddie. How do you sleep at night alone here? Aren't you scared?'

'No, not really.' Which is true, although sometimes when I'm up in the night, like I was last night, the dark places in this house can stir me.

'Most burglaries happen at night, while you're in bed. You have no alarm.'

'Stop it, Hal. Anyway, there's not much for them to steal here, the TV, video.'

'But think, people in your house while you sleep. You don't have a panic button by your bed?'

'What's the point in thinking about it until it happens?'

What scares me when I'm alone is what comes from inside not from outside, and I've learned about that, learned how not to press the panic button.

'It's big,' says Hal. He's only been here once before, last year just before Annie and Jack left for the States. They had a farewell do, I took Hal along, a real live American, a sort of preview to their new life. I tend to see Hal either at the gallery or at my studio. Sometimes I go round to his flat; four rooms in a basement in Holland Park, bars on all the windows. I can see why he'd hate to be here alone. This isn't my house, I'm housesitting. Annie and Jack bought this place fifteen years ago, before anyone wanted to live round here. When they moved in there were pigeons nesting where I now sleep. They've patched it up over the years, though there's still a suspect stain in the corner of my bedroom that seems to grow when it rains.

'I think Annie and Jack were burgled once so maybe we've been done. Anyway what burglar would bother to come up and find me asleep in the attic?'

'How's it going with Annie?'

'Spoke to her last week. It's not confirmed, but they're pretty sure Jack's project will get another year's funding.'

They will need the whole house when they return. They were a couple when they left, now they have two bonny babies. Clever of Annie to have twins, one of each. I could hear them squealing in the background when she phoned.

'So I won't be homeless in August. I'll have another year here, more perhaps; enough time to do the exhibition.'

The exhibition.

It's coming up fast now, which is why Hal has been here since lunchtime; we've had a marathon session sorting out the slides of all my work. Everything from my college degree show up to the present. There's to be a 'substantial publication'. That's what Jude said in her last letter. By which she means more than a pamphlet, not quite a book. Anyway, I'm going up to Liverpool next week to discuss it.

'I know what you mean about chronology,' says Hal, 'but I guess that at some point, since this is a survey, they're gonna want to lay it all out in a line.'

'It's not a line though, is it? It's a circle, or a spiral, up and down, round and round . . .'

'Hey, look, it's gone eight. I sure could use a drink,' says Hal. His concentration is finished.

'Do you want to eat?' I say.

'Sure. Takeaway? Thai?' Hal smiles.

'I can't be bothered to fetch it, can you?'

'Guess not.'

'I'll do pasta.' Now that food has been mentioned I realise I'm famished.

Down in the kitchen Hal sits at the table which occupies the centre of the room. Annie made the table from some old door, or was it a fence. She reclaimed the planks, pitted with bumps and marks, she stripped, sanded, waxed and then fixed them to the base of an old Sixties table she found in a skip. Annie has a way of making things look good on no money. She painted the splayed legs brick red. I miss Annie. We grew up together in Chester, came to London about the same time. We've sat at this table so often, laughed and told our secrets. She painted the cupboards in here yellow, they're filled with the pottery she's collected over the years. No two cups or plates are alike in this house.

'OK, so I'm a bit behind on the housework.' Hal's making a big deal of how the floor is tacky under foot. He fidgets the soles of his shoes on the chequered floor.

'Here, open this,' I say, handing him a bottle of red wine and a corkscrew. I fill a large pan with water, set it on the hob with the gas full on. While it comes up to boil, I lay two places at the table, then grate Parmesan into a bowl. Funny how it smells like sick but tastes so good, I love its saltiness.

I'm ravenous. I could eat the table.

The kitchen's the best place to be in this house. I don't spend much time here; I'm either in the studio or teaching at college. Most of the time I am here I'm asleep, way up in the attic. Burglars could be in and out and I wouldn't stir.

I did stir last night, but it wasn't burglars. It was this shifting ache, that I want to say is in my back, but it moves. It starts deep in my pelvis. I got out of bed, made my way to the bathroom in the dark. Didn't look at the clock, didn't switch on the lamp. It was deep night. Hands before me, feeling my way, feet careful on the stairs down to the bathroom on the floor below. Sitting on the toilet, even with the light switched off, I was not in the dark. I could see that the tissue was clear.

No blood.

Light from the moon spread through the frosted glass; a thin, cool brightness. A beam of light cast, it seemed, for my own convenience. Are we ever fully in the dark?

Definitely no blood.

I wiped a second and third time to make sure, mentally juggling the dates. There was enough light, even in the dark, to see that there was no blood.

Hal holds up the glass to the light, checks for cork, then hands it to me.

'Cheers,' I say. We sip red wine, watching the steam rise off the pan. When the water bubbles I drop handfuls of penne through the steam and a drizzle of olive oil.

'Pass me a bowl,' I say.

'Which one?' Hal moves towards the shelves cluttered with bowls and plates.

'You choose, something for the salad.'

Hal hands me a wide, shallow bowl, pure white. On a heap of salad leaves, I sprinkle chopped onions and cherry tomatoes.

'Want me to make a dressing?' says Hal.

'OK.'

He finds garlic, balsamic vinegar, olive oil. Hal would make someone a wonderful wife. Anyone looking in on us might mistake us for a happy couple. Whatever that might be. Hal carefully measuring the proportions of oil to vinegar, me stirring the pot. Except I'm about a foot taller than him. Exaggeration. Three inches. He's five-seven, and stoops, I call it his anxious stoop. I tease him sometimes and say if he were less anxious he'd be as tall as me.

'Have you given any thought to Berlin?'

'It's time away from the studio, Hal.'

'It's the summer festival, a great time to be there, and we'll pave the way for when we show in the autumn.' Hal's doing the new art fair in October for the first time. He's networking like mad, wants me to go with him to Berlin next month, to see and be seen.

'The art scene is shifting. In five years Berlin will be the centre of gravity in Europe, Maddie, you just go and show your face.' I've never yet learned to work out this tension between making the stuff and selling it. What's bothering me is the new work, the work that isn't made yet; it's still only an idea in my head. Two days in Berlin talking about work I made last year or the year before steals time from the new pieces.

'Studio time is what I need, but I'll think about it.'

'You were going to tell me about the new work.'

'I don't know.'

'Superstitious?'

'A bit. You know what it's like: the idea in my head seems perfect, I can see it. I could tell you about it, but that might make it not happen.'

'Only if you want to.' He shrugs. I know that shrug. What it really says is: tell me or I'll have a fucking tantrum. He knows I'm more likely to tell if I'm not pushed.

'Well, I'm going to use the glass.'

'Oh yeah?'

Hal knows the story of the glass.

Made by Frank. Broken by Faith.

My inheritance.

He knows what the stuff means for me. He nods, knows he'd better not push me now.

'Lighting it will be tricky. What are the art handlers like up at the MCA?'

'This is The Museum of Contemporary Art, Maddie, not some naff neighbourhood arts centre. Listen, it's a great team up there. They'll work with you. Anyway, what's with the lighting? What are we lighting?'

Now I shoot him a look that says: I'm telling it my way or not at all.

'Sorry,' he says, holding up his hands. 'By the way, how long?' He nods at the pasta.

'Five minutes.'

He puts the jug of salad dressing on the table, takes out tobacco, papers, stash and rolls up.

'I thought you'd given up.'

'Just one to sharpen the appetite. Want some?'

'No thanks.'

He leans back in the chair. 'Go on, you were saying.'

'All I know,' I say, 'is that the process has started. All I can tell you at the moment is the way my thoughts are going. It's starting to happen. It's exciting, but scary too.'

I've always known I would use the glass for this exhibition but I'm beginning to see how I can do it, things are beginning to connect. It's funny how the thoughts come, like last night when I couldn't sleep and I was thinking about the dark. The quality of darkness. I want this new piece somehow to be in total darkness. Well, maybe. I walked around the house checking how dark the darkest room would be at the darkest hour of the night. I wandered down through the house, not just the rooms I use, but the rooms filled with Annie and Jack's stuff. I'm living around the edges of their old life. I noticed, in my night wanderings, that it wasn't fully dark in any of the rooms, but especially at the back where there was moonlight. As I stood in the kitchen another kind of light suddenly beamed through the glass panel in the back door. It startled me, then I saw that a cat walking the fence, had triggered the infra-red beam on next door's outside light.

'I want to light this piece in some way so that the viewer triggers a beam, activates the light, you know, walks in and lights the space.'

'Sounds interesting but . . . but I'd kinda like to know more about what it's lighting up.'

'You'd think they would learn where the beams are, even though they can't be seen. Do you think cats like lighting up the night?' I'm hoping Hal takes off on this, he has four cats of his own. His children.

'That's it? You've had a great idea about how to light it, but what is it?'

'I'll come to that, but what I'm saying is it's strange the way ideas grow, you know, when I get involved in a piece the ideas come from the most unexpected places. I know I'm on to something.'

I won't tell him, even though I want to, that as I stood there in the bright light from next door, I looked down at my bare feet on the chequered lino and shivered. I was wearing the baggy T-shirt that Annie sent me for my birthday, white with an image of a steaming cup of cappuccino, below it the word *regular*. I won't tell him, yet, how I ran my hands around my middle as the ache seemed to be everywhere again, tightening like a belt around my back. I pulled the soft cloth of the T-shirt tight; my stomach was slightly swollen, the surface of the coffee cup bulged a little, the word stretched: r e g u l a r.

I would like to tell Hal, say it outside of my head. I could trust him. He wouldn't tell a soul. '*Entre nous*,' he'd say. 'Strictly *entre nous*.'

Hal would love the drama of it. Hal would love a baby.

'Anyway, I went right down to my space in the cellar.'

'You went down there alone at night?'

'Stop being such a baby.'

Baby. It's not a word I use.

It's getting dark, I pull the blind down to make the room cosy; its wooden slats rattle.

'Ready.' I drain the pasta, stir in tomato sauce from a jar. 'Let's eat. Afterwards I'll take you down to the cellar, if your nerves can stand it, and show you more.'

We sit facing each other, happy couple again. What a pair we are. He's in love with a boy half his age and I'm possibly pregnant by someone else's husband. At least Hal hasn't asked about Dom.

'What's with you and Dom these days?'

'Are you a mind reader?'

'What?'

'Nothing. Nothing new. Boring, boring. You tell me, tell me about Michael.'

'Gorgeous, I'm telling you. Gorgeous. Maddie, I'm in love.'

I want to say: Again? But that would be cruel. I couldn't be cruel to my dear Hal. Hal is practically family. He's more family to me than my real family.

Our feet clatter on the bare wooden steps as we go down below. I shift the blue velvet that's heaped on the old armchair.

'Sit there, I don't want you pacing,' I say. There isn't room in here. This is my thinking space, it's like having someone walk around inside my head. It's not my studio, but a space I cleared where I could make a mess in someone else's home. I can only work on a small scale, but it's good to have somewhere to go when ideas come in the night or when I don't want to spend a day at the studio. Sometimes I come down here without switching on the light. I don't mind the dimness while the ideas grow, like mushrooms pushing up through compost.

It's a sort of office too. My desk is a piece of fibreboard spanning two old filing cabinets. It's strewn with papers, notebooks, sketches and bits of broken glass. There are letters I must answer: invitations to lecture, queries from students. I don't like to take paperwork to my studio; being there means becoming absorbed in the work.

There is a small window down here and a door that doesn't open. The window and the door are covered with sketches and some of my research notes. When I stood here last night it was the darkest room in the house; but even then not fully dark, not cave or dungeon or deep-space dark. The orange street light leaked through the sketches, made my skin look green.

'I want an enclosed space, somewhere people have to walk into. Or maybe there could be some kind of window that invites you to look in on the space. It's still fluid. I want it to be a kind of visual drama.'

We talk about how I might achieve the darkness, how I might

line the space with velvet, or even raw pigment: Prussian blue, so that it's not only dark, but depthless.

'Is that the glass?' Hal turns the lip of a jug over in his hands.

'Some of it. Mind you don't cut yourself.'

'Research?' he says, pointing to the list I have written in large letters, pinned above the desk.

Glass is a poor conductor of heat.
Glass may be transparent or opaque.
Glass is neither a solid nor a liquid; it is amorphous.
Glass becomes rigid when cooled but may be heated back to a liquid.
Glass must cool slowly from its molten state,
otherwise internal stresses occur. It might crack.
Glass has a memory. It remembers the actions performed on it.

'It remembers; I like that,' says Hal.

I take a piece of the glass to show him how I want each fragment suspended.

'I must find the right thread,' I say. 'This wire is no good, you can see it, it distracts. I want each piece of glass floating in space.'

'This is knock-out stuff. Go with it.'

'That's what I'm trying to do. Studio time, Hal, studio time.'

'I have such a good feeling about this exhibition, Maddie, the Nationals will review it. Might even get some TV. It's going to put you on the international circuit.' He doesn't mention Berlin, but I know that's what he's thinking. I'm lucky to have Hal as a dealer. He's behind me and the work one hundred per cent whether it sells or not. He's shrewd, astute but he's also a friend. I've had solo exhibitions before but nothing this big; I can see why he wants to make the most of it.

'A mid-career survey,' is how Jude put it to me when she first rang. 'You have enough work now to look back, I'm interested to show the shifts in medium. You've worked in so many different media.' The Museum of Contemporary Art, Liverpool. Of course I would prefer it to be The Museum of Contemporary Art, London but they want to make something of my regional connections. I taught at the art college in Liverpool after I graduated, and I was born in Chester. Hal thinks the MCA show will make me more collectable. A major show in a top public gallery with critical acclaim, prices will go up. Since I stopped painting, my work doesn't sell as easily. Once I've shown at The MCA, Hal is sure that European collections will buy and some of the big private collectors.

'I told you about the Rosenbergs and the Wilsons in Chicago? I would say more than showing an interest. Dora Rosenberg is going to be here for the opening.'

'All these people getting interested, I wish I was further on with the work.'

'Come on, Maddie, these are strong ideas pushing up from that deep pool of yours.'

I turn off the light by my bed. I'm not really sleepy. Hal's right. I must trust the process, follow the ideas. There's a lot to think about. I lie back and watch the night sky through the skylight. A few thin clouds scud by. Soon it will be clear, I can already see the stars. As the street lights go out, they will become sharper, pin-pricks of ancient light in a depthless blue.

It is dark inside me where no light can reach.

Dark with the build up of blood that is waiting to come; or, if not, dark with the blood that is making a lining, for what? A few cells, a dark speck that is splitting, growing.

It.

It, if it exists, is in the dark.

So am I. It's strange but, for the first time in my life, I'm happy to keep it that way.

A Little History 5

'Did I wake you?'

It's Dom.

'Mmm,' I make a noise, let him know I'm here, but I don't want to speak. I don't want to lose the dream: a vast building at night, a factory. Hal is with me. So dark the building is a solid black edifice rising before us. We look up as a light goes on in a single window; an orange glow from within the black mass. Part of the window is open. Hal says: A burglar could get in there. I say: It's too small. He says: A child could fit. I say: Shh, listen. There's a faint sound coming from the open window but I can't make it out. Then, along the bottom of the frame, someone moves. I'd know that outline anywhere. Faith's bun, neat, tight on the top of her head. Faith's head as a silhouette. Solid, black.

'Sorry,' Dom says. 'I woke you. Thought you'd be going to the studio. Shall I call back?'

'No, wait.'

That's it. I don't remember any more, except the sensation of straining to hear.

'Hang on a second,' I reach for my sketchbook, do the outline of the window and scribble: *black wall, orange light, open window, Faith's head, silhouette. Was she speaking?*

'What time is it?'

'Eight-thirty,' he says.

'You're at college, already?'

'No.' There's a pause. If he's calling from home there must be an explanation; what he says next will be a moment of trespass into his other life.

'Tessa's down at her father's. Went last night. Things aren't looking good.' Tessa's father has been in and out of remission for almost as long as I've known Dom. A slow tumour in the gut.

'Oh, I'm sorry,' I say. There's an uncomfortable ambivalence around Tessa's sick father. I don't want to think too hard about how a dying man makes time for Dom and me. Don't dramatise, Maddie. It's not like that. Tessa knows, has known for some time. We all know what we're doing. It's only a matter of time, for all of us, not just Tessa's father.

'I was up late. Hal was here, sorting out slides for the catalogue. I'm off to Liverpool next week. Funny going back over my work. Exhausting.' Dom makes a weak joke about having dinner with another man which I don't find amusing.

'Can you manage a drink at lunchtime?'

'I don't know, Dom, maybe. Where?'

He mentions a pub near the university.

'But I'll be at the studio.'

He sounds deflated, disappointed.

'Things start to get busy next week,' he says. 'You know what it's like at exam time. Can't you manage an hour?'

'What about later? This evening?' I suggest somewhere else, halfway between my studio and the university. 'We could maybe have something to eat.' I'm assuming Tessa will stay down in Bristol for a few days.

Another pause. Then I remember. Joe.

'I promised Joe we'd have a session tonight.'

'How's it going?'

'He's putting in the work. First paper next week. History.'

Hardly relaxing. A snatched hour, Dom with his eye on the clock, thinking about getting back to Joe.

'I'd love to,' I say. 'Only, I've promised myself a day in the studio. You know what it's like, if I get into it, I'll want to work late. I can't predict.' If I get into the work I won't even notice the time. I don't want to go to the studio knowing I'll have to stop at five in order to meet Dom.

'I'll be in college until six, call me if you can make it. We could have an hour,' he says.

'OK.'

'Bye. Go back to sleep,' he laughs.

I want him here in my bed, now. I want to feel his tall, lean body next to me. I want to hold him.

'Bye.' I put the phone back on its cradle, snuggle under the duvet.

I know I won't go. I'll have some coffee, call him back. I need a full day in the studio. Let Joe have the evening with Dom. After all, everyone, including me, wants Joe to get his grades. Joe is following in his father's footsteps; going to study history. Cambridge, if he gets straight As. Dom will be proud, it will have been worth it, staying in his marriage, making sure there are footsteps for Joe to follow in. A strong clear line, not one that was broken off at a critical moment five years ago. *Thirteen, Maddie, he's only thirteen. What an age for a father to walk out on his son.* I've never met Dom's own father, but when Dom said those words, I thought he must be speaking as his father would. Thinking of it now, I hear the words with a slight Irish accent. Whenever Dom quotes his father, his voice changes; it's the intonation. Dom was born here. It was the pull of Dom's past that kept the present steady for Joe. Soon Joe will be eighteen. An adult. He'll become an academic like his father. Professor Dominic Cotter.

Dom believes in history, though he's not one of the old guard, he doesn't subscribe to the Grand Narrative. Equally he's no high-priest of theory. He's been through the theory phase and come out the other side, which is why he's so highly thought of. It's another thing he and I have in common; we are wary of 'the clerics', as we call them, the evangelical theorists who've lost sight of the object of their study.

'Theory makes us critical thinkers, but we must go back to the material. There's stuff out there, evidence; there are many ways of looking at it. Each generation asks its own questions, breathes its own breath into the material. Primary sources, analysis, narrative. History is endless stories.' Dom was saying this as I came into the lecture theatre. It was a sunny October afternoon, light streaming through the windows. I was stuck, needed a new direction. I'd been wondering where to go with my obsessions. To be honest I'd reached the point where I felt trapped by them. Part of me wanted to let go: what did it matter, in the scheme of things, that Stella left Frank. Who knows why. If Faith knows, she's not telling. But, I can't quite let go. This single event had such an influence on us all. Or rather, her keeping quiet about it. Also, what keeps me circling around silence is that it's not just my family. Ask anyone, most families have something hidden, hushed up. A family is a breeding ground for secrets. Spoors of silence grow, forming an invisible fungus that pushes its way into the lives which follow. We need our history, the story of our family, but there is always someone who wants to forget.

It doesn't work.

Those next in line want to know, they feel the absence.

Silence creates the desire to know more.

'We need to imagine a span of time which is longer than our own span. It's like needing food or water. We need history. Who are we without a sense of the past?' Dom's words held the audience of fresh new undergraduates. I'd seen the reminder on the Humanities notice board: *Why History?* I went on impulse. Dom wasn't looking at lecture notes, he spoke with passion yet it was intimate, as if he was talking to each of us individually. Goose pimples rose on my arms. I scribbled down snatches of what he was saying. History starts with our own lives, he said, our parents, grandparents. We can find a way into the past through ordinary lives. Those who came before lived in different times.

'This is where history starts,' he said. 'With a curiosity about the gap between the familiar and the strange, kinship and remoteness.'

He asked us to think of the oldest living member of our family.

'Is there a story, an anecdote which connects this person to a larger event: First World War, The Depression, Second World War?' he asked, and suggested we try to picture them caught up in whatever it was. Frank might have been in the First War. Frank's dead, a shadow. I thought of my mother and father, Faith and Ernest, meeting at a VE day celebration. Without the Second World War I wouldn't be me.

'Our existence, past and present, is a collective enterprise,' he said. 'How could we live in a vacuum, alone in the present?'

Tell that to Faith.

Music to my ears, I wanted to hug him.

There were four more lectures in the series. I went to them all. We recognised each other as familiar figures at the coffee machine in the Senior Common Room, but I couldn't say I knew him. After the second lecture I hung around like a smitten student. I was greedy, couldn't wait until the following week. I went up to him, he was polishing his glasses, the ones he still wears with the gold wire frames. He gave me a myopic look with his soft, grey eyes. When he put the spectacles on again he became a sharper version of himself, pushed his dark hair off his forehead. He had no grey then. Now, his hair is beginning to match his eyes. He smiled and I noticed the way his mouth slides up to one side. I couldn't take my eyes off his mouth. I wanted to kiss him. That was five years ago and I haven't tired of kissing Dom.

'Basic stuff,' he said, almost apologising. 'Some of them don't know why they're doing history. I like to fire them up in the first semester, connect to their own lives. Ego-bloody-maniacs.' He laughed. That's me I thought, *ego bloody maniac.*

'What's your interest in history?'

'Oh, you know, looking for a fresh take on the past.'

'Why?'

'I suppose because my work is about the effect the past has . . . Do you have time for a drink?' I said to change the subject. I hate explaining my work. It sounds overstated. We went to the pub down the road. The one where Dom wants us to meet this evening. I asked for a glass of red wine. He bought a bottle. I was determined not to go on about myself but the wine worked.

'You have a past?'

'Well, that's just it, I don't know. Let's say there are shadows over my family history.'

'A common experience.'

'That's what keeps me going.' I told him how I worked from the fragments, like the photograph of Faith and Irene.

'I try to imagine from the little evidence I have.'

He quoted someone, I can't remember who, but I remember exactly what he said: *very little history is better than no history at all.* From a few shards of pottery, he said, pictures of lost societies have been built. Do individuals have a history or only memory? Does history begin where personal memories gather around a larger event? I could have listened to him all night. He said that the history of ordinary people was important, to weigh against the official version.

'History needs stories. History needs imagination,' he said.

I told him I didn't have many stories. I never had the soft lap of a grandmother to climb into, old photos in silver frames on the mantel, new ones in envelopes waiting to be stuck in albums, talk of great aunt so-and-so who never married but had a secret lover for fifty years. None of that. My father was the only child of parents who both died of tuberculosis just before the Second World War. My father, Ernest, was seventeen at the time. He used to say that the army became his family. We had three photos of Grandma and Grandpa Armitage in cardboard frames; one on their wedding day, another with Grandma Armitage holding the new-born Ernest and all of them on holiday in Skegness when Ernest was three. They were jolly, round people. Grandma Armitage had a large bosom and big arms. Grandpa Armitage carried a little too much weight and smiled the same wide grin in each picture. Ernest used to say it was a blessing they went together, otherwise the one left behind would have died of a broken heart. He talked about them easily, openly. This was the Armitage story, it didn't have many chapters, but at least I had the satisfaction of knowing it.

'On the other side,' I said. 'I have a black hole. Guarded by Faith.'

'Can't you ask her?'

'It's not possible.' I tried to explain the effect of Faith's silence. How it has a physical presence, like an insurmountable wall. Only the wall is not made of bricks, it's a huge wall of water. The water stays up there, a tidal wave the second before it crashes. If I were to speak the water would crash down on us all.

'It's powerful,' I said, and told him how Ernest had gone to the other side of the world to get away from it and that Edward, my brother, lives in a world of speechless insects.

'And here I am, trying to say the unsayable in the work.'

It's only words that can make the wave break.

'You know nothing at all?'

'Very little. All I know about my grandfather is that his

name was Frank Lilley, he was a glassblower and his wife, Stella, left him with two little girls. One of whom was my mother.'

'People make their own history,' he said, 'but often, it's in conditions which are not of their own choosing.' He was quoting again; Karl Marx, I think. He asked if I'd ever thought of going to the place where Frank had lived, finding out about where he worked.

'Would the facts of his existence not give you something or at least somewhere to do your imagining?'

I didn't know, then, where to go. Five years ago, when I first met Dom, I didn't have the glass. The glass only arrived a couple of years ago. It was finding the glass again that led me to Bagshott's and Featherbridge. It was because of Dom that I tracked down Bagshott's glass factory. I now know more about the facts of the place where Frank worked, but the shadow is still a shadow.

It's nearly ten. The new work for the exhibition won't get made lying here, day-dreaming about Dom. I'm going to look through my research before I go to the studio. I'll have a coffee then call Dom, tell him I'm not coming. I want to push on with the glass. I might look at the Bagshott's material, that's one way in. Or, better still, the stardust stuff.

Down in the kitchen the tidiness comes as a surprise. I'd forgotten. Even the floor is clean.

'You can't leave this till morning, Maddie, what a slut,' Hal said after we'd eaten. He tucked a towel around his waist for an apron, washed up and put everything away.

I sit at the table and sort my post. The usual stuff: letters from someone doing a dissertation, an invitation to lecture in Birmingham. They can wait. I add these to the pile on the table.

I start to make coffee, but my heart's not in it. The screech of the grinder has my teeth on edge, and, when I lift the lid, the smell of freshly ground beans doesn't have its usual appeal. I carry on, go through the motions, push down the plunger, packing the grains tight at the bottom of the cafetière. Before the cup reaches my lips it comes upon me, rises like a wave, from nowhere. I stand up, move towards the sink, hand to my mouth.

Three, four times, I retch. Nothing comes.

Silence In Prussian Blue

5

When I wake again it's late afternoon, gone five. I've slept for most of the day. After the nausea came the bone-deep tiredness. I never did call Dom. I wonder if he's hanging around the office, waiting for me to phone, to say I'm on my way to the pub. I don't want to speak to him now and admit I've spent the day in bed. He'll wonder why. I didn't promise to go for a drink. This is how it is. We have a part-time life together and, as time goes on, I'm not sure I want it to be any different. Not having it all means taking more care of the bit I, we, have.

I get out of bed, glance around looking for something to wear, but what I see is a heap of clothes waiting for the wash. I pull on the least dirty T-shirt. I won't make it to the studio now. I'll work here, take a look at the star stuff.

I pad down to the kitchen, feet bare. I'm hungry, really hungry. I cut two thick slices of bread to make toast. I grate cheese into a heap on each slice then watch it bubble under the grill, catching it at the moment when the cheese has browned, just before it burns. As I munch the cheese on toast I think about the star stuff as a way into the glass pieces I want to make. I have a sketchbook down in the cellar, with a few rough ideas and notes from the lecture. Jack put me on to it. The Royal Society, not somewhere I'd been before but Jack said I should go, I'd be impressed. He was right. I've browsed Jack's book, *Tracking The Universe*, but I end up looking at the pictures of galaxies. My favourite is a swirl which is red at the centre then moves through blue, purple and on to the blackness, scattered with millions of pin-pricks of light. The last works I did, that might still be called paintings, were inspired by images which Jack had shown to me. These were three large canvases, my 'cosmic' works, Hal calls them, *Eclipse, Dark Matter, Event Horizon. Event Horizon* was the only one I was happy with because it seemed to say what I wanted to say about Faith. An unsurpassable space-time barrier, is how Jack describes an event horizon in his book, which seemed to me a good description of Faith's silence. I worked with raw pigment for the first time. I wanted these paintings to have depth, texture. I used the darkest blue I could get, a blue that was almost black. I had to wear a mask and goggles but still the stuff got everywhere, in my ears, nose, under my fingernails. The finished piece is a field of Prussian blue pigment; emerging from beneath the density of blue, slicing across the canvas from bottom left to top right is the finest arc of yellow. A thread of light, barely visible, always being overwhelmed by the density of the blue. For me, looking at it feels like being with Faith. I've told Jude that, of the three, I want *Event Horizon* in the exhibition.

The stardust idea is different. It's not so much the image but the idea of stars and what happens to them that's got me thinking about the glass, making connections. I won't look at my notes, not yet. I'll have a bath, see what I can remember; what I remember without looking at the notes is always a good place to start.

In the bathroom I light a candle, put it on the edge of the bath and watch the flame's reflection in the white tiles. I turn off the electric light and run the water, deep. I pull my long hair into a scrunch. My hair is bushy, wavy. It needs colour but I can't be bothered with henna tonight. With the colour it looks more distinctive, without, it's simply mousy. 'Lady of Shallot,' Dom used to tease when we first met. The window and mirror have misted over, it's as good as a Turkish bath in here. I ease myself through the steam, stretch out and watch my legs and my belly turn pink.

'The catastrophic death of stars makes life possible,' was how Professor Julia Caulfield began her lecture.

But for the death of stars, we wouldn't be here.

She left it hanging, paused. If she hadn't been a leading professor of physics, rational scientist of international repute, I would have said I was in some New Age gathering. She knew how to tell a story. She waited as the silence of our attention gathered and then she brought it down to us, to our bodies.

'What chemical elements are present in the human body?' she asked. Hands went up. Not mine, I should say. I felt like I was back at school. People called out the names of elements, she made a list on her overhead transparency – iron, sodium, potassium, silicon – some of which, I already knew, were present in glass. These chemical elements originate in stars, they fall to earth when stars explode. We are ninety-three per cent star stuff. Stuff that fell to earth when stars died. Stars are dying all the time. Sprinkling their stuff from the heavens on to the earth.

'They're dead by the time we see them, you know,' Edward, my brother, knew about stars. 'We go on looking at something we think is there when really it has long since died.'

Stella, Faith's bright star. Gone.

How far back do I want to go? Back to the death of a star.

Stella, dying star, a catastrophe in little Faith's universe. But she wasn't dead. She moved away where her light couldn't reach Faith and Irene. Faith must have looked out for the light of Stella coming back, eager child at the window. Day and night. When Stella did not appear there must have come a moment when Faith refused to look any more.

She turned her back.

'What's past is past.' For Faith, there's no going back. She clears up the past as she goes, Hoovering, damp-dusting, polishing each day away as it happens. Faith spreads the day out like a clean linen tablecloth, at the end of each day it goes into the wash. Faith might have been happier as a goldfish with a thirty-second memory span.

'Why must you dwell on things so?' she would chide.

Dwelling on things means you have an inner life. I sometimes think that Faith dare not have an inner life beyond thinking about the day ahead, the next task. She can't afford to close her eyes, allow the space behind them to open up, expand. If I think about the space inside her head it's like the corner of an attic where no one goes; dark, empty, claustrophobic. Not a space where you would want to linger. When I was younger I lived mostly in the space behind my eyes; at school I would drift off in lessons, I was only ever half there. *A disappointing year. Madeleine remains preoccupied with something which appears to be of far greater importance to her than academic achievement,* said my report. At home with Faith, behind my eyes was somewhere I could go on the days when I was shut up in the house with nothing but the washing or the cleaning ahead of me.

'You dwell on things too much,' Faith would say and draw me into her tasks. 'Here, take this.' Another sheet to squeeze through the mangle. Faith shunned the automatic washing machine. She needed to have her hands in the water.

Doing.

No dwelling on things. She would draw me away from my thoughts and my awkward questions into the strange intimacy of her tasks. Rarely talking. Together and yet apart, conversation was not in words but was limited to the lexicon of Faith's chores. All that activity to keep whatever was inside her at bay. Sometimes it felt like the thing inside her was a solid, heavy sadness. Other times it felt like she was all molten liquid, seething.

Melting wax gathers in the well of the candle, brimming to the edge. It dribbles down the side of the bath; a sizzle as it hits the water. I watch the trail of wax cool, set hard on the side of the tub. I pick it off, drop it back into the heat of the flame. The water is cooling. I pull the plug, let out enough water so that I can top it up again.

Dwelling on things is my life now. I am lucky it worked out that way. If not, well, I don't like to think about where I might be now. I imagine myself shuffling along a bare corridor, polished lino floor, no visitors. Or perhaps a care-in-the-community case, taking my bags from bench to bench. I remind myself how lucky I am. I have Hal who has always believed in my work. I have a job, a studio, I keep on making the stuff.

My work in The Museum of Contemporary Art; all my best work to date. It's beginning to sink in what this exhibition will mean.

'It will do wonders for your profile,' Hal keeps telling me.

I think myself back to the art room at school, try to imagine what that Maddie, then, would say if she could see me, Maddie, now.

I stop the water before it's too hot, lower myself deeper,

shoulders under. When the water cools again I will plunge my head underneath, dare myself to let the water close over my head and count to ten before I come up. It's a test I do every now and then, I check out the level of my aquaphobia.

'Aquaphobic,' said the swimming teacher and gave up on me. I was excused. To my twelve-year-old eyes, the pool was as unfathomable as Faith's silence. Down, down, down. If my feet ever did hit the bottom would I come up again? I'd only have to smell the chlorine and the panic would rise. I was good at art, but being good at art was not a good thing to be, not at the Grammar School. It wasn't a real subject. Being aquaphobic and keen on art had me singled out as odd from the start. I didn't mind. The art room was the only place I wanted to be and it was empty at the same time as the swimming session. I would help Mr Horrocks; Clive, as I later came to call him. Clive was a slight, wiry man with a pointy beard. I would wash brushes, sort pigments, fill palettes. When I'd finished he would give me a sheet of paper and some charcoal and I would sketch whatever he had set up for the next lesson. A bowl of fruit, a piece of driftwood, shells.

'You have talent, Maddie,' he would say. 'You have a way of looking closely, you pay attention.' It was funny to hear him say that because all of the other teachers said: *Madeleine Armitage, you're not paying attention.* Clive watched out for me all through school. I got just enough O levels to stay on and take A level art with Clive. There were only two of us, me and a boy called Trevor. In some lessons Clive would talk to us about what real artists did. He would show slides of their work. 'What do you think the artist is trying to communicate?' he would ask. Clive loved to talk about abstraction. His own work was abstract. Jackson Pollock, Mark Rothko, Clyfford Still. These were his heroes. The names sounded exotic. I wondered if you needed an exotic name in order to be a real artist. Madeleine Armitage did not have the ring of Jackson Pollock. Clive would stop at one of Pollock's drip paintings, talk about how Pollock worked somewhere between dream and reality, that what he created was a self-contained universe; we were invited to enter, to find our own place within. Clive said we should look upon Pollock's paintings as if they were events.

'You have to find a vocabulary, a way of saying what you have to say, to put across your view of things.' Clive said that if we were true to our view of the world, we might produce something which allowed others to see things in a new light. He said that looking at a boiled egg could be made interesting if you found a new angle. I sort of knew what he meant, I trusted him, it sounded right. I've never forgotten Clive Horrocks, he believed I would become an artist. He was the only one who made me feel it was possible, desirable, even. Not mad, bad, doomed to failure.

'You must be true to yourself,' he would say. 'Go where the work takes you.'

He would ask us to talk about what we were trying to do, not in a wordy way, but after we had worked on something for a while he would make us stand back and look hard.

'You need to be enough of a critic of yourself so as not to be overpowered by the criticism of others,' he would say. 'Criticism from others is sometimes useful, sometimes not. You must learn to tell the difference.'

He would set us projects. He encouraged me to build up a portfolio that would get me into college. Those two years with Clive were productive years. Thanks to Clive I did go to college and once I began to work at it, I found I could keep the chaos at bay. I had fewer panic attacks, less of the night terrors which otherwise would have had me shuffling up that corridor, trailing from bench to bench.

Clive took me and Trevor to his own studio where he worked on large abstract canvases. He built them up, layer upon layer: red, blue, yellow, purple, black, white. He worked back into the layers revealing bands of hidden colour. He gave them intriguing titles such as *James After the Party*, or *Suzanne Leaving*.

'I'm not aiming at the literal person but a sense of the person, the atmosphere of the event,' he would explain. After the visit he set us a project. We had to do an abstract portrait of someone close to us, someone important in our lives. He suggested that we approach this from a number of angles. We might ask them to sit so that we could draw them, or we might choose an object we associated with them and make a study of that. We ought to think, he said, about the colours we associated with this person. Perhaps we could find a colour equivalent to some aspect of their personality. However we approached it, the final piece had to be abstract.

I began with my bedroom curtains; heavy, blue velvet drapes that always made me think of Faith. She believed I would sleep better, have fewer of my 'disturbances' at night if no light could get in, especially in the summer months. She said my disturbances were because I was light sensitive. She bought the velvet curtains at a house clearance sale. They gave me nightmares, became another cause for terror as I lay awake in the small hours. I would imagine the folds swelling, deepening. I might fall in. Faith had to alter them to make them fit my window. She kept the offcut in her bit-box. I studied this remnant closely, arranged it to create folds, did studies of the undulations, carefully shading in the dark crevices. Later, at college, I learned that a fold is both surface and depth; a continuous surface containing volume.

Next I drew Faith. I said we had to do studies of figures for homework. She wasn't happy. I said it wouldn't take long, and if she liked I would do it while she was washing up so she needn't even see me do it. I sat at the kitchen table as Faith stood at the sink. I exaggerated the proportions of her back to fill the page. I wasn't much concerned with the lower part of her body. I didn't want an accurate figure-drawing so much as the feeling of Faith having turned her back.

The colours I already knew: Ultramarine, Indigo, Prussian. All the blues.

For the final piece I worked in oil pastels; they don't make dust, they are rich, pliable. You can work lightly or thick, creating layers. I loved the oily smell that lingered on my fingers.

From a distance the final piece looked like cloth, deep folds of velvet, but as you got closer you could see that beneath the layers was a person; the outline of Faith's back. I used a 2H pencil. Hard and unyielding compared with the Bs. I set myself to draw the outline of Faith's back in a continuous line, which meant being accurate in one go. At the first attempt, my hand slipped, the line veered off the page. It took me four goes. I superimposed the soft undulations of velvet over her back, mainly in Prussian blue. Curves and dips, dark places. The pencil had left a precise mark that resisted the softness of the pastel. Even when I worked deeply with the blue, the outline of Faith's back remained visible.

I called it *Silence In Prussian Blue*. It was one of the best things I did at school. I got an A grade in the exam, and Faith eventually accepted that art was what I was good at. She understood that people would buy paintings to hang on their walls, even if she personally would not. She was pleased when I got a teaching job in Liverpool. Now, she accepts that I am an artist because I still teach part-time at the university.

'I don't know why you gave up painting,' she said when I moved on to the way I work now. The installations do not make sense to her. She would not see that working with the broken glass has a direct connection to the piece I did at school which got me an A grade.

If she could, I wouldn't need to make it.

I still have *Silence In Prussian Blue*, I'd like it to be in the catalogue, I think.

My skin is starting to pucker. I climb out of the bath, wrap myself in towels and go up to my bedroom. Dom will be at home with Joe by now. I could take a chance, call him, but what if Joe answered. I don't want to unsettle him days before his first exam. Instead, knowing he is not there, I call Dom's office voicemail. When he picks up the message in the morning he will know that I thought of him.

'It's me,' I say. 'Sorry I didn't make it. Catch up with you soon.'

Lying on my bed I can see there are no clouds. Tonight will be a clear, deep sky. Plenty of stars.

'A ball of stuff,' said Professor Caulfield. 'No bigger than a speck of dust.' From that speck of dust (I want to say, splinter of glass) comes all energy, all matter. Where was the speck of dust when it exploded? I see Faith with a new duster the colour of egg yolk. If Faith had been there with her duster, none of us would exist. She would have polished the speck away before it exploded. I see it on a skirting board, or mantel shelf. Faith with a damp cloth. She always wet-dusted so the particles wouldn't fly. I liked to watch dust motes dancing on a beam of sunlight, pretty as a toy snowstorm in a glass dome. Faith didn't sit around long enough to notice dust dancing on sunbeams. If she did, I swear, she would have turned the vacuum nozzle on the air itself.

Was the first speck of dust one of many dancing in a beam of light or was it alone? I write in my sketchbook: *perhaps the form of the stardust piece could be as if a beam of light, glass pieces dancing like dust motes.*

It occurs to me that I know more about how the universe began than I know of my own origins. Or should I say of Faith's origins. Is it her history, or mine? Who owns history? Who owns a family's history?

A little history is better than none. We need to know what came before. *A span of time longer than our own span.*

The glass is part of what came before. The glass belongs to all our pasts. Our belongings. Our personal effects. It was made by Frank, laid on the table by Stella, before she left. Stella the dying star. Faith's explosion came later. Her cosmic moment, is how I'm starting to think of it, the time Faith broke the glass. The bits of broken glass were once real objects in all our lives. Frank, Stella, Faith, Irene, Ernest, Edward, me, we have all eaten and drunk from those things.

Glass has a memory. It remembers the actions performed on it.

There are scenes too, events that I know happened. I was there.

The visit to Stella in our new car.

Stella turning up at our house, unannounced.

Faith smashing the glass.

Stella's funeral.

I can run these scenes through my head like a film. Disjointed scenes. The bits in between were cut, or never shot. That's where I work, in the in-between. Between distance and intimacy, fear and fascination. Each piece I make is an attempt to expand from what is known; push, push at the edge of what is known. Where there is nothing, imagine. Shape the silence, otherwise I might not exist.

'Keep your shape, Maddie, keep your shape,' Ernest would say when I had my upsets. Crying was not allowed.

My shape is changing. These breasts belong to someone else.

It can't make a noise yet. A dark, silent thing. Growing in darkness but not silence. Listen, listen from the very first. It will hear the thump and pump of my blood, the swish and gurgle of my gut. Can a cluster of cells hear? It can't hear until it has ears, but it must be sensitive to rhythm, movement, even if it can't process sounds, can't separate heartbeat, music, speech. If an egg responds to a sperm, if cells cluster, split, grow, it must be affected by sound. Is it listening now to my breathing? Can it hear my uncertain thoughts? I will have no choice. I can't let it grow until it can hear. It cannot be. What would I tell it if I did carry on? Listen, this is what I know. Faith has worked hard to forget; the past has been tucked tight under sheets on the bed, rolled up with mothballs in the blanket chest, pegged out to freeze with washing in winter, swilled down the drain with bleach, scrubbed from the doorstep. Faith's busied the past to oblivion, she thinks.

The professor can't see the distant dark star; but, knowing it is there, she tracks its influence.

5 Sea View

'You're out early,' says Sevgül, solid behind the counter. I've never seen her stand. I've made an effort today. Out of the house before eight. It's one of those clear, fresh mornings. Bright sun, clean sky. I'll be in the studio before nine.

Sevgül sits, seven days a week, taking cash for bread and newspapers, trading stories; slices of her customers' lives swapped for a glimpse of her own.

'I need to catch up with myself,' I offer, knowing she will want more.

The rickety fan, like the propeller of a small aircraft, stirs the air above Sevgül's head. She's caught between the billowing heat of the bakery and the build-up of traffic fumes, the urban fug that will expand, push its way through the open shop door as the day goes on. A mournful Turkish love song wails from the speakers on the shelf above her head. Her sons bake bread and cakes beyond the bead curtain. Each new batch is stacked on the shelves that line the back wall of the shop. Sevgül doesn't need to move. Customers are drawn to her warmth, her ampleness, the smell of baking. The Hot Shop, is what everyone calls Sevgül's place. She sells things people need every day, things with a short shelf-life: bread, cakes, newspapers.

'Teaching today?' She needs to keep the plot going.

'No. I've finished until the autumn. Working on my exhibition.'

'When you a famous artist, Maddie, I'll say: I knew her.'

Sevgül knows more about me than Faith does; it's a kind of intimacy once-removed. She even contributed to a piece of work I made, *Comfort Blanket*. I collected wads of fluff from the tumble driers of friends and people I come across on a daily basis. I cut them into squares, as if I was making a quilt, lined an enclosed space. It was like a friendship quilt, but more intense. In the absence of family, we take comfort from friends, and even strangers.

'Don't know about fame,' I say.

'Here in the papers,' she waves her hand towards the piles of tabloids and broadsheets. 'They will write about you, Maddie.'

'They might.' A review on the arts page of a broadsheet is hardly fame. I'm not sure I want fame, whatever that is.

'When, Maddie. When is it?'

'January.'

'Next year. Long time away and you working hard already.'

It's a story she can come back to, meanwhile she offers an instalment in the running saga of her family: her nephew's forthcoming wedding. How can they all go to Turkey and keep the business running?

'Might have to shut shop for two weeks,' she says shaking her head. Ten years Sevgül has been here, closed only on the first of January, otherwise open each day, seven until nine.

'Spoilt for choice?' Sevgül points to the front window display of cakes, golden and oozing honey, sprinkled with pistachio or dusted with icing sugar. On days when I walk to the studio I treat myself. After the walk, the reward: sticky sweetness against bitter black coffee.

Today, I can hardly bear to look.

'Here, Maddie. Day in the studio, you need baklava? Very good.'

What I want is bread. Dry bread to keep the nausea at bay.

'I'll take these,' I say, reaching for a packet of sesame bread sticks.

'And some baklava?'

'You have no flat bread?' I say to avoid her question.

Am I Faith's daughter, or what?

'Ten minutes. He's just put a batch in. You wait?' Ten minutes chatting to Sevgül and she'd nudge at my reluctance. It wouldn't take much for her to discover why I haven't bought baklava.

'I'll take the bread sticks. Would you keep a flat bread for me? I'll collect it on my way home tonight, I might be late. Sevenish.'

'Long day, Maddie. Don't work too hard.'

Sevgül has seen me enough at either end of the day to know that being in the studio is a day's work. Faith thinks it's a cranky hobby. If I had asked Faith for the fluff from her tumble drier she would have been appalled, as if I'd asked for her dirty knickers.

I start to take coins from my purse.

'Pay me tonight,' says Sevgül, leaving the script open, laying down the possibility of another episode later.

I need the walk. It feels good to be out of the house; I don't want to spend another day calculating ovulation. My periods aren't regular enough for me to reach an accurate conclusion, and anyway I can't remember the date of the first day of my last one. A vital piece of information. I know in my bones, though, that the days Dom and I spent in Norfolk were long enough after the last one ended for it to be possible.

Before I set out it always seems such an effort to walk to the studio, but I'm getting into my stride now. I love the clutter along the way, the jostle of different lives. I munch on a bread stick as I go. There's no logic to the shops round here: locksmith, sauna, fishing tackle, dentist, funeral parlour. At the chemists, a young woman, tall on her platform trainers, finds the right key on a huge bunch, opens up the door setting off the alarm. I hurry past, catch a whiff of perfume and soap. I could go in there now, buy a test and know for certain in the time it takes to piss. I don't want to know, which is odd, not like me at all. 'Curiosity killed the cat,' my dad would say, 'Maddie, you ask too many questions.'

I don't want to ask my body what it's up to. Not yet.

Outside the undertaker's a sleek hearse waits, its black bodywork and chrome bumper shine like it's never been on a road. First funeral of the day. It seems too early to get buried. Funeral parlours always make me think of Stella, mute and motionless in her plain pine coffin, her grey hair draped around her. Both times I'd seen her alive her hair was up, plaits coiled on either side of her head. I wondered whether she would mind being seen with her hair down. I've never seen Faith's hair down. She has it up in a bun before coming out of her bedroom each day. I don't even know how long Faith's hair is; it used to be almost black, now it's a steely grey. Stella's hair was a soft grey and wavy, like mine. I've no idea what colour Stella's hair was when she was younger. Amongst the tales I used to spin, around why she left Faith and Irene with Frank, was the one about a long-lost lover, given up for dead in the Trenches. I fancied that he returned to claim Stella but wouldn't take on another man's children. A more florid version was that Stella had a secret love-child hidden away, so when the lover came back she had to choose between the family she had with Frank, and being with her true love and their child. As I stood there watching her dead, I imagined the love-child turning up, proving me right. In all my versions it had to be that Stella did it, left Faith, for passion. There is always a man in these fantasies of Stella. Sometimes I feel as if I've met him. Why else would a mother leave her two little girls with a working man? I watched Stella as if I was waiting for her to wake up. She was more still than a statue, skin like a church candle. She was there, right there in front of me.

'Take your time,' the undertaker had said.

I could stay all day and she would remain the same, my grandmother, known and yet unknown with the real story locked inside her stone-cold head. There I was, alone with her at last. I could ask: Why did you go?

'Why did you leave your children?' The words even came out of my mouth; a feeble noise that fell into the soundlessness. She's not going to tell me anything. It's like losing precious photographs and then finding the negatives have also been destroyed. As my question faded, the silence that gathered around Stella was beyond quiet.

There isn't a word for it.

A car draws up alongside me, stops at the traffic lights, window rolled down, tape-deck on full, speakers thumping a bass which sends waves of solid sound through my body. In the school yard boys shout at each other, tussle over a football. Outside the Neighbourhood Centre mothers with buggies cluster, waiting for it to open. One angry toddler writhes, pulling at the straps. The mother carries on talking to the woman next to her.

It's not as though there are many days in the last month when we had sex. Sharing Dom, as I do, with Tessa, I tend to remember each time. Not that I keep a note or anything but it's not that frequent. Dom had a conference which gave us three legitimate nights away. He was giving a paper early on the second day. He said that once he'd delivered his paper he could fade in and out of sessions. He would speak to the right people at lunchtime, appear for drinks one evening.

We left London early on the Thursday morning. He dropped me off in the centre of Norwich, while he went off to register and attend the plenary session. I looked round the castle, climbed right up to the battlements hoping the view would stretch to the coast. It didn't. We met again at four. I was looking forward to being by the sea.

We could see the humped ridge of the dyke for miles across flat fields and reed beds.

'I thought the cottage was by the sea,' I said.

'It is.'

'Where is it?'

'After the pub.'

'No. Not the cottage. I mean the sea. Where's the sea?'

'Over there.' He indicated the other side of the endless mound that now ran alongside the road we were on.

'I want to see the sea,' I said. I hadn't meant to sound like a sulky child impatient to arrive at the holiday destination but that's how it came out.

'The sea is five minutes' walk from the cottage,' Dom said. It belonged to a colleague in the department. Dom and Tessa used to go there when Joe was small. They haven't been for years.

We pulled up outside the converted barn with its trim thatch.

'Where's the sea view?'

All I could see were more reed beds that ended against the hump of the dyke.

'Dom, are you sure the sea is there?'

'Of course it's there.'

'I don't believe you.'

'We'll walk down there tomorrow.'

I was agitated. I had a strong need to move in order to stave off the rising panic.

'I want to see the sea. Now.' I didn't care if I did sound like a child.

The sun was low. It would soon be dusk.

'Now?'

'Doesn't it feel strange to you, knowing it's there and not being able to see it or hear it?'

I knew I would feel better, once I could hear the crash of waves, see them fizz along the shore, smell salt and seaweed.

Dom looked tired, preoccupied with his paper. He wanted to read through it again before tomorrow.

'I won't be long,' I said.

I had to move.

He thought I was winding him up. He carried on unloading things from the boot. I set off, legs striding, arms swinging, up the dirt track that led to a gap in the sea defences.

From a distance the dyke looked man-made. As I got closer I could see that it's a bit of both, the dunes held in check by concrete reinforcement. I walked quickly, skipping over puddles and muddy patches. My black suede boots were soon spattered. I carried on until the path petered out into sand. At the gap in the dyke, a concrete ramp rose up and then down to the beach. There was a steel gate that could be drawn across against an angry sea. I stood at the top of the ramp, heart thudding. The wind was strong now that I was almost on the beach. I could hear it tugging at the Marram grass on the dunes, it made my skirt stick to my legs and my skin tingle, my hair whipped my face. As soon as I saw the sea, I felt calmer. I like to know what I'm up against. I stood for a moment as my pulse slowed down. It was a wide, flat beach. I could have walked for miles. I skipped down the ramp and jumped into the soft sand. It's difficult to walk quickly in dry sand; it's like being in a dream where you think you are running but getting nowhere. In my head I was speeding along but my feet were toiling against the drag of the beach. At the water's edge, where the sand was firm, I took off, ran along the shoreline, jumping to dodge incoming waves. I ran until I reached a row of the wooden pilings that sectioned the beach, stopping the drift of sand. These ranks of great timbers patterned the beach in a regular sequence. I decided to run as far as the next row before turning back. I was out of breath, thinking I might just perch on one of the wooden pilings, when I noticed a fat black thing between two posts. I thought it was alive, even though it was quite still. It was too big for a fish. An eel, leathery and dead. It had shrivelled in the middle, like a collapsed tube with the air sucked out, yet its tail and head were quite intact. One dead eye was milky white, scoured by salt water. The other had been pecked hollow. The sand around was cross-hatched with the marks of gulls' feet. The eel lay in a curve, frozen mid-movement. If only it could join its head to its tail again, fill out its missing middle. Was it trying to get from sea to marsh, or marsh to sea? Whatever, it was in the wrong element; drowned in air. If it could inflate its middle section it might slither off, live again.

'Maddie!' Dom sounded demented as he rushed up the beach. 'What's the matter? Why did you go tearing off like that?'

'I wanted to see the sea.'

'Why?' He was panting, his chest rising and falling beneath his sweatshirt. His greying hair flopped over his forehead.

'Don't you think it's odd to arrive so close to the sea and not be able to hear it or see it? Being near something so immense and not having sight of it, I mean . . . don't you . . .' I wasn't sure what I wanted to say, or who it was I was speaking to. For a second I thought, who is he? Who is this man? What is he to me? He's standing so close but the distance chills me: there are many things we don't know about each other. He doesn't know how I feel when I'm near the sea. Why should he, how could he? We're always in London, in my bed. Sometimes in a cinema, restaurant, art gallery, the college bar. In bed there's the intimacy of bodies, few words. We are close at night in the dark; fluent bodies. No need to talk of the sea. If we had a full life together in the world outside, we might disagree on more than the sea. Why should he know about me and the sea?

'Are you all right?' I couldn't tell if he was cross or concerned.

'I'm fine, now I'm here.' He held both hands towards me, took hold of me, smiled like he does, his mouth turning up at one side. I kissed him, hard and deep. I let the weight of my body slump against him. I wanted his tongue to be bigger, to keep on filling my mouth, fat as an eel. His hand moved down my thigh till he found the hem of my skirt. Nimble fingers slipped into my tights, stroking, easing me apart, finding their way inside. One, two. I gulped the sea air. I came quickly.

I couldn't have conceived then.

We walked back, arm in arm, leaning in on each other, silent.

We had supper in the pub and fell into bed early. We made love slowly, sleepily. The next thing I knew it was three in the morning. I was sticky with Dom, hot. I was careful not to wake him as I made my way first to the bathroom, then to the kitchen for a glass of water. I stared out of the window for a while. There was nearly a full moon and the sky was vast across the reed beds. I pulled on Dom's jeans, my sweatshirt and then Dom's sweater over that. I found a scarf on the pegs in the hall, stuffed my feet into someone's green wellies.

It was cold.

I crunched across the gravel courtyard, crossed the lane and stood on the edge of a field, looking inland at the flatness. The sky was huge. A fathomless dark blue with its pin-pricks of iced light. I thought of my portrait of Faith, *Silence In Prussian Blue*. I listened, checked out the silence. No traffic. I thought I could hear the sea but it was muffled by the dyke. A swish in the reeds; an eel or some small marsh creature. The sound of my own breathing and a high-pitched note, deep inside my ear. When you can hear the sounds of your own body there is very little external sound.

As a child I would wake early before everyone else. I would listen to the silence of our house. Before the others woke the silence was passive, a lull, a stillness. It was simply there. Then sounds would creep in: the ticking of radiators, pipes expanding as the heating came on, Ernest's alarm clock. Once Faith was up, in would come her silence; active, aggressive sometimes. If there'd been an 'incident' it would be her punishing, rigid silence. A silence that made me feel as if I were looking into a dark mirror; cold and hard, it would not give back my reflection. She would never discuss the incident. Whatever we had done, and sometimes it was not clear what had upset her, we had to work it out. This brittle silence would gradually break up. It was not pleasant to be on the receiving end of the dark mirror silence, but, on balance, I preferred it to the other kind of silence. The 'don't ask' silence. The deep blue silence. This was how Faith was most of the time. Her deep blue silence was vast, compelling, like the night sky or a tidal wave the moment before it breaks. It draws you in, creates the desire to know more. It's like no other silence, and I have observed many kinds of silence: on the Underground, when a train stops short of the station, waits in the tunnel, there is the anxious hush of a hemmed-in crowd; after a snowfall the world is muffled; I've listened to a blank tape as it gives off white noise; the irreversible muteness of Stella in her coffin. Silence is something I touch, smell, taste. Silence is a state, a place I go when I work. It's a struggle to name it, put it in words. Faith's silence is large, amorphous, continues to grow; an unseen drapery with folds which could swallow me up; it's the dark sky at the end of the universe when all the stars have gone.

I stood there on that cold, Norfolk night and dared myself to see how long I could gaze into the night sky before I felt dizzy, taking myself to the edge of panic, daring myself to stay there, not to run off. So many nights as a child I would wake hardly able to breathe, knowing only that I must find the door, find the way out. Caught up in the blue velvet curtains, fumbling, trying to open the window, simply to breathe. Once, I ran downstairs, pyjamas clinging to my body with sweat, out of the back door; I was down the end of the garden when Ernest caught up with me.

'Madeleine!' By the time he reached me I was wide awake, shaking. I stared up at the sky and wondered how we could all calmly get up each day, do things like eat and drink, how could Faith polish, scrub, bake with all those stars up there; where was the edge? Another time, I stood out in the garden with a torch. I shone the torch on the night sky as if it were a ceiling. I thought of it as a bigger version of the solid blue wax crayon that filled the top of my pictures. If the sky was the dark ceiling of the world then I could shine a torch up there and the beam would hit the ceiling, like it did when I shone the torch as I lay in bed. But the light from the torch dissolved, disappeared, did not come back.

I don't know how long I was out there under that big Norfolk sky, but the air inside the cottage felt warm and welcoming as

I shut the door on the cold night. I pulled off my clothes, left them where I stood. Dom stirred. Climbing in next to his hot, firm back was exquisite. Dom. Solid enough to hold on to so I won't fall off into the depthless night sky, lose myself beyond the stars. He mumbled in his sleep.

'Dom, Dom?' I whispered, kissing the back of his head. I ran my hand down his side, slid it round to his half awake penis. He was soon aroused and all I wanted was him deep, deep inside. I didn't give it a thought, I didn't want to get out of bed again. Afterwards, as I lay there, I thought of my diaphragm, where I had left it, on the linen chest beside the bath.

He left early next day to deliver his paper. I spent the day alone, mainly walking on the beach. It was sunny, warm for April. I sat with my back to the concrete wall that keeps the dunes in check. A family camped near by; mother, father, a girl of about seven and boy of ten or eleven. The mother walked off up the beach, the girl followed her, they left a trail of parallel footprints along the shoreline. The large ones just ahead of the smaller ones. Once they were out of sight I took photos of the lines of footprints, mother's and daughter's. I was pleased to be on my own. I needed time to think through some ideas for the exhibition. I knew I would use the glass, but nothing was fixed. I've always wanted to do something based on the sea, so I watched, noticed things, took photos, sketched. I took images of my shadow on the sand, some at the water's edge, where half my shadow was on the dry sand, half submerged in the shallow water where the energy of the wave was played out. In the shadow my legs were extra long, out of proportion to my body; my hair, pulled up in a scrunch, swayed out to one side. The sea rearranged sand, pebbles, shells but it could not rub out my shadow.

I cross the main road, by the Mosque, sun glinting off its copper dome, slim crescent poised on top. I zig-zag, cutting through a jumble of housing old and new; maisonettes have balconies crammed with geraniums and satellite dishes; a restored terrace has been done up so it looks as if it's just been built. A terrace that reminds me of Dom's house. I've never been inside, only driven past. Geranium pots line the front step; Tessa's the gardener.

Annie says Dom's weak, why should I put up with this part-time life. Early on I would have said that I wanted all of him. When Tessa found out I was almost glad. Two tickets to the Hayward Gallery found in his jacket pocket. She didn't make a big scene. She must have had them for a couple of weeks before she said anything. They were reading the Sunday papers, apparently she looked up and said: 'Let's go to an exhibition.' There was nothing unusual about this statement, so Dom said: 'All right.' And she said: 'Yves Klein at the Hayward sounds interesting.' Dom says he could feel the heat rising in his neck, but he was hidden by the newspaper. He said: 'Mmm,' in a noncommittal sort of way. Then she said, in a cool, even voice: 'Perhaps not, you wouldn't want to go again would you?' She laid the ticket stubs on the table and walked out of the room. The marriage hadn't been good for some time. She was caught up in her work teaching media studies at a college of further education. She'd had a fling with a younger man in her department, but it was over. Dom said he would have preferred a row, some passion. She said: 'Get it out of your system.' They never considered separating because of Joe. If I'd asked him to leave Joe, I would have lost him. We've fallen into this way of being, I can't imagine life with Dom there every night. What scares me is how we've settled into a part-time relationship with the future never coming, never quite shaping up. Until now. Always the understanding, which has become vaguer with the years, that when Joe went to college Dom would leave Tessa. Leave to go where? If we moved in together, became full-time, would the good things become worn, lifeless with over-use.

As I reach the cobbled cul-de-sac, I see a woman coming out of her house; an African woman, sixtyish, with a child who can only just walk. She laughs, scoops the child inside a length of bright fabric, patterned with dots and swirls of blue, yellow, green, black. She swings the child on to her back, easy as putting on a jacket. The child melts into its grandmother's body.

When you get to forty-one, well, you don't expect to be pregnant. I could simply be late.

At the dead-end of the cobbled street are the steel gates of the studios. We used to have wooden gates with the words PIANO FACTORY STUDIOS, painted in rainbow letters, but they rotted, couldn't keep out vandals. The new steel gates have a human-sized door within them and a letter box. I unlock the door, letting myself into the yard. Someone else is here already because the mail has gone. Inside the yard stands the converted piano factory, home to twenty artists now. A three-storey building with a metal staircase that zig-zags up to each floor where it meets a metal walkway. Balcony would be too grand a description, it's purely functional. Each studio has a double glass door which opens on to the walkway.

Inside my studio I open the glass doors, the sun does not come round until later, it's pleasantly cool. I am on the top floor. One half of the roof is sloping glass, which makes the place light, but cold in winter. Along one wall is a sink and a fridge. When I'm really into the work, I stay for long stretches. I've sometimes slept here. Another wall has bookshelves where I keep outsized art books that never seem to fit anywhere else, and exhibition catalogues. Another wall is full of sketches, notes to myself and suchlike; my thinking wall. There's a door in this wall that leads to a corridor of other doors, other studios. I have two paint-spattered chairs and a small table. In the corner is a plan chest full of old drawings, and stacked next to that are some of the earlier canvases. I've cleared the floor space in order to work on the glass. The four tea chests are lined up next to the plan chest. I start to lay out pieces of broken glass.

The phone rings down the corridor; an insistent ring, a chink in my concentration. Someone answer it. I don't want to lose my thoughts. It stops. I hear footsteps, a tap at the inside door.

'Yes?'

'Maddie?' Patrick opens the door. His studio is right by the phone.

'Hi, Patrick. Who is it?'

'I didn't ask.'

'Man or woman?'

'Man.'

'American accent?'

'No.'

Not Hal, then. Dom.

'Could you say I'm not here?'

Patrick shrugs.

'Please.'

Piece Work 5

I'd rather not talk to Dom until I've had more time to think about things.

Things.

A euphemism.

A Faithism.

Things: a late period and an odd sensation 'down below'.

'You might feel uncomfortable, *down below*,' Faith said with her back to me as she slipped a packet of sanitary towels into my sock drawer. 'There's more in the airing cupboard, under the pillowcases.' We never spoke of it again. That was the sum total of our discussion of menstruation, reproduction, intimate relations. That was the first time I noticed Faith's habit of saying important things with her back turned, her hands busy with a chore.

'Your dad's leaving,' head bent over the sink, Brillo pad frantic against the greasy grill.

I can't imagine looking Faith in the eye and saying: I'm pregnant, Mum.

Mum.

I've called her Faith ever since I left home. My act of rebellion. It makes her uncomfortable. To her, the use of her first name is shockingly intimate. To me, it would now seem more intimate to call her Mum. Perhaps I'll wait until her back is turned: Faith, guess what? I'm pregnant.

It's Dom I'd have to face first and I'm saying nothing until I'm sure. My breasts are tender, swollen but when I looked at them in the mirror this morning I was relieved to see they don't look as big as they feel. They feel different. Still, there's no point offering

Dom a maybe. If the bleeding comes he need never know and I will never be so careless again.

I swear.

Dom's busy for the next month with his students: assessments, dissertations to mark, exam boards. May is a month in which Dom disappears. My teaching at the university has finished, which means I have no reason to be there, so we can't easily meet for lunch or have a drink in the bar at the end of the day. He will phone, keep in touch, like he did just now, but it's easy to avoid him. I'll keep the machine on at home. Here, the phone is so far down the corridor that someone always gets there first; anyway, I tend to ignore it when I'm working. It's not unusual for us to have no contact for a week or more, given our situation. He knows I'm preparing for the Liverpool trip next week. He knows it's important. Jude wants a planning session with everyone concerned: publicity, education, the graphic designer, the art handlers.

'We need to start putting the final shape on the project,' Jude said when I rang to confirm my train. It's nine months since she invited me to do the exhibition.

'That only gives you a year and a half,' she said. 'We normally work two years ahead, I know it's a bit tight.' To me, then, it seemed a luxury of time, an incentive to begin a new series of work. As soon as Jude asked me I thought of the glass: this is it, Maddie, use it or let it go. Four tea chests of broken glass, kept in Annie's parents' garage in Chester for over twenty years.

'Madeleine, dear,' her mother called me, a couple of years ago. They were moving to the coast. 'I just wanted to check, those boxes of yours, is it all right if I get rid of them?'

'Boxes?' I had to think a moment about what she meant. I've never forgotten about the glass, but it wasn't something I thought about day-to-day.

'If I remember rightly, they're full of glass. Very heavy, dear.'

'The tea chests.' My skin tingled.

'Only, the house clearance people are coming to sort out the garage.'

I hired a small van and drove up there. On the way back I stopped at a service station for coffee. I was nervous with the van out of my sight, afraid it might be stolen. A heap of broken glass that's all it was. I drove straight to the studio. Patrick helped me bring it in. I try to avoid Patrick, or, let's say, not to encourage him. I get the impression sometimes that he'd like to get beyond being studio neighbours. He's younger than me, not really my type at all, but I had to ask him, it was too heavy for me to lift alone.

'Where d'you get this?'

'My inheritance.'

'You're going to use it?'

'Maybe.'

Stored in that heap of glass, I knew, was a story, waiting to be released, pieced together. When Patrick left, I cleared the floor, laid down sheets of black paper and I began to take out the fragments, carefully, piece by piece, making piles on the black surface. Last time I'd handled this glass, I was anxious to clear it up so Faith would not have to look at what she'd done; Edward and me sweeping it into piles. There it was, where we'd left it. If I found a handle or a spout intact I set it aside in a separate pile. Next, I began to sort the fragments by colour: blue, pink, green, amber. I examined individual pieces; some were jagged, others more like crumbs. I studied the surface of some of the larger pieces through a magnifying glass. What looked smooth to the naked eye, was pitted and scratched, scored with tiny marks. Signs of use. Who had made these marks: Frank, Stella, Faith, me? I held bits up to the window to see how the light changed it. I wanted to get a feel for the stuff, to know its weight, its colour. I cut myself, not badly but I nicked the ends of my fingers. I didn't mind, I was hooked. My skin tingled; a sure sign that I'm on to something because it hit me all over. I paced around, my head buzzing. This is how it is when new work starts; it's not a clear thought, more like a disturbance, a turbulence that moves through my whole body. At the bottom of the chest were flakes of glass too small to separate one colour from the next. If I could have sorted the pink from the green, and so on, I would have layered them in a clear cylinder, like a souvenir I once bought in the Isle of Wight, layers of coloured sand in a glass lighthouse. Evidence that I had been there. I knew that what I had was live material. It can take a while to come to anything. So when Jude invited me to do the exhibition with a year and a half to produce something new, it seemed like plenty of time to work with the glass.

The exhibition is not only about new work, I have to look back over all my work and select 'representative pieces', as Jude calls them. Now, half that time has passed and I've a long way to go. It's nine months to the opening but Jude wants to see work before then. She'll need something to photograph for the catalogue and for publicity. Jude is talking about August, which will be tight. She can have existing work by then, the early stuff and loans. That's if I can decide exactly which pieces of my old work I would be happy to see brought together in one place and called representative. Representative of what? Having to revisit the early stuff is more unsettling than I'd thought.

'Do you think some of it still stands up?' I asked Jude. 'I'm not so sure.'

'As far as I'm concerned,' said Jude, 'the problem is not what we put in, but what we leave out and yet still give a sense of your development as an artist. Of course I have my own ideas, but we want to work with you, and Hal.' Hal, bless his Armani suits, is thrilled. He's spoken informally to the private collectors who bought early work. We've each made our long lists. Jude and Hal are keen to show more of the early paintings than I am.

'For sure, Maddie,' Hal insists. 'We must.' The collectors who bought the early paintings might look again at the new work once they see their purchases acknowledged in The Museum of Contemporary Art: Collection, Mr & Mrs Loads-of-Dosh, London. Hal's sure that this is the moment when the Rosenbergs and the Wilsons in Chicago will buy. I mustn't be cynical, Hal says. Thank God for Hal. He loves to generate excitement around new work. It's genuine, he couldn't do it if he wasn't behind the work one hundred per cent. He's got an instinct for who will buy. He pitches it right. Not too low, because that says the work isn't serious enough. Not too high so they become suspicious of the hype. I try not to get involved in that side of things. The work is what I have to do, otherwise I'd go nuts. Of course I want to exhibit; if not, I'd be talking to myself. Selling it, well, that's a bonus. It's something that seems to happen, despite me.

My list puts emphasis on the last five years, and the new

glass work. Jude agrees with Hal and wants to show my early paintings, especially *Family Album*.

'People expect artists to paint,' says Jude. 'The fact that you did, and did so successfully, then stopped, says a lot.' The education department, apparently, sees me as a challenge. Jude says that part of doing this exhibition, as far as The MCA is concerned, is to show how an artist like me moves on, isn't necessarily held by a discipline or medium.

'We want to show that there's a connection, that you didn't stop painting on a whim,' says Jude. 'Why move from a narrative form in two dimensions to work in three dimensions? There's plenty of scope for events and supplementary material here: the relationship between objects, memory, narrative. That sort of thing.' Innovation, access, education, is Jude's mantra.

She wants all of *Family Album*, and some of the *Shadow* series. It's getting close to decision time. We have to edit the lists soon if Jude is to secure loans.

'I don't want to ask collectors for loans if we don't then include the work.' When I go to Liverpool next week we'll spend time in the gallery, check out the space, decide how much I'll need for the new work. What doesn't go into the exhibition could go into the catalogue. Jude says her new assistant, Ward Joffitt, is to be in charge of this. He wants a section on source material, like the photograph of Faith and Irene. I've never shown sources before. What is Faith going to think: public exposure of things that aren't meant to have happened, things I'm not meant to know about. She must know that I have the photograph, she must have missed it by now.

I was about nine or ten at the time. I was looking for evidence. I found a round leather box at the bottom of Faith's wardrobe, an old collar box which used to belong to Grandpa Armitage. One day, when Faith had nipped to the corner shop, I decided to see what was inside. When I lifted the lid all I saw was a pile of junk: a pair of Ernest's broken cuff-links; lots of odd buttons, mainly from Faith's frocks; hair pins; a leather finger stall; a compact with hardly any powder left in it. Beneath this heap I could see a folded piece of paper. I pulled it out. It was Faith and Ernest's marriage certificate and beneath that was the photograph of Faith and Irene.

Treasure.

After that, I would regularly check the box, whenever the opportunity arose. Finally, when I was about sixteen, seething with anger at Faith and her secret life, I took the photograph. If she wanted it back she would have to ask, I thought.

She never has. She must know I have it. Or maybe she doesn't. Maybe she's not looked in the box for years. She has seen the *Family Album* paintings; they are almost abstract, not literal copies of the photograph. I'm not sure Faith would necessarily connect the details which I painted to the scratchy old photograph. It will be a different matter altogether to see herself as a child reproduced in the catalogue.

I wish I was spending more time in Liverpool. Jude invited me to stay the weekend with her, but I'd already told Faith I was coming.

Cancelling Faith would be harder than going.

It seemed like a good idea at the time. I haven't seen Faith since last Christmas at Edward's. She wanted me to come up last month, over the Easter weekend. I couldn't face it. It was just before the Norfolk trip with Dom. I said I needed to put in time at the studio during the vacation, making work for the exhibition and, quick as a flash, without stopping to think, I said: 'Anyway, I'm coming to Liverpool in May. I'll see you then.' It's not as if travelling to Yorkshire from Liverpool is that easy, I'll have to change at Manchester.

Now I can't think of anything worse than being stuck halfway down that steep cliff of a moor for a wet weekend with Faith, and me having morning sickness. If that's what it is. I've convinced myself that putting off the test is the best thing, because I don't want to meet either Jude or Faith next weekend knowing that I'm pregnant. Pregnancy and preparing for an exhibition are not compatible.

Not compatible.

Maddie, get real. The exhibition will be the least of your worries. Lone parent, aged forty-one, no fixed abode, of uncertain income, uncertain partnership, emotional potential as parent highly questionable.

Why is my body doing this to me?

After the Liverpool visit, after I've seen Faith, I'll buy a kit from the chemist and move from a state of uncertainty to certainty. It will be either positive or negative. There are no degrees of pregnancy: almost pregnant; slightly pregnant; a partial pregnancy. Pregnancy is a definite. Until it's definite I will put in time on the new work.

The enclosed spaces might be domestic in scale, possibly. A room within the gallery. A space which stirs the imagination, dream-like, theatrical; the inside walls lined with velvet or pigment. Prussian blue to draw the eye in. The fragments of glass will be suspended. I want to piece them together somehow, the lighting will be part of the drama. I want to create two of these rooms, at least. Possibly three. In one room I want the glass to be in the form of the original objects, bowls and plates. I think of this as *Piece Work*. It's a working title. If I was being paid by the piece, as Frank was, I'd have earned nothing. I'd have lost my job.

I see the other room more like an explosion, *Death of A Star*, is what I call it for now. I want it to be an explosion like the dying star, or the moment of impact, when the glass hit the wall. I can see both of these rooms, vividly, in my mind. What I have to do is make the images happen in the gallery. There's a lot to be resolved. I've thought about it enough, I need to start making something. I sift more of the broken glass, think myself back into the work. I wear gloves some of the time, leather gloves, to protect my hands. Now and again I take them off; I need to feel the glass, its sharp edges, smooth surface, its coldness.

Glass is a poor conductor of heat.

I sort out the recognisable bits – stems, lips, handles – from the smaller crumbs. Twenty years in Annie's mum's garage. I knew I had to keep it. My only thought at the time, if it was a fully formed thought, was that if Faith needed to smash this stuff it must have been important.

Faith's most dramatic act.

Faith made a mess.
Faith made a noise.

It was only the glass she broke. She was thorough. Some of it was in the kitchen cupboard, some in the dining-room cabinet and there was more in the cupboard beneath the stairs. It was the glass which we set on the table each day, but I'd never made the connection to Frank until Faith smashed it.

Frank, Faith's father, my grandfather, made this glass.

I believe.

As Faith smashed the glass against the wall, one word came to mind. A word that I had seen handwritten in faded blue ink: glassblower. I'd seen it in the leather collar box, written on Faith's marriage certificate, under the column headed 'father's occupation'. Faith has never mentioned him, this glassblower. Not once, ever. As she smashed the glass against the wall, things came together in a new configuration. As the pieces flew I knew I was watching my family history condensed into a single, potent act. Faith was breaking up what remained of her past, annihilating it, she thought. Smashing it to smithereens. It was shocking. I feared for Faith, in such distress, but there was also a thrill. The thrill of watching real, raw feeling. I knew that if I could discover where that massive energy had come from, if I could trace the events which led to that fierce shattering of glass, I would start to know who Faith was. Is. I knew it, then, in my gut. I couldn't have put it into words, analysed it, but I've been thinking about the mess and the noise Faith made for over twenty years.

It was the long hot summer of 1976. Edward and I were both home from college for the summer break. It hadn't rained for a month, and the temperature that day was into the nineties before breakfast. There were cracks in the lawn. Ernest, my dad, stood in the kitchen, frozen. The back door was wide open. Faith stood just outside, hurling bowls, jugs, vases, a vinegar bottle, a jelly mould, at the brick wall.

'Whatever is it?' Mrs Thornton's voice came from the other side of the wall, too high to see over.

'Faith? Ernest?' She called for Ted, her husband. The thought that the neighbours might complain or, worse still, call the police, shook Ernest out of his paralysis.

'Faith, Faith. Come on, love.' I'd never heard a term of endearment pass between them before. I'd never seen him touch her. He reached for her shoulders, laid his hands there to steady her. The doorbell rang. Betty and Ted from next door. I let them in.

'Madeleine, whatever's the matter?'

I shrugged. 'It's Mum.'

'Faith, Faith?' said Betty, hurrying through to the kitchen.

Faith carried on. She brushed Ernest away, took no notice of Betty and Ted. She carried on until everything was shattered. She cleared the kitchen cupboard, the dining-room cabinet and then she started on the boxes under the stairs. No one moved. We were frozen around her. When there was nothing left, she stood for a moment, looking at the pile of fragments. Her eyes didn't seem to see. She was shaking. She slumped down on to the doorstep, weeping. I say weeping but there were no tears, and there was no noise. But that is how I remember it, as weeping. Her body shook. There was no sound.

After a while Betty said in a kind voice: 'Come inside, love.' She took Faith's hand and led her into the sitting room. Ernest was in a state of shock, but he managed to call the doctor. He left Faith with Betty and came out into the yard where Edward and I were looking in disbelief at the heap of glass.

'We should clear it up,' I said.

'Not now, what about Mum,' said Edward. He called her Mum then, now it's Mother. 'Shouldn't we be with Mum?'

'I don't think so,' said Ernest.

'She won't want us in there,' I said. 'She's probably dying of shame already because Betty's here. I'm telling you we are doing her a favour if we clear that up, because when she comes to her senses she's going to flip at the mess. She won't want to see the mess that she's made.'

'You've got a point there, Maddie,' said Ernest.

'Edward and I will clear it up, Dad.'

'What will we do with it?' I could see Edward wasn't keen.

'We'll take it to the dump,' I said, 'she won't have to see it again.'

'Mind you don't cut yourselves.'

'Come on, Dad, we're not kids. Can we have the car keys?'

'If you're sure. I'll have to stay with your mother until the doctor comes. But you're right, Madeleine, she won't be happy to see that mess. To tell you the truth, the way she is at the moment, I don't think she rightly knows what she's done or where she is.'

Edward found tea chests in the garage. I took the stiff gardening broom, swept it into heaps and I wore gardening gloves so I could pick it up in handfuls.

'It'll take us all day at this rate,' said Edward. It was hot work, sweat trickled down my arms. We improvised, used the hood of the lawn mower. Edward held it steady on the ground while I swept the pieces of glass towards it. We tried to do it quietly but it made a brittle clanking sound. Glass on glass; glass against the tinny metal. It was heavy. I know now what goes into glass: lead, sand, quartz, lime, silica. Frank spent his life making it, Faith smashed every last piece.

It was never spoken about again.

Faith never explained her behaviour; never asked where the broken glass went. Next day, when there was nothing to lay on the table it wasn't remarked upon; she put out the best bone china as if that were entirely normal.

I cornered Ernest.

'What's going on?'

'Leave it alone, Maddie,' he said.

'Dad, she smashed all that glass. Why?'

'She's not well, she's very upset.'

'What's upset her?'

'Leave it, Maddie.'

'So, we just carry on. It's entirely normal to do what she did, is it?'

'I don't think she wants to be reminded.'

'Perhaps not, but you can't say it's unreasonable of me to ask.'

'Will you leave it.'

'Why, why did she do it?'

'She's upset.'

'Why is she upset?'

'It's her mother.'

'You mean my Grandma Lilley?'

'Yes, love.'

'What about Grandma Lilley?'

'She's dead, love.'

'Dead? When? How do you know?'

'Telegram. That's what set her off. Funeral's on Thursday. She won't go.'

'I'm going,' I said.

'Madeleine, please don't upset her any more.'

'I want to go, we must go. Someone must go to her funeral.'

'She's adamant,' Ernest said. 'Go if you must but keep it to yourself.'

Faith wasn't herself. The doctor kept an eye on her, while we all walked on eggshells. Who would dare, which one of us would dare to push her?

Today, I will try out the nylon thread. It could be what I use to suspend each piece of glass. I've tried other kinds of thread and wire; all too visible, too intrusive. The nylon thread absorbs the light, it disappears. What you see is the piece of glass in mid-air.

I see *Piece Work* almost like a table setting; bowls or plates of different sizes, suspended. If the thread works, it should look as if the bowls and plates are floating, the formation will suggest a table, but I don't want a literal table. Today I will piece together a small bowl form. Each suspended fragment must be close enough to the next to imply the bowl, but separate enough from one another also to suggest that the bowl is falling apart. That is how I want all the pieces to look, so you think: Are these objects falling apart or are they about to solidify?

Glass is neither a liquid nor a solid.

Seven bowls, maybe, in a circle; a table set for a family dinner: Frank, Stella, Faith, Irene, Ernest, Edward and me.

I take a piece of glass, tie the nylon thread around as if wrapping a parcel. Next, I add a length of thread long enough to hang from the ceiling. I will need a grid, wire mesh, hidden in the space somehow. I can use the grid to adjust the distance between the threads. It's exacting, time-consuming work, but I don't mind, that's part of the process for me.

The other new piece will be based on the star stuff. Larger, I think. What I see in my head is the moment of impact.

Glass shattering.

Freeze frame.

If it were a photograph it would be a blow-up of the moment when the glass exploded off the brick wall. As the objects shattered, fragments flew away from one another, momentarily held in the air until gravity pulled them to earth. I've thought of recreating the act on video. I could play it back, slowing down the tape. It won't do.

I want the objects in there.

The actual glass objects, made by Frank, set daily on the table by Irene and Faith, obedient little girls, and then brought by Faith into our lives. These things – sugar bowl, milk jug, sundae glasses, salt and pepper pot, sauce boat, cake stand, jelly moulds, trinket bowls – were witness to it all. Our lives have accumulated around these everyday things. Frank's rage, Faith's fears, my anxieties. *Glass has a memory*. It has to be the real thing.

I wonder if Faith will recognise the glass. I don't mean Faith any harm. I worry that I might unhinge her and I wouldn't want that to happen. I think of her unseeing eyes as she stared at what she'd done. The weeks afterwards on medication, more silent than usual. There is always this tussle inside of me: part of me wants to protect her from the angry part of me that wants to know. Is it her story or mine? Sometimes I think: Don't try to shine a light where it's not wanted. Faith is happy with the shadow across her memory.

She's never been comfortable around my work; never comments, rarely comes to my exhibitions. I send her the catalogues. She never asks why I do it, or what it means. She sees the making of art as something I do in my spare time. As far as she is concerned, I am a teacher in a university. This is respectable. Part of me thinks: It's a generational thing, it's no big deal.

My exhibition at The Museum of Contemporary Art will be hard for her to avoid. It's a big one, and public. If she comes, will the new work disturb her? This concerns me. When the light goes on in *Piece Work*, will her past tumble out, take her by surprise? She might be relieved, angry, indifferent. Most likely she won't come.

I can't believe Faith has forgotten. However hard she's tried,

I think it's all still in there, beneath the shadow. Memory needs things, we attach our lives to things. We save things in order to save bits of our lives. We can't help it. Faith smashed the glass; shattered the past to fragments, banished the fragments from her thoughts. Faith knew what the glass had witnessed: Frank hot by the furnace, gathering up the molten toffee, not too much, not too little. Hot. When the shift was over, he had two little girls to look after. Faith and Irene laying the table for tea: sugar bowl, milk jug, filling up with their chatter and the brooding silence of their father. Later, Faith would ask me to lay the table. Cake stand on a Sunday, salad bowls in summer. I polished the glass many times. Carefully lifting each piece from the draining board, fresh linen to wipe away the water, and to polish each piece to a shine. Faith watching, making sure I put the clean glass away in the right place, bowls and plates, neatly stacked.

'Mind you don't break anything, Madeleine.'

Deep Water 5

'Ah, good. That's everyone,' says Jude, as a young woman with tangerine hair slides into the last vacant seat. Kathy from publicity has a skirt to the floor, slit to the crotch, back and front, its black and white irregular check is like a Mondrian. She's put thought into her vivid appearance; it comes with the job, I suppose. I, meanwhile, feel like a bag lady in jeans and a linen jacket which has seen better days. My feet are on fire. I wish I hadn't worn socks. It's hotter now than when I set out. I had to leave so early, I didn't give much thought to clothes, being more concerned not to miss the train.

Jude is on form, she smiles around the table, a unifying, motivating smile. Her teeth make her attractive; white and straight, except the front two cross ever so slightly which gives her an interesting edge, otherwise she'd look like a toothpaste ad. She's tiny, doll-like with long blonde hair, fringe in her eyes. Always one step ahead, is Jude. We first met when I was teaching in Liverpool and she was dogsbody at an arts centre which doesn't exist any more. She helped organise the first exhibition I was in, a group show. She's always kept an interest in what I do. Now, here she is, Deputy Director of The Museum of Contemporary Art. She pushes up the sleeves of her leopard-skin print top.

'Do help yourself,' she says pointing to the stack of white cups and a filter machine laid out behind us. 'Then we can start.'

This meeting room feels formal; interrogation room. Nothing in it but the large table, around which we have all gathered, plus the chairs we're sitting on and the coffee table. Most of the wall opposite me is taken up with two windows which overlook the river. If I sit up straight, stretch my spine, I can see the water. If I slump, all I see is the skyline of Birkenhead. A seagull glides across the piece of sky framed by the window. I follow its arc. Its movement calms me, lifts me beyond this group of eager young things who are weighing me up. The artist. Call it paranoia, but the way a couple of them regard me it's as if they would prefer me not to be here. I can imagine how the presence of a living artist could be an irritation, especially since some of the time they're dealing with the work of the recently dead. Well, maybe that's unfair on Jude, but Ward Joffitt, her new sidekick over there, sees me as an inconvenience, I'm sure. There's a man who's happier dealing with the dead. I need to get my head together before he comes on the agenda.

We have an agenda.

1. *Marketing and Publicity*
2. *Education and Gallery Events*
3. *Catalogue*
4. *Final selection deadlines*
5. *Revised schedule.*

Jude is making the most of my visit.

Kathy with the tangerine hair circulates a draft press release which seems appallingly early to me.

'We need images of the new work if we're going to excite the magazines,' she says, turning to me. '*Contemporary Art 4* will probably pick this up. We should get an in-depth interview with colour spreads, but they work four months ahead.'

They all look my way.

'Well,' I say, 'won't we talk about photography under number three, "Catalogue"? Would that make sense?' I only want to have to say once how far behind I am. Kathy moves on, clarifies how much of her budget will be allocated for press train tickets and who will they target? Might the rail company sponsor?

'Critics won't budge out of London unless you take their hand and sit them on the train at Euston.' Jude will not cut the train fare budget.

'I want this show covered.' Jude drums her fingers on the pale ash table, black nail polish gleaming. I think about the review

I read this morning on the train coming up, a piece by Isolde Maddox. I wonder whether Isolde Maddox would take a train from London to Liverpool. I've never been on Euston station so early, practically dawn. I had half an hour to spare and all my stuff to lug around: overnight bag, a holdall full of source material – notebooks, photos and so on – and a small suitcase with some of the glass. I want to do a test in the gallery, see what the drop is, where and how I might conceal the mesh I need to hang the threads. That's what I came here for, and I would much rather be doing that than sitting here having to think about how I will get 'covered' as Kathy keeps saying. How to increase 'exposure'. Seems like a contradiction to me, how can I be covered and exposed at the same time?

I do care about what others will say, which is why, despite being weighed down with bags, I made sure I bought a newspaper before catching the train. It's review day, with a full-page article by Isolde Maddox. Jude has mentioned Maddox as a possible contributor to the catalogue. I can think of worse people who might write about me. I read the piece on the train. It's about the New Generation Exhibition, due to start its European tour in Berlin. The show Hal thinks I should be in, would be in, had the MCA show already taken place. As critics go Maddox is of the creative, rather than the parasitic, kind. I marked a paragraph which struck a chord.

> *Irony, used for its own sake, is overplayed by many of these artists; the joke is wearing thin. Irony is powerful when used to expose the pompous, the false, the politically dangerous. Too often here, it's a shield, self-protection. A 'what-you-see-is-what-you-see' attitude prevails; they don't want to be caught believing in anything. To refuse to move beyond the surface is to refuse to take risks, to refuse the imagination and it leaves us becalmed. The most interesting work here speaks of its process, takes imaginative risks. To paraphrase William Blake: art is unceasing practice.*

Towards the end of the piece she listed what she called 'serious omissions' from the exhibition, and my name was there. I can't wait to show Hal. I tore it out, tucked it in my notebook. I wonder if I should show it to Kathy, but we're moving on now to Education and Gallery Events. I'll save this for Ward Joffitt.

I'm still hot, even though I've taken off my jacket, the sun is strong on the window, the air in here is thick.

'So, Sarah,' says Jude, 'tell us where you're at.' Sarah has a stud through her tongue, and one through her bottom lip. I wonder where else she has them.

I need air.

'Ward could you open the window?' So it's not just me; either that or Jude reads my mind.

Ward gets up from his seat, turns to open the window, giving us a prime view of his tight little bum. He swings the window wide, letting in a waft of cool river air. Once Sarah is done with Education and Events it will be Ward's turn.

'The students will be easy with this one, don't you think?' Jude says to Sarah who has outlined a series of talks for undergraduates. 'I want schoolchildren and the general public in here. Access, access, access.' Sarah fumbles amongst her papers, produces rough notes for a worksheet: *What is an Object?*

'And regional links, the industrial past, connections to the port et cetera. We must do all we can to connect the objects in the exhibition to life out there. Maddie, perhaps you can come in on this, tell us more about the glass.'

'Well, yes. It's industrially produced glass that I'm working with. Made in Yorkshire, Featherbridge.' Raw materials – sand, lime – could have travelled from Liverpool along the canal and the finished glass might have travelled back along the canal for export.

There's a welcome breeze through the open window, it ruffles Jude's papers. I notice the gulls again, watch two of them rise and swoop. They are following the river inland. There were gulls at Featherbridge, along the canal.

I was in Featherbridge, walking along the canal with Wilfred Nowells, two months ago. New work takes time. There's thinking time and studio time. I need both. Thinking means looking at the glass from different angles to see how it connects to the world beyond me, Frank, Stella, Faith. I needed to know how and when the glass was made. I found the name J.M.

Bagshott embossed in a piece of the glass. I remembered the name, I'd seen it in the base of a vase we had on the hall table when I was a child, always filled with the same display of dried honesty. Bagshott's wasn't in the phone book. Dom suggested I contact the local museum. It turned out they had a 'living history' display of life in the glassworks and holdings of glass. Bagshott's was taken over in the Sixties. It's all changed, but the factory is still there, along the canal at Featherbridge. I told the man at the museum that I was researching my family history, because it was easier than explaining about my work. I wanted to find out more about my grandfather, I said. He put me on to an amateur historian, Wilfred Nowells. Wilfred Nowells had worked at Bagshott's from the age of fourteen. He's retired now and taken it upon himself to record the history of the glassworks.

'Talk to Wilf,' said the museum man, 'he'll tell you what you need to know, might have known your grandfather.' This seemed too good to be true, after all these years; could it be this easy?

'Do you think he would mind?'

'You'd be doing him a favour, the work he's put in saving the story of Bagshott's. He'll be glad of an audience.'

Dom reckoned that Wilf sounded like a find. 'Obsessive usually, the amateur historian. Not much interpretation or analysis but thorough on data collection, and full of good stories.'

He was right.

Wilfred Nowells lives at the end of a terrace which gives him a reasonable-sized garden for his prize roses and his wife's small aviary. The cooling towers of a power station rise just beyond his potting shed. He was looking out of the front window as I parked awkwardly.

'Miss Armitage?'

'Maddie.'

'You found us then. Cup of tea?'

In the back room, where we sat, there was a cabinet full of the same glass that had filled the shelves of my childhood; the glass which is now in fragments in my studio. It was like being in the dining room of our old house, the house where I grew up and where Faith broke the glass. Wilf has the history of Bagshott's in his head.

'I was a lad in short pants when I went to Bagshott's. My job was to bring beer to the men. I'd go over to The Unicorn, fill up their pint cans. When I first started, I'd faint on account of the heat. But still it were a cut above going down the pit, and better paid.'

I could see the shadow. Frank, hot by the furnace. Maybe Frank had started at Bagshott's as a boy bringing beer to the men. Maybe Wilf took beer to Frank.

'Lilley you say his name was – Frank?'

He didn't remember the name, but then Bagshott's had been large in the Thirties; five bottle shops and the crystal ware. We sat with the curtains drawn, and the constant whirr of Wilf's ancient projector as he showed me slide after slide, which he'd had made from old photographs, newspaper cuttings, catalogues of the glass. Wilf gives talks to schools and local history societies.

'This'll give you a general impression,' he said.

There were pictures of the work's football team: rows of men, arms folded, brilliantined heads; women in the packing sheds, bundled under headscarves; men at the furnace, gathering molten glass on the end of long iron rods. The blowers, cheeks puffed up to the size of a grapefruit, filled the molten substance with the power of their lungs. I let the image of the shadow, which I know so well, slide over these images of men at work.

I was putting some volume, some texture on to the shadow.

'Blower you say, you sure?'

'As far as I know, he was referred to as a glassblower.'

'Likely he'd be on the big stuff, mouth blown.' He showed me a slide of a large man, trousers held up by braces and a thick leather belt, kerchief round his neck to soak the sweat, blowing into moulds so big they were sunk into the floor.

It could have been Frank. The hair on my neck stood up.

'Five-, ten-gallon carboys. Supplied the chemical industry. Bagshott's specialised in the big stuff,' said Wilf.

'Maybe he worked on the crystal,' I said. 'Our house was full of Bagshott's glassware.'

'Happen not if he were a blower. Craftsman. Blown crystal didn't last long. Pressed stuff,' he pointed to the cabinet of glass, my sort of glass.

'That's the stuff,' I said. 'Pressed?'

'Poor man's crystal they called it, semi-automated. Blowers objected, they'd served an apprenticeship. Pressed glass handed half the job over to a machine. Unskilled men could do the job, get paid the same.'

I thought of Frank, de-skilled and de-wifed.

'Likely he was a union man, Glassblowers Protection Society, it were called. I've a loft full of union stuff.'

Angry Frank.

Wilf's wife, Doris, made another pot of tea and laid slices of Battenburg on a Bagshott's cake stand, clear green glass embossed with a leaf design. Pressed, not blown.

Later, Wilf walked me along the canal, showed me the site of the factory. It's been rebuilt and the area along the tow-path has been landscaped. Frank wouldn't recognise the place. We walked along until we reached one of the locks, watched a coal barge pass through. There were gulls perched on the lock gates; if they flew west, they'd end up in Liverpool.

The gulls I'm watching now, out there above the Mersey, seem to be headed towards the sea. Sarah scribbles away and then hands round the draft introduction to the events leaflet.

'I think we should use the industrial link to remind people of this building's past. I mean, it was originally a warehouse for raw materials and goods. Now, the objects stored here are about ideas rather than trade.'

Tell that to Hal and the Wilsons, the Rosenbergs of Chicago, I want to say.

'Some of that industrial stuff, Maddie, we could include in the source material in the catalogue, do you think?' suggests Jude. 'Could we get hold of some of those images, glass production as it was?'

'Maybe.' I think of Faith seeing her hidden life published, laid out as source material. The tidal wave might break. I used to think that what held the wall of water in place was not saying, not speaking. What will happen if others speak on my behalf. Will that count?

I sip my fizzy water.

It's Ward Joffitt's turn. Tight-arsed American. He's in transit, passing through, a necessary stretch on a career path that wants him running The Museum of Modern Art, New York, by the time he's thirty-five. He will co-ordinate the catalogue. Jude has delegated this to him and he's the sort that will take it seriously, want to stamp his mark. Collarless shirt, bloodless lips and one of those haircuts that's always the same, a millimetre short of a shaven head. Rimless spectacles underline his academic credentials. Yale, then doctoral work at Massachusetts Institute, hot-bed of art theorists. I've met his sort before. Career curator who forgets the artist. Thesis is all. Make the work fit the thesis, not the other way around.

'Two, possibly three, newly commissioned essays,' Ward's accent is clipped, East Coast. He suggests Richard Park to write about the early works, the paintings. Well that's all right. Park once wrote something for Hal, he's well thought of.

'The other main piece, in my plan' – note the *my* – 'would be around objects or installations as narrative. Something along the lines of: *Narrative strategies: from painting to the dramatised encounter with the object*. Norman Dixon will be perfect. He's over here on a Fellowship at The Courtauld.'

One of his MIT mates. Careful, Maddie.

'Well,' I say, 'what happened to the idea of using Isolde Maddox?'

'Maddox has lost her theoretical edge if you ask me,' says Ward.

'Oh?' Here we go. Mr Readymade Critique. I want to say: You mean she's seen the limits, not got stuck in the evangelical stage. Cleric. I pull out the article from today's paper.

'I can't agree,' I say, offering the cutting. 'She strikes me as a creative critic.'

'Oh, all that death of irony shit.'

Good, he's ruffled.

'She's strong on process, on art as something beyond language.' I should have kept my mouth shut, spoken to Jude first. No point in having a confrontation, not if I want Maddox in the end.

'There is the possibility of a third piece,' Jude comes in, 'which could be on process, on the need to fabricate, the search for new media, et cetera. Perfect for Maddox.' Ward shunts his spectacles up his shiny nose. Sorry, Ward, but I am inconveniently alive. I know what he thinks: too organic, too pre-symbolic, or perhaps he would want to say sub-symbolic. I've seen the likes of Ward Joffitt give conference papers on the hair's-breadth of difference between the two. I can use the jargon, if I choose. I prefer to put my ideas into my work, not words. My theory is that the likes of Ward Joffitt forget that. I see it from the other end at college. Students come from theory lectures into the studio with a pile of books. I say: Start with the work. What is it that tugs at you? What makes you have to get up off your seat and make something happen? Explore it in your work, save the words for later. It's not theory I object to, it has its place; it's the theorists, the clerics, like Ward Joffitt.

Art is unceasing practice. I quote Maddox and say, 'She'd do a good piece on the way knowledge doesn't always come through words.' I want to say: Experiencing the work directly is the point, not layers of explanation. What matters is being in the studio, trying to get the image in my head out there in the world in a form that others might recognise.

I watch the flint-coloured river through the smart new black railings. The great mass of The Museum of Contemporary Art rises behind me. Once a warehouse, its solid brick has been recently cleaned, its rows of arched windows reglazed. A cast-iron door on each storey, closed off now, indicates where goods were hauled up and down. Ornate iron brackets swing out above them, remnants of the hauling gear. I came here years ago on a geography field-trip from school. The dock was derelict then; it's been remade, given a second chance. My exhibition will be up there on the top floor. The walls are thick so that each arched window has a sill deep enough to form a seat. People can sit and look at the exhibition, but they can also look out towards the estuary; they can watch the river as it heads off into the sea. I like the idea that people can look inwards and outwards from the same place, at the same time. I hope my work will release their thoughts, memories, stories. I hope people will have their own different versions of what the broken glass means to them. It's not easy to put it in words. Being raised in silence means I'm careful with words.

I'm glad of a break after all the talk of this morning. I'm meeting the art handlers soon to discuss the installation. That's what I need to do now, find out how the glass pieces will work in the gallery, make them relate to this building, this place.

Even the cobblestones here have been cleaned and repointed. Along the black railings at the water's edge, there are orange life-belts, brand new, never used. There are signs at the point where stone steps descend to the river. One shows a man standing on the edge of a jetty, beneath him squiggly lines suggest water: DANGER, DEEP WATER, it says. The other is a series of squiggly lines with an arrow passing down and through them: DANGER, STRONG CURRENTS.

The sun is warm on my arms. The river laps against the stone below; a gentle slap, slap, slap.

I will go inside soon but first I want to read the other article I tore from the newspaper. *Grandmother's Footsteps*. The human race owes its success as a species to women beyond childbearing age, it claims. We wouldn't have progressed beyond the Savannah without our grandmothers who, during droughts, foraged for food while their daughters gave birth. Grandmothers chewed berries and roots to a pulp, weaned their grandchildren so their daughters could bear more. A vital link. In times of plenty grandmothers modelled figures from clay, props in the stories they told to their grandchildren. Stories of wonder and warnings, of what came before. Today, the article concludes, grandmothers are essential for our sense of identity, continuity and reassurance in a complex world. I think of the woman I saw near my studio, scooping the child on to her back, the child melting into her body; Stella in the funeral parlour, skin like a church candle, her stone-cold head full of stories never told, beyond recall.

I see the catalogue Ward Joffitt will produce. He will fish at the story behind my work. He's talking about using a detail of the photograph of Faith and Irene for the cover.

It's out of my hands. This exhibition is happening, almost despite me.

Exposed. Covered.

Deep water, strong currents.

If a tidal wave breaks is there always loss, injury?

Maybe it's possible to give a warning.

A police patrol boat speeds by. In its wake the slap of water increases to a smack. Drops of the river splash my jeans.

Touch-Me-Not 5

Even though I'm expecting it, the stone of Faith's kitchen floor comes as a shock through the soles of my bare feet. I shiver.

'Sleep well?' says Faith pulling cling film across a bowl, tight as a drum. Barely glancing in my direction she turns the bowl to seal the rim, puts it in the fridge, then scuttles to the cooker where a pan lid tinkles, dancing on steam.

'Giblets,' she says, though I haven't asked.

I'd know that smell anywhere; it wafts back down the years, past each family roast lunch. Faith lifts the lid, quietens its insistent jiggling for a moment, takes a spoon and skims the scum from the bubbling surface.

'Like a log,' I say. Since she did ask, I will answer. 'Like a log.' Which isn't entirely true, but I collude. Keep to the surface. Cheery, buoyant. No jumping in the deep end, letting go of the side and plunging down, together.

She wants to know that I've slept, that I'm no longer tired. She does care. If I hadn't slept well she would be sympathetic, suggest I go back to bed; she'd tiptoe around to make sure I wasn't disturbed. But she wouldn't want to delve, to know why, come close. Faith can't bear to be touched. She cares from afar. Physically present but not connected. It's unsettling. She likes me near; close by is not the same as intimate.

When I was a child she would sit on the edge of my bed, tuck the sheets under my chin. If I were to wriggle my shoulder free, dare to release my arms towards a possible hug, she would bristle, tuck me up again. When I was fifteen, dumped by my first boyfriend, grief-stricken, beyond caring what kind of spectacle I made, I shut myself in my room and cried, flooded with feelings too big to keep in. She put her head round the door, 'Do try to eat.' I reached towards her, she stiffened, her arms stayed at her side. Her eyes were cold, glassy, fixed, like a doll with its eyelids forced open. Lost in something never to be shared. It was a greater rejection than being dumped by the boy. 'Do try to eat,' she said and scurried inside herself, turned her back. 'I'll warm some soup.'

So, I tell her that I've slept like a log, sealing off the possibility of open-ended, loose talk that might go anywhere. I'm beginning to see that I'm as adept as she is, which disturbs me.

She doesn't want to know that I woke at dawn thinking: What a prick Ward Joffitt is. She doesn't want the messy details of the dream: me on a loo in a wide open space trying to shit, with Ward dressed in priestly robes insisting he watch. I won't tell her how scary it felt trying not to shit in front of Ward Joffitt, even though I was bursting. It wasn't simply the discomfort of clenching a loaded bowel, it was like constraining the entire contents of my skin. She'd be proud of me, I'm sure, for my restraint, keeping myself to myself. She wouldn't like the next bit: me realising that if I dumped, I'd make him sick, he'd leave. Suddenly, from all around, not just from me, there's shit flying.

Covered. Exposed.

Faith scrubs the toilet after she's used it, opens the window wide. I've never smelled her, seen a single skid-mark on the porcelain, never seen her menstrual blood, her sweat. I don't catch the scent of her body, just the bleach, the deodorant.

No point in trying to start a conversation about my disturbed night, my messy dreams.

Faith doesn't do conversation.

Conversation feeds on memory. Talking about this morning can lead to yesterday, last week, last year, a lifetime. *Do you remember when . . . ?* Faith avoids conversation, instead she reports. Information scrolls from her like a protective layer: the tasks achieved, those still to be tackled, events at Stonebank, Edward's family, village life. Telegraphic headlines.

'. . . bookings are down this autumn . . .'

'. . . starts school in September . . .'

'A hundred and one last month, Mr Booth. Still collects his own pension . . .'

Concise, leading nowhere. We don't want to imagine what it must be like for Mr Booth to be a hundred and one. Think of all the past he has. If bookings are down at Stonebank what of Faith's future?

She's been at Stonebank for twenty years, lived here for more years than she's lived anywhere else. She wanted to sell up, leave Chester as soon as Dad went off to Australia with Marjorie Allen from the Abbey National. It was at the end of my second year at college, a year after she broke the glass. She waited until I graduated, which to her meant that, technically, I'd left home. Situations vacant in *The Lady*. A retreat. A mixture of Buddhism and psychology. Brian was starting up and wanted someone to be housekeeper and bookkeeper. *Would suit mature, single woman*. He liked the fact that she thought he was an oddball who needed sorting out. The pay wasn't much but the cottage came with the job. Faith didn't hide the fact that she thought the whole enterprise was cranky, but since the guests undertook not to speak during their stay it hardly mattered. She was pleased to find a job where her bookkeeping skills were valued.

She has never said so but I think she wanted to be back in Yorkshire. Once we'd all left Chester she didn't want to live her days in that alien place, where she'd only ended up because of Dad's promotion to Deputy Branch Manager. There was always the feeling that Faith was uneasy in Chester, which is surprising because it is a Faith-like place: neat, tidy, its limits defined by ancient, immovable stone walls. She never lost her Yorkshire accent. It was smoothed down, but anyone could hear that she wasn't from around there.

Where is Faith from? Where could she go back to?

Not Bickersthorpe, the village where Stella lived and now lies in her grave. Bickersthorpe was never Faith's home. What about Featherbridge where she and Irene and Frank lived in the black hole of Stella's absence? A place I'm starting to get to know, having visited Wilf Nowells. I might go back again, especially if Wilf finds evidence of Frank in his loft.

'No Wilf, think of your back,' Doris Nowells was not happy when Wilf offered to climb into the loft to see if he could find Frank amongst his boxes of union records. It was tantalising to think what might be up there, but I could hardly insist. Wilf promised that the next time his son visited he would ask him to bring the boxes down. Wilf has had a letter from a university asking him to donate his collection of material to its archive of labour history.

'It's a job that needs doing. We haven't the space,' said Doris.

'I've photographs of Protection Society Committees from 1925 to 1939, I think,' Wilf said. He promised to telephone if he found anything but he hasn't called.

Going to Featherbridge felt like a betrayal. Prying into Faith's secret life. If she knew I'd been, it might crack her shell, puncture the membrane.

Isn't that what we've steered away from these years? Dad buggered off to the other side of the earth, Edward is buried in his insect world listening out for the wingbeats of moths, and I have my art. Making things, avoiding words.

Faith wants me to visit her but I'm risky to have around. I've learned never to ask directly, but she knows, I'm sure, that I watch her and wonder. All the stuff we've avoided, for years, stacks up. The unsaid inhibits conversation. Sweep things under the carpet for long enough, the contour will show.

Unanswered questions don't go away.

A natural curiosity, I think.

Poking around in what doesn't concern me, she thinks.

So I make art; I use other kinds of language. I make coded things, hints, clues. Like the people of Laputa in *Gulliver's Travels*, who communicated through objects not words, holding up things to say what they meant, I show my work. I hope Faith will see and understand.

Faith couldn't go back to Featherbridge. This is close enough; she's in the right county, her words sound like everyone else's. Down in this valley she's safe behind the humped back of the moor which lies between here and Featherbridge.

Faith's cottage is a thick-walled, stone haven that clings to the side of the cliff, embedded. It is lower down the valley than the main house. This is the appeal, I'm sure. She belongs to a community whilst being set apart. Faith could never live entirely alone. In complete isolation it would be impossible to keep the past at bay.

The village is twenty minutes' walk away, a steep climb, but she has the car. I worry about what will happen when she has to stop driving. No sign of it yet, though. At seventy-five she could have retired long ago, especially as Brian has someone to manage the place now. Faith still keeps an eye on the books and the post, goes up to the office for a couple of hours a day. When she first came she did a bit of everything. She set up the office, the accounts and dealt with the bookings. She drove down to the cash-and-carry and stocked up the larder, supervised the cleaners on the Saturday turnaround, mucking in herself, helping to remake the beds. Faith is an expert bed maker; sheets and blankets, of course. She was miffed when Brian finally bought duvets.

Faith doesn't hold with duvets.

Here, in her cottage, the beds are properly made with pressed linen sheets. Ironed flat, then folded and re-ironed with each folding. Spreading the sheet out to make the bed, Faith will line up the centre fold down the middle of the bed, so that it hangs evenly each side. She will tuck it tight beneath the mattress, lifting the ends to make envelope corners. She does the same with each layer: bottom sheet, top sheet, one, two blankets, depending on the season. Inside these stone walls it's always chilly. In her neat parcel of a bed, orderly in the corner of her room, Faith is held tight beneath the blankets' weight. The top layers are turned back to make a tidy cuff pulled up against her chin, secure against her dreams.

When I was a child, Faith would sometimes change all the sheets twice a week. It was as if the slightest stain was too much evidence of life going on. Sometimes I don't change my sheet for weeks; each stain a diary entry. And, I have a duvet. There's no work to duvets, thinks Faith; no way to make the room look straight, and at night, in bed, there is nothing but a soft weightlessness, open on all sides.

Besides my dream of Ward Joffitt, I woke last night because the envelope corners had worked loose, blankets and sheets had slid halfway to the floor. I must have been restless to rumple a Faith-made bed. It was almost light, birds beginning to stir above the murmur of the river. It is a murmur from up here; down below it will be a roar as the river swells with spring rain, thunders across ancient mossy boulders. Edward will want to take the boys down there tomorrow, William and James. He'll turn over stones to show his sons the hidden world of insects. The boys will giggle and squeal as the beetles writhe, surprised by the sudden light and the insects will scuttle away, seek the dark. Edward would be happy to live with his moths and beetles, to crawl into the darkness under a stone, or into the crack of a tree's bark. You have to admire a man who has narrowed the world down to the winter wingless moth, his current research project.

When I taught in Liverpool I would sometimes come here for a week or more during college vacations, though it's never felt like my home. It would take a few days to get used to the sound of the river. I would hear it in my sleep and dream that someone was trying to tell me something. I could never see the person. It felt like Faith whispering, her mouth close to my ear, not quite touching, breath cold when I was expecting warmth. She was saying something I could never quite hear. I would wake, realise it was only the river, the persistent sound of running water at the edge of my hearing.

I hauled up the sheets and blankets then I lay quite still, concentrating on the gathering birdsong of the dawn chorus. I wanted to see if it was possible to shut out the sound of the river. I went blissfully, deeply back to sleep.

'I've one or two things to do round here this morning,' says Faith rummaging in the cupboard under the sink.

'Anything I can do?'

'I don't think so.'

'Sure?'

'You could give me a hand when the next load of washing has finished. Lovely drying day.'

'It's the weekend, take it easy.'

'I like to keep busy.'

Need to, she means.

'Thought I'd go for a walk before lunch, while the sun's out. Want to come?' I say.

'Oh no. You go. I've things to do here and I want to pop into the office and sort the post. You enjoy your walk. I thought we'd go to town this afternoon.'

She's found what she was looking for. A bottle of lavender-coloured liquid. I don't know why I expect conversation. Why not fall in with the fluent chatter of her tasks. Wash, polish, scrub, iron, fold, knead, knit. Strong verbs. She opens the back door, shaking the bottle as she goes.

'Poured down yesterday before I'd time to finish the outside.'

'Couldn't you get someone in to do that?'

'Not worth the trouble, easier to do it myself.'

'You must have someone to clean windows up at the Centre, couldn't they do the cottage at the same time?'

'I hadn't planned to do the windows but this weather, well, I must make the most of it . . .' No, she hadn't planned to clean windows. She's not dressed for doing what she calls 'the heavy'. She's wearing an overall to protect her going-to-town clothes. I can see the hem of her navy, knife-pleat skirt.

I don't know why she still affects me so much, it's not a surprise, she's always been like this. She's not going to change. I wonder if it's me; is she worse when I'm around? Her sensors are on full alert. She can smell my desire to talk, pungent as bubbling giblets.

What would happen if I said: Come in Faith, leave that, let's have a chat, let's catch up. Remember when you broke the glass, all those years ago in the long, hot summer? Well, I'm going to put it all back together again. Or: I think I might be pregnant, you know, having a baby. Another grandchild. I might have a girl, to go with Edward's boys. Would you like that? A little girl. You could knit a bonnet. That's if I have it. Do you think I should? Will I know how to be a mother? The father's married already, so that's tricky. An impossible fantasy of a wise mother, who could tell me what to do next. We can't do it. Inside my potentially wise mother lies a seething child, back against the door, eyes staring, fierce. She's keeping the wall of water in place. We don't want the wave to break. We're stuck, Faith and me, both in our solitary confinement, exiled, on either side of the invisible membrane, cling-filmed off from one another.

Faith's cottage is too far down the valley for me. It's not so bad today with the sun shining, but when it's wet the outlook is overbearing. Faith wakes up each day, confronted by the rock mass of the cliff. So little sun gets through. Trees rise from the river, tightly packed like heads of broccoli, then the green density gives way to a stern outcrop of rock against sky. Millstone grit. What I see when I look out of the window is trees and rock; dense, dark. Faith was a midwinter baby, born into darkness on the shortest day. Spring and summer must have come as a shock. I was born in March, month of madness, the day the clocks changed. Here in Faith's cottage, if I want to see the sky, to reach light, I must make an effort, look up to where rock meets sky. There's a row of fence posts, so high I can't see the wire that joins one to the other, but I know it's there, keeping the sheep from the cliff edge.

Faith gives the bottle one more vigorous shake, then unscrews its white cap, lets the creamy liquid pour on to a soft, white rag. She dabs it on to the window. Making circular movements, she smears the Windolene round and round; streaky white clouds gather across the valley wall. Faith disappears. She makes a line round the edge of the pane, to be sure the glass is coated. She pauses, admires her handiwork; the Windolene dries. She takes a clean yellow duster and circles again over the chalky deposits. She comes back into view as the clouds disappear. It's as if she's waving.

Annie always said I should ask her in a straightforward way: Tell me about Stella, why did she leave? What was Frank like? But the past, which intrigues me, doesn't exist for Faith; it lies in permanent shadow. If I did ask, she would say: it's none of your business, before your time. What's done is done. Least said, soonest mended.

Nothing said, nothing mended, I would like to say, but never do.

I'm forty-one years old. I could open my mouth now and make those words come out. I could say them gently, hold her so she wouldn't fall off the edge. I wouldn't let her fall. If I put my arms around her and spoke the words she would stiffen, run to the airing cupboard and wash sheets that are already clean. I shudder when I think of that time I tried to hold her after Stella's funeral. I can't bear to think of it. Her rage, silent rage. This is how it is, the wanting to speak weighed up against the consequences.

If I speak now the tidal wave might flood the valley, water rising up to the sky.

'Aren't you having breakfast? Shall I poach an egg?'

'Toast is all I want, I'll do it. Do you have any herb teas?'

'There's a box of those fruit sachets. You left them last time you were here.'

'Can I make you a cup?'

'No, nothing for me. I'll pop up to the office.' Perpetual motion, folding rag and duster as she scurries through the kitchen, puts them away under the sink alongside the bottles of bleach and disinfectant. *Kills all known household germs*. The past is a bacteria to be wiped out. She turns off the gas under the giblets.

'I'll leave you to your toast and your walk. We'll have a sandwich around one-thirty, I thought, and then get off to town. I'll make an apple crumble later.'

I will walk down to the bridge, cross the river and climb the lane up the other side of the valley, to the cliff edge. Rise above it. Here, in Faith's home, it's like being on a shelf. We can only sidle along the narrow strip of land which extends to form a garden to one side of the cottage. A place of safety for Faith where the past can't find her. She's out of reach, steady on her ledge; dusted and polished like a glass figure on a mantel.

To go anywhere from here means a steep walk up or down. Best not to think about the gradient of the lane, remember that the view from the top is worth the effort. It's all right after the first, steep drag. The trick is not to look up. I will keep my eye on the verge. I noticed, as I arrived yesterday, the cow parsley is as high as my shoulder, the first shoots of Himalayan balsam pushing through beneath. When I was here last September the lane was flanked with balsam in full bloom; dusky pink petals on tall stems, blossoms which look like a mouth open for a kiss. As I reached to touch one, its hidden torpedo pods exploded, showering a hail of white seeds.

Touch-me-nots, that's what they call them round here.

Lupins 5

It is beautiful. If this were my home I would want to live here, high up, not with my nose pressed to the valley wall, like Faith. Up here I could fly. The ampleness of the moor stretches around me like a broad-backed creature, huddled on its haunches, dozing. Faith's cottage has disappeared, down amongst the tight-headed trees which form a dark scar on the creature's flank. Faith is hiding, like one of Edward's beetles, happy under the weight of rock.

I could sit here all day, but I'd better get back soon, help Faith to hang out the washing before we set off for town.

In memory of Eleanor Strickland, 1906–1996, who enjoyed this view until the day she died, says the small brass plate on the bench where I sit. Eleanor Strickland must have been a sprightly ninety-year-old to make it up here every day; perhaps someone drove her here. A name, some dates and a single piece of information; enough to make me curious, to recall Eleanor Strickland. She's here in the landscape, part of the view. I've often wondered whether anyone put up a headstone for Stella. Perhaps Ernest sent money.

Stella was buried, laid in the ground. I know because I stood at the edge of her grave, black earth, cleanly dug, cracked by the drought. The plain pine coffin was lowered, awkwardly, bare and forlorn. I didn't feel like me. I was in a play, a dream, watching someone like me. As I watched I thought: Stella's not in there, she's not stiff, lifeless, irreversibly mute in a box. No, she's slipped away from the funeral parlour, back to her old folks' bungalow, glad of the opportunity to straighten her hair.

'Man that is born of a woman hath but a short time to live, and is full of misery,' said the vicar and I wondered why he was carrying on now that Stella had left. 'He cometh up, and is cut down, like a flower; he fleeth as it were a shadow . . .'

Illogical though it seems now, I remember thinking: She died to shock us, make Faith realise that it was time they settled their differences. Now that she's made her point, I thought, she's waiting for us to visit. I imagined her sitting before the mirror in her bedroom. She'd thrown off her shroud, put on her own clothes; skirt and cardigan beneath a wrap-around apron with its swirling floral print and strings tied in a bow in the small of her back. Even as we stood there listening to the vicar's pious drone she would be brushing her soft grey hair, dividing it into strands to make plaits, one each side of her head. I must be patient, I thought, allow the vicar to finish the ceremony. '. . . the soul of our dear sister here departed . . .' It would have been rude to leave. When it was over, I decided, I would go to the bungalow, talk to Stella, listen to her story so I could explain it to Faith. I thought it would be best not to tell Stella about the broken glass. I would take a message from Stella back home to Faith. Faith might be cross, at first, that I had gone without saying anything, but I would explain, she would understand.

A neighbour of Stella's, Edith, had approached me as we made our way from the church to the burial plot.

'Are you Madeleine?'

I couldn't speak, so I nodded.

'Stella would be so glad you came.'

Stella?

I wasn't sure who she was talking about, because up until that moment the woman who everyone thought was in the box, but who I knew was elsewhere, had been Grandma Lilley to me. I always wondered about her name. I almost wrote to ask her once, at the bottom of one of my Christmas Thank You letters: P.S. Would you mind telling me what your first name is? Of course, I didn't. Well, I thought, now I know.

After the service, back at Stella's bungalow, there was only Edith, no Stella. Edith made pots of tea and set out plates of bridge rolls and whist pies. Amongst the neighbours, and friends from church, I was the only relative and I knew her the least. I was having tea in my grandmother's home but she wasn't there. Also, it was new to me, it wasn't the house we had visited when I was eight years old; the one and only time we had visited Stella, the day we had a picnic by the reservoir and Ernest had insisted we drive on to Bickersthorpe. Even though I knew from Stella's letters and cards that she had moved, I had expected to see the same old terraced house we had visited, not this new bungalow. I was hoping to see that house again because it was dim in my mind, still is. I don't remember much beyond us pulling into the yard behind it, Edward being sick on his *Beano*. Standing in the new bungalow after Stella's funeral I wondered if I had imagined this other house. The Council would be eager to move someone else in soon; this was to be the one and only time to see my grandmother's home. Edith said I was to take anything I wanted from Stella's belongings.

'You'll want something personal, I expect,' she said.

There wasn't much. I didn't know what to take. It felt like stealing. I've often wondered what I might have taken if I'd dared. I was only nineteen. I thought I was so grown up. Actually going to the funeral had taken all my strength, all my courage; it simply didn't feel right, looking through her belongings. Her personal effects. There was a glass trinket tray on her dressing table, in it a pile of hairpins threaded with her soft grey hair. By the bed her slippers sagged in the shape of her bunioned feet. It didn't seem possible that she was dead. The hairpins, the slippers, waiting for her, alive. In the bathroom amongst the denture paste and corn plasters I found some ancient talcum powder. It looked like something from a museum. The container was made of cardboard. The white background was faded to grey, there was a huge flower print and the word *Gardenia* in flowing script. I unscrewed the lid. There was a piece of gauze through which to shake the powder. It smelt of nothing, the gardenia had long since faded. The lover, I thought. This would have been a gift from the lover, that is why she kept it. I wondered what happened to the lover, if there really was one. I have spun this version so often, I feel as if I have met him. Sometimes I think I have met him.

By her bed there was a photograph in a silver frame of me and Edward. I must have been about five or six. We were standing either side of a large snowman, togged up in thick winter coats, woolly hats, gloves and scarves, knitted by Faith, our trousers tucked into Wellington boots. Ernest was leaning into the picture from one side. I remember making the snowman. I remember that Ernest had bought a new camera and he wanted to take a picture of Faith but she wouldn't let him. I looked at my six-year-old self and realised how much I looked like the six-year-old Faith, but I was smiling; a broad grin and my eyes looked bright, bursting with curiosity. I'm glad I smiled for Grandma Lilley. To think that she lived with this winter version of us. I imagine that Ernest sent it. I didn't find any more photographs. To her I was always six and it was always winter.

I didn't know what to take; in the end, I took the apron hanging on the back of the kitchen door and the spectacles on the sideboard, because that's what I remembered about her when we visited her. Her spectacles and the apron that went right round her body. I held it up and imagined the soft warmth of her flesh inside it. The garden at Stella's bungalow was small but well tended with a border of forget-me-nots, wild geraniums and a bird bath in the centre of a patch of grass, too small to call a lawn. I stood with the kitchen door open and a blackbird appeared on the fence.

'Will you look at that,' said Edith, her eyes brimming. 'She tamed them you know. If she was here he'd come right inside. Talked to him for hours, she did.'

Two crows, sleek black feathers ruffled by the wind, land on the fence that marks the edge of the valley cliff, ready to soar or dive; they could go either way. With the wind lifting them high they could cross the moor in no time, swoop down on Bickersthorpe, Stella's garden, someone else's now. This was the landscape we drove through the one time we went to Bickersthorpe, visited Stella in her old house, the one I find it hard to picture now.

I was eight. Dad had recently passed his driving test and bought his first car.

'A hole to throw your money in,' said Faith. Ernest needed a car because he had been transferred from the Chester Branch to Denbigh. Faith saw the car as a functional thing, a way of getting to work each day. She agreed that having a car was better than moving to a foreign country, which was how Faith viewed Wales. Ernest saw the car as a way of widening our horizons.

'Come on, Faith,' he would say. 'Let's go for a spin.' Going for a spin was a flagrant waste, to Faith. I'd like to think she was an environmentalist ahead of her time. For Ernest 'motoring' was a hobby. He took me and Edward to the coast. We drove up The Wirral on the Dee side, stretched our legs on the sands at Hoylake before driving back down the Mersey side; such a contrast between the polite semis of the outward journey and the cranes of the Cammell Laird shipyard on the return. Once, we drove through the Mersey tunnel and on up the coast to Southport. We walked for miles on firm, flat sand looking for the sea, which we never reached, my cardigan itchy on my skin. One weekend Ernest announced we were going somewhere different, inland. It was something he'd read about in the papers; a new dam, a reservoir, a spectacle of engineering.

'Educational,' he said, 'for the children.' He had made up his mind.

'We'll make a day of it,' he said. I don't know how he persuaded Faith, but she agreed to come, reluctantly made egg sandwiches and wrapped them in the waxed paper that came off the loaf. She filled a large thermos flask with tea. The first part of the journey was boring, but the other side of Manchester, as we climbed higher, it started to look like this: bare moor, a few stone cottages. It made me feel sad and excited at the same time. Edward and I played I-spy, until Edward said he felt car sick and Faith said I was to leave him alone.

'He needs to concentrate,' she said, 'if he's not to be sick.'

We reached the new reservoir by late morning. The dam was a vast, curved wall, holding back millions of gallons of water. Ernest told us of the fuss there had been about having to flood the valley. A village had been sacrificed for this: a farm, a school, a row of cottages, lost now under the weight of water. Most of the twenty inhabitants had got a better deal from the relocation so it didn't matter, but one woman who was nearly a hundred had protested. It was in all the papers, but they moved her anyway.

'You'd think they could have waited, she wouldn't have lived for ever,' said Ernest.

Edward and I played hide-and-seek amongst the gorse bushes. The grass was coarse and clipped, nibbled by sheep. Faith made a fuss about setting the tartan rug down on sheep droppings. In the end they spread it out next to a clump of boulders, and Faith lay back against the rock.

It was my turn to hide. Edward couldn't find me. I was squeezed between two boulders right by Faith. I knew it was a good place, so near to Mum and Dad that Edward wouldn't think of looking.

'It's not an hour's ride from here, Faith,' Ernest was saying. 'She's your mother.' Faith had that doll's-eye look, fixed on the still water; she was somewhere else. Somewhere she kept to herself. She said nothing. Not a word. Ernest kept on: 'She's only seen the children the once, and they were babies. It's not right. You haven't seen her since Irene died.' I wondered who this Irene was. I didn't know then about the photograph in the collar box; I hadn't found it yet. I wondered when Irene had died, and what it had to do with not seeing our grandmother who, to me, was a birthday card and a line of loopy writing. *With love from your Grandma Lilley*. Ernest's words pushed against Faith's silence; it felt dangerous. 'I think they would like to meet their grandmother. You could swallow your pride for an hour. She might not even be in.'

The more silent Faith was, the more Ernest talked. I wished he would stop, he might go too far. When she looked like that it was as if she was crying inside, the tears welling up inside her. She might burst. I once made a piece of work about Faith's hidden tears.

Thinking now about that visit to the reservoir, it was as if Ernest had always intended to visit Stella. The new reservoir was an excuse to pitch us within striking distance, wear down Faith's considerable defences.

'Anyway,' he carried on. 'We can't stop here much longer.' He pointed to the gathering darkness in the sky. Within a few minutes the dry stone that I was wedged between was spattered with dark spots that quickly joined up. Fat raindrops landed on my bare arms.

'Hurry, Madeleine, you'll ruin those new sandals.'

As we bundled into the car the rain grew to a torrent. Even more water pressing down on the drowned village. I hoped that the old woman's house was still standing, that it hadn't been crushed by the weight of water. There would be fish swimming in and out of her broken windows.

As we set off, nobody spoke. We could hardly see for the rain. We could have been anywhere. After what seemed ages, though it can only have been half an hour, the rain eased up, but the silence remained. The silence came from Faith. It was vast like the moor, dense as the dark sky. It filled the car, pushing its way into every corner, forcing out the air. I thought I would stop breathing. Each breath felt shallower and shallower. The only way for me to breathe again would be to speak, say something to puncture the invisible mass. But if I did that then something worse might happen, so I hummed quietly. A tentative, barely audible sound that came out through my nose; my mouth stayed shut tight. Faith and Ernest wouldn't hear it because of the engine noise. Edward was looking out of the window so as not to be sick. A hum to keep me alive, push away enough of the silence for me to breathe. In my head I said my name over and over to myself, in case the silence, not content with taking all the air, might swallow my memory.

Madeleine Armitage, Maddie Armitage, Maddiearmitage, mitagemaddiearmitagemitagemaddiearm. It speeded up, faster and faster inside my head until it sounded like nonsense, the letters turned to liquid, drained away so the sounds no longer attached themselves to me. When I thought I could bear it no longer, I realised the car was slowing down. The sun was out again. We were coming into a village. We passed an old church, which I would see again, over a decade later, the day Stella was buried. We passed beneath a railway bridge. 'Left here, isn't it?' Ernest said. Ordinary words but they sounded strange against the silence. Faith said nothing. We passed a large black mountain of coal and there were terraces at right angles to the road, short terraces which backed on to an area of common ground, a dirt yard. As we turned into one of these yards the car wobbled over the uneven ground. Me, Edward and Ernest shook from side to side. Faith sat with her head erect, shoulders stiff, back pressed against the passenger seat, not moving.

'Look,' said Ernest, 'she might not be in.' As the car stopped Edward was sick; it landed on *The Beano*, which lay open on his lap.

Tomorrow, Edward will bring his two boys here; William, aged two and James, aged four. William and James know their grandmother. I expect they are looking forward to coming. I've never clicked with Nancy, Edward's wife. There's no hostility, we just don't have much in common. She's quiet, sweet-natured. It seems to me that she's playing house, happy to shape herself around the demands of Edward's career. She gave up her job to be a full-time mother. Edward is getting to look like Ernest.

'Right lads,' I imagine him saying, 'let's go for a spin. We're going to Grandma Faith's. Auntie Madeleine will be there.' They will pile in the car, climb up away from the city, semi-detach themselves from their suburb on the outskirts of Manchester, drive up over the bare back of the moor. It's basking in the sun at the moment, but more often it's set hard against wind and rain. Now, with the sun out, it seems a benevolent creature, it draws me in, makes me feel at home. I forget that underneath the rain-soft green lies unyielding stone.

The walk back down to Faith's cottage is almost as strenuous as the walk up. If I was a car I'd be in a low gear. The effort of resisting the gradient puts a strain on my knees. I could fall forwards any moment, tumble head-over-heels. If I fell I wouldn't be able to stop until I hit the bottom. Round the next bend Faith's cottage comes into view. What is she doing? She makes her way along her ledge of a garden, laden with what looks like a basket of washing. What she can't see is the weather coming in from across the moor, banks of cloud, hanging low, getting darker, creeping this way. The sun is still shining on her strip of land. She is too low down to see the change that is headed her way. Within the hour it will be raining. If I shout she won't hear. As I get closer, I can see that she's hanging out blankets. Washing blankets is a bad sign. She washed blankets in the days after she broke the glass. She washed blankets after Stella made her surprise visit to us.

I was twelve, the summer holiday had just begun, at the end of my first year at Grammar School. We weren't going away that year. Dad was off work for his annual two weeks and we were having a holiday at home. It was the day the Americans were going to attempt a moon landing. Ernest said we could stay up and watch. 'This is a historic day,' he said. 'You will be able to tell your children about it.' Because of the moon landing we hadn't gone out for the day. Stella arrived out of the blue, late morning. Faith had one load in the washing machine already, she was setting up the line in the garden, and Ernest was catching up with his weeding. Stella arrived with a man I had never seen before. He brought her in his car to our house. I learned later, at Stella's funeral, that he was her neighbour, Malcolm, Edith's husband.

Ernest showed them into the front room. Faith banged around in the kitchen making a pot of tea. Edward and I were sent in to say hello.

'Go and say hello to your Grandma Lilley,' said Ernest.

We stood there, awkward in front of her. She had horn-rimmed glasses, her hair was in two plaits coiled either side of her head. She wore a blue skirt and a ribbed, white cardigan that looked hand-knitted. It had pearl buttons. As we stood there, I could feel Faith come in the room behind me, she put a tray of tea things down on a side table. We were all standing.

'Won't you sit down,' said Ernest.

Nothing else was said. With Faith in the room the silence changed from a normal, awkward silence to a stiff, starched-collar sort of silence. It chaffed.

White noise crackled around us.

There was a tear in Stella's eye, a resolve in Faith's jaw.

'My, how you two have grown,' Stella managed to say, and she handed us five shillings each.

'Off you go now, you two,' Ernest said.

I took the two half-crowns and put them in my money box. Edward went to his bedroom, shut his door and busied himself with his Airfix kit, pleased now he had enough to buy another

Spitfire for his fleet. I listened from the landing. I couldn't hear what was being said, only intermittent mumbling and once, a sharp sound that was Faith raising her voice.

'Well, you know where I am.' Stella's voice was suddenly clearer, nearer as the sitting-room door opened and the four of them fumbled into the hall. Ernest walked them to the car. I watched from my bedroom window. No sign of Faith. I thought the man who turned out to be Malcolm looked kind. He stood tall over Stella, the brass buttons on his blazer gleaming. He held her gently at the elbow, walked round to the passenger door, and steadied her. Stella looked pained as she eased her stiff joints into the car seat.

Faith bustled upstairs, flung open the doors of the landing cupboard, and took out a couple of blankets.

'Has Grandma Lilley gone?' I said.

The words were out before I could stop them. I was shocked by my boldness. Why hadn't I thought before I spoke? 'Grandma Lilley.' I heard the words as Faith would hear them.

Over-familiar. Impudent. Disrespectful.

It was worse than if I had sworn. She was my grandmother but she had been kept a stranger and here I was claiming her, being familiar with her as if Grandma Lilley visited us every week. It would have been better if I had sworn. Faith had her glass-eyed look, staring at something no one else could see; something that, if revealed, might finish us all. She pulled out another blanket.

'I thought you were going to Annie's.' She was wearing a summer frock, a blue background with a pattern of white flowers. A shirt-waister, fitted on top but with a full skirt and a deep, tight belt. With a swish of crisp cotton she busied me away.

'I've things to do.' She had washing to hang, a step to scrub.

I banged the front door but didn't go out, I wanted her to think I had gone to Annie's. I sneaked down the garden and hid, crouching behind the lupins, my back pressed against the fence, which smelt of creosote. Ernest was proud of his lupins, cones towering in the July heat. He staked and labelled them. I read the words he had written on white tags: Noble Maidens, Russell, The Governor.

Faith heaved out a basket of damp towels, Ernest was in the

vegetable patch, ridging and mulching his potatoes. 'You've to keep out all the light,' he once explained to me. He leaned on his fork.

'She is your mother,' he said to Faith's back.

Up went another towel.

'Faith, did you hear what I said?'

She went inside for more washing. Sheets. She pegged them, the corner of one overlapping the corner of the next. A borderline of white linen the width of the garden.

'When all's said and done, she is your mother.'

Faith had a peg between her teeth.

'She came all that way, Faith. Doesn't that tell you something?'

Up went the last sheet.

The blankets were already swirling in the machine, they would be next.

'Whatever happened, it's past. Something and nothing in the first place, if you ask me. So why keep this up? Life goes on, you know. They're landing a man on the moon today.'

Faith had said nothing up to now, but when he said this she turned and spoke in a tight, cold voice. I was scared. The words didn't make sense. The voice didn't sound like the voice of anyone I knew.

'My mother might as well have lived on the moon. I've had to manage without a mother since I was six years old. Why would I want one now?'

My nose was up against one of the giant varieties, pouches purple as church robes swirling from the fat, pink stem. I touched one, ever so lightly. Its hood fell away to reveal a black-tipped stamen; a tight curve, a well-kept secret. I squeezed it. Orange pollen spiralled from its tip. You must know where to put the pressure, there is so much in a single pouch.

'Would you mind shutting the door,' says Faith, as she settles down behind her knitting. Faith hates to see an open door. I'm only too happy to oblige as it keeps out the smell of damp blankets draped on the airer in the kitchen. Faith works fast, her fingers animating the needles, looping the wool, over and over: loop and slide, loop and slide. Clickerty, click, working her way up the back of a sweater for Edward; grey, ribbed, sensible. It's almost finished.

'He needs layers when he's out on field work,' she says. The ball of wool is nearly used up, there isn't enough for her to complete the back, even though she's only rows away from casting off.

'You need more wool,' I say, 'where is it?'

'It's all right, I'll get it.'

'Tell me where it is, I'll fetch it for you.' It's as if she'd rather not be in my debt, if I do something for her, does she think she will owe me?

'The cupboard under the stairs,' she says.

It's a relief to leave the room, if only for a few minutes. The effort of staying within Faith's limits makes time expand, slow down, go backwards.

In the cupboard there are many shades of wool stacked on the shelves: navy, red, cream, brown. Some in small tight balls, left over from previous sweaters, others still as skeins waiting to be wound.

'Is this it?' I say, returning with a skein the same colour as the sweater back.

'That's it. While you're up would you mind switching on the television?' There's a documentary about to start, wildlife in Antarctica. Faith likes documentaries. I suggest the film on another channel but I can see she's not keen. Faith is not at ease with stories of any kind. She might fall into a story, become caught in its web. I flip the channels, adjust the tuning; reception is patchy this side of the valley. Her television is old, a big box. On top sits a polished wooden ornament: Three Wise Monkeys. One with its hands over its ears, the next with hands over its eyes, the third clasps its mouth.

I get a good picture. *Weekend Review* has not quite finished. This is the arts programme Kathy, with the tangerine hair, hopes to get me on. The presenter is talking to a writer about her latest book, which he can't quite categorise. Is it fiction or fact, he wonders. The cover of the book, showing a wide-eyed child, is blown up as the studio backdrop. The writer says that most of it is based on her childhood experience of abuse and abandonment but the novel form allows her to imagine. The presenter wants more, he looks at his fingernails as if checking for dirt.

Faith is running out of wool. I will wind a ball from the skein.

'Here,' I say. 'Come on.' I indicate that she must hold out her hands for me to loop the skein around. She does so, awkwardly, reluctantly, but, gently, I insist. The skein hangs between her outstretched arms. I take up the end of the yarn, wind it around my fingers until I have enough to start a ball. Faith taught me how to do this. She taught me to knit too. Who taught Faith to knit? She might have learned the rudiments from Stella before she left. I didn't get along with knitting, row upon obedient row; you can't take risks with knitting. If you do, the sweater will fall apart.

'Fact or fiction,' the presenter is saying, 'it's a compelling read. Join me next week when . . .' He lists a film, a new biography and the exhibition which is about to open in Liverpool at The Museum of Contemporary Art. Kathy knows how to get results. In a few months' time, she'll have me sitting where the writer was.

Exposed. Covered.

I don't have anything as tangible to talk about as the writer. I can't dish up the dirt. The only way I know how to talk about silence is in the work, Laputa fashion, holding up my objects.

The wool in my hands is now a sizeable ball, I have more of the wool than Faith does; the strands of the skein are thinning out.

Of course they might interview me in the gallery; I could deflect to the work. Back in the studio he might have a critic to read between the gaps, the cover of the catalogue filling the screen. Faith and Irene staring out at millions, if Ward Joffitt has his way. I ought to warn her. When I arrived on Friday Faith said, 'Had a good day?' She hasn't asked me about the exhibition. But then, I haven't told her. Not for the first time this weekend, I see myself in a different light. Curious Maddie, always asking, probing, challenging. Yet, if I had to sit where the writer sat, I would be as mute, as protected as Faith behind her knitting.

I was up with the birds. The sun is strong, not a cloud; it's going to be a hot day. I hung out the blankets for Faith before she woke, so they will be dry by lunchtime, before Edward and his family arrive.

'I'm off to church now,' says Faith, pulling on white gloves, adjusting the navy straw hat, perched on her bun. I don't think she believes in God. Going to church is part of village life, part of the routine that keeps her safe. She knows better than to ask if I will go with her.

'I'll be back by 11, but would you switch the oven on so it's ready for the joint when I get back.'

'Anything else I can do?'

'I don't think so.'

I wait a few minutes after the sound of her car has faded. I take out the card of the mini-cab that brought me up from the station on Friday. Not a Sunday lunch with Edward and his family. I can't stay here a minute longer. I need to be back in London.

I need to know.

I don't like the way I'm avoiding not knowing. If I stay here any longer I will become Faith. When I looked in the mirror this morning I would not have been surprised to see Faith's bun, tight on the top of my head, instead of my own frizzy mop.

'The cottage just below Stonebank,' I say, giving clear directions. 'Ten-thirty. You will be prompt won't you? I have to make the London connection.'

Window Boxes 5

The train throws me from side to side. I hold on to a paper carrier bag which contains an egg sandwich and a cup of tea. I didn't think I was hungry until I heard the steward announce that the buffet car was about to close. Next stop, Watford Junction.

I did what I could to soften the shock of my departure. My note was apologetic, effusive. Hal had called, I lied. American collectors had arrived unexpectedly and were keen to see work which was stored at the studio. They were flying back to the States tomorrow, so this was the only opportunity. Hal was sure they would buy. I thought she would prefer this note to having me barge into church. I was so sorry, I wrote, and underlined the words, but if I'd waited to tell her I would have missed the connection at Leeds. I promised to phone this evening and said I would call Edward too. Then, propelled by guilt and the overwhelming urge to get away, I did what I could, in the hour that remained, to help with the lunch. I pulled the dining table away from the wall, extended its dropped leaves, and spread a good, starched linen cloth over its shiny surface. I set places, putting out the best bone-handled knives, I even cut a few bluebells, put them in a white jug and placed them at the centre of the table. Not something Faith would have done; Nancy will appreciate them. Though the blankets were a touch damp, I brought them in from the garden. Faith would hate Nancy to see washing on the line on a Sunday. I put them in the airing cupboard, then went back to the garden to pick mint. Faith tends to forget something on these occasions, usually the mint sauce. I plucked and chopped the leaves, added wine vinegar, sugar, a dash of lemon, spooned it into a sauce boat which I set on the table with the flowers. As the taxi driver loaded my bags in the boot of his car, I switched on the oven and moved my note to where I knew she would see it as soon as she came in.

I fight with the plastic box until I recover the trapped sandwich, then fish the tea bag from the plastic cup and add milk. The sandwich tastes of nothing much. At Stonebank lunch will be over; it will have been an awkward affair. Faith gets to a pitch before a meal such as this, though she would never admit it; anxiety rises from her like steam from the green beans, new potatoes and carrots simmering on the hob. Now she will be stacking dirty plates in the kitchen. Nancy will be insisting that Faith sit down while she, Nancy, does the washing up. Edward will be keen to take the boys outside. He will walk them up to the Centre; there are no punters in residence on a Sunday, so the boys can play on the swing behind the old barn. When they've had enough, he will take them through the wood, with its carpet of bluebells, down to the river to look for bugs. Edward, having brought red wine and drunk a glass too many, will be glad of the walk. Later, he will leave the boys with Nancy and Faith, settle himself in an armchair behind the Sunday paper and work hard to conceal how pissed off he is with me.

Primrose Hill, almost there; past the Roundhouse and in under the hood of the station. The sight of those white stuccoed houses with their colourful window boxes, always sends a wave of relief through my whole body. I'm back in London, one in millions, where window boxes are in the majority. In London it's acceptable to live a window-box life; hardly anyone expects you to be an established shrub in a mature garden. I'll be home soon. Home is not an accurate term. I'm not sure I can say where home is. I have attachments to several places – Chester, Liverpool – and, I might add, Featherbridge, Bickersthorpe. Stonebank, even. Places I'm associated with, where I have ties of blood, but not where I belong. I don't belong anywhere, except my current window-box, and even that isn't mine.

I put the debris from my snack into the carrier bag. At last I have something to offer to the man with a black plastic sack who has passed through the carriage a dozen times.

It seems so long since I was in London, longer than the

forty-eight hours I know it to be. It's as if I've been in a different dimension. Sitting with Faith last night I was in the room but somewhere else at the same time, escaping behind my eyes, then back in the room, weighing my words; time slowing down, stretching, extending. All I had to do was open my mouth, speak. I almost did as I wound the wool, taking the yarn around one of Faith's hands then the other.

The nearest to an embrace we'll ever get.

Close up, almost holding her, I wanted to tell her: I have the glass, I've found a way of piecing it back together. I thought of possible ways in casual, conversational remarks such as, 'It was Bagshott's where Frank worked, wasn't it?' or 'Do you ever feel like going back to Featherbridge?' Innocent sounding openers, but I'm not supposed to know about the town, the factory, the man. Anything I said would catch her off-guard like a punch, a blow. She wouldn't be prepared. I carried on winding the wool that hung between her arms. If I spoke, Faith would no longer feel safe, embraced; more likely she'd feel as if I'd tied her hands. This is how it is; I think I'm getting there, that what I want is within reach, when really it's always just beyond my grasp. Round and round, I wound the wool, the new ball growing in my hand. She kept her eyes on the skein as it disappeared, shrunk, never once met my gaze, her back firm against the chair. I said nothing. I complied. Knit one, purl one, knit two together. Keep to the pattern, that way the sweater will have a back, a front, two sleeves. We don't want the garment to unravel.

I'm hoping the chemist on the station will be open. I bought tissues in there on Friday on my way to Liverpool and I checked: they do stock That-Which-I-Have-Been-Avoiding. Whatever the brand, they turn out to be a version of something like a colourless felt-tip pen; a swab on a stick, that sucks up piss to a window, which then displays the result. There's already a blue stripe in the window, if a second blue stripe appears you're pregnant. With another brand it's pink dots, a third stays blank if you're not, develops a purple smudge if you are. If they weren't so expensive I would buy them all, make a pattern: blue stripes, pink dots, purple blobs in full confirmation.

'Can I give you a hand?' says an earnest young man, rucksack towering behind him. I'm blocking the exit with my assorted luggage but I can't open the door of the train. He squeezes past me and with one effortless movement we're on the platform.

I push the pound coin into the trolley, there's a clatter of metal as the thing breaks free, it veers towards the platform edge, on its swivelling wheels. I anchor it with the weight of my belongings, join the swarm up the ramp to the concourse. There are eager faces at the barrier looking out for loved ones; creased brows, searching eyes suddenly relax as a familiar face is spotted amongst the many. For a moment I find myself scanning the crowd, hoping, though I know it can't be possible, that Dom will be there.

Why Wait? it says in large, white type. There's a queue at the till, there would be; but I'm staying in it. *Reliable as clinical tests. You can't go wrong.* If I didn't have the trolley I could do it here at the station but I'd rather be at home. I'll take a taxi, be there in ten minutes.

'Both?' says the woman at the till.

'Yes,' I say.

Blue stripe. Purple blob.

There are two pints of milk on the doorstep; I thought I had cancelled. Never mind. Keys, keys. I fumble in my bag. Now that I've made up my mind to do it everything conspires to hold me up. The mortice lock is stiff and I must pull the door towards me and turn the key at the same time. Inside, I stumble on a pile of post. Most of it is for Annie and Jack. I leave my bags where they fall from my hands. On my way to the bathroom I notice, through the open door of Annie and Jack's study, there are faxes waiting, but I carry on.

Open Here it says, but there's nothing to get hold of. The cellophane is tight against the box, it's worse than trying to unwrap a new video cassette as the programme you want to record is starting. I bite the corner, eat my way in.

Ninety-nine per cent accurate.

The blue stripes will appear in one minute, the purple blob, three minutes later. I hold them both, firmly, in the stream of my piss, drenching them.

As I wait, I go down to pick up the faxes. One is from Ward Joffitt, the other is from Dom. I start to read Dom's but I bang into the makeshift light box which is still in here from my session with Hal. I catch the glass just in time before it falls, crashes to the floor.

Back in the bathroom, I look at myself in the mirror, still no bun. I'm still me. Behind me, on the window sill, is the information I've been waiting for. Come on Maddie, don't turn your back. Prove you're not Faith.

The second blue stripe is crisp, clear.

Minutes later the purple smudge starts to grow.

I want to tell someone, to hear my voice say: I'm pregnant. I could have a baby, be a mother. For a moment I am relieved, simply to know, pleased at this confirmation of what my body has been telling me. I'm not prepared for the turbulence which follows; torn between two equally strong currents, pulling me in opposite directions. Exhilaration, euphoria; I've been given a present I never expected to receive, didn't even know I wanted. Equally and at the same time, I'm stunned the way I imagine I would feel if I'd just been told someone important had died, my mind unwilling to take in the unthinkable, appalling news.

I remember the milk on the doorstep and wonder if it has turned. I don't think it has rained here. I take the bottles into the kitchen, press down on the foil tops; sour, both of them. I pour milk down the sink, watch the white gather, then disappear down the drain. I run the tap until the white becomes cloudy then clears. Watching it reminds me of the dream I had last night at Faith's. In the dream I am eight or nine, standing on a chair by the kitchen sink, helping Faith do the hand washing. She lets me do the rinsing. I lift each garment from the rinse water and wring it out until no more water comes. Edward's sweater, a petticoat, my school cardigan, in a heap on the draining board. When I have finished, I pull out the plug, watch the water swirl down the drain.

Faith has disappeared.

I can feel her presence but I can't see her. I know that I have swilled her down the drain. I'm drawn towards the dark hole by an invisible force. The chrome rim around the plug hole swells to the size of a giant metal doughnut, shiny. I see my face, enlarged, reflected in its curve. I lean further in, the hole is now wide enough for me to fall down. I stare into the darkness which is not black but night-sky, Prussian blue, fathomless. I am drawn to it. There's a sucking sound. It is both the most scary place in the world, and the most desirable. I am hot, liquid bliss and rigid, petrified, all at the same time.

I answer the phone automatically, a reflex action. I'm still in the dream. I stare at the receiver in my hand and wonder what I'll say if it's Dom.

I say nothing.

'Maddie, Maddie?'

Edward.

'Hello,' I say, relieved that it's not Dom.

'Maddie what the hell are you up to?'

Not now, Edward, please. Nothing comes, I can't think of a single thing to say. My mind is filled with the image of a clear blue stripe which means the same as the word, pregnant, baby. Gift. Disaster.

'Maddie, are you there, say something?'

A voice, which sounds like someone pretending to be me, says, 'I'm sorry. I had to leave. Something came up here.'

'What?'

'Something with Hal, he needs a piece of work from the studio,' I say, sticking to the script.

'Feeble, Maddie. That's the story you gave Mother.'

Mother. He will call her Mother.

'OK, cover blown.'

'Mother is upset.'

'Is she?'

'Of course she is.'

'How do you know?'

'She'd worked hard to make a family occasion.'

'I know.' And I want to remind him that I did the shopping with her yesterday, laid the table, made the mint sauce, wound wool for his sweater. I did more than you, Edward, I want to say, but don't. 'She had you and Nancy and the kids. She was only one short.'

'She was hurt.'

'How do you know?'

'Anyone would be.'

'Faith isn't anyone. What did she say?'

'Does it matter?'

'Yes.'

'She rarely sees us together. She'd been looking forward to it. You gave her a shock sneaking off while her back was turned.'

'Her back is always turned.'

'What?'

'Oh, never mind.' Knit one, purl one, knit two together.

'Will you ever grow up, Maddie?'

Probably not if being grown up means being like you, Edward, I want to say.

'I left a note. I'll phone her later. All right?'

'No, it's not all right.'

'Why not? What did she say?'

'I don't know.'

'Try to remember. You're the scientist. If Faith was a winter wingless moth, you'd describe her response down to each single antennae movement. So what exactly did she say?'

'I can't remember.'

'You can't remember because she didn't say anything. She carried on.' I can't say how happy I would be if Faith had cried, or said something with feeling.

'Hang on a minute,' I say. I see that I've left the tap running, the sink is filling up. The foil tops have floated into the plug hole. I fish them out, release the water. I watch the receiver dangle on its spiralling cord; I might leave Edward hanging there. But I see him, earnest child in grey flannel shorts, lining up his soldiers, building models, storing things in his massive brain, facts that he would toss out, like protection. *Did you know female grasshoppers have ears on their legs?* Which made me wonder if what was wrong with Faith was that her ears were somewhere else, in her legs, perhaps. Maybe she couldn't hear in quite the same way as us. I wondered what would happen if I whispered a question into the hollow behind her knees. At least I wouldn't have to see her doll's eyes freeze over. Edward will be standing by Faith's front door with one eye out for the others coming back; jerking his left shoulder like he always does when he's nervous, as if easing out a painful knot in a muscle. It's a tic he's had as long as I can remember.

'Sorry, I left a tap running.'

'You will phone her tonight?'

'I'll try.'

It's on my lips to tell him. I'm pregnant, Uncle Edward. That would shut him up. For a while. Then he could really disapprove; his wayward sister with her no-way-to-earn-a-living job, her nomadic life, and now tainted with a married man's sex. The words are forcing themselves into my throat. I'm going to say something.

'Edward, do you remember the day Faith broke the glass?'

'What?'

'She stood in the yard and belted jugs, bowls, vases at the brick wall.'

'That was years ago.'

'Do you remember how we swept it up, used the lawn-mower hood as a shovel, packed it into tea chests?'

We drove to the dump, but it was closed. I knew Edward wanted to get back home, so I suggested we take it to Annie's house and do it another time.

'We can't take it back home because Faith will see it,' I had said, and he agreed. He doesn't know what happened because I dropped him back at our house and said I would take the stuff to Annie's. Later, I told him Annie's dad had offered to get rid of it. We were all too busy walking on eggshells around Faith to worry about what happened to the glass.

'It's turned up again,' I say, 'the glass.'

'What are you talking about?'

'The tea chests full of broken glass. They've been in Annie's parents' garage all these years.' I tell him that the new work for my exhibition will be made from the glass.

'What?'

'It's potent stuff.'

'It's a heap of old glass that Mother will not want to see again.'

'It's more than that,' I say, but then I stop. Edward is in no mood to listen to my thoughts on the new work, on the idea that an object is a powerful way to tell a story. The work I want to make will tell a story but not in a straight line. Instead, it will be a cluster of past, present, future; saying many things at the same time, and not a word spoken.

'I would like to tell Faith what I'm doing,' I say. 'I'd like her to know.'

'You're kidding, aren't you?'

'No.'

'You are so selfish, irresponsible, you don't live in the real world, do you? It's all make believe. I do wonder, sometimes, if you're quite sane.'

'I'm as sane as the next person, Edward.'

Insane is what I would be if I couldn't piece the glass together.

Bank Holiday 5

Hal and I have an arrangement. On a Bank Holiday Monday, if neither of us is doing anything else, we meet up. Hal hates British Bank Holidays, says they're made for families; such days rub in his lack of one. They are not good days for me either as Dom disappears into his family. It looks like Hal's new lover, Michael, is cooling, which makes things even worse today.

We sit on low-slung, blue and white striped deck chairs in his patch of garden which we've climbed up to out of his basement; plants spring up from gravel beds. We're only just in the sun, soon we will be in the shadow of the tall, stuccoed terrace. We're having lunch later down Portobello. He says I mustn't ask about Michael, he wants me to take his mind off the possibility that he might not see him again.

'There you go. Sure that's all you want?' He hands me a glass of sparkling water, takes a sip from his glass of iced coffee. 'This is so good, even if I say so myself. Are you sure you don't want some?'

'This is fine.'

'I told you Jakob was a good contact.' Hal's had a call from Berlin. I've been invited to fill a slot in some panel discussion, and it's come about because Jakob, the guy who has the new gallery in Mitte, put my name forward. So now going to Berlin is something Hal can pin me down to, rather than something I might do some time.

'Like I said, Roz Whitehead has pulled out. Jakob suggested you. I said, I was sure you would agree. I have to phone him tomorrow.'

'Studio time, that's what I need right now, not going away.'

'I know that. Look, do I ever waste your time?'

'No.' It's true, he protects me from all kinds of undesirable invitations. He rarely makes demands unless he thinks it's important.

'This is good timing with the MCA show coming.' He says the summer arts festival is a great time to be in Berlin, and the discussion is at the Hamburger Bahnhof gallery where the New Generation Exhibition has just opened.

'You should be there, Maddie.'

'It's such short notice, barely two weeks.'

'You get to see the New Gen show, meet people, meet Jakob. This is a major European public gallery. Things are moving towards Berlin. I wouldn't ask you to take two days out of the studio if I didn't think it was worth it. I'm talking long term here. Look, it's a free air fare.'

'There's no such thing as a free air fare.'

'I wish you were more enthusiastic. It's part of the festival but also one of the events around the New Generation show. "Serious Omission", as Isolde Maddox pointed out, this gets you in there.'

'What's the deal?'

'Roughly translated from the German, the theme is: New Narrative Forms. Do a fifteen-minute spiel, show your slides, you've done it a hundred times, Maddie, then be part of the panel discussion.'

'Who else is on the panel?'

'A photographer, a performance artist and some novelist.'

'All men?'

'Yes, but that's all the more reason for you to be there. Do your usual enigmatic statement per slide, let the work say the rest.'

'It's not that bit that worries me, it's the questions afterwards.'

'It's going to be chaired by the curator there, good contact. He'll see your work. And I'll be there afterwards to remind him of your MCA dates.'

'I'd have to answer questions in German.'

'Speak English, they'll translate, they all speak English anyway. Look, the performance artist and the novelist will do the talking.'

'I don't know.'

'I have to phone him tomorrow.'

'I have an appointment tomorrow which might mean I'm not able to go to Berlin.'

'S'cuse me?'

'I'd rather not go into it.'

'What?' I don't know how I thought I was going to spend a day with Hal and not say anything.

'I'm pregnant.' Hal blinks, says nothing for what seems like ages, looks at me as if I'm a stranger.

'I'm pregnant,' I say again, in case he hadn't heard properly.

'How, when?'

'The usual method.'

'You never said . . . I thought . . .'

'Not planned, an accident.'

'You had unprotected sex?'

'It's Dom's, not some one-night stand.'

'You have unprotected sex with Dom? I hope you've seen his test results.'

'Hal please.'

'You straight people think you're immune. You should know better. I don't know what to say.'

'Nothing to say.'

'Are you sure?'

'I've bought a test.'

'But have you seen a doctor, are you absolutely sure?'

'Yes, I have seen my doctor. And yes, I am absolutely sure.'

'So what's happening tomorrow?'

'Abortion clinic. Which is why I can't give you a straight-forward answer on Berlin.'

'You're having an abortion tomorrow?'

'No. I'm going to fix up for one. I'm not sure how pregnant I am, so they'll do a scan, talk through the options. I'll probably have it done in a couple of weeks, so Berlin might not be possible.'

'How many years have you been shagging? You know what happens.'

'We all have moments of carelessness.'

'And you're sure that's what you want? What does Dom think?'

'Dom doesn't know.'

'What?'

'I haven't told him.'

'How long have you known?'

'A week.'

'Am I hearing this right? You plan to have an abortion but you're not telling Dom?'

'Look, it shouldn't have happened. It's my carelessness. I'll deal with it.'

'You'll tell him eventually though?'

'I don't know. Maybe not.'

'You'll carry on with him and never say anything?'

'Don't go all moral on me.'

'I'm not squeamish about termination. A woman's right to choose and all that, and I've no doubt that Dom isn't going to force you to have his child. He's going to be with you whatever you decide, but not telling him, Maddie. Think about it, keeping a secret like that.'

'He's got a lot on at the moment: Joe's A levels, Tessa's father. It's exam time for his students and now there's this TV and book project.'

The fax from Dom, waiting when I got back from Faith's, was to wish me luck for my meeting at The MCA but also to tell me he has been asked to join a team of consultant academics on a new television history series. Dom will work on two programmes covering the history of history as an academic discipline, also, he will write a section of the book that will accompany the series. He's pleased. It's an opportunity to take his research out of the seminar and into the living room. *So*, he wrote, *we have something to celebrate . . . let's have some time together soon. Love you, Dom*. I spoke to him on the phone in the week; they've all gone to Bristol for the Bank Holiday, Tessa's father wants to see Joe.

'Tessa's father's probably dying. I don't want to bring Dom down.'

'Bullshit. Aren't you doing what comes naturally here? Not telling, not talking about it. I can't believe you.'

'I'm having a termination, what else can I do?' I don't want to have an argument with Hal. I'm churned up enough as it is; pulled in two directions at the same time. I've decided that it's best not to be fooled by the excitement that I felt when I first did the test, the thrill of receiving an unexpected gift. I'm not going to accept it, much less unwrap it. It's probably a trick of the hormones that makes me feel this way. If I'm not keeping the gift, the fewer people who know it was even offered, the better.

The stunned sensation is still as strong as the excitement.

Pregnant.

It's unthinkable that another human being is growing inside me. As shocking as if Hal were to drop dead right now before my eyes.

'I'm not mother material, how can I be, I'm Faith's daughter.'

'Well, you sure are a keeper of secrets.'

'That's not fair.' It is though, he's right. I run my fingers through my hair, still my frizzy mop. Any day now, it will come, I'll wake up and the bun will be right there on top of my head.

'Maddie, whatever you decide, I will back you, but this feels rushed. Slow down, talk to Dom.'

'Too much of a dilemma for him. Once a Catholic. Why lay that on him?' That's not the whole reason, it's a tiny part of it. Why I can't tell Dom is more complicated, I'm only just beginning to realise. It's still a muddle in my mind, I can't unravel it. I'm not going to try to explain it to Hal.

'You have to talk to someone. You only told me because I was pushing you on Berlin. Talk to Annie. Call her, do it now.'

'It's eight in the morning there. Anyway, phoning Annie lately has been impossible, there's always one twin or another demanding her attention, and Annie's not a phone person, she's not good on the phone even without the babies and the time difference.'

'Fax her. Say you need to talk, fix a time later on. There are ways round this, you need to talk it through.'

'You sound like my GP.'

My doctor had listened, her eyes steady on mine; soft, caring eyes. She asked who had I talked to.

'No one,' I told her. 'Look, I'm forty-one, on my own.'

'Not ideal circumstances,' said the doctor, 'but I've known worse.'

'I want to fix an abortion.'

'There's no need to rush,' she said. 'You're an intelligent woman. You might not be in the ideal circumstances to have a child, but it might be your last chance. What's going on here? Is your pregnancy an accident? Why was someone, who has been careful for more than twenty years, suddenly careless? Don't decide in a panic, don't rush to tidy the thing up.' I see Faith scuttling around her kitchen, folding, polishing, scrubbing. 'If there's no one you're prepared to talk to, and you are set on an abortion then perhaps you should make an initial appointment at the clinic,' said the doctor. She gave me a phone number and a leaflet. She said they would offer me counselling if I wanted to talk to someone.

'Well, I think you should talk to Annie,' Hal insists.

'Can we leave this? Let's have lunch.'

'Shit, Maddie, I'm sorry.' We stand up to go back through his flat, and out to lunch. His arm comes round my shoulder, he pulls me close, gives me a hug. My eyes sting with the effort of keeping back the tears, hot tears. I won't let them come, not yet.

'My appointment's early,' I say, sniffing. 'I'll phone you at lunchtime. I'll have a date. If I can go to Berlin, I will.'

One Small Step 5

I'm early. The clinic isn't open yet, but I want to get this over with. There are two other women besides me. We sit on chairs of moulded plastic, grubby orange, laid out in rows. We're not in any order, but scattered about, keeping our distance from each other. We don't look up, don't acknowledge one another's presence. A fourth woman appears, carrying two steaming plastic cups. She's with the woman furthest away from me. The woman bringing the drinks is an older version of the one sitting down, her big sister. I could do with a big sister right now. Hal phoned late last night, offered to come with me.

'I can't say I feel good about you not telling Dom and all, but if you want someone there . . .'

It didn't seem a good idea to me. I said no thanks.

I read the leaflet again. It's written as though the writer knew the words would have to be heard through tears and distress. A clear, calming tone. The important points are in bold, black type, surrounded by a box, so that however much you're crying or not concentrating, you can't help but notice them: **You will not have the abortion at your first visit, but all the necessary arrangements will be made.** I will be seen by a nurse, a counsellor, a gynaecologist. **Be prepared for a long visit, from one and a half to three hours.** I can't hang on to my bladder for three hours, that's for sure.

The sisters have finished their coffee. The older one has her arm round the younger one who looks upset. If Annie was in town I would want her here, the nearest thing to a sister I will ever have. Hal was right, I needed to talk to Annie. I did get through.

'I want to say congratulations,' she said, 'but I guess it's not that straightforward.'

'I'm going to the abortion clinic tomorrow,' I said.

'I wish I could be there,' she said.

'I've no choice. How can I have this baby?' She made sympathetic noises, a lot of 'oh Maddie'. Then a pause.

'Only you can decide,' was what she said next, but it sounded strained, like she'd read a book on counselling or an abortion advice leaflet; they were not her words. Not what she'd say if we were sitting at home, elbows on the kitchen table, halfway through our second bottle of wine. I could hear the strain in her voice, keeping something back.

'You think I shouldn't do it, don't you, you think I should have the baby?'

'What I think is not the point.' Leaflet-speak.

'You are my oldest friend, and you think I ought to have this baby.'

'I wouldn't put it like that.'

'How would you put it?'

'It's not rational, not helpful for me to say this, but . . .'

'Yes?'

'Look, you're asking the wrong person.'

'Well, if I can't talk to you, who the hell can I talk to? I'm going nuts.'

'It's just that for me, having the babies is the best thing, the best thing that ever happened. I know they're not a year old and I'm still crazy in love with them.' Annie had waited for so long she'd almost not minded whether she did or did not have children. She was thirty-nine, hadn't realised time would run out. It was Jack who wanted to give it a try. They had agreed they would give it a year, and if nothing happened, well, they would live with the choice they had made.

'Every now and again this shock comes over me,' she said. 'I find myself thinking: I might not have done it. I might have missed out on this. It scares me how close I came to not having them. I feel so lucky. Perhaps that's not helpful, Maddie, but it's what I feel. I suppose I want you to have what I have.' Then she back-tracked and said she could only speak for herself, that she lived a different life. She was right, it wasn't helpful. We agreed that we'd hit the limit of what could be said on the phone with all that ocean between us. I wanted to see her, look her in the eye. When I put the receiver down it was hot and sweaty from my tight grip. Her saying that about the twins, being the best thing that had happened to her, stirred up the excitement. Maybe I want to keep my gift, I thought. Maybe she's right. When I woke up this morning, I realised that Annie is still in the grip of the same hormones that are playing tricks on me. Unreliable evidence, maybe.

They want me with a full bladder for the scan, but I'm not sure how much longer I can hold on. I'm wondering if I could let a bit out, ease the pressure. Once you start, is it possible to stop the flow?

Another woman arrives, she can't be here for a termination, she's well into her fifties. She looks hurried, she's late. She wears a beige raincoat, a shapeless thing, her hair is unkempt, a dull grey and her spectacles make her look like an owl. She's staff. She goes behind the reception desk, switches on lights, disappears through the office. Perhaps she's the cleaner, late, should have done and been out of here by now.

'Madeleine Armitage?'

A young nurse appears at reception, says she will book me in, then I can see the counsellor.

'I have to go to the toilet,' I say.

'We need you with a full bladder.'

'Can't I just let some out?'

She says it's up to me, advises me not to empty the bladder entirely, and then to drink lots of water. Also, I must be prepared to wait if I don't have a full enough bladder for them to do the scan.

'How do you feel about the fact that you are pregnant?' asks the counsellor in leaflet-speak. Here we go.

'I'm not sure,' I say. On the table between us is a jug of water, a tower of plastic cups, a box of tissues. I pour myself some water to fill my bladder. The plastic cup is brittle, shiny. I squeeze it. It clicks. She watches me do this over and over, trying to translate the clicks. I squeeze too hard and the water splashes my face and my jacket.

'Here,' she offers me a tissue, sits back, the question is still hanging there, she hasn't forgotten. No amount of silence or clicking will move it away. I look up at her and see a speak bubble over her head, she's become a Roy Lichtenstein Pop Art painting; she's made up of dots, magnified, a bubble rises from her mouth, clear black type says: *How do you feel about the fact that you are pregnant?*

She looks at me, patiently, her slim ankles crossed. Marjorie Allen from the Abbey National had slim ankles. This woman opposite me, who is called Jean, has the same build as the woman who seduced my father. A big woman, ample bosom, attractive face. Another person with the same body mass would look fat, but she has long legs and slim ankles, which means she's more elegant than fat, just like Marjorie Allen. Ernest and Faith were both motherless creatures which might have been what brought them together in the first place, but they couldn't give each other the mothering they needed. Marjorie Allen was the mother Ernest hoped for. I reckon that Ernest was happy to drown in Marjorie Allen's bosom after bird-like, brittle Faith. Jean waits, unafraid of the silence, like an understanding aunt. Or, how I imagine an understanding aunt to be, since I don't have one. When I think of my only aunt I see Irene, smiling at the camera, her dress hanging below her coat, eight years old. There is no Irene now. This temporary aunt, sitting opposite me, has a blonde bob and an open face with no make-up. She's fifty, fifty-five. She leans forward slightly, her hands relaxed in her lap. She can wait; so can I.

I can do silence.

What she wants is a feeling word.

'Confused?' I say. It comes out like a question.

Her head moves, not quite a nod.

'Can you say more about the confusion?' Jean wants to know.

'Not really, it's a muddle. Look, I can't have this baby, I can't.'

'Why not?'

'I'm forty-one, I live alone, I work irregular hours.' Sound, practical reasons why not to have the baby. Jean doesn't say that, but I hear the practicality of it, so I add: 'I never intended to have children. I've always been clear about that. I never intended to be a mother, I'm not maternal, I'm not mother material.'

'How did you get pregnant?'

I tell her about Dom and the time in Norfolk.

'A careless moment,' I say. I don't tell her about me running away up the beach, the dead eel, damaged in the middle, unable to join its head to its tail, me out gazing at the night sky, listening to the silence until all I could do was find Dom, hold on to him so I wouldn't fall off.

'He isn't here today?'

'No, he doesn't know I'm pregnant.'

'I see. Have you had time to talk this through with anyone? Your mother?'

I laugh.

An angry, tight laugh which scares me. I don't want to sound like this. I sound like Faith that time I hid amongst the lupins. *My mother might as well have lived on the moon. I've had to manage without a mother since I was six years old. Why would I want one now?*

The tears come.

I'm drowning in my own tears, enough to flood a valley. There are no windows in here. I want Jean to say something to stop me crying. If she doesn't, I can't be responsible, the room will fill up, we will both drown. She hands me a box of tissues.

I'm on the orange plastic chairs again, there are more people here now. It's not possible to sit alone. Ten or fifteen women, some flick through magazines or stare at nothing, waiting inside themselves. I'm grateful to have stopped crying but my eyes are scalded with tears. There's a pain in the corner of my skull, a burning. I feel as if I'm filling up with a hot molten substance. Jean says I can talk to her again, says I should give myself time. I'm going ahead, booking in for the abortion. Jean says I can pull out any time, even as they wheel me down to the theatre. When I've had my scan I'll know how long I've got.

The nurse puts a new strip of paper on the high examination

couch, pulls on a fresh pair of rubber gloves, then checks my details.

'Miss Dawson will be here soon, she's the consultant.' In walks the cleaner, the shapeless beige raincoat replaced by a shapeless white coat. She looks at me through her owl glasses.

'This will be cold,' says the nurse, she squirts clear gel on my belly, then she moves a hard cold thing across my flesh, pushing it this way and that; they both watch the monitor screen. A scratchy, black and white picture like the first telly we ever had. I can see Edward twiddling the knobs for better reception the day the men landed on the moon. I half expect to see Neil Armstrong's foot coming down the ladder, making the first mark in the dust.

'There we are,' says the cleaner. 'Eight weeks I'd say, but let's check.'

They zoom in, make the picture bigger. I can see it.

It.

What I see is a blob no bigger than a grape. Pulsing.

'There's your baby. We have a heartbeat,' says Miss Dawson.

One small step.

The gallery is only four stops on the Underground, I'll tell Hal in person. The termination is the day after I would get back from Berlin, if I went. Suddenly going to Berlin seems attractive, I'm not going to do much work until this is over. Going would be a distraction, keep me away from Dom. Hal will be pleased.

My eyes sting from crying.

'It's never easy,' said Jean. Her voice was kind, like a hug, like she held me with her words. I found myself wanting to say irrational, childish things, like: I want my Mum; I want a hug.

Dangerous things, hugs.

I remember the time I tried to tell Faith that I'd been to Stella's funeral. I wanted to tell her the next day. I'd stayed the night at Annie's and the next morning I felt strong, because I'd been. I'd seen Stella's hair, her bulging slippers, the faded gardenia talc. I wanted to tell her. Ernest said I was to do no such thing. She was too fragile.

'Don't upset your mother, don't push her.'

'I'm not going to push her. I want to tell her that I was there, that I went on her behalf. What is all the secrecy about?'

What could be so bad?

'Nothing, really, it's how they were, how they came to be.'

'Why?'

'Why must you go on so? We are where we are, Maddie. Leave the past.'

'I can't leave the past because I don't know what it is. Perhaps if I knew what it was it wouldn't seem so important.' I wasn't taking no for an answer. I said if he didn't tell me I would tell Faith because I didn't see how telling her that I'd gone on her behalf to her mother's funeral was a bad thing. It seemed to me that not telling her was more dangerous. That's when I found out that Stella had left the family when Faith was six.

'Walked out, no explanation. Never came back,' said Ernest.

It made sense of Faith's outburst on the day Stella visited us.

'Why?' I imagined Faith, my motherless mother, abandoned at six. A terrible thought. I wanted to find her, to hug her. To stop her falling into space.

'I've no idea.' I really believe that Ernest doesn't know. 'Something and nothing, I've always thought. They had a stand-off, neither could back down. Something and nothing.' Stella never came back to live in the house as a family, though she always kept in touch.

'It broke Stella as much as it did your mother, I reckon, but Faith can never see it that way.' It was Irene who made sure that they never lost contact with Stella.

'Irene was a gentler soul, not as stubborn as your mother. It was Irene who insisted we visit after each of you was born. But once Irene went, well Faith cut off from Stella.'

'Went? Where did Irene go?'

'Maddie, it does no good knowing. It'll upset you.'

'I'm nineteen years old, and I can assure you that not knowing upsets me. Not knowing means I imagine the worst.'

'Irene took her own life. You were only a baby.'

'How?'

'Oven.'

Ernest said I wasn't to let Faith know that he had told me any of this. Faith refused ever to talk of her family again.

Ernest had tried to do what he could but Faith did not want to see Stella.

'She wanted to stop Stella sending stuff to you and your brother, but I put my foot down, I said it wasn't right. So at least you've had that.' But I couldn't let it go. I knew better than Ernest. He was set in old ways. I had dared to go to Stella's funeral, I was going to break through this silence once and for all. It was like Faith was in exile, cut off from us. Trapped inside herself. I wanted to let her out. Let us all out. I was sure I could do it, a hug and some kind words, I could do it. It was a while after I'd spoken to Ernest, things were getting back to normal after the glass breaking. I'd been round at Annie's and I'd made up my mind that I would talk to Faith. I was so eager to be in the house that I almost rang the bell, but that would irritate her. 'Use your key,' she would say.

As I opened the door I could smell hot linen; she was ironing.

'Mum,' I said. 'Why did you never tell us about Grandma Lilley and what happened?'

I willed her eyes to stay soft, not harden. I could see her stiffening.

'Mum, don't, please don't,' I was sure that I was strong enough, that now I knew she would be relieved. I stood close to her, put my arms out to hug her, as if she were a child, six years old, her mother gone away. I spread my arms to take in all of her. Brave, sad, lonely Faith. I waited for her to slacken into my arms, to loosen.

Nothing.

I waited; didn't know what to do with the weight of my outstretched arms, they began to ache.

Her face froze, the jaw tight, eyes dead but alive at the same time. She stared at me. The same eyes as in the photograph. A look that said: Don't touch, get back, leave me alone. Clearer than any words.

I have replayed the scene many times wondering whether she did slacken slightly, ease a little. She didn't. It would have been enough for her to brush my arm, a slight reciprocation.

Nothing.

She can't go back on the deal she made with her angry six-year-old self, back pressed to the door, eyes fixed and fierce.

My eyes fill up again, burning.

The woman opposite me is talking to herself, though I can't hear what she's saying above the clatter of the train. She takes out a cosmetics bag, inspects her face. At first glance she seems young; she is well into her seventies, but dressed as if she were twenty. Her hair, a mass of ginger bubbles, is a wig. It is cut through with a white velvet band which accentuates the bubbles. She has large hoop earrings, a silver choker round her neck. High cheekbones and wide-apart eyes suggest she must have been beautiful once. Her skin is dry as chalk, etched with lines that are filled up with powder; she dabs more powder on her nose, cheeks, chin. She wears a black velvet skirt that stops just above her ankles and a black taffeta top. Her white patent-leather handbag matches the strappy white sandals that bind her swollen feet. On her lap a cigarette holder, with a cigarette waiting to be lit when she gets off the Tube. She's talking to someone who isn't there, might not have been there for decades.

Strawberries and Cream 5

'Here,' says Dom. I open my mouth, suck in the strawberry he's offering. We picked them this afternoon. He's here for the night, our first night together since Norfolk. We're celebrating; the television project, the end of his term, the end of Joe's exams. I notice, it's the endings that prevail. Tessa is in Bristol for the weekend, Joe has gone sailing with a friend, won't be back until Monday.

Dom divides the strawberries into two bowls, hands me one, then peels the foil off a tub of cream.

'No, I want them as they come. Naked,' I say.

We sit facing each other, at the kitchen table, as if this was how we always lived.

'We should have picked more,' I say.

Late morning we had headed for the coast but never made it. We stopped at a pub for lunch, sat in the garden there talking. We didn't notice the time. We were catching up on each other, mostly about Dom's project but also the exhibition. We do this well, Dom and me, listen to what the other is passionate about.

'How else will young people take an interest in the past if we don't make a good story of it?' Dom said, breaking the fresh bread roll, piling on cheese and pickle. He was looking forward to the challenge of this project. 'We've got to make it accessible, give it narrative drive, without losing the ideas. History is about telling stories,' he said. Dom makes a story out of verifiable facts. I imagine something from the missing, never-to-be-recovered facts. As I talked about the exhibition and the new work I found out something about myself which I hadn't quite realised.

'I don't suppose it was important enough to him,' I said. Talking to Dom I had to admit how disappointed I was at not having heard anything more from Wilf Nowells. I'd been hoping that he would find Frank amongst the union records. Dom said maybe I should phone him again, offer to go through the material myself. Besides the sex, this is what we do best, talk and listen. What we each do is of interest to the other, but there is no competition, no envy.

Out of London it was easy not to think about the baby. It didn't feel as if I was keeping something from him. We relaxed into each other's company. Back here, I feel the knowledge of it, a tissue, an invisible fabric stretching between us. I don't like it. I don't want to tell him, but neither do I like the fact that it's so easy to keep it from him. Once in place, will the tissue, this layer of stuff, be permanent?

We left the pub around four, saw a sign for the strawberries. As we filled the punnets, hands sticky with juice, laughing, seeing who could pick the most, we were creating a story, the story of us. A piece of past. In a week, a month, a year, one of us might say: Do you remember when we picked strawberries? We will, do, have a past; we are creating it all the time, this meal, this night, another chapter. It's a story known, in the main, only to us. But will we have a future? If we do, then this past of ours will also have a secret in it. There is a secret waiting in the future. A secret which only I will know.

'They taste so good,' says Dom.

'They taste,' I say. 'That's why they are so good, they have a taste, not like those watery things in the supermarket.'

'You don't want cream?'

'No, thanks. Maybe, come here.' Dom has a smudge of cream on his lips, I reach across, lick him. We kiss, a strawberry-flavoured kiss.

'I've missed you,' he says.

'Me too,' I say, which is both true and not true, since I've worked at avoiding him.

'And now you're off to Berlin. Perhaps I could come with you?' This is not what I expected him to say. I try to look pleased. I can't tell him that I'm going to Berlin to keep out of his way before I get rid of our baby, the baby he knows nothing about.

'Could you?' I say, then peevishly: 'What lies will you tell?'

'Don't.'

He probably wouldn't have to lie too much since Tessa is spending more and more time in Bristol with her father.

'I'd like to be in Berlin with you, see you talk about your work.'

'It's only two nights, I'll be preoccupied with having to perform, it might not be such a good idea.' I try to sound as if I wish it was. 'Do you think Joe will get his grades?'

'I think so.'

'He'll be gone in October.'

'Yes.'

'What then?'

'Tessa's looking for a new job.'

'Again?' I say. She's done this before. Every now and then she circles jobs in the situations vacant, leaves it around for Dom to see. Often they are out of London. She never leaves. She's in the same job she's been in since returning to work after Joe.

'She might go back to Bristol,' Dom says. 'She could go anywhere once Joe leaves.'

'What then?' I say.

'Us you mean?'

'It scares you doesn't it?'

'What do you mean?' says Dom.

'We've become comfortable with our part-time life. We've shaped ourselves around each other. Tessa included. Joe going, well, it changes the shape, doesn't it? We'll have to rearrange ourselves around the space he's left.'

I want to say something that has been growing in my mind. I want to say: Have you ever thought that Joe's going away might be the end for us? This thought, as much as anything, is keeping me from telling him about the pregnancy. It's hard enough after five years of our part-time arrangement to work out if full-time is what either of us wants. This is what neither of us can quite say. I can't believe the pregnancy is meant to force a decision, that doesn't feel right; but that is how it will look. Even when I feel as if the baby is a gift, it is not about Dom, not entirely. It's coming from somewhere else, too. It is as if Dom is caught up in something which is nothing to do with him, he's an innocent bystander. This is why I'm not telling him; it would be too difficult to explain, I can barely explain it to myself. I don't want him to think the pregnancy is about forcing the issue; the issue of us. I don't know how I could explain this to him. I think Annie might understand what I'm talking about; but trying to tell this to Dom would be like trying to walk into a room when the door is shut. Is that a female/male thing, or is it me?

Dom gets up, walks around my chair, starts to massage my back. He knows how to find the knots. I've often thought that the way to get through to Faith might be to massage her back. Her muscles will be hard, tight with the effort of bracing herself against the door.

'Love you,' Dom says quietly, next to my ear, his hands easing out the tightness from my neck. I reach back, squeeze his thigh in answer. Feeling words do not come easy. Lack of practice, Faith had no words for feelings. She must have thought that if she lost the words, she would lose the feelings. Her back is formed by anger. Compressed, embedded, like geological strata, layer on layer of rage held in. If Faith's back were to be massaged it might cause a seismic shift, a volcanic eruption.

'Come on, let's go up,' says Dom. 'I could do this better if you were lying down.' He goes up ahead of me. I put the cream and the few remaining strawberries in the fridge. Dom is an occasional treat, like freshly picked strawberries. If we have more of each other, the taste might change, become watered down, hot-house forced.

In the bathroom I brush my teeth. Dom's been here already, water drips from the toothbrush he keeps here. Most nights it hangs stiff and dry beside mine. I reach into the cabinet for my diaphragm. I flick open the white plastic lid, my leg is already up on the side of the bath, my other hand clutching the gel. As I squeeze the gel inside the rubber dome I think: Hang on, why? Because I don't want Dom asking questions, because I'm doing what I always do. Doing what I always do, except for one abandoned moment in Norfolk.

'Why do you think you were careless that time?' Counsellor Jean's question won't go away.

'I don't know. We are careless, sometimes we forget and regret it.'

'Is that what you feel, regret? Do you regret being pregnant?' I couldn't say yes to regret because I had already offered her confusion.

'Give it more time,' Jean said. 'Come and see me again before you go ahead.'

I rinse the rubber mushroom under the tap, shake it dry, put it carefully back in its plastic case and back in the cabinet. But I leave the gel on the sink, like a lie, to reassure Dom that I've done what I always do. This is not deceit. He doesn't need this now. It's better I decide. Better I act quickly and put right something that should never have happened, wasn't planned, doesn't come into the equation which is complicated enough.

Dom is already in bed, lying with hands behind his head. The duvet is pushed back, almost on the floor. It is hot up here in the attic. I open the window in the roof, letting in a rush of air that is fresher than the room but still warm. It is a clear night, immense blue.

'Come here.' He pulls me down next to him, starts to kiss me, his hands find my breasts. I'm still wearing the dress I've been wearing all day. I feel dirty with sweat.

'It's so hot,' I say, but hesitate before I undress. What if he can see the changes to my body? I pull away gently, kissing his forehead. With my back to him, I take off the dress and leave it on the floor.

'Won't be a minute,' I say.

I'm not ready for this. I so much want him here and yet it's hard with the layer forming between us. We have few opportunities to be together, how can I pull away from him, appear less than enthusiastic? I can't bear it if he asks me what's the matter.

I pull up my hair, tight to my scalp, it feels like wool. I pull it through a scrunch, winding it into a knot on top of my head. I don't want to get my hair wet, it takes so long to dry. I stand under the shower with my head clear of the cold water, rub soap under my arms, between my legs.

When I step out, dripping, Dom is there. He's hard already, looks impatient, puzzled.

'I was so sweaty,' I say reaching for a towel. He gets there first, kisses me hard. Despite the cooling shower I feel the heat rush between my legs, my breasts burn.

We lie, limbs entwined, sticky skin on sticky skin. His warmth leaking between my legs. Millions of sperm that didn't make it. There are millions more, the strong eager ones, forging ahead. They can't know that they don't stand a chance. They can swim as hard as they like, they are doomed. All that effort for nothing.

'All right?' he says, a sleepy whisper.

I say nothing, kiss his shoulder.

We snuggle into sleep position, me turning away. He follows. I can feel his softened penis against my bum. His hand strokes my belly. I squeeze his hand in an effort to hold on to the words that are forming in my head, making their way to my throat.

I'm pregnant.

The words are in my mouth. I mouth the words. There is no sound.

Light In A Dark Place 5

'Je-sus,' says Hal. 'What kind of shit is this?'

'It's an airline breakfast,' I say.

'It's a contradiction. *Ham* on a bagel.'

'I've seen you eat bacon.'

'If I choose to eat pig, that's one thing. I want the choice.'

'Don't eat it, then. You won't die, we're almost there. Here, I'll have it.' I left the house early, no breakfast, not even a cup of tea. Dom was barely awake. I left before he had time to surface, moving quickly, aware that with each moment his potential for full conversation was increasing. During the weekend I kept finding myself on the verge of telling him. I couldn't trust myself in his company for much longer without saying something. Part of me wants to tell him, blurt it out, because I know that not telling him will have consequences. But telling him also has consequences. At the moment the consequences of not telling him seem easier to handle. I never thought I'd be so glad to come to Berlin. 'Good luck for the talk,' Dom had said sleepily, 'call me when you're back.' When I do call him, I will have done it; got rid of our child. Not a child, a pulsing blob, a heartbeat. He need never know. I've done the right thing, I keep telling myself; I don't regret it, I say over and over. Today is Monday, I fly back on Wednesday, the operation is booked for Thursday morning. When I speak to Dom on Friday, it will be done.

'Eating for two,' says Hal, as I take his bagel.

'That's cruel, Hal.'

'I'm sorry, it slipped out.' We agreed not to talk about it.

It.

That was the deal. The decision is made. I'm here to take my mind off it.

'Forget the food,' I say. 'Look.' I stack up the tiny packets of salt, pepper, sugar, creamer, wipe, none of which I want. Hal hasn't used his either.

'Think of the effort that's gone into producing these.' Dark blue paper with white words in five languages. Somebody designed them, thought how to make them this small, how to make the letters fit; someone else checked how to spell salt, pepper, sugar, creamer, in five languages; yet another person sorted them out, one set for each of us. These things came into the world, not to be used but just in case we might want to use them. We didn't. All that human effort has gone into making something that will be thrown away; we discard them without a second thought.

'For chrissake,' says Hal, as I start to take his salt and pepper and add them to my pile. The stewardess is making an announcement; she wants to collect our small change, no matter what currency, this way the airline collects millions of pounds for sick children.

'I could ask her to collect all the salt and pepper packets while she's at it,' I say. 'I could ask the airline to do it worldwide. Think of the installation I could make.'

'Like the pyramid of garbage in Manhattan you mean?'

'I could call it *Lost Appetites*.' I could see it now, a giant salt and pepper pot, built from tiny blue packets, millions of them.

'*P-lease*. You're not yourself, Maddie. You are up to doing this presentation?'

'Don't worry, I won't embarrass you,' I say, stuffing the sachets in my pocket. I'm disappointed that Hal doesn't appreciate *Lost Appetites*, the coming together of corporate sponsors and social conscience.

The plane starts its descent, plunging, nose forward. We're falling. I can see Berlin, it's getting bigger. In no time we're almost level with slab upon drab slab of high-rise housing, and the television tower. It looks like a golf ball on a concrete tee; there's a spike rising from the golf ball, red and white striped, and satellite dishes above it. A strange assemblage which hasn't quite worked: *Golf Ball With Barber's Pole and Wok*. Someone had a vision once. There's a bump, we're on the ground. People are on their feet, the click of overhead compartments and the rise of conversation, relief. We did not die. Hal and I seem to be the only English-speaking people, there's an explosion of German. If these words were things they would have sharp edges.

'I feel like we're in the middle of a quarrel,' I say.

Since I'm on expenses, I've taken the hotel room. I could have had the sofa-bed at Jakob's apartment where Hal is staying, but I don't want to be in Hal's company all the time. I need to sort out my slides, think what I'm going to say.

The hotel is like something out of a black and white movie, an old building that survived the war. The woman on reception is the owner too, I think, dressed in black crepe, amber beads resting on her bosom, her white dog yapped at my ankles as I registered. It's not a smart enough establishment to have someone show me to my room. Up I went to the fourth floor in a lift that is old, a gilded cage on the outside, but inside it is lined with new steel doors that snapped shut when I pressed the button. Hal says the building was once grand apartments, that Generals lived here during the war. Jakob told him this. I got out of the lift at the fourth floor and found my room. The maid was still mopping the floor, a worn parquet. She gave me a guilty look, as if to say: Sorry, I'm running late.

'I'll wait outside,' I said, indicating I would sit in the chair along the landing, which upset her even more. She hurriedly finished. As she straightened up from her mopping I saw the mound of her belly. Further on than me, halfway, perhaps; beyond termination. I didn't like to walk on the wet floor, an insult to her effort. I tiptoed to the bed and lay down.

That was an hour ago. I haven't moved.

I gaze up at the high ceiling; this was probably an elegant drawing room once, there's a huge fireplace with a high mantel. I see a German General leaning against it, smoking a cigar. The floor is dry now, a threadbare rug runs between the twin beds. I get up and open what I think is a cupboard, but it's the shower and toilet. I must get ready, Hal will be here soon. We're going to do some sightseeing, ending up at a private view at one of the new galleries Hal keeps telling me about. It belongs to a friend of Jakob's, over in the old district, Mitte, which is where Hal is staying.

As I stand under the shower I run my hands over my belly; it's thickening. I wonder if I would have noticed that the maid was pregnant two months ago? What's inside her will have hands, feet, eyes.

I think of the blob. Dark, pulsing. Working hard at splitting and growing, working hard to come into existence. It doesn't have hands, yet, it doesn't have feet; well, not visible to the naked eye. Frog-spawn is not a frog. *There's your baby*. She didn't say: There's your blob. *We have a heartbeat. A viable foetus. Eight weeks.* Viable was a word that stuck in my head. I looked it up: *Capable of living, able to maintain a separate existence*. In three days' time it will no longer be viable. Sluiced away down the hospital drain, into the sewers. It will not be a foetus, viable, capable of life, but its particles will be out there somewhere, rearranged. One day these particles will be sucked back into the atmosphere to become a star. There's no going back. It's all fixed up. Even though Jean says I can pull out any time. *Even on your way to theatre*. There can be no baby, no separate life. It's not easy, I'm not relishing the thought of having my insides vacuumed; but the consequences of not going ahead are also not viable. I am caught between two non-viables. This is what Hal would call a lose-lose situation.

I rub myself with the towel which is not quite big enough and laundry-stiff. I won't put my jeans back on because it's getting so they are not really comfortable. I put on a dress and notice that my bare arms and neck are white. Ghostly. Hal will be here soon. I need sunglasses and some money. I check my jacket pockets, find them stuffed with airline sachets. *Have you asked yourself why you allowed yourself to become pregnant?* They both asked that, the GP, and Jean the Counsellor. I have tried to think of an answer. What I do know is that I haven't done it because of Dom. This is so clear to me; but that's what anyone would think, that's the obvious answer. Not to me. Salt, pepper, sugar, creamer, I can't bring myself to put them in the bin, I toss them on to the bedside table. An appalling thought: did I get pregnant to see whether I wanted a child, to give myself the option? *It might be your last chance*.

The telephone makes a buzzing sound; that will be Hal.

* * *

We rise up from the S-Ban station at Potzdammer Platz, and there it is, the Info Box, the story of a city reinventing itself, a pillar-box red portakabin on shiny black stilts. We climb up the metal steps.

'We'll go right up,' says Hal, who has been here before. 'It's the view we want.' We leave the multimedia display to the swarms of tourists. We climb up more metal steps, along gantries, until we can see the whole city.

'Will you look at that,' says Hal. We turn towards the Reichstag, its new glass dome glinting in the sun through a forest of cranes. I stop counting the stiff-necked giraffes once I get to thirty; they swing back and forth, lifting and lowering. Below us colour-coded pipes take building materials around the city so as not to bung up the streets; pink and blue. Boy or a girl, I try not to think of the sewers.

'I'm telling you it was amazing. You imagine that building, minus its dome of course, wrapped up. Like some strange gift.' I've heard Hal talk about this before but, now we're here, I can connect to it. Hal was in Berlin when Christo wrapped the Reichstag in '95, that's when he met Jakob. He watched as trained climbers tipped the bolts of fabric over the edge of the building then followed the cloth in a synchronised abseil.

'It changed all the time depending on the light,' says Hal. 'Grey when it rained, pink to gold at sunset. It was like Woodstock, only better. Everyone hung out, there were musicians, Jakob and I sat up one whole night and just watched it change.'

'It must have been quite something to have that scale of vision and to see it through. It makes my work seem much more do-able,' I say.

There is a good breeze up here; we lean on the railings and watch the cranes swinging, swarms of men in hard-hats, the half-built tower blocks rising from the excavated no-man's-land where The Wall once was. A city transforming itself, coming to terms with its past. Things move on, nothing stays the same.

'Do you think that was enough, wrapping up the past?' I say. 'Might it not have been better to pull it down and start again?'

'I'd have agreed with you if I hadn't seen the wrapping.' Hal reminds me that though the building has been restored, some of the marks of war – graffiti, bullet holes – have been left visible on the stonework.

'It's a cone of mirrors,' Hal says, as I try to figure out the structure inside the new glass dome. A cone of mirrors which reflect light into the heart of the building; bringing light to a dark place.

'Apparently you can see parliament at work,' says Hal. Transparency, no secrets. That's the idea, the vision. We'll see.

'I'm not sure about this,' I say. We look at the new corporate headquarters rising from the wasteland. Name a corporation and it's here. Name an architect and he's here. When it's finished this area will be like a living textbook of late twentieth-century architecture. I can see Hal thinking about all the lobbies and boardrooms that will need art. We move along the gantry towards the Sony Tower; a huge glass edifice rising before us.

'Feels, well, aggressive to me,' I say. 'All that money in one place, all those shareholders needing to be satisfied.'

And yet it is beautiful, this curved wall of glass.

Hal is loving it, wine in hand, moving through the crowds. I've told him I've had enough. I can't do another stilted conversation in slow English with my few words of German. I've come out into the courtyard to get some air. Hal's right, this area is buzzing. The buildings around this courtyard have been restored, colourful mosaics in brick and tiles, each façade different. There are networks of courtyards, each one a surprise. It's more intimate than Potzdammer Platz. We've been round so many new galleries, some are more serious than others. It's like SoHo was in New York twenty years ago. I'm relying on the fact that Hal will want to leave soon, I know he and Jakob plan to go to the sauna. I could get a taxi, but he wouldn't forgive me for leaving without saying anything. Hal is at home here, getting into his roots. His grandfather lived in Mitte, before the war, got out in '36, traded in oil cloth. He went to New York then ended up in Chicago where Hal was born. When Hal first started dealing in paintings the family joke was that he was carrying on the business by other means.

'Maddie, you are alone.' It's Jakob.

'I don't mind, I need some air.'

'What do you think of Berlin?'

'It's a surprise, all the building, ambitious.'

'Needs vision to put the two halves back together.'

'I thought there would be more evidence of the wall. It's hard to imagine it now.'

'Still a long way to go, it takes longer to come down in the mind,' Jakob says. 'Do you know they say that there are still police sniffer dogs who know where it is, could follow the line of it even though it's not there.'

I wake early as the traffic below builds up. I've been thinking about the third piece for The MCA. A glass wall made up of the pieces, but I want the form to suggest something more fragile, amorphous, transient. I want to imply a wave, a tidal wave. So, a wall of glass with the top edge curled over. Wave and wall in one.

Hal's coming over to take me to lunch and then on to do the talk. No doubt he's had a busy night: sauna, clubs. I will not ask. I have a couple of hours until he arrives. I'll go for a walk, there's a museum near here I want to visit. First, one more run through my slides. I'll start with *Family Album*, then the *Shadow Series*, then some of my early installation work like *The Uncried. The Uncried* was one of the first things I showed that wasn't painting. I saw a documentary about the human body; apparently, on average, we cry sixty-five buckets of tears in a lifetime. This made me think about Faith who never cries. Where have all the tears gone? What would her non-tears look like? If an average person cries sixty-five buckets, then Faith must have, given what happened to her, an above-average tear-count. I arranged one hundred empty zinc buckets in the shape of a teardrop. I made a soundtrack which mixed the roar of the sea with sounds inside the body, amplified. One hundred empty buckets. I always imagined her tears, uncried, had seeped inside her, a leaking sadness, pent-up salt water.

I'm not sure whether to include *Comfort Blanket*, the piece I made from tumble-drier fluff; it's not a good slide, too dark. I'll leave it out. I'll put in the three cosmic pieces, they always go down well. I'm not writing a script, the images will do the work. I want to say as little as possible. I put away the notes I started to make, in amongst them is the fax from Annie.

Dear Maddie,
I said all the wrong things. I'm sorry. As far as having children is concerned there's no such thing as good timing. If you really don't ever want a child, then go ahead with the termination. But, if you have a fraction of doubt, then be sure you know why you're doing it before you go through with it. I don't think this is a situation where you ever get it right. What I mean is you'll have fall-out either way. If you think you can't be a mother because of Faith, it will be different. The child will not be you, you are not Faith. I hope this helps. Do call again soon. Let me know what you decide. I'm thinking of you.
Much love,
Annie.

I've managed so far not being a mother; I know how to do that. I make art. It has a purpose. It feels purposeful. Being a mother is something I am wholly unprepared for. I don't know what reserves I would draw on, emotional I mean, leaving aside the practical stuff. Yet it scares me, what I'm choosing to do. It's like giving in, saying that I am Faith's daughter; daughter of silence.

'You were great,' says Hal as he bundles me into a taxi. 'Leave the networking to me.'

I must collect my stuff from the hotel, and catch the six o'clock flight. I will sleep in London tonight, wake up early for my next engagement.

I take the lift up to my room. The pregnant maid is working her way along the corridor. I put the slides in my suitcase, change into something more comfortable for the flight. I've asked the woman in black at reception to have a taxi here by four-thirty.

Your last chance.

We never get it right.

No such thing as good timing.

I look at the phone beside my bed. Too late, I've paid the bill. I pile myself and my luggage into the gilded-cage lift. The internal steel doors snap shut. I press the button for the ground floor. The lift doesn't move. I try again. Nothing. I'm trapped in the steel case. It is dark. The only light comes from the fluorescent buttons.

Don't panic. I try the button again. Nothing. I pull off my jacket, I'm getting hotter by the minute, I can't breathe. Don't panic. I try the button again. Nothing. I press the emergency button. Way off in the distance I hear a bell ringing. I will have stopped breathing by the time anyone reaches me. I can't see how I can get out, short of a can opener. There will be no baby, no me, no intricate, time-consuming works in glass. The exhibition will become a posthumous show of all my work to date. I see Hal at the private view, dressed in black, subdued, regal. My finger is permanently on the luminous emergency button. Perhaps I don't exist any more apart from my finger. Surely this is the last breath, one more perhaps, one more. Who am I anyway, did I ever exist? Madeleine Armitage, Maddie Armitage, Maddiearmitage, mitagemaddiearmitagemitagemaddiearm. I hear voices shouting at me in German. Then in broken English, a button, which button? I flick a switch and the steel doors flip open. I blink at the bright, corridor light. There stands the woman in black, bosom heaving; she has run up four floors. The pregnant maid looks as if she will cry.

'This door,' says the heaving bosom, pointing to the gilded gate, 'you must push hard, not shut properly.' She wants me to go back inside the lift.

'No thanks,' I say. 'I'll walk.'

She and I puff our way to reception. The taxi is here, but I don't mind, he can wait a moment.

'I need to make a phone call,' I say. 'To England.'

I get through straight away.

'Armitage, Madeleine,' I say.

'We're expecting you tomorrow,' says a kind voice. 'How can I help?'

When it comes to it, I can't say the right thing.

'I wanted to check what time I must book in,' I say, still hoping the right words will come.

'Eight-thirty. And remember, nothing to eat or drink.'

'Right.'

'Are there any changes in your circumstances?'

'No, no. I just wanted to confirm the time. Thank you.'

Part Two

Stair Rods 5

I select a nugget of green glass the size of a sugar lump; part of a sundae glass, I think. Judging from its thickness, I'd say it was from where the stem joined the bowl. I have eaten Faith's trifle off this piece of glass, my spoon scraping the last of the jelly and custard until I could see my hand beneath. I take a reel of nylon yarn, cut a length and encircle the rough lump, first one way, then the other, as if it were a parcel. I tie a secure knot and make a small loop. Later, through the loop, I will attach another length of the thread so the piece of glass may be suspended, take up its place amongst the others to form the wave-wall. That's how I think of this one. It doesn't have a title yet. When I've tied this knot I will have a rest. I need a drink. Also, I must close the doors, rain is starting to trickle in from the build-up of water on the walkway. The air is heavy, muggy. I don't want the door closed but I don't want the place flooded, the photographer is coming tomorrow. He will take pictures of what I have produced in time. A detail, only. I haven't enough even for a detail, yet.

I've been here all day, tying these tiny parcels. I've been at the studio most days for weeks now, since I came back from Berlin. You could say I was in hiding.

One of my students was meant to help today but she called in sick. To be honest, I'm glad to be alone. If I keep up a steady pace I will have enough nuggets of glass ready by this evening. Hal said he would drop by to see how I'm getting on, to see how it looks.

'It's so exciting,' he said, 'to see new work.'

Well, he'll have to temper his excitement and put in a bit of graft. Hal will not want to handle the broken glass, he will fuss about cutting his hands. He can help me suspend them, fixing them the right distance apart to make the form I'm aiming at. I will let Hal climb the step-ladder, dangle each piece on its thread, while I judge the drop, decide where it needs to go in order to build up the mass.

I'm nervous, these days, on the step-ladder.

The rain is coming down hard now, a thundery, August rain pelting the glass section of my roof, until the blobs of bird shit begin to dissolve. The noise of the rain is the first thing to have broken my concentration all day. I tend to shut out noise when I'm working.

'Don't know how you do it, Maddie,' Hal says. 'I'd go out of my skull.'

I don't mind the repetitiveness. I play games. First, I notice how I become more adept at wrapping the thread around, getting the tension right. Sometimes I see how many I can do in ten minutes, half an hour, an hour. By the time I get bored with counting, my hands have found a rhythm, seem to know what to do without me. I drift off. Thinking time. A precious, private space. I forget myself.

When my jeans wouldn't fasten this morning I knew there was no point forcing myself into them. I can't drift off into thinking time if I'm physically uncomfortable. Frankly, with this humidity, I would rather work naked. I found some of Jack's old overalls: big, baggy. I cut out the sleeves, cut off the legs at the knees, like shorts. I am naked inside this baggy blue sack.

I was miles away until the rain cut in, thinking about the layout of the gallery. There will be the three enclosed spaces. The proportions have still to be decided, also the relationship of each to the other. I don't want to impose an order of viewing, a route which people think they must take. I'm going to Liverpool early in September for a meeting with Jude. I want something else besides the three 'rooms'. I've been thinking about an area between the rooms, not enclosed; there might be a real table, laid for high tea, with the glass as it was. The Museum of Contemporary Art could borrow from the Featherbridge Museum. Also, I would like there to be something which connects to how the glass was made at Bagshott's, a sense of the workplace. I would love to be able to blow a piece myself, but it's unrealistic. Patrick, down the corridor, has friends who make hot glass, they have a workshop in Dalston. I went to see them, Matt and Carol, but their furnace isn't lit at the moment. They're working on a window commission, etching, blasting not blowing. They're not sure when they'll light it again.

'Have to wait until we have enough orders on the books,' said Carol. 'Not worth the gas bill otherwise.'

I want to have a go, at least, even if I don't produce anything. I want to feel what it's like; what it felt like to be Frank, the shadow. The more I work with these jagged pieces, the more curious I become about the stuff.

'Glass is always moving,' Matt said. 'It's a super-cooled liquid.'

There is something about the behaviour of particles, what they do or don't do when they cool; held in a glassy state, technically neither quite solid nor liquid.

For now I must work with my nuggets. They are laid out before me on the table which Patrick helped me to fix up. Last week I had the glass arranged on the floor on sheets of black paper. The constant reaching to the floor, bending and stretching, was getting to be uncomfortable. Patrick and I have talked a lot lately with me being here most days. I like to stop for a break in the late afternoon, sit out on the walkway if it's fine. He sometimes makes tea, asks how I'm getting on.

'Slow. It's time-consuming.'

'Why don't you get some help?' he said. I had the sense he was offering, but I couldn't work with Patrick.

'I could get a student, I suppose. I don't mind doing it. It's the deadline,' I said, standing to stretch my stiff back.

'Be easier if you had the stuff to hand,' he said, as he watched me go back to my piles on the floor. Next day, he came around with a large sheet of plywood from his studio. The four tea chests form four sturdy legs. I've spread the black paper and laid my table with heaps of glass sorted by colour, size, or recognisable parts of the original objects. I have more handles than anything else. Lined up along one end are reels of nylon thread. I've been sitting at my table since early this morning. I left the house even before Sevgül had opened the Hot Shop.

* * *

I walk over to the double doors which are wide open on to the walkway. There will be no sitting out for a cup of tea with Patrick today. I take a broom and push off the gathering water, pull the doors together, so the rain can't leak in, but I don't quite close them.

Jude wants an image for the catalogue, the poster and the private view invitation. We all agreed that a detail would work well.

'Intriguing,' Jude said.

I'm doing a pilot of the wave-wall piece, assembling a section of it in the corner of my studio. It will give Jude the image she needs. It will also give me a sense that what I've seen in my head can work, can come into being. I can't mock up the whole thing but I've created a corner of it, lining the darkest corner of my studio with blue velvet; old cloth, worn in parts, it bears traces of other lives. I've chosen velvet, rather than pigment, for this piece because I like what it does to the sound. Walk into an enclosed space lined with velvet, and sounds change. The tap of feet on the floor sounds further off, voices more intimate. Velvet confounds hearing, you listen more intently; it's like after a snowfall when the world sounds different. In a confined space, velvet walls create an ambivalent atmosphere; comforting in a way, the softness, the warmth, yet claustrophobic. There is no way through, only the folds to fall into; like the deep folds in the curtains which Faith hung in my room to keep out the light. Curtains which she bought at a house clearance auction. They smelled of another place, another time, other lives. I would stare at the folds through the darkness of my room until they became waves or the night sky, but mostly they were Faith's silence made real. Faith's silence hung heavy around us all, an invisible drapery with unsettling folds which hid the unsayable and into which I could easily fall. I used to think: If only I could pull back the curtains I would see what the silence was hiding.

I think of this one as the wave-wall but that's not the title. The caption will have to read: detail, pilot installation, glass, nylon thread, velvet. By the time the photographer comes I will have made enough to imply a wall of glass which curves over, becomes a whitecap, a cresting wave. I want people to feel it as a physical presence, bodily, as much as to see it with their eyes. I've roughly worked out where to hang the threads so that the pieces are spaced as I want them to be. When Hal comes I will direct him.

Reaching up is tough on my back with you inside me.

The worst thing is the tiredness, a deep tiredness; as if I have walked for miles. Earlier, I had to put my head down on the table, I dozed for a while. It helps.

A few things have become clearer but an awful lot more is still a muddle which I can't begin to unravel.

So, I work. Every day.

One thing I know clearly is that I kept you because I wanted you, for your own sake. I couldn't shake the image of you. Pulsing, embryonic blob. That's how I still think of you, though I know you're bigger now. Now, you will have arms and legs, you are floating on the end of your rope, swimming safely.

Another thing I know is, now I'm going to have you, I'm glad you're Dom's. I don't know what the future is but we have a past, Dom and me. I've thought a lot about Dom, over the last few weeks, what he means to me. I've thought about the time in Norfolk when I came in from my night wanderings and had to hold on to him. What I love about Dom is his tenderness, the ease with which I can rest against his flesh, sink into him. It is not something I have experienced often in my life. When it happens, when we are alone enough, safe from watching eyes, it happens. You have come into being out of that. The scary thing is, if I want that closeness too much, too often, perhaps I won't be able to have it at all.

I am glad that you are Dom's and I am glad you are still there.

The rest is a muddle. I don't know how to explain to Dom that having you is not about trying to hang on to him. I've tried to explain, but I didn't make a great success of it. That's why I can't see him.

'What do you mean stay away?'

'I can't see you, Dom, not now. Not for a while.'

'When?'

'I don't know.'

So I hide, here in my studio.

I still think about what I had planned to do and I shudder to think that you might not have been.

The last morning in Berlin, before my talk at the festival, I went to the Käthe Kollwitz museum. It was once a grand old house, now each floor is given to a phase in Kollwitz's artistic life: drawings and prints depicting war, work, poverty. I kept going back to the room of charcoal drawings of her and her children; the volume of plump new flesh eased into being with a single line on a piece of paper; muscle dissolving into muscle. A ferocious closeness. It scared me. It was something I had barely known, something I wanted to know.

Then in the lift when I thought I would suffocate, through the panic, I had one clear, fierce thought: I had to live in order for you to live. It didn't make sense, considering where I was going the next morning, but it was strong. When I called the clinic from the hotel reception I lost it, couldn't do it. There was the disapproving impatience and heaving bosom of the owner, flushed from her mercy-dash up the stairs, but also I thought: Anyone can have rash thoughts trapped in a lift in a foreign country. When the calm English voice at the other end of the line said: *Are there any changes in your circumstances?* I wanted to say: Yes, I'm having this baby, I want it. But I could also see myself landing at Heathrow, heavy with regret.

As I waited in baggage reclaim I was thinking: This time tomorrow it will be over. I started to shake. My legs felt like lead, I expected to keel over. Here I go, I thought. I could see myself going round and round on the carousel, unclaimed baggage. The feeling I'd had in the lift came upon me again, stronger this time. I knew the only way to stop myself becoming unclaimed baggage going round and round on the carousel, was to phone the clinic, cancel the appointment. I knew it through my skin. I haven't got beyond that certainty, the certainty of keeping you. I knew I had done the right thing. I was dog tired. I went home and slept like the dead.

I've no idea what comes next.

Dom doesn't want to disown you but I can't see how it will be. I don't want to play house like Nancy and Edward. I don't want Dom simply to do his duty, I become Tessa. He stands by me because of the child. Think how easily we might slip into that. I don't want to play Happy Families.

Things didn't go well when I told Dom, mainly because I had no time to think. He surprised me, turned up the next morning. When the doorbell rang I thought it was the postman. Still half asleep, I opened the door and there was Dom.

'Dom,' I said and hung back.

'You don't seem pleased to see me,' he said.

'It's so unexpected,' I said and made myself go towards him, drew him in, kissed him, tried to behave normally. All I could think of was that, right at that moment, I should have been lying in an operating theatre getting rid of our baby. He knew something was up.

'What is it, what's wrong?'

So I said it: 'I'm pregnant.'

He said nothing. His face froze, brow creased, as if he was trying to work something out. Perhaps he doesn't know what the word means, I thought.

'Having a baby,' I said. 'Say something.' Before he had time to say a word, I realised what was puzzling him. Of course he knows what it means to be pregnant. What doesn't seem clear is whether it has anything to do with him. I could see that he thought perhaps I was trying to tell him I was having someone else's child.

'Ours,' I said. Then a torrent of words. My decision, I was prepared to take it on. An accident, yes. Did he remember in Norfolk, when I'd been outside in the middle of the night. Did he remember, I woke him up. His face softened at the memory, the fierce tenderness of our lovemaking.

'I forgot, just forgot, it was in the bathroom . . . I . . .' Quiet, then. There was so much to be said, neither of us spoke but we could hear each other's thoughts. I cut in, 'I'm supposed to be having a termination, right now.' And the look on his face changed again.

'You can't . . . we haven't . . .'

Molten fury sprung from nowhere. I surprised myself.

'We? Who is this We?'

* * *

The rain is getting stronger, a fierce pounding. A cloudburst. 'Stair rods,' that's what Ernest used to say when it rained like this. The force of it makes the doors swing open again. I get up to close them. As I step out on to the walkway, a determined rain hammers on my arm, it hurts; the noise of it now on the glass roof, it's as if someone is scattering gravel.

I stop and listen to the rain, watch it run down the glass roof. I can't believe the force of it could increase any more, but it does; a clap of thunder, white lightning. The release of so much water; vigorous, urgent. The thrill of it makes my heart race. Elation. I want it to go on and on, become stronger and stronger. I want it to rain so hard that the roof will shatter. I'm high on the possibility of this, high on the danger.

It's a feeling I recognise.

The thrill of watching Faith break the glass against our back wall. I was appalled, yes, to see Faith in such distress, but thrilled too at the display of raw feeling; feeling that up to then had been channelled safely: scrubbing, polishing, ironing, sewing, knitting.

The Dream Jar 5

'The three glass pieces amount to a major body of work,' says Hal. 'The pilot piece is sensational. Isn't that a great image?' He holds up the contact sheet. The photo session last week went well.

'But I think there needs to be something else,' I say.

'That one,' says Hal. 'That would be my choice.' He puts a self-adhesive red dot next to the frame on the sheet. 'I mean, why put more pressure on yourself at this point?'

Why doesn't he say it: *in your condition*.

Since the photo-shoot went well and The Museum of Contemporary Art has images, there have been sighs of relief all round. There will be a poster, Kathy with the tangerine hair is working on the magazine editors. Apparently *Contemporary Art 4* is considering what Kathy refers to as 'a major piece'. She's sure the pictures of the new work will clinch it. The designer is working on the poster and catalogue cover. I want to say to Jude, to them all, that having a poster is one thing; it's no guarantee of an exhibition, no certainty that the new pieces will work. We won't know that, finally, until we install them in the gallery.

'There's something missing,' I say and try to explain to Hal my thoughts about laying a trail through the gallery, connecting my dramatic, imagined spaces to a sense of home and workplace.

'I've been thinking about the gallery, seeing it as a series of spaces which can be moved in and out of in any order. Each will be about a different experience of the same thing: how Frank made the glass, how it was used in the home, how it might be reimagined.'

'But isn't that implied by the work?'

'Yes, but I want to lay a sort of trail, moving from the real to the surreal, maybe it won't work. We'll see. Jude likes the idea.'

'Blowing glass takes years to learn, sounds kinda hot. Hard work.'

'Yes, and no.'

'I would say, yes and yes,' says Hal with a look that means he's humouring me. A look that says: it's her hormones.

'Anyway, it might not be possible. Matt and Carol don't have the furnace on at the moment.'

'All I'm saying is I hope it doesn't dissipate the energy.'

'I want to work with molten glass. It's not separate from the broken glass pieces, it's another way of following the ideas through. I'd like to move beyond the broken glass for a while.'

Especially since I had the dream.

'It was a powerful image, I can't shake it. So I'll follow it,' I say and I tell Hal about the dream of the bubble, bottle, jar; I don't know what name to give it. A beautiful object, strange. In the dream it seemed like something I'd never seen before, and yet at the same time, there was something about it which was utterly familiar. It appeared on the table in my studio. Finely blown glass, blown beyond the limits of what is known to be possible. Not a bubble, more of a tear-drop shape, like the carboys, giant glass bottles, in the chemist shop window. Instead of coloured water the fluid inside it was clear. To call it clear does not describe the luminous quality; a liquid that was more pure light than liquid. In it floated a tiny, perfect child. In the dream I wasn't afraid, it didn't seem strange or science fiction-like as it does now to my waking mind. In the dream it was happening in parallel with the real child growing inside me, it was part of the process. It was part of growing a child. It was a beautiful thing. I couldn't make this thing, even if I could remember it exactly; it is beyond the limit of my skill. In a dream things can be two things at once. The womb jar, which is what I call it, was a fine, fragile glass, delicate as a single flake of ice, but it was also soft, yielding; a material which is not familiar, not known at all. Not glass, not cloth, although it could be taken for either; not skin or a membrane, not organic and yet alive. It is one thing for me to imagine such an object, but how can I realise it as a piece of work?

'It made me think of Frank. I'd like to have a try. Maybe I won't be able to blow something myself, but I could have a hand in making something, something which relates to Frank, whatever. We'll see.'

We go through the contact sheet one more time, putting stickers on the ones we prefer. At least Hal and I are in agreement on that.

'I'll go now,' I say, 'I want to catch Jude and tell her about these.' I put the contact sheets in my bag. I want a word with Jude about the catalogue cover. Last time I mentioned it she said: You'll have to speak to Ward. I have already spoken to Ward Joffitt. He's briefed the designer to use the image of Faith and Irene for the catalogue cover. I'm not sure. Now that we have these shots of the new work I hope he'll make the cover the same as the poster.

'It's going well,' says Hal as I pick up my stuff to leave. 'You're on a roll.'

'That's how it goes as the deadline looms. And I want to get ahead in case Annie comes.' There is the possibility that Annie and the twins might come over later this month.

'Good,' says Hal with rather too much emphasis.

'Why, "good"?'

'You and Annie can do girl talk.'

'Say what's on your mind, Hal.'

'Look, it's great that you're so into the work but there are other things going on in your life.'

'Meaning?'

'Your health?'

'Don't fuss.'

'You've hardly mentioned it.'

'It?'

'The fact that you are pregnant, with child. I mean, are we allowed to speak of it? I can't tap-dance around this much longer, Maddie. I mean pretty soon you're going to be able to see the physical evidence of this pregnancy. Can we talk about it or not?'

'Hal, not now. I must get home and talk to Jude.'

'You're doing it again.'

'What?'

'You know.'

He's right.

I keep setting deadlines in my head which allow me to put off doing anything: after I've made the pilot, after the photo session, after we've agreed the poster. I've been hiding behind my work and I can't think of another deadline, I can't think what I'm supposed to do. The tears come.

'Hey, hey,' says Hal, shutting the door which opens on to the gallery. He puts his arm around me, walks me into his office. I sit at his desk.

'I didn't mean to upset you,' he says. 'You've been working flat out since Berlin. You need time off.'

'I don't know what to do,' I say between sniffs.

'You have regrets?'

'No, no. That's the one thing that's certain, the thing I hang on to. I want the baby but I can't get any further.'

'You're still not seeing Dom?'

'He's left messages but I don't want to see him yet.'

'Why?'

'I can't say, it's not rational.'

I think of what Dom said, or started to say, when I told him. I hardly let him finish. *What are we going to do?* I took hold of the word: we. All the time he and I have been seeing each other the one thing we haven't been is a 'we'. Not a legitimate 'we' in the real world. I flipped.

'Don't you think you might have been over-reacting a little?'

'Of course,' I say. 'But I have to be able to do this on my own without Dom. It wasn't something *WE* ever planned.'

'I don't get it – you're freaking out because you think he's coming on heavy, taking control, or what?'

'I don't want this baby to be what decides whether we stay together.'

'It's kinda hard to put it out of the picture though, isn't it?'

'Like I said, it's not rational.'

'Let's take another angle on this. Aren't you supposed to see a doctor? Have you registered this pregnancy yet, made it official or whatever you're supposed to do?'

'Booking-in, it's called. Yes, I've booked in. I'm supposed to go for a test next week.'

'What kind of test?'

'For abnormalities. At my age the chances are quite high.'

'And if . . .'

'I'll cross that bridge when I come to it.'

'Do you think you ought to be even thinking about blowing glass, working at a hot furnace?'

'I've no idea what I should be doing.'

'Those would be my preference,' I say giving Jude the numbers from the contact sheets. 'Do you think you will use the same image for the catalogue cover?'

'I'll put Ward on,' says Jude.

'But Jude,' I say, 'I'm not sure about the *Family Album* photo for the cover.'

'Talk to Ward.'

I've come to realise that Jude has a blind spot as far as Ward is concerned. There's silence on the line as she transfers me to his extension.

'Maddie, how are you?'

I've no time for niceties: 'I'm not sure I want the photo used so prominently. I thought it was going inside for the section on sources?'

'Both, I hope. What's the problem?'

'I've been thinking. Maybe I don't want it used at all.'

'I thought we'd agreed.'

'I can change my mind.'

His tone softens.

'I think you'll like what we come up with. I've seen the roughs.' He describes how a detail of Faith and Irene will be blown up and bled into the image of the new work.

'I can send you proofs this week. Let's talk then.'

'If he's doing more than one version, would you get him to do one that just uses the new work?'

As I put down the phone, I realise I've not handled this at all well. If I don't want the photo used then I ought to have said so. It's not that simple. I can see what he's doing. Part of me can see that what he's suggesting makes sense. If I hadn't wanted him to use the photograph I shouldn't have given it to him at all; shouldn't have painted it; shouldn't have taken it from the collar box in the first place.

I think about what I would say if I phoned Ward back. I could pick up the phone now, tell him I want it back, the photograph is not on offer any more. I think of words to say this, rehearse my tone; neutral, level. The phone rings. I half expect it to be him having read my thoughts but it's Annie.

'Annie?' How good it is to hear her voice.

'I thought I'd call before the day starts,' she says. 'They're still asleep.'

'It's so good to hear from you,' I say and realise how much I miss her. 'So, are your flights booked?'

'Maddie, I'm sorry. We're not coming.'

'Why?' And she explains how her parents have decided to go out there instead and Jack's not sure he can get away for long enough, and now a colleague of Jack's has offered them a beach house for the rest of the month.

'To be honest I'm relieved, I'm not ready to travel with these two, not after what happened last week. I could do with a quiet time.'

'What happened?'

'Can you believe it, I went out in the yard to pick up their toys, left the door open. It's a glass door. Sarah pushes it; it closes. I see her fiddling with the key but I don't think she's strong enough to turn it. Tommy watches her. I'm pleased they are both occupied so that I can finish outside. Maddie, she locked the door. Can you believe it? Locked them both in, me out in the yard.' Annie is still upset, I can tell by the way she is talking. Fast. Like she needs to get this outside of her head. I know she will have gone through this many times. Telling the story over and over to get rid of it, talking it out.

'Of course, they laughed at first because I was outside, waving to them.' She doesn't pause for breath. 'I talked to them through the glass, mimicked turning the key. They laughed. Then the game went sour. Sarah had her hands outstretched for me to pick her up. Tommy looked bewildered. I didn't know what to do. I didn't want to let them out of my sight. I mean, think what they might get up to left alone in the kitchen. But I had to get help. There was a small window open, but I couldn't get through it. Seeing me try to squeeze through the window upset them; they were both crying. Serious crying. Their faces, I will not forget their faces. They looked so abandoned.'

In the end Annie climbed the fence, used the neighbour's phone to call 911.

'I stood on the other side of the glass door talking to them, trying to explain what the banging was. The most distressing thing was that the fireman got to them first. It was awful, seeing their hands outstretched, pleading to be picked up and I couldn't do it.'

'That's awful,' I say. Not being able to imagine at all what it must have been like. 'But it turned out all right. They'll forget.'

'That's just it, children don't forget, do they? I mean, think about it, anything that happens to you at that age, it's so intense. I always pick them up, often both at once. They don't know that I *couldn't* pick them up; they just know that I *didn't*.'

'Do they seem upset still?'

'They're OK now, but they were inconsolable at the time. We had a couple of bad nights.'

'I'm sure they'll be fine. They know you're there now.'

'That's what everyone says but I keep seeing it from their point of view. Practically begging me to pick them up and I ignore them. I never leave them to cry like that. It scared the shit out of me.'

'Sounds like you need a break. Annie, I do miss you. I'm sorry you're not coming.'

'Why don't you come here?'

'I'm working flat out on the exhibition. Can't say it's not tempting. One way of not seeing people.'

'How's it going?'

'All right. I'm tired no matter how much I sleep.'

'I remember it well. It passes. But I meant you and Dom.'

'I'm having the amnio next week.'

'Is Dom going with you?'

'I haven't seen him.'

'Still? You still haven't seen him?'

'He keeps leaving messages.'

'You can't avoid him for ever.'

'I know.' In the background I hear the robust cry of a child; it might be happy, it might be sad, hard to tell at this distance.

'I'll have to go.'

'I'm sorry about what happened. I'm sure they'll be fine.'

'I hope so.'

I think of Annie, trapped on the other side of the glass, try to imagine what it must have felt like. Two little infants, barely able to walk, reaching out to be consoled, Annie not able to touch them. Inconsolable, Annie said. Inconsolable at the time; not the same as unconsoled, no arms to pick you up, ever again. Still, they can't talk like Annie can, anxious talk, to get it out of her system.

Down By The River 5

I've agreed to meet Dom. Annie's right, I can't go on hiding in the studio, lost in my work, ignoring his messages. I want to see him. I miss him. These last few weeks have been good for my work and for me to adjust to my altered state, but I miss him. I realised how much when I spoke to him yesterday. What scares me is that he'll go all dutiful. I couldn't bear that. I said as much on the phone.

'I don't want you to take this on as your duty.' He didn't say anything for a while, I heard a sigh at the other end, then he spoke.

'If I walked away I'd be the feckless lover, if I show concern I'm being dutiful. What can I say? I don't know what to say.' There was sadness in his voice.

'It's all gone your way, up to now,' I said. 'Us. Always driven by you and your duty to Joe.'

'I've had the impression lately it suited you, that the little we had together was enough.' I didn't like the edge that was creeping into his tone.

'Maybe.'

Neither of us said anything for a while; it seemed pointless, getting into a row on the telephone. Then Dom softened.

'We're good for each other, you know,' he said.

'We're good for each other because we don't waste the little time we have,' I said and bit back the rest of what I wanted to say: if we had more time, we might be like every other couple, we might be just like you and Tessa.

'I don't want to talk on the phone,' he said. 'I'd rather see you.'

'See you tomorrow then.'

Quite a bit of me needs Dom. With Dom I can look at the night sky, plunge to the bottom of the pool and know I'll come up. With Dom there is the possibility that I won't, necessarily, become Faith.

I've arranged to meet him at the greasy spoon around the corner from my studio. I'm late. He's sitting at a table by himself, with a cup of tea in front of him which he stirs but does not drink. His newspaper is spread open on the table, but he's not reading. I go over to where he is, but I don't sit down.

'Hello.' He almost smiles.

'Sorry I'm late.'

'You're here.' He folds his newspaper, tucks it into the pocket of his jacket which hangs on the back of the chair.

'Sit down.' He pulls out the chair beside him.

'Can we go somewhere else?'

'Where?'

'I don't know, I have the car; out of town maybe. It's hot. I'd rather be outside.'

'All right.'

We walk to the car saying nothing. As he eases himself into the passenger seat I catch the scent of him; I think of a dozen times we've taken off like this, had a day somewhere, easy in the presence of each other. It would be easy to drive home, spend the day in bed.

I don't know where I'm going, headed north. Cambridge, says the sign. We could take a boat on the river. Out of town is always safer. If Joe's results come through, Cambridge won't be safe. We'll have to avoid Cambridge. Unless, of course, things change. The traffic is heavy, nothing moves; it will take for ever to get out of London so I turn off at the lights, head towards Springfield Park. We can walk down to the river; the Lea is not the Cam but it will have to do.

We leave the car in the shade of laurel bushes, which tumble over the high brick wall of the park, and enter by the side gate. We stand halfway up the hill, not sure whether to go up or down. Neither of us wants to start this. Dom picks at a thread which trails from the cuff of his jacket. If we start, pluck a little harder, the whole garment might unravel.

At the bottom of the hill there is an expanse of grass, dotted with encampments of women and children. School holidays. Older boys have a fiercely contested game of football. Along the pathway walk groups of Orthodox Jewish women with their growing tribes, dressed smartly in suits, high heels, wigs and hats. In this heat. A young woman passes; she has a brand-new pram, a shiny blue carriage bouncing on white wheels. Her first. The woman who walks alongside her already has four others tumbling around her pram.

'And I'm worried about having one,' I say, almost laughing. 'I envy them.'

'You're not serious,' says Dom.

'I am. It's all laid out, follow the plan.'

'You'd hate it.'

'Knowing you had to produce a tribe. They look happy to me, they belong, they know where they came from, where they are going.'

'The unshakeable belief in tradition – doesn't sound like the Maddie I know.'

'You know why they wear wigs, keep their heads covered like that, even in the summer?'

'Modesty?'

'If a woman doesn't show her hair she believes she will be rewarded with children who are spiritual and holy.' We watch and talk about other people, easing back into ourselves, shaking off the estrangement of the last few weeks. I look at him, watch his face relax. We can start, we can open it up now.

'I don't know about spiritual and holy,' I say. 'I'll settle for a baby that arrives in one piece.' We move away from the clusters of people, head back up the slope, across the grass to the bandstand in the shade; everyone else wants to be in the sun. We stand inside the bandstand, lean on the rail looking out over the marshes and urban rural sprawl.

'How are you? I mean physically, everything OK?'

'Better now the nausea's passed. I get tired.'

'It's still sinking in, Maddie,' he says plunging his hands into his pockets.

We haven't quite touched, yet.

'For me too,' I say.

'So everything's OK then, you've had check-ups?'

'Yes. Got myself a right-on community midwife, benefits of living in Hackney.' Monique is from Mauritius. She says I should eat plenty of fresh pineapple to tenderise my womb so I'll have an easy birth. I had imagined that midwives were large, matronly, capable. Monique is tiny, lively. She smiles a lot.

'She gave me a form to fill in. Nearly every section I had to leave something blank.' First came questions about the family history. Apart from Grandma and Grandpa Armitage's TB and Faith's silence there wasn't a lot I could tell her. Then we moved on to medical history of the partner. Again, I had nothing to offer. I had to tick a box saying if this was a planned or an unplanned pregnancy. If the latter, why had my contraception failed? I wanted to say: to stop me falling off the edge, into the night sky.

'Monique and the GP are urging me to have the test, you know, for abnormalities.'

'Will you?'

'I've been resisting.'

'Why?'

'There's a risk of miscarrying.'

'Wouldn't you rather know?'

'You'd think I would, wouldn't you? I've surprised myself. It isn't straightforward. None of it is.'

'When's the test?'

'Should have been this week. I've pulled out.'

'So you've decided.'

'No, not really, the doctor has asked me to think again, I have another appointment next week. It needs to be done soon. Do you think I should have the test?'

'What does it matter what I think?'

'Well, I'm asking you.'

'I think it might be wise to know.'

'Damaged goods, get rid of it if it's not perfect?'

'Wouldn't you rather know?'

'Tessa didn't have to do this did she? What was she, twenty-five, twenty-six when she had Joe?'

'Maddie.' Dom tries to say more but I can't hear. A power mower appears from nowhere. The park-keeper, proud of his shiny red vehicle, is taking the chance to mow the grass, long overdue because of the rain. The smell of fresh-mown grass hits us, Dom starts to sneeze. We move off down the hill away from the noise. There's a row of benches halfway down, each one is hidden inside a kind of alcove formed by a box-yew hedge. We find an empty one. The hedge is higher than our heads, it feels as if we are in a private cubicle; the bushes have grown out sideways, knitted together to form a solid wall of dark green. Below us the river, the marshes, hedgerows and high-rise blocks; a sprawling jumble which the eye reads differently each time: rural overtaken by urban or is it urban trying to be rural.

'Look, Maddie, I don't know what to say about the test. You must do what feels right.'

'Not you too. It's like everyone's read the same counselling leaflet: "it's your decision, whatever feels comfortable". Dom, say what you mean.'

'I think we need to go back to the beginning.'

'The beginning of what? Us, the baby, the universe and life on this planet as we know it?'

'Maddie, I didn't expect this. You being pregnant. It was a shock. I'm getting used to it. I don't know what you want of me, what you expect of me. I want to do . . .'

'Go on, say it. You want to do what's right, you'll do your duty. Yes, you'll do your duty. We know you're good at that. I don't want you to do your duty. I don't want to become your duty.'

A Hasidic matron passes by, pulling her children away from our raised voices.

'Calm down, Maddie.'

'Don't patronise me.'

'OK, over to you. You say what it is you want because I'm lost and everything I've said so far has touched a nerve. Tell me what it is you expect, what I'm supposed to do.'

I see the strain on his face, the look of sheer frustration. I'm being a cow, not giving him a chance but I can't help it.

'I'm sorry,' I say, taking hold of his hand. 'Come on.' I

stand up. 'Let's walk along the river. I feel shut in sitting here.'

We walk down the path, holding hands, behind us the pick-pock of tennis balls, a match in progress between a man and woman. She slams the ball home, laughs; he shrugs. The touch of Dom is something I have never tired of. Why am I trying to push him away when I would like to fold myself into his lean, kind frame and stay there.

It's quieter along the tow-path. We leave the noise of the park behind. Past the marina, past the café at the water's edge, a little way along we stop and sit on the grassy bank.

'Maddie I really care about you; about what happens.'

'Do you? Sometimes I think I'm simply the marriage repair kit. You know, basically bearable at home, as long you've got a bit on the side.'

'You believe that, you really think that?'

'In my bleakest moments, yes.'

'It's not true.'

'It may not be the whole truth but I think there's a grain of truth in it. I wonder if staying for Joe is the real story.'

'You want the truth?' he says, plucking a long blade of grass.

'Go on.'

'I've never really thought much about the future for us.'

'You don't want us to go on?'

'I'm not saying that. I'm saying that "us" always seemed to be what it was. I've enjoyed every minute I've spent with you. Looked forward to seeing you.'

'And now?'

'I told you, I've never thought much about the future.'

'Why?'

'One reason being that I thought you would tire of me.'

'Tire of you?'

'I thought you liked what we had, despite the difficulties. I've got the impression that you wouldn't want me around every day.'

He's right. I've grown used to the mixture of uncertainty and commitment. I can't imagine what it would be like, day in day out. I am used to being on my own.

'Do I have to see you every day in order for us to have a future?'

'Having a child will change things.' He stretches his legs, lies back. 'You never wanted children, you seemed so certain.'

'I thought I was certain. Scary, isn't it?'

'What do you mean?'

'That you can be so sure you don't want something, then find that you do want it, want it badly.'

'You can't do this alone,' he says, sitting up again.

'I can if I must. Don't start your dutiful stuff.'

'I can't pretend that I wasn't shocked – badly shocked – by the news.'

'I'm sorry.'

'It's the thought of starting again,' he says. 'It's so long since Joe was a baby.'

'What's the worst thing? It scares you, drags you down, traps you – what?'

'How to manage it all,' he says.

'We're to be managed are we, me and the baby?'

'Give me a break.'

'You know what I think?' I say.

'What?'

'That when it comes to it you don't want to leave Tessa. You'd rather stay in a lifeless marriage – and I've taken your word all these years that it is a lifeless marriage – than go through the upheaval.'

He says nothing, plucks another blade of grass which he sucks. I take his silence to be agreement.

'I knew it,' I say.

'There's some truth in that,' he says. 'But it's not what you think. Twenty years together, Tessa and me. We've had Joe. It is a lifeless marriage, sometimes I feel like I'm living in a shell, a husk. But we have our work, we don't see much of each other. We get by.'

'Sounds unbearable to me.'

'When Joe's gone, there really will be very little to take Tessa and me forward.'

'Sounds to me like you're staying anyway.'

'It's the cutting off I dread. We've had good times, half a

lifetime. I suppose a bit of me still feels loyal. It would be sad. It would hurt, not because we wouldn't be going on together but because we would be cutting off from the past. It would be sad because of what has been. There's a kind of grief I'd have to bear.'

'And you can't face it.'

'To be honest, no. Like anything unpleasant we put it off.'

'I suppose you have to feel it,' I say, 'the sadness, I mean, before you let it go, move on.'

He stretches out on the grass again, I snuggle beside him. He slides his hand under my T-shirt, feels the bump, and smiles.

'So you don't altogether recoil from this union of our flesh then?' I say and we both laugh and kiss for the first time in weeks.

'I've missed you,' I say.

'Your own doing.'

There's applause from a bunch of teenagers as they pass by in a rowing boat.

We walk back along the tow-path, arm in arm.

'I'll come with you, for the test, if you want me to.'

'Will you?'

'Course I will. When did you say it was?'

'A week today.'

He takes out his diary, flicks the pages. Says nothing.

'What is it?' I say.

'Joe gets his results that day.'

'Well, you can't come, then, can you?'

'What time is the appointment?'

'First thing, nine.'

'That's all right then, I'll be there.'

'Not if it's going to be difficult.'

'I want to come. I'll work it out.'

We walk back to the car through the park, the tension eased. I notice a little girl, six maybe, going on sixteen. She's laughing, running on, leaving her mother behind. The girl wears purple cut-off shorts, a yellow crop-top, white baseball cap, sunglasses with hot-pink frames, on her feet are sparkly pink plastic sandals.

She keeps going, gets way ahead of her mother. She walks like a confident young woman in a child's body. She turns, smiles at her mother, the mother smiles back and waves.

Waving 5

'I'll come in with you,' says Dom.

'I'd rather you waited here. Having you in there will distract me.'

'If you're sure.'

'I'll need all my concentration if I'm going to let them stick a needle through me.' He looks disappointed; it's the way he pulls his mouth in, so you can't see his lips for a moment. He sighs, air forced down his nose because his mouth is tight shut.

'Look, I'm glad you're here. I really appreciate you coming.'

We sit amongst other couples and I wonder if they are all happy couples, real couples with a house and a double bed into which they both snuggle each night. Real couples have underwear mingling in the wash; his and hers toothbrushes in the bathroom; dinner parties with mutual friends. I wonder if any of these are part-time couples, with a 'his' toothbrush that hangs in the bathroom unused for weeks on end, and a social life that rarely extends beyond themselves.

I lie on the examination table, beached whale.

'Will it hurt?' I say. 'Don't I get an anaesthetic?'

'Giving an anaesthetic would hurt you more than this,' says the doctor holding up a long, fine steel needle with a precise, surgical point. The needle is hollow. The fluid inside me will be sucked up its hair-fine shaft and caught in the cylinder attached to the other end. The nurse spreads gel on my mound. It's cold; I flinch. She spreads the icy gel with the sensor, tunes in. My insides will appear on the screen. I close my eyes. I will disappear, let them get on with it, these skilled mechanics. I will dissolve into the space behind my eyes. I stare into the orange void. Orange as the sun; I think of nothing but the orangeness. I've done this before. If you stare long enough the orange turns to crimson, then a hole appears, a bright orange dot amongst the crimson. Then a tunnel forms and fine black lines dance in the tunnel, like filaments in a light bulb, a restless jumping and crackling.

'Ready now. Relax. Keep perfectly still.'

I say nothing, concentrating on the space at the back of my eyes.

A sharp prick, then nothing.

It didn't hurt, but nothing, nothing ever felt so strange. I wanted to say: Be careful, don't poke its eyes out.

'Drawing off the fluid now,' says the chief mechanic.

Down, down the tunnel, the orange has turned to crimson, the crimson gets darker, the tunnel brighter.

'Sorry,' she says. 'No suction, faulty valve. Won't take a minute.'

I can feel her fumbling with the cylinder at the end of the needle. I feel like a kebab. Skewered.

Mechanic number two squeezes my arm.

'It's nothing,' she says in a bright, reassuring voice that has me worried.

'Look,' she says in that high, bright voice. A voice you might use to distract a frightened child.

'Look,' she says again.

Without thinking, I open my eyes, turn my head to the monitor.

You float across the screen.

A bud-like hand bounces off your tadpole nose. How you've changed since I last saw you. I still think of you as a blob. Look at you: a face, arms, hands, legs. Waving. If they gave me a print-out I could start a picture album. I don't need a replica, a reminder. I will never forget what I have seen. I want to tell them to stop, not to take the fluid, not to bother. What for? We're in for life now, you and me, no matter what. No choice. I hope we haven't damaged you trying to find out if you are damaged.

'That's better,' says the chief mechanic as she draws off the straw-coloured fluid. 'Needle's coming out now.'

'Ouch, that really hurt.' Steel dragging against muscle, fat, skin. 'That hurt more than when it went in.'

Mechanic number two helps me off the table.

'Bed-rest for the next forty-eight hours.'

I am given a card with the number I should call in three to four weeks. That's how long it takes for your fluid to yield its secrets.

Dom looks at me, eyes tentative behind his glasses. He gets up from the plastic chair, takes my arm.

'You all right?'

'Fine,' I say. 'Well, a bit wobbly.'

'It's done.'

'Waste of fucking time.'

'Why?'

'Let's get out of here.'

On the street the air is thick. Muggy August London air. I could lean on it, even in my bulky state it would support me.

'Do you want a drink?' Dom says, pointing to a sandwich bar.

I can't face the idea of hauling myself up on to one of those high stools.

'I want to go home,' I say. Home; where is that?

Dom is waving, hand in the air.

'What are you doing?'

'Come on, get in,' he says, and runs to open the door of the black cab.

I lie in the cool north-facing sitting room. Dom makes himself a coffee and brings me iced water with a wedge of lime. The ice tinkles in the silence between us.

'It makes no sense,' I say.

'It's best to know.'

'To ask me to look, to point to that fragile thing inside me. They know why I am there, where it might lead. What if I wanted a termination? Wouldn't you think they'd have some sensitivity? Somehow because I've already chosen not to get rid of it once, this all seems, well, silly. Illogical.'

'I still think that it's best to know.'

'Dom, I saw her.'

'Her?'

'I'm sure it was a her.'

'Wishful thinking,' says Dom and I can see the word 'hormones' flashing behind his eyes. He knows better than to say it.

'A face, a real face, something so face-like, they ought not to let you look.'

'My eyes or yours?'

'Don't take the piss. I hope she's all right. That needle, so close to her.'

'They know what they're doing.'

'I willed her to stay still. She waved, Dom. Like this.' I show him the action. Her hand touched her nose, seemed to bounce off then back again. She had hands, fingers fat as camellia buds.

I remember Faith cleaning the windows at Stonebank, her hand going back and forth, back and forth across the glass.

'Waving,' I say.

'You need to rest.'

'I'm scared.'

'If you rest, you'll be all right. It's a very slight risk of miscarriage.' Dom read the leaflets while he was waiting.

'No, I don't mean that,' I say. 'What I feel for her. What I wouldn't do to protect that little thing. If I feel this much now, what will I feel like when she's here in my arms?' I see myself holding a baby that is you. Only now your stubby, bud-like hands have separated into slender fingers. They clutch at air. I see wisps of hair on your bald head. Your eyes are bright, wide open. You're swaddled in a blanket, tucked in my arms. Will I dare to put you down; dare to let you out of my sight? I remember the little girl waving to her mother in the park.

'Listen, I'm sorry, but you know I have to go,' says Dom. 'Will you be all right?'

'I'll be fine, but will she?'

'Rest, go up to bed, why don't you?'

'I'll stay down here.'

'Only I must go,' he says. 'I have to get up to school before lunch.'

I've forgotten in all this, Joe. Joe's A level results are out today.

'How did you get away at all? What did you say?'

'Does it matter?' He looks awkward. 'I'd love to stay but I have to get to the school, meet Joe.'

'I know, I know.'

'Look, Maddie, let's talk again. I could come round on Sunday, maybe.' Things are easier since our walk by the river, but I can't say we're any nearer knowing what to do.

'Edward's coming to stay on Sunday, remember?'

'I'd forgotten. How long will he be here?'

'I'm not sure.'

'I'll phone you later today. Let's try and meet up at the end of the week, after Edward's gone.'

'He will get them won't he, Joe? His three As?'

'I think so.'

Lucky Joe will have his results by lunchtime. I have another three to four weeks to wait.

'Does he know he's about to have a sister?' I can't stop myself saying it.

'Maddie. Anyway, it might be a brother.'

'Don't avoid the question.'

'Of course he doesn't know. He knows that his mother has written off his father, he knows I'm sleeping in the spare room.'

'I'm sorry. You go. Call me. I'll have my fingers crossed for him.'

I hear the thud of the door. I lie back on the sofa and sip iced water. The phone rings. I let the machine take it.

'Hi Maddie, it's Ward, Ward Joffitt at The MCA. Need to talk to you over the next couple of days concerning the catalogue.'

'Fuck off, Ward Joffitt.'

The Leg Power Of A Flea

5

'Here, take these,' I say, handing Edward a set of keys. 'The mortice lock is stiff. You'll need to pull the door hard towards you.'

He still hasn't noticed.

He arrived late last night, tired from the drive. I made him hot chocolate and we sat at the kitchen table, as we are now. His eyes were weary from hours on the motorway; all he could think of was getting to sleep. I was wearing this same baggy shirt. It hides a lot. My height helps. Naked, my bump is obvious, but I can lose it under the right garments. This morning, even though he is fresh after a good night's sleep, he hasn't noticed, but he hasn't seen me standing. I was already here in the kitchen, munching on toast, when he emerged and helped himself to cereal.

'What time will you be back this evening?' he says.

'Not late.'

This is my first day attempting to work since the amnio. I had a couple of days in bed, feeling sorry for myself. Yesterday I got up, pottered around here catching up with letters and stuff. I was also thinking about what might be possible with the hot glass, because Matt called. They've got a big order from Japan and he's relit the furnace. Today, I'm going to watch him blow glass, get an idea of what might be possible for me to do. If anything.

'Are you coming back here to eat this evening?' I say.

'If that's all right.'

'Don't you want to do something while you're in London? A film, theatre?'

'It's not that sort of trip.' He's here to discuss funding for the next phase of his research and to plan an international conference with others in his field.

'Let's eat out, then,' I say.

I don't want the evening here, cooking for Edward, making stilted conversation. There's only so many times I can ask him about Nancy and William and James. We did that last night. At least if I take him out to dinner there will be other people to watch and remark upon.

'Plenty of good places around here,' I say. 'I'll wait till you get back.'

'All right.' He's indifferent. I expect he'd hoped to come home and find a dinner, made by me, to Nancy's standards. Having eaten, he would prefer to lose himself in his papers, consider what his conference contributors have to say on the breeding habits of wood lice or the social interaction of fleas. If I'm honest there are moments when I envy Edward. Here we are living in a manic, congested world, with so much to take in, to sample. How to choose from the cacophony of sounds, images, performances, real or virtual; a crisis of choice, some might say. Not Edward. Edward ignores most of what is going on around him. He simply shuts it out. His head is full of what matters most to him. He's an international expert on the winter wingless moth. The female, apparently, lives in the trunk of a tree; sidles up and down cracks in the bark with her rear end hanging out, waiting for a passing male. She lays eggs and it all starts over again. What a life.

Edward developed this ability to shut out the world from an early age. I remember once I had a row with Dad about staying up to watch *Sunday Night At The London Palladium*. I wanted to see the Tiller Girls with their long legs going up and down, never out of sync, like a giant centipede. Dad said it was too late, things got quite heated. Edward had his head in a book. As Dad's voice rose, Edward looked up calmly and said: Do you know that if a duck had the leg power of a flea it could leap across the English Channel?

He looks at me now across his cereal bowl.

'I was wondering if you'd like to travel back with me,' he says. 'Spend the Bank Holiday weekend with us. Mother is coming. Thought it would be nice for the children, family get-together.' He doesn't add: after your performance at Stonebank. The unspoken accusation reverberates round the kitchen, echoing off Annie's pottery collection.

'Not sure,' I say.

'It would be nice to know. I'd like to give Nancy some warning.'

'I have to put in more time at the studio, going away breaks the concentration.'

'It's a Bank Holiday.'

'So?'

'Couldn't you spend some time with your family?'

My family.

What he doesn't know is that I'm hoping to have time with Dom this weekend. My family? What he doesn't know is that the half-brother of my unborn child has been dealt a blow: two As and a B. It looks as if he won't get into Cambridge, but they won't know for a couple of weeks. Joe has gone into the Summer Pool; he has to wait and see what's left over at Cambridge when those who did get As have accepted their places. I learned this much in a call from Dom, snatched in a chink of time between heavy sessions with Joe, Tessa and the school. The Summer Pool. It sounds pleasant, as if he's been offered a holiday, floating around in warm blue water, waiting for a call from quad. He got the B for history, which has them baffled. Poor Joe, a B in history sounds like an achievement to me, a hair's breadth from what he needed. Dom, like the school, doesn't trust the result, but equally he doesn't want to make things worse for Joe by coming the heavy parent with the exam board, raising hopes that the result might have been a marking error. Dom is torn between helping Joe accept that the reserve place at Durham does not represent failure, and his own niggling sense that something has gone wrong in the machinery.

For once, it seems, Tessa and Dom are in agreement. They've agreed that Joe needs to take his mind off it. Tessa is taking Joe to Bristol for the weekend. I wonder if being around your dying grandfather is much of a break. Dom says Joe likes to see the old man. Dom and Tessa have agreed that Dom should stay in London, the pretext being that he'll put in some time on the television project, but they both know that he's going to consider starting the procedure to challenge the result. So much agreement between Dom and Tessa is unnerving. *We've had good times, half a lifetime.* One thing he and Tessa won't have agreed upon is that Dom will come over here at some point, most likely on Sunday or Monday. I ought to tell Edward I have family matters which keep me in London this weekend, but I don't.

'She's getting on, you know. Mother,' Edward says.

'She's fitter than I am.'

'I don't know how long she can carry on at Stonebank. She's seventy-five.'

'She likes it up there. It suits her.'

'You hardly ever see her.'

'She hates coming to London, won't come. It's not easy for me to get up to Yorkshire.'

'She's your mother.'

There is something about the way he says it. *She's your mother.* He sounds like Ernest. I see Faith and Ernest, sitting on a tartan rug, their backs against the boulders, Faith's doll-eyes staring at the reservoir which has drowned a community. *She's your mother.* Faith in the garden, peg between her teeth, one sheet overlapping the next on the line. *She's your mother.*

'I know she is,' I say.

'You could make more of an effort.'

'I'll think about it. Want some more tea?'

I get up, put the kettle on, swill out the teapot. Let him notice the bump, let him see that I have things on my mind.

As I put the pot of tea on the table, I stand and will him to look up. There's an expression on his face, puzzlement, he's trying to work something out.

'Yes. I'm pregnant.'

He stares at the bump. Says nothing. He jerks his left shoulder like he always does when he's tense, up and back it goes. He pours a cup of tea then looks me in the eye.

'What are you going to do?' he says.

'Do?'

'You're keeping it?'

'I hope so.'

'What do you mean, hope so?'

'I'm waiting for the amnio results. But, yes I'm keeping it. Even if the results are negative. I'm keeping it. Her. I've seen her, Edward.'

'Her?'

'Not confirmed, it's a feeling I have. That's how I think of it. Her. She waved at me. I can't tell you what it did to me.'

'And the father?'

'Dom.'

'A married man.'

'Technically married, yes.'

'He still lives with his wife?'

'He does.'

'Where will you live, how will you manage?'

'I have a job. There's a crèche at the university.'

'You'll need more than that.'

'These things work out.'

'You can't leave these things to chance.'

'I'll manage. I always do. I want this baby. This is a wanted baby. Did you see William or James when Nancy had a scan?'

'No.'

'It was so clear. Had to be, so they wouldn't hit it with the needle. I was afraid that we might hurt it. To think, Edward, we were like that inside Faith. I mean, think about it. We've all been there. We must remember it, don't you think, at some level?'

'I don't give it much thought,' he says and lets his head fall forward into his hands. I notice his hair is thinning, a patch of shiny scalp is beginning to show through.

'We once floated like that in Faith's womb, and she in Stella's.'

Edward shifts in his seat. I've been thinking: If Stella had seen Faith waving could she have left so easily?

'Do you think the technology changes things?' I say.

'Eh?'

'I saw my baby as an eight-week embryo, a pulsing blob. Then at sixteen weeks, waving at me. It means we start further back, we get to know them sooner. The first bit of our lives used to be unseen, unknown.'

'You're getting a bit fanciful. It strikes me we know too much,' says Edward.

'You're an academic, how can you say that? How can you know too much?'

'I mean in everyday life, maybe it's easier to live if some things are left alone.'

'You wouldn't say that about your moths. You keep prodding away at their lives.'

'That's different.'

'I'm talking about something that's curled up inside me, growing. I've never known such intimacy.'

He looks embarrassed.

'Pass the sugar?' he says.

'I suppose it's just biology to you. Animal reproduction. You'd be interested if I were a wood lice.'

'Louse. Does Mother know?'

'No. I want the results before I tell her, which is why I don't think coming for the weekend is a good idea. It might have taken you nearly twelve hours to notice, but Nancy and Faith will spot it right away, which won't make for a cheery family get-together.'

'This is a mess. A mess,' he says, elbows on the table, head in hands.

'Mess? I can live with mess,' I say. He glances around the dishevelled kitchen, shakes his head.

'I'm not sure you know what you're taking on, having a child.'

'I've a lot to learn, I'm sure.'

'Shall I tell Mother?'

'Absolutely not. Promise me. You tell no one, not even Nancy.'

'Thought you didn't approve of keeping secrets?'

'This is temporary.'

'All right, but you promise me that when you have the results you'll go up and see Mother.'

There's a thud in the hall. The post. A ring on the bell; a package needs signing for. It's from The Museum of Contemporary Art, mock-ups of the poster and two versions of the catalogue cover for me to consider.

I clear a space on the kitchen table, lay them out.

'What do you think?' I say. 'The poster for my exhibition. It's the glass. See?' What he sees are particles floating against undulations of dark blue velvet.

'Hmm,' he says.

'Doesn't it make your skin tingle to see it again?'

'Do you know what you're doing?'

'I think so.'

'You're taking a risk, aren't you?' says Edward, looking hard at me. I think about him, Dad, the neighbours, me, frozen around Faith, watching her smash the glass. Helpless. Afterwards, her eyes staring but not seeing; the noiseless, tearless weeping.

'On balance it seems a risk that's worth taking.'

'You're not thinking about Mother.'

'Oh?' I show him the two versions of the catalogue cover. One shows the image of the glass; the other uses the glass image bleeding into the picture of Faith and Irene. I hate to admit it, but Ward and the designer are right; this makes a strong cover. Objectively, it's very good.

'I am thinking carefully about Faith. I'm going to ask them not to use this, even though it makes a good cover. I will ask them not to use it because I'm thinking of Faith.'

'Have you ever asked Mother about using this stuff?'

'Give me a break, Edward.'

'It's hers, what right have you?'

'That's our mother as a child, with her sister, our aunt.'

'It's not yours.'

'It is, and it isn't.' When I found the photograph, hardly more than a child myself, it became part of me, something to hang on to in the silence. Here was the evidence that Faith had existed before she was my mother. It was an enormous relief to find that she had been a little girl. The photograph feels like part of my life.

'You should have talked to her about using this stuff.'

'I wish I could. I'd love nothing more. She's never acknowledged I have the photograph. And, as far as she is concerned, the glass didn't exist. She says nothing about anything. Why pretend she does?'

'Why are you so destructive?'

'Destructive?'

'Self-indulgent.'

'Can't you see that piecing that glass together is like trying to repair something?'

'It's meddling, poking around in someone's painful past.'

'You agree there is a painful past. That's progress.'

'You can't leave things alone, can you?'

'It's our past too. It's the way I am. There are times when I wish it were otherwise. Why do you poke around moths' backsides all the time?'

'Why always come back to Mother, the past – aren't there other themes you could tackle?'

'I come back to it because it's unknown.'

'Invading her privacy, it's aggressive. Destructive.'

'I do think about Faith. All the time. I've played along, colluded with her silence. I've never pushed her.'

'Why does it matter so much?'

'It's a big part of me, of our lives. Aren't you curious?'

'I am, but not in the way you are,' he says. 'Sometimes I wonder, but I wouldn't probe.'

For the first time it hits me; why haven't I realised this before?

'I don't think it affected you in the same way. It was different for you,' I say.

'What do you mean?'

'It didn't affect you did it, her sadness?'

'Sadness?'

'Couldn't you feel it? I could. It was always there, beneath the silence, a deep sadness inside her.'

'You've always had a vivid imagination,' he says in a tone so patronising I consider pouring tea on his thinning hair.

'I felt it. It leaked into me, it affected me. Maybe she was protecting us by pretending there was no past. But it didn't work, she handed it on anyway and in a much more powerful form. She handed it on to me, a heavy wrapped object. I'd like to know what I'm carrying, I'd like to put it down.' And I see that Edward really doesn't understand what I'm talking about. But then it was always me at her side, helping with the chores. Edward would take himself off to his room, line up armies of toy soldiers and pretend that he couldn't hear when called. I would be with her, sorting the washing, peeling potatoes. She would stand beside me, far away, far off inside of herself. I wouldn't dare speak. It felt like she was crying but there were no tears. I imagined her tears seeping inside her, a leaking sadness, pent-up salt water. Over the years the sediment has silted up, ossified. Soft creatures, under pressure, become fossils.

'It didn't affect you in the same way, did it?'

'Can't you just get on with life? You're happy aren't you?'

'Happy? What is happy?'

'I'm happy enough. I have the work I want, the family I want.'

'It didn't leak into you.'

'Perhaps this baby will be good for you. Dose of reality. It won't be easy.'

'Easy? I'm not expecting easy. I've had nothing easy, so easy is not in the picture.'

We both look at the proofs of the poster lying between us on the table. Can't he see what I'm trying to do? This glass provides the key to our family history. Those ordinary things, which were laid on the table each day, have gathered our lives around them. These simple objects accumulated so much that Faith had to destroy them. Isn't he curious about why she felt so strongly, what was lost when they were broken, what might be recovered by piecing them together?

'I've been finding out about Frank Lilley, our grandfather, where he worked. If I can put together enough of a story I'd be happy to leave it alone, move on.'

'You want to put pressure on an old woman.'

'Aren't you curious, in a factual way to know what he was like, this glassblower, our grandfather?'

'Grim, is how I imagine it,' says Edward. 'Grim and best forgotten.'

'Doesn't that rather negate his existence? Ashamed of your working-class roots? Now who's being selfish?'

'Mother has left it all behind, found a way to be.'

'Has she?'

'She is content in her own way.'

'If you say so.'

'You're risking her happiness.'

'She's not happy.'

'You can't say that.'

'Look at it this way,' I say. 'Imagine what it feels like to hold it all in.'

'It's what she chose, it's how she is.'

'So, we collude with holding on to her pain, her anger?'

'She's not asking for this, Maddie.'

'Even if Faith longed for comfort, for release, for love, she wouldn't dream of saying so. She's like an unconsoled child. She is an unconsoled child.'

'You're so intense.'

'Childhood is intense, hers was.'

'Which is why she has chosen to put it all behind her. You ought to respect that.'

'It's not behind her. Keeping it to herself makes it more powerful than it needs to be.'

'You're overstepping the mark.'

'Perhaps. I hoped I was doing something positive. She can't polish Stonebank for ever, keep the books neat. She's lucky to have gone on this long. Imagine Faith with nothing to do. She can't tolerate it. Wouldn't it be something if she could relax enough to simply sit and enjoy the view?'

'Most of this is in your fevered imagination.'

'Why is there so much which can't be done around her, can't be said, can't be referred to?'

'That's a generational thing, Maddie. You're getting this out of proportion.'

'It's so total with Faith. If it's nothing. Edward, why does it matter that I'm concerned with it?'

'This is too much, too early, for me. I have to go,' he says.

'You see her differently, I realise that now. You've never noticed how she can be, have you, washing blankets, washing sheets that are clean?' Is Faith the unconsoled child, or is it me?

'I'll be late,' says Edward, getting up from the table.

'I don't know why you're getting so het up,' I say. 'The reality is that she won't even see the stuff, she never goes to my exhibitions. I'm a teacher with a cranky hobby. It will pass her by like the rest of my work.'

'Perhaps. Look, you've given me a bit of shock, you know, the pregnancy. I can't really . . .'

'Go, Edward, go to your boffin friends and your bugs. I'll survive. Don't forget these.' I hand him the keys. I ought to remind him about the lock. It's tricky, the locking and the unlocking. Let him work it out for himself.

'It's hot in here,' I say.

'Over a hundred,' says Carol.

'Wait till you get nearer the furnace,' says Matt.

Matt and Carol's workshop is in what was once a row of garages, all knocked together now, tucked away down an alley behind a terrace of houses. Double doors are pushed wide open and every window is up as far as it will go; even so, there is a tremendous heat. I take off my jacket, but I'm not sure where to put it.

'What's that clicking noise?' I say, though they don't seem to notice the insistent click, click, click.

'The lehr,' says Matt pointing to a large metal cupboard. 'That's where we put the glass to cool down.'

'Here,' says Jim, their assistant. 'Give me that.' He takes my jacket, and hangs it on a peg in the corner to the side of the lehr.

I'm keeping my distance from the furnace, I'm hot enough. It's a rotund, homely creature, growling away in the corner. Gas jets roar as if several central heating systems had been turned on simultaneously. It's smaller than I had imagined, like a tandoor or pizza oven. Standing on the stone floor is a metal cylinder about five feet in diameter, on top of it a bricked 'roof' with a sloping side. In the slope, there's a hole the shape of a large mouse-hole, about eighteen inches high. There's a door which can slide over the hole, it's half open at the moment; beyond it the fierce glow of pure heat.

'Come closer in,' says Jim, as Matt and Carol start to make a piece.

'I don't want to distract them,' I say.

'Once they get going they're oblivious.'

I'm not sure I can stand more heat. When you're hot anyway, why move towards the fire? Matt takes up a blow-pipe, one of several which sit with one end resting in a box by the furnace.

'It heats the tip,' says Jim. 'He can't put a cold pipe into the pot.' Inside the furnace, just beneath the mouse-hole sits a crucible of molten glass, the massive heat keeps it soft and runny, like honey. The furnace mouth glows, white and orange, an intense heat which I can feel as Matt slides the door open and Jim nudges me to move closer. Matt shows no sign of the heat bothering him; it's as if he doesn't register any change in temperature. His T-shirt has white rings beneath the armpits where sweat has dried. A damp patch grows on his back, as fresh sweat seeps from him.

Matt dips the pipe into the crucible to gather molten glass on its tip. His fingers move constantly, a nimble turning of the pipe, round and round. A delicate action. He might be twirling a drinking straw in a cocktail. The pipe looks heavy but in Matt's hands it seems weightless. He's pure concentration, turning, turning the pipe, then he hauls out a glowing orange ball, a gob of glass. Swiftly, he swings the pipe away from the furnace, rests it on a small steel table, rolls it back and forth, back and forth then, in what seems no time at all, he moves to the bench, a seat with metal-plated arms extending from it. Turning, turning all the time he rests the pipe on the side of the bench, lets it take the weight. Carol is ready for him, supporting the hot gob of glass, holding it through a thick pad of sodden newspaper, steam rises, hiding her face.

'He needs to even up the weight, get a good sphere before he starts to blow,' says Jim. 'Once the heat's gone, you can't shape it. He'll have to go back to the furnace.' And he tells me that the heat is best the first time, evenly spread throughout the glass. You can go back in, reheat, but each time you go back to the furnace you apply the greatest heat to the outside of the piece, it's cooler on the inside.

Matt and Carol work quickly, not saying a word, each in tune with the movements of their bodies.

I think of Frank, shadow man, plunging his blow-pipe into the furnace, day after day, swinging the pipe to the bench, shaping and turning, preparing to blow; taking the piece back to the heat, but try as he may, the centre stays cooler than the outside. As I was leaving the house this morning the phone rang. I was going to ignore it, thinking it was Ward Joffitt. After my tussle with Edward I was in no mood for Ward; but, it was not Ward, it was Wilf Nowells, the man from Featherbridge, unofficial historian of Bagshott's. 'My lad's been round, cleared the loft,' he said. 'I reckon I've found him.' He has a photograph from the 1930s, of a group of Bagshott's workers, amongst them, F. Lilley. I'm going up there next week. It might not be him. We'll see.

Matt rises from the bench, the glass is too cold to work now. He goes to the glory hole, a heat chamber which stands alongside the furnace. Matt turns and reheats the sphere of glass, makes it pliable again.

Frank, plunging his blow-pipe into the furnace, trying to reshape his life around the hole left by Stella, day after day in this heat.

'There's no margin for error,' I say. 'They have no time at all to shape it.'

'It's like working with a ghost, a shadow,' says Jim. 'One minute, it's moving, you have it, then it's gone.'

Matt swings the pipe to the bench again, his hair is stuck to his forehead with sweat, his eyes fix on the gob of glass. He doesn't take his eyes off the ball; an effortless co-ordination of lung, eye, hand. His fingers are delicate on the iron, as if playing some wind instrument. A strong, steady blow. Carol holds the pad against the gob. Matt blows. Blow, turn, blow, turn. Steam and smoke rising from the pad, the smell of singed newsprint. Matt empties his lungs into the hot glass, making it hollow, the size of a balloon.

'He's going to cut it now,' says Jim. Matt knocks the balloon from the blow-pipe then fuses it to the glowing tip of a different rod which Carol offers him.

'He'll open up the form now,' says Jim.

Matt spins the pipe so the balloon opens up into a wide, generous bowl. Jim goes off to help, takes the bowl to the lehr. It must cool very slowly, anneal, for a day. The lehr is an oven in reverse, going from five-hundred degrees, ever so gradually losing heat until the bowl is warm enough to hold, like a freshly baked cake. If the glass cools too quickly, flaws occur, internal stresses in the structure, which cannot be reversed. It will be brittle, too fragile to use. It must cool down slowly, so it won't crack.

'I'll never manage that,' I say to Matt. He takes a break, swigs on a bottle of water.

'You should have a go,' he says. 'Not today, we've an order

to finish. Come along at the end of the run.' He says I can stay and watch for as long as I like. He says I should stay to get used to the heat.

'That's half the battle,' he says. 'The heat. You'll never be a glassblower if you can't stand the heat.'

'Thanks,' I say.

I watch as they make more bowls. They work hard for what they earn, but they love it. This is what they've chosen to do with their art school training. Would Frank recognise this as the same job he had?

A generational thing, Maddie. Perhaps Edward is right.

The Glassblowers Protection Society

'Like I said, photos of committees going right back. I knew they were up there,' says Wilf, proud of his squirrelling. 'Come in. Let's see if it's him.'

He pulls off his gardening gloves, shakes my hand. He's been dead-heading roses.

'You've made good time, then,' he says, nodding to the car I've parked at his gate. I picked it up at the station, couldn't trust my own car on the long motorway haul. I don't like driving at the best of times but with my bump a long journey is out of the question.

'I came on the train,' I say. 'It's hired.'

I'm here for two days. It's good to be away. I'm trying to forget about results; Joe's, and mine to come.

Two days I've given myself to find out what I can, get this out of my system.

This is about me.

It's me who needs to find out, not Faith.

I've booked into a bed-and-breakfast outside Featherbridge, on the road to Bickersthorpe. I'm going to take this in stages. I might lose my nerve and head back to London tonight. First, I need to see what Wilf has found.

Part of me doesn't want to look. It's only a photograph. I'm expecting too much. If it is Frank it's not as if I'm going to meet him, sit down and have a chat, make up for lost time. It can only be a disappointment. If I'm still up for it when I finish here, I'll check in at the B & B and go to Bickersthorpe tomorrow.

To find Stella's grave.

To look at where she lived.

To see if anyone remembers her.

I could have come back years ago. Now that I'm here I wonder why I haven't done this before. For one thing it was forbidden; how easily I accepted the unspoken law, instinctively. For another, I was scared. Not that I might discover some awful secret, but scared because there might be nothing, nothing at all. Ever since Stella's funeral I've thought of going back to Bickersthorpe, wondered about contacting Edith, Stella's neighbour, but I never did, until now. It occurs to me, there may be people still living who know more about Stella than either Faith or I.

'In you go, Doris'll get a brew on. Doris?'

Wilf goes back up the path, collects his secateurs, then heads for the kitchen door at the side of the house where he takes off his boots. Doris invites me to follow her through the front door to the dining room where Wilf gave the slide show on my last visit. Boots replaced by carpet slippers, Wilf joins us. Doris notices my bump. She looks awkward, uncertain whether she should say anything.

'January,' I say. 'It's due in January.'

'Congratulations. Your first?'

'Yes.'

'Lovely.'

I see her eyes flit to my left hand; or that could be my paranoia.

Wilf looks embarrassed.

'Here,' says Doris, 'let me shift this.' Chairs, table, floor are covered in boxes, box-files, manila folders, ring binders. I remember what Dom said: obsessive, the amateur historian, thorough on data collection.

'Got me loft cleared at last,' Doris says, giving me a knowing look. 'Off to some archive now, this lot. A university isn't it, Wilf? Wilf knows.'

'Aye,' says Wilf. 'Good timing. Glad you could come 'cause we're off to Scarborough next week. Marvellous. Scarborough in September. Marvellous.'

'I've never been,' I say.

'Let me get sorted. There's other stuff you might care to browse through. Don't know if it concerns him directly, this Frank Lilley, but it covers the time he were at Bagshott's. There's all sorts: newspaper cuttings, brochures of the new lines, works notices and such like. You're welcome to go through it. But I reckon you want to start with that photo.' He reaches for a box marked Glassblowers Protection Society, 1925–1935. The box is full of photographs. Some are the size of postcards, others are bigger. Some are pristine, others are bent and stained.

'Here he is.'

The photograph Wilf hands to me is thick, more like cardboard than paper. It's grey and grainy. The back is grubby with finger marks. There are names written in pencil, faint now. Also, there's a crack right through it, as if someone has tried to fold or tear it.

'Here, I've typed out the names. Easier to read.' The typeface of Wilf's typewriter is not much blacker than the pale hand-written pencil marks on the photograph. Some of the letters are solid where the typeface is clogged, others are raised above the line, a jumble of jumping pale letters. My eyes come to rest on these: Lilley. F.

'See, third from the left, committee member: Lilley F.' says Wilf to confirm what I've read. I go back and read it all this time: Glassblowers Protection Society: Shop steward, treasurer, secretary, committee members, top row left to right: Briggs. H., Stenton. J., Lilley. F., Cunliffe. B., Shaw. G. and so on. I check that Wilf Nowells has them in the right order. Then I locate the man himself, counting in from left to right.

One, two, three.

I stare hard at the man between Stenton. J. and Cunliffe. B.

He is a stranger.

I don't feel anything much. I look again, at the dark-haired, brooding man. What did I expect: a warm flood of recognition? He is a stranger. I think of the shadow in the photograph of Faith, the shadow I have studied and painted. The shadow is more familiar, more Frank to me, than this man. It will take a while for me to fit this solid, brooding, burly man into the familiar outline of Frank's shadow. There is something of Faith in his jaw line, also the strong wavy hair I recognise; but he is a stranger. A hard-pressed, hard-working man with a dispute at work and a dispute at home. What would he think of me tracking him down. He'd say: Call that a day's work?

A generational thing.

My eyes wander over the rest of the picture. Two rows of men. All looking straight ahead, no smiles, their arms folded proudly across their chests. Togged up in jackets, caps and mufflers, they stand outside in the works' yard. Some wear a waistcoat beneath their jacket which wouldn't have stayed on long by the furnace. I think of Matt in his T-shirt, sweating. Perhaps the men dressed up for the photograph. A blackboard rests at their feet, the chalked letters read: J.M. Bagshott and Co Ltd., Featherbridge, Glassblowers Protection Society 1935. Lilley. F. has a thick head of dark hair and a heavy moustache, so thick it hides his mouth.

I run my finger along the crack down the photograph.

'Can you credit it?' says Wilf, shaking his head. 'Looks as if someone tried to fold it.'

The fold has left a white line through the image where the surface has broken. Cunliffe. B. has a crack through his face, all you see is his lower lip. Shaw. G. has no face. Another couple of centimetres and that would have been Frank.

'Likely you'll want to get a copy made?' says Wilf. 'I can arrange that for you.'

'I could do it,' I say.

'I'd better keep it with the rest,' says Wilf.

'I'd look after it.'

'Anyway, there's all sorts here. Have a look, see what else you can find.'

'I expect she wants some time alone,' says Doris.

'Right, right,' says Wilf. 'I'll get back to me roses, call me if you need anything.'

'Take as long as you like,' says Doris. 'Would you like another cup of tea?'

'No, I'm fine. Are you sure you don't mind?'

'Not at all. Pleasure. I'm glad we could help.'

It's four o'clock. I must go if I'm to make it to the museum. I've been lost in the history of Bagshott's. I've worked my way through Wilf's files of cuttings, works' bulletins, brochures. As I pieced together the story, I looked up from time to time to check out Frank. I've been learning his face. He's giving nothing away, mouth hidden beneath his moustache, eyes neutral, looking straight at the camera. I wish Wilf would let me take it. I must be the only person to have looked at it in fifty years.

I've sorted out cuttings about the dispute, I'd like to make copies. Bagshott's produced bottles of all shapes and sizes, big stuff, ten-gallon carboys, but alongside the bottle-shops there was a lead-crystal shop; this was where the best craftsmen worked, the skilled blowers. Making lead crystal used their skills. But Bagshott's couldn't compete, couldn't make it pay. So they introduced pressed glass. Poor man's crystal, they called it. The semi-automated process made Bagshott's a success. The craftsmen didn't like it. Blowers resented having to tune in to a rhythm set by a machine. They didn't like seeing unskilled operators on the same wage as them. This was at the heart of the dispute. A craftsman had served an apprenticeship, earned nothing for years but had the promise of a good wage later and pride in his skill. The local paper reported the disagreement, which went on for weeks. Frank would have been involved. Started at the end of 1929, it went on into the next year, the year the photograph of Faith and Irene was taken. Bagshott's wanted it settled, there was a Royal Visit planned for Spring that year. I would like to copy these newspaper cuttings; one in particular, where the reporter sat in on a secret meeting of the Protection Society, held in the back room of a pub. It's full of unnamed quotes. Any of these might be Frank speaking.

I worked for next to nothing as a lad, so as I could earn a decent wage later. I've worked hard for Bagshott's since I were fourteen. Now anyone can earn as much as me.

He had learned how much hot glass to pick up from the furnace, the skill was etched in his muscles. He learned how to blow, prided himself on his steady blow. Though it was hard and hot, there was more pride in glassblowing than in breathing dust in a dark place all day underground.

Now I've to do what a machine tells me.

The blowers still gathered molten glass from the furnace, enough to drop into a mould, then the machine operator activated a plunger to spread the glass. There was still finishing to be done by hand: spinning out a vase, turning the lip of jug, crimping the edge of a bowl. The men were paid by the piece. Piece work. With each new line the target rate, the 'doggie', was fixed; anything over the doggie and the men were on a bonus. Since the judge of the gather was by hand and eye, the glassblowers argued, they should be on a higher basic rate; the man at the machine should take less.

The glassblowers were united at first, but weeks into the dispute came dissent amongst Protection Society members.

We must hold out for more.
Look at it this way: there's work. The order book is full.
It's not what I served my time for.
If we don't do the work, others will.

Bagshott's glass was popular, it sold all over the country. They began to export. They were on to a winner. Inexpensive household items, caught the light like real lead crystal, but cost a fraction of the price. Bagshott's expanded, brought in a colour chemist from Italy, there were new ranges in green, blue, pink, amber, opal.

I've put aside other cuttings of stories which caught up the whole community. Like the one about searching the workers' homes for filched glass and the girl who was drowned in the canal. Stories which put flesh on my mother's shadowy childhood. Reading these I feel Faith and Frank in the story.

'I've a nice bit of smoked haddock for tea, reckon it could run to three, will you join us?' says Doris Nowells, pulling me back to the present.

'Sorry,' I say. 'I've out-stayed my welcome.'

'Not at all. You're welcome to have a bite to eat before you go.'

'No. Thanks. I must be going.'

'If you're sure.'

'These,' I say, pointing to the pile I've put aside. 'I'd like to photocopy these, could Wilf do it for me? I'll pay.'

'Look, love, you take whatever you need,' says Doris.

'But Wilf said . . .'

'Never mind Wilf. Long as we have the originals by the time we're back from Scarborough, it's all the same to him.'

'And the photograph?'

'Reckon it's safer with you than most.'

I've cut it a bit fine, the museum is only open for another hour, but while I'm here I'd like to look at the displays again. With Frank. With my head full of these stories.

I walk up the museum's stone steps against a crocodile of school children with clipboards. They've been learning about how their grandparents and great-grandparents lived. I wonder if they care.

I walk through the ground floor, through a re-creation of stone-age Yorkshire and on to the rooms that hold the Bagshott's glass, my feet squeaky on the shiny lino. The guard looks at his watch as I pass.

I've spent so long working with the glass in fragments, I'd like to see it again as it was, to look at objects I might ask to borrow if I go ahead with the table setting for the exhibition.

One case shows how many versions of a sugar bowl Bagshott's produced: plain, twin-handled, flanged, covered. Another shows many versions of the trinket set. Each set had seven pieces: ring tray, main tray, large powder bowl, two smaller powder bowls and two candlesticks. I remember Stella's hairpins in the glass tray. There are cheese dishes, honey pots, biscuit barrels, a pair of owl bookends. In the last case there are seaside trinkets made by Bagshott's, jugs and mugs embossed with the words: Whitley Bay, Bridlington, Scarborough. There is a commemorative dish which was given to all workers on the occasion of the Royal Visit. I think of Faith and Irene in their winter coats. Is that why the photograph was taken? Were they off to see the King; to line the main street of Featherbridge and wave a flag?

At the end of the Bagshott's display I come out into the corridor at the foot of the stairs. A sign points to the upper floor: *Discover how families lived in the days before television, cars, washing machines. What was it like to work full-time from the age of twelve?* I go upstairs to lives reconstructed from belongings left behind. Objects, rescued from ordinary lives, arranged to suggest scenes. There's a kitchen with a blackened range, a copper pot sits on mock coals. Beside it stands a ribbed metal barrel, a rubbing board and a stick to stir the wash. Faith must have learned early how to do the laundry, to wash the salt sweat from Frank's shirts. I can see her rubbing the cloth against the ridges of the board. You don't need much to stir up the past. Life accumulates around things. Belongings. Who is to say what is worth saving, what can be thrown away? Is there a choice, or do we make what we can of what is left?

The local Oral History Society has gathered quotes from people who still remember the heyday of glass and coal in Featherbridge. People who are now Faith's age or older.

Wash day was worst. Ask any of the women. Getting salt out of a glassblower's shirt was worse than washing pit grime. I washed my father's clothes. No matter how hard you tried, you never got all the salt out. We used to scrub and rinse, scrub and rinse but when you took the shirts from the line they were stiff. Stiff with salt. My mother used to say, 'Think on it's not pit grime.' At least you could see coal dust.

There's a life-size cut-out of a man in working clothes, baggy trousers held up with a thick leather belt, collarless shirt with sleeves rolled to the elbow.

My husband used to have to climb into his trousers each day. Solid with salt, they were.

Also, in the kitchen, hanging on the wall, is a zinc bath tub.

Me and my sister would fill the tub from the copper on the range. Dad first, then my brothers. Not every night. We placed the tub near the range which made it easier to scoop water from the copper. Me dad would roar at us if it weren't right. It were freezing taking a bath in the back kitchen. You'd think they'd want to cool down after a day by the furnace.

I see Faith and Irene, filling the zinc tub for Frank, struggling to ladle jugs of hot water from the copper to the tub, getting ready for Frank coming home at the end of his shift.

'We close soon,' warns the librarian, her fringe so straight across her forehead I hardly dare argue.

'I need to photocopy these, please.' I stand my full height, put a hand to the small of my back to emphasise my condition. It's worth a try.

'Ten pence a sheet,' she says. 'You'll have to be quick.' She looks round, I'm the only one there. She takes pity.

'Here,' she says. 'Give them to me.'

She is brisk and efficient, copying the cuttings, piling them up.

'You're interested in local history?'

'Yes.'

'Have you seen the book?' She points to a display which I must have walked past on my way in. On a pin board, a series of old photographs, beneath it a book open for anyone to inspect. I take a look. *Featherbridge: Picturing the Past.* It's a compilation of old photographs from the turn of the century to the 1950s.

'They're for sale,' says the librarian, handing me two piles, originals and copies.

'I'll take one.'

I see a traffic warden noting my number.

'Only just over,' I say.

'You're all right,' she says, 'I'd have to give you five minutes.' She smiles and moves on. I've never met a cheerful traffic warden before.

There's a woman loading shopping into the boot of the car parked next to mine. She has already strapped her three children into their seats. The baby squeals, its arms and legs writhing. The two older children squabble over a bag of crisps.

'There's only one,' says their tired mother. 'You'll have to share.' She's about my age, so is the traffic warden. I think: If Stella hadn't left, if Faith hadn't wanted to get away, I might know these women. We might have gone to the same school, lived in the same street.

I think of Faith meeting Ernest, wanting so much to forget. She was offered a new start. She took it, she left this palce, she forgot. Who can blame her. I would probably have done the same.

I'm struck by the ordinariness of it all. How unexceptional it is, which is a relief, and a reason, I think, to make the work, beyond my own obsessions. Testimony to the ordinary, the unconsoled, the painful but unexceptional lives which don't get mentioned, but retreat into silence because it's easier. A painful, unexceptional silence which grows out of circumstance. *People make their own history, but often it's in conditions which are not of their own choosing.*

I can't stop now. Even if Edward is right, I can't stop. Underneath the doubt, I feel something is starting to flow. It's as if a boulder has been trapped over the mouth of a cave; it's shifting, light rushes in.

This is something I must get out of my system. I don't want to hurt Faith, yet I can't stop either. It's not my intention to cause damage. I'm trying to mend something, not break it.

The bed-and-breakfast should be the next left after the traffic lights. You couldn't quite call this countryside. I've left Featherbridge but I'm not at the next place yet. I turn down a side road, an estate of new semis. According to the directions I was given there is a track off one of these roads. There it is. It leads to an older, stone house that was once a farm. The track is overgrown with willow herb, it opens out on to a patch of ground, thick with buddleia on one side and a parking bay with six spaces on the other. I squeeze myself into the last space.

A woman in her thirties comes out to greet me. She's wearing pink jeans and a Lycra top that hugs a roll of flesh above her waist. Her hair is cropped short, platinum blonde.

'Miss Armitage?'

'Yes.'

'I'm Sandra. Here's your key. Number five,' she says, pointing to the door of an extension which is tagged on to the garage. 'I'm full of regulars tonight.' She nods towards the house. 'If you want a meal, the pub you passed by the traffic lights serves dinner till eight. I start breakfast at seven.'

'I won't be up so early,' I say, the tiredness makes my bones ache.

'Anytime till nine,' she says and points to a path which leads to the kitchen where breakfast is served. 'They'll all be gone by then. You'll be needing your sleep.' She nods at my bump.

'Yes.'

'Holiday is it?'

'No. Not exactly.'

'Travellers I have, mostly travellers. What work are you in?'

'Research. I'm looking up my family tree,' I say.

'I've had a few doing that, it's getting popular.'

She opens the door to my annexe. There is a double bed with a vivid floral-patterned duvet. She points to louvred doors which push back to reveal a shower and toilet. On a ledge in the corner is a kettle, and sachets to make tea and coffee. A sagging armchair on splayed legs sits before a massive television.

'I think you'll find everything you need.'

'Thanks.'

I take in the view from my window: fields, motorway, landscaped slag heaps, pylons, a rugby pitch, the new housing estate. It isn't anywhere exactly; tucked into a corner at the intersection of the motorways.

I shower, make myself a cup of tea and lie on the bed to read the stuff I photocopied. I have Frank's photo propped up beside me. It's him I see, and cross little Faith, as I read these stories. Like the time Bagshott's management threatened to search the workers' homes. They were sending the police, they said, to look for filched glass. Up until then it had been accepted that workers helped themselves to seconds. There was resentment still about low piece rates and workers began to take prime stock. The packers especially were good at this, mostly women, they would hide bowls in their bras. I wonder if Stella had been a packer, was that how she met Frank? When the search was announced, it was reported, the workers went round their homes collecting up the glass. After dark, men, women and children were seen along the canal, throwing away the hot stuff. I look at Frank and think maybe he was too proud to creep around at the dead of night; he thought the glass was his by rights. I could see this man with his big moustache, ready, waiting to argue his case.

There was the tragic story of an eight-year-old girl who fell in the canal while carrying a hot dinner to her father on the late shift, six till two. It had been common practice to send children along with home-cooked food for their dads. An eye witness saw her fall but was too far away and on the wrong side of the water. By the time they reached her she was dead. The suet pudding floated on the surface, air trapped in its muslin wrap.

Grim, best forgotten. She's not asking for this.

I wake at around seven and doze, listening to cars leaving. I'm hungry, looking forward to breakfast, but I want to be sure the others have gone. I have a strange taste in my mouth. I get up and clean my teeth. It's still there, beneath the toothpaste. It's the taste from my dream. So vivid, I almost believe it happened.

Last night I went up to the pub, ate scampi and chips from a plastic basket, then came back and watched television; the last episode of a drama serial and I hadn't seen the previous three. A stern father lay dying in bed, his daughters gathered around, the priest came and went. They were waiting for the eldest son to arrive. The son had long been estranged from his father; neither could forgive the other for a stand-off which happened long ago. The girls knew that the father would die easier for having his son's forgiveness and the son would live a freer life for letting go of his angry pride. The son turns back, does not go. The father dies, raging.

After that, I found it hard to sleep and when I did, I had vivid, busy dreams, so real I can't believe they've evaporated. In the dream, I was in a kitchen like the one in the museum. A coal scuttle, black as black, as if made of coal itself. Compressed coal. I sat by the hearth and bit into this strange object as if that was a normal thing to do. I bit it. It tasted dry, bitter. Like eating burned biscuits, only worse; no hint of sweetness.

Sandra is cheerful, her pink jeans replaced by an identical pair in lime green.

She sets the plate before me, a full fry-up: bacon, black pudding, eggs, fried bread, tomato. She brings a fresh pot of tea.

'More toast?'
'No. Thanks, this is more than enough,' I say.
'Right. Well, if you'll excuse me, I've things to fettle.'
I eat, to take the dry, bitter coal-taste from my mouth.

Sherbet Dip

5

It's no more than fifteen minutes' drive to Bickersthorpe, says Sandra; that's if I don't get lost.

Breakfast has left a different kind of aftertaste; salty, smoky, greasy. I have eaten too much. There must be somewhere around here where I can buy a bottle of fizzy water and an apple. Tomorrow, I will order a boiled egg. I've confirmed that I'm staying for a second night.

'No problem,' said Sandra. 'I'm never full on a Wednesday. Some of them go home for a midweek break.' Midweek fuck, I thought she said, and she was off to fettle her washing.

Fettle.

That's a word I've not heard for a while. A word Ernest used. *Get that homework fettled, Madeleine.* Ernest kept his Yorkshire sayings. Faith didn't. Even though she still spends her days fettling, it's not a word she uses.

I will start at the church, find Stella's grave. I'm trusting that, once there, I will know where to go. I will remember. I want to see her name carved in stone, to prove I didn't imagine her. I don't believe in an afterlife, I don't believe Stella is up there watching me driving towards her village, the place where she lived for over half a century. I do believe in the presence of those who once lived, a presence which is vital in our memory. Our memories are the sum of who we are, who we have been over time. *A span of time longer than our own.* Maybe what we need is to imagine another three-score and ten on either side of us; to know the story as it started before us, and have a sense of where it is going afterwards. Any further beyond a life-span in either direction, is interesting, fascinating, but not a necessity. Not vital.

Faith refuses to allow Stella's presence, her memory. She has shut Stella away, beyond recall. Why has it taken me so long to realise there are others, still living in Bickersthorpe, who would have known her? Someone my age might remember an old lady. Perhaps Stella is a presence in the minds of others besides me. Edith. I wonder if Edith, her neighbour, is still alive. I've been trying to recall Edith. When I met her at Stella's funeral, she and her husband had recently retired. They were new to the bungalows having moved from a terrace on the other side of the village. They had known Stella for years through church. If Edith was in her sixties when Stella died then she could still be alive. The vicar who buried Stella was young with a smooth, line-free face and a shock of red hair. As long as Stella can be recalled by others she has a presence. Why have I never done this before? In matters of Faith, up until now, I have been a good girl, careful not to say the wrong thing, careful not to make the wave crash. Stella left her children: earth shattering. The aftershock has not been played out. Faith blocked it. The wave needs to crash, dissipate its energy. I don't believe it will harm us. Then again, there is the risk that it will. Stories affect people in different ways, whether they are told or untold. I know what the effect of the untold story is, I'm curious to know what will happen if the story gets told. All this and a full fry-up is churning inside me as I keep to a steady fifty miles an hour along a stretch of dual carriageway. A metal barrier runs along the central reservation, I must keep going forward.

Without warning there is a break in the barrier, the offering of a right turn: Bickersthorpe 2, says the sign. It has taken no time at all. To think Stella lived so near to Faith. Sixty years ago there was no dual carriageway, no car for Stella. A bus once a day, once a week and the cost of the fare. It shocks me to think she was living so near to Faith.

I'm on a B road approaching a junction. I try to remember the journey I made to Stella's funeral twenty years ago with Annie navigating. It's not the same journey; we were coming from the north then, now, I'm approaching from the south.

The sign says that Bickersthorpe is to the left, a further half mile. The tick-tick, tick-tick of the indicator is in time with my pulse, my hands are shaky on the wheel. My legs turn to jelly as I pass the village sign which tells me I'm now in Bickersthorpe.

I studied the map last night and have an image in my head of how the village is laid out. It is a sprawling place which doesn't appear to have a centre, it's strung out around a triangle of roads. The longest side of the triangle runs parallel to the canal. There used to be a pit on that side of the village, closed some years ago. I slow down. There is a rugby pitch to my left, which nestles in the right-angle of the triangle. Next, I turn right into the road which runs parallel to the canal. A strange feeling; something familiar, I can't quite grasp it. Whatever it is, it remains just out of my vision. I try to recall; I remember feeling as if I couldn't breathe, smothered by Faith's silence, and my name slipping and sliding till it made no sense. Faith's head stiff above the car seat, Edward reading his *Beano*. I've been here before. Ahead of me a railway bridge crosses the road. As I pass beneath it now I can hear Ernest say: Left here, isn't it?

I turn left. There are terraces between the road and the canal. I pass by the site of the old pit. The black mountain I saw as a child is now green, landscaped. I slow down and read the sign: remainder heap, it says. Slag heap.

Some of the terraces have gone. In their place are council houses. I drive to the other end of the village, through this mixture of old terraces and new semis. At the junction I turn towards the church. There are more terraces around yards. I pull up at the gap between two rows of houses, but I don't drive in. I get out of the car and look. There are ten to twelve houses to a row; two rows face the road. I stand at the gap between them and glimpse the backs of two more rows which face a field. All four rows are set around an unmade yard the size of a football pitch, dented with puddles. I don't go any further, but turn back towards the road. There's a shop on the corner. Spar open 8 till 8, says the sign above the window.

Inside, a woman in a sari sits at the checkout. It's not a big shop but it's filled with everything from fresh fruit to sacks of smokeless fuel. This woman is too young to have known Stella.

From a humming fridge I choose a diet Coke. There's a small display of fruit and veg; I select a firm, green apple.

'£1.20,' says the woman at the till. I hand her two one-pound coins and as I do I hear another voice, feel another coin pressed against my palm. A scene arrives, as if from nowhere, as if it's been waiting there all the time.

Mind you don't spend it all at once. Stella gave me and Edward a threepenny bit each; a thick coin clutched tight in my palm, a portcullis on its tail side. Edward and me standing in the shop, staring at the jars of sweets. I chose sherbet and a liquorice stick. A barrel of a woman in a grubby overall plunged a scoop into the jar. She weighed an ounce; a brass weight clinked on one side, pink grains stacked up on the other. I watched as the side with weight came up, steady against the pan of sherbet. Fizzy pink dust and a shiny black liquorice stick. I can taste it.

As I leave the shop I hesitate. I want to drive the car into the yard, have a closer look. I'm a stranger round here, with a swollen belly and a shiny new car, too conspicuous, a trespasser. I climb back behind the wheel, head for the church.

A gate in the stone wall opens on to a path through the churchyard. There is a sign beside the gate, blue with gold lettering: The Church of St Michael And All His Angels. Vicar: Rev. Alison Booth. There is a telephone number. A woman. New to the job, then. Not the man with red hair and pious voice who buried Stella . . . *hath but a short time to live, and is full of misery . . . is cut down, like a flower . . . fleeth as it were a shadow . . .*

Stella Lilley. Dying star. Cut flower. Shadow. Giver of threepenny bits.

I glance at headstones as I walk towards the church. Marble: liver-coloured, white; most have the same black lettering. I notice a row where all the dates are in the 1970s. I scan each one, but I don't remember it being this close to the church. I move out to the margins where the grass is longer and the headstones more crooked and mossy. Every now and then there's the odd well-tended grave. All the time my eyes scanning for the word Lilley, so easily found on the photograph of Frank. I find two more rows of headstones all in the 1970s. Nothing. In the next row the dates jump back to the 1930s; there is no logic to the layout. I could be here all day. I make my way to the other side of the church, furthest away from the road. Here, the grass is even longer. The dates are in the 1880s and early 1900s.

On this side of the church there is a door, open. I go inside. The door is thick, dark wood, studded with iron. Now that I'm here I've no idea what to do. There is someone shuffling about near the altar. A man looks up, sees me.

'Morning,' he says.

I nod, manage a smile.

Where I stand at the back of the church, there is a table set out with information about its history. There has been a place of worship on this site since Saxon times; part of the foundations date back to 1200. A chart records how much has been collected for the restoration fund. There's a long way to go to reach the target. Beneath it sits a huge glass bottle in which to drop money.

The place has the smell of many lives; damp, musty. I sit in a high-backed, wooden pew. Along the side aisle are effigies of those who were once local dignitaries, monied families able to have a likeness preserved in stone. No point looking for Stella amongst them. I hope she's in the parish records. All those who have been christened, confirmed, married or buried here will be listed as names and dates. I will ask the man at the altar about the parish records.

As I stand I feel an odd sensation. It's like nothing I have ever felt before. I grip the solid wood of the pew in front me. There it is again.

It's as if a butterfly is stirring inside me.

Again. I feel its wings brushing against the folds of my insides.

The baby, it's moving.

Kicking, waving?

I see your hand bounce off your nose. Your arm is longer

now, has a longer reach. Your camellia buds are fingers, feeling towards the limits of where you are. Or perhaps you have stretched your legs, swimming. I run my hand over the bump. Again, then again.

It's you, moving.

'It's moving. It's moving. I can feel it,' I say and realise I've said this out loud. I wonder if you can hear me. Not a sound that comes in through your ears. It will be muffled by muscle and fluid. Vibrations. You will feel the sound of my voice, a tingle on your skin, a sensation, stored, remembered.

My words bring the man from the altar.

'Did you want something, love?'

'Sorry,' I say. 'It's the baby, it was kicking. I . . .'

'You're not about to deliver are you?'

'I hope not.'

'Reg Holt,' he says extending a hand. 'Church Warden.'

'I was wondering if I could see the parish records?'

'Not from round here, are you?'

'No. But my family was.'

'You'll have to talk to the Reverend Booth. It's all the same to me, but you'll need to speak to her first.'

The plump woman with short dark hair has a warm smile above her dog collar.

'You'll need to make an appointment with our Warden. A Mr Holt,' she says and starts to write down a phone number.

'He's in the church now,' I say.

'Well, if Reg doesn't mind,' she says. 'There is a fee, you know.' She looks it up, tells me how much it will cost.

'Family tree?' she says, looking knowingly at the bump. 'I get quite a few in your condition.'

Reg Holt leads me into the vestry. Inside, it is dark. The only window, a glass slit, is above our heads. A wooden table is cluttered with vases, candlesticks, piles of faded red hymn books. To one side of the door is a pile of blue velvet hassocks. Reg pulls back a plum-coloured curtain which is drawn across an alcove. There are two small safes, one on top of the other. He picks his way along a bunch of keys, opens the safe and brings out several leather-bound ledgers. I know the date Stella was buried. We look it up in the record of funerals. Stella Lilley died on 11 July 1976, Age: 81. She was buried at St Michael's church on 15 July. She died at home, the address given is 29 Moor View Lane, Bickersthorpe. The number of her entry in the register of burials is 380.

'Is Moor View Lane still there?' I say.

'Aye, that's bungalows.'

'Do you know anyone there?'

'There's not many I don't know.'

'Is there someone called Edith, living in the bungalows?'

'Edith Ridge you mean?'

'I don't know her last name. Next door to number 29.'

'Edith's at 27. I do a bit of gardening for Edith. Frail, she is. Eighty-five. Not been so good since her husband died last year.'

'How frail?' I say. 'Do you think she would mind if I called on her?' I explain how I met her years ago, at my grandmother's funeral.

'She'll not answer the door to strangers, love. If you can wait till this afternoon, I'll come with you. She knows who I am.'

'Would you?'

'I'm on duty here while three. Vandals. Vicar doesn't want church shut up, we have a rota.'

'It doesn't say where she's buried,' I say, going back to the records.

'No. Different book. The plan of the graveyard is kept at the vicarage. You'll have to see Reverend Booth for that.'

'She's out for the rest of the day,' I say, recalling what she said this morning; that I'd been lucky to catch her. I hope that Reg will offer to find it for me.

'I can't help you there. But like I say, I'll take you to see Edith Ridge. Three o'clock.'

'I'll come back here. I owe you money for looking at the records.'

'Robbery. You weren't but five minutes.'

'I don't mind.'

'Look,' he says. 'We need one hundred and fifty thousand pounds to put the church right. I'll not ask you for it all, but that's where to put your money.' He points through the door, towards the glass bottle at the back of the church. I slip a note into the bottle as I leave. I'd hate the church to fall down. Think of how many people's history is kept here and nowhere else.

I'm no nearer finding where Stella is buried. The graveyard is too vast for me to search without the plan. Each time I think I remember where it is, I'm wrong. At least I've confirmed that she was buried here on the day I remember. I know she's here, somewhere. I watched the coffin as it was lowered into the cleanly dug trench. There was a pause. I became aware of the pause and of Edith nudging me, signalling for me to throw earth on to the coffin. I was rigid. I couldn't do it; fling dirt at my grandmother when I hardly knew her. It seemed disrespectful, the symbolism of earth to earth was lost on me. I had bought flowers from a roadside stall, on the way. So I threw them in, one by one. Larkspur. Soft shades of pink, cream, blue. Delicate heads, layers of petals which seemed almost to be made of cloth; a summer frock for her to wear. I wanted to remember her in a summer frock not a heap of dirt.

I don't see much point in wandering the graveyard until three. I'm going back to the yard behind the terraces, the one near the Spar shop. I will wait for Reg before I look at the bungalow in Moor View Lane. I will see if I can recall the other house, the one we visited the day Edward was sick over his *Beano* and the car shook as Ernest drove over the unmade yard. Faith's head didn't move. I see it now, rigid, above the back of the car seat.

I turn into the yard, drive past the Spar. I drive slowly but still the car wobbles over this rough, common ground. I half expect to see Edward sitting next to me with his head in a *Beano*. I'm aware of how the car stands out, gleaming, too new. I want to say: it's not mine. I stand there studying the houses, seeing if there's anything that will distinguish the one we visited. The backs of the terraces are a jumble of drainpipes, satellite dishes, dustbins, washing lines. Some are more cared for than others. One house, straight ahead, has matching frilly blinds upstairs and down, and a glass porch newly built over the back door. Each house has its own small patch of ground and a gate which opens on to the common area. The house with the frilly blinds has a trellis round its gate which builds to a peak, roses climb around it. The next house along doesn't have a gate, simply a gap in the brick wall. I turn to look at the terraces on the other side of the yard. Here, most of the houses still have the original privvy and a coal shed.

I stop in my tracks.

Light-headed. A flicker. A feeling as if I'm coming round from a faint. For a fraction of a second I wonder who I am. I shake my head and think: I'm still here, still alive, still me. I'm waiting for the meaning to slide back into the letters of my name: mitagemaddiearmitagemitagemaddiearm, Maddiearmitage, Maddie Armitage, Madeleine Armitage.

I concentrate, take a deep breath. I'm back there, I can hear Edward's voice.

'Don't open it, Maddie,' he is saying.

I can taste the mixture of sherbet and liquorice in my mouth.

'Why?'

'It's not ours, it's trespassing.'

'I want to know what's inside.'

I walk towards the thing which has caught my eye, snagged at my memory, unravelling a knot tied long ago. There, set in the brick wall of one of the houses, is a wooden door, no more than two feet square, as if there is a cupboard in the wall. I stare at this square wooden door in the brick wall. It comes back, flooding in, as if it's been there all this time. Waiting. When I last stood here, all those years ago with my sherbet dip, the door was above me. I remember having to reach to open the catch. I had to be on tiptoes to see inside. Now it's in line with my bulging belly. The wood has weathered over the years, dried and cracked by wind and sun. It's hanging on to its metal hinges, which look like elongated Vs laid on their sides. A peg of wood on a screw keeps the door in place, round and round it can spin, I remember, like a propeller.

'Here, hold this,' I can hear myself saying to Edward as I hand him my sherbet dip. The catch was stiff against the door, I had to put my hand against it and press a little, then the catch spun round on its screw. The door swung open. Inside, it was black. It smelled of dust. I couldn't see much, straining on my toes. I picked up a stick from the ground, poked it around in the coal dust like dipping my liquorice into sherbet.

'Madeleine!' A shrill, angry voice. Faith. Faith who didn't raise her voice. I felt as if I had done something terrible. I couldn't imagine what. What had I done? Trespassed? What did that mean and how could I put it right? How could I tell her I hadn't meant to do anything, really, I hadn't. I wanted to say I was sorry. There was nothing in the coal hole, I was sure. How could it matter?

Now, I reach over to the catch on this door. I feel as if there are eyes in every window, watching me. Trespasser. I slide my fingers under the door, there is a gap where the wood has shrunk. I open it, look inside. Junk, household junk: a buckled bicycle wheel, the sides of a cot, a broken chair, a coil of hose.

'Looking for something?'

I spin round.

'I'm sorry,' I say. 'I'm looking for the house where my grandmother lived. It was a house like this.'

'Not from round here are you?' says a young woman with a tired face.

'No,' I say. 'Stella Lilley. She lived in Bickersthorpe most of her life.' The young woman is in her twenties, weighed down with shopping.

'Never heard of her.'

'Sorry,' I say. 'I was only looking. I was miles away.' I point to the door in the wall. 'It reminded me of something.'

'You'll find nothing in there but junk.'

I sit in the car, with the door open, take a swig of Coke and let the knot unravel. Faith gripped my arm, she was rough, she marched me back to Stella's house. I see it now like a tableau. There was a man sitting on the sofa who hadn't been there when we arrived. He'd appeared while Edward and I had been to the shop. No one said anything. He wasn't introduced. Ernest and Stella stood behind the sofa. The man on the sofa said nothing.

He had one leg.

I remember now. The light was dim, the sun was not on that side of the house. It felt chilly after the heat and dust of the yard. It wasn't cold enough to light a fire but there was a fire laid ready in the grate. The one-legged man had a suit on; his Sunday best. He didn't say a word. He stared out of the window, as if we didn't exist. His good leg rested on the rug, a foot firmly planted; one hefty shoe with a shiny black toe. I wondered if, in a cupboard upstairs, there was the other one, never to be used. His left leg stopped at the knee; the trouser leg was folded back, pinned. A great wooden crutch with a leather pad, on which to rest his armpit, lay propped beside him ready to be his leg.

Stella half turned, as if about to go through to the kitchen.

Ernest tried to look normal. He was going bald and had a tuft of hair in the middle of his bald spot, the tuft seemed to stand higher than usual. His scalp was damp with sweat.

'You've been keeping well,' he was saying to Stella, who wore a wrap-around apron. It was white cotton printed with swirls of pink flowers and had green piping along its edge. It was tied with a bow at the back. Her stockings were thick, her slippers a worn tartan.

'Rummaging in the Shaws' coal hole,' said Faith, looking daggers at Ernest, as if to say: I told you so, why bring us here?

'Look at you,' Stella's voice was kind. My hands were black. 'We'll soon have you clean again. Nothing soap and water won't fix.' I would have done anything to fix the damage. It felt as if I had turned Faith into a madwoman, Ernest prematurely bald and I'd cost this silent, unknown man his leg. If I could put it all right by having a wash, what a relief. Eagerly I headed for the door in the corner of the room; the stairs were behind the door, I knew. Even though I'd never been up them, never been here before, I knew because the door was raised up and a step jutted beneath it. I reached for the latch. It was not a big house, I would find the bathroom easily enough, I thought.

'Not there, don't go up there,' said Faith. I wondered why. Was it because up there was the place where Stella slept with the one-legged man?

'Here,' said Stella, and she led me through to the kitchen. I washed my hands at the deep white sink. The big brass taps were stiff, the sink had a gingham curtain beneath it, like a skirt. The water was icy cold.

'Just a moment,' she said. 'Let me fill this.'

I pulled my hands out from the flow of water while she filled the kettle; the tinny sound of water on aluminium, a proud high spout. I wanted to say: who is he, who is that man and where is his leg?

I said nothing.

'These grandparents of yours, you know what I reckon?' says Reg Holt as we walk to my car. 'A stand off. Stubborn. Things get said, can't go back on them. Something and nothing. That's what you'll find at the bottom of this.'

I'm thinking about the man with one leg. Since this morning, when I told Reg my sketchy family history, I've found the one-legged man. He sits inside my head alongside Frank. The one-legged man in his best suit saying nothing; Frank, proud, arms folded across his chest, mouth unseen beneath his huge moustache. The two mute men in Stella's life. Hard-working Frank, craftsman, master blower, abandoned for a man with one leg. Perhaps he still had two legs when Stella left Frank. To think the one-legged man was there in my head all these years, no wonder I felt so sure about my fantasy; the lover-returned-from-the-Trenches version of the story. I always hoped that Stella had done it for love, left her children for love.

Never in all these years has this one-legged man been referred to, not even in the hissed exchanges between Ernest and Faith. I remember how he terrified me. It was as if, by opening the coal hole, I had let this man into our lives, conjured him from the dark.

'I can't remember which terrace she lived in,' I say to Reg as we drive through the village to Edith's. 'I only came once. It might be any of these. It backed on to a yard, each house had a coal hole in the wall, an outside loo. No bathroom.'

'They were all like that, love,' says Reg.

'I thought I found it this morning,' I say and describe the houses near the Spar.

'Like I say, I don't remember anyone with the name of Lilley.'

'I've remembered something,' I say. 'Stella Lilley, my grandmother, she lived with a man who had one leg.'

There, I've said it. The world is still turning.

'Stan Kelsall?' says Reg.

'I don't know his name.'

'Stan Kelsall. Everyone knew Stan with his peg-leg. I thought you said Lilley, the name was Lilley.'

'Stella married Frank Lilley, but she left him. Maybe she lived with Stan Kelsall.'

'Stan Kelsall never married,' says Reg.

'Well, perhaps it wasn't the same man.'

'There's only been one peg-leg in Bickersthorpe this last fifty years. Stan Kelsall.'

I try the name on to my image of the man on the sofa. I see him again, right from the toe of his shiny black shoe, up to his staring eyes. Stan.

'You know about the Kelsalls don't you?' says Reg.

'No,' I say and Reg doesn't offer to tell me.

'Stella? You mean Stella Kelsall, tall woman, glasses,' says Reg, suddenly getting the picture.

'She had her hair in plaits coiled each side of her head,' I add, determined to make sure this is my Stella we are talking about. My Grandma Lilley.

'That's her. Stella Kelsall, she lived with Stan.'

'But I thought you said he didn't marry.'

'He was her brother.'

'Brother?'

'Stella and Stan Kelsall, brother and sister.'

I want to say: What, not her lover, gone to the Front, believed dead so she married the wrong man.

'Stan Kelsall never married. They say he were "that way", if you get my drift, batted from the wrong side.'

'Gay?'

'Some call it that. Kelsalls lived in one of the yards off Pit Lane.'

'By the Spar?'

'That's right,' says Reg. 'Here we are, left now.' He directs me into a road which soon forks. On either side are bungalows, each has a well-kept patch of garden at the front. Reg tells me to stop as we reach number 27. I turn off the ignition.

'Sad family the Kelsalls.'

I'm having to adjust quickly. The Kelsalls. One quarter of me is a Kelsall.

'How did he lose his leg?'

'Pit.'

'How?'

'Stan had a bad time in the war, the first one, I mean. He was never right when he came back, so they say. Story goes he were distracted, didn't see the train coming, you know, the trucks that bring the coal up. Walked right under it. They say he rolled over, picked up his own leg, but I think that's just in the telling.'

It seems Stan had a brother, Ezra, who had been melancholic even before the war. They both came back from war, never married but lived with another sister, Freda.

'Freda wasn't right in the head, they say, but she kept her brothers.'

'What was she like?'

'I never knew Freda. Freda was before my time.'

'When did Stan die?'

'I remember that, still had my post round then. Talk of the village.'

'Why?'

'Canal. Some say he fell, others say he jumped. But there was more thought he'd jumped, because of his brother.'

'Ezra? What happened to him?'

'Ezra cut himself, like, with a razor, if you get my meaning.'

'When?'

'A good ten years before Stan, I'd say.'

Edith's garden has roses, marigolds, stocks and a bushy pink hydrangea by the front door. I glance over the fence to 29 where Stella lived, half expecting to see a border of forget-me-nots. There is a single pink rose-bush at the centre of a patch of grass.

I lock the car.

Stella's brother. The one-legged man is Stella's brother. And there were others. Ezra. Freda.

Grim, best forgotten.

Grim and getting grimmer.

Easter Eggs 5

I've dropped Reg off at the church and I'm sitting on a low stone wall by Bickersthorpe Post Office. Edith can't see me today; I have to go back tomorrow.

She took a while to come to the door.

'Hello, Edith,' said Reg. 'This young lady here, name of Madeleine Armitage, she'd like to talk to you.'

'Oh?'

Edith was barely recognisable as the woman I'd met over twenty years ago. She has doubled in size, and her hair, now white, has thinned so much she is almost bald.

'Maddie. Stella's granddaughter,' I said and smiled to reassure her. She looked confused. 'We met at her funeral. Stella's.' I couldn't bring myself to call her Kelsall and didn't want to confuse things by calling her Lilley. 'I'm sorry to descend on you like this.'

Edith thought for a moment then said: 'Used to live Chester way didn't you?'

'That's right. I live in London now. I was hoping I could talk to you about Stella.'

'Lovely woman she was, Stella.' Edith didn't move. She was holding on to the door frame. She went quiet then said: 'My legs are bad.'

My head was bursting with questions about Stan and Ezra and Freda but I couldn't insist, couldn't barge my way in. I looked at Edith's thinning hair and thought: Inside her head there are stories which can be recalled. Edith was frail but she was not stone-dead like Stella in the funeral parlour.

'Doctor's been this morning. My legs are bad. I was on my way to lie down.' I was torn between wanting to know and concern that she was about to fall over any minute. I didn't want to keep her on her bad legs any longer than necessary. I looked down at her ancient feet, bulging in worn slippers, her legs were swathed in crepe bandages.

'I'm so sorry to have disturbed you,' I said.

'London you say. Long way. You're going back now?'

'No, I'm here for one more day.'

'Lovely woman, she was, Stella.'

'Thank you.'

'If you could come in the morning, first thing. You're the image of her, you know.' Edith smiled for the first time. 'Tall, she was as tall as you. Come tomorrow, first thing. I'd like that. My legs are never good in the afternoon.'

I can wait until the morning. I'm still absorbing the Kelsalls.

As I drove Reg back to the church we passed the row of shops and he said: 'See that wall there, I can see him now, Stan Kelsall with his peg-leg, sitting on that wall. Day in day out. Didn't say much.'

I've come back to sit like great-uncle Stan on the wall outside the Post Office. An old lady drops letters into the red pillar box. I think of Stella coming here to buy the cards and the postal orders which she sent to us, all of them dropped into that box. Sometimes she would send money at Easter with a note to say that we must buy a chocolate egg. One year a parcel came. I was nine, I think, it must have been the Easter following our visit to Bickersthorpe. Faith had just plunged her arms into the suds of a hand-wash.

'Who's that now?' she said as the doorbell rang.

'Shall I go?' I said. She didn't like us to answer the door to strangers. She shook the suds from her hands, wiped her hands on her apron.

It was the postman with a parcel for Edward and me.

'Whatever's this?' said Faith, frowning. I knew it was from Grandma Lilley, I knew her writing. We set it down on the kitchen table. It was wrapped in tough brown paper, tied up with string, the knot was fixed with red sealing wax.

'Whatever is she thinking of,' Faith muttered.

'Can I?' I said, taking the scissors from the kitchen drawer. I snipped the string, peeled off the layers of brown paper. She had wrapped it so carefully. I took the lid off the box, lifted the tissue paper to find a heap of chocolate shards; a yellow ribbon and an artificial flower lay amongst them.

'Silly woman,' said Faith.

I wanted to cry, but I daren't. I wanted to cry for Stella, thinking how sad she would be if she could see the broken eggs. I thought of Stella choosing the eggs, buying brown paper, string, sealing wax; finding a box; packing the eggs; taking a match to the sealing wax, watching it drip, drip. At the Post Office she would take out her pension, have the parcel weighed, count out the price of the stamps. And when she'd finished she would find Stan on the low stone wall.

'Come on, Stan,' I imagine her saying. 'Come home.'

I've had dinner at the pub again; chicken and chips followed by bread-and-butter pudding with custard. I ate to stop me flying away. I'm light-headed with all that's happened today. Stories are multiplying in my head as fast as cells. I lie on the bed flicking through the pictures in the book I bought yesterday at the library, *Featherbridge: Picturing the Past.* It's arranged in sections: *Home, Work, School, Shopping, The War, Glass* and *Coal.* There are no words apart from the occasional caption. Some of the pictures are dated, others are not. I flick through each section looking for Frank, Stan with his one-leg, and Faith. I turn to *Shopping*; several pages of shop fronts with proud shopkeepers posing on the street outside. Albert F. Dean, tailor and habit maker, stands in his doorway, tape measure around his neck, rows of hats and caps hang in the window. Caps like the one Frank wore in the photograph. Pike's Grocery Store has a poster in the window saying that Pike's Special Blend is two shillings and eight pence. Haslams Pork Butcher has fancy lettering over the door which says wholesale and retail, ranks of sausages swagged across the window. There's even a travelling ice-cream van: a man with a motorcycle and side-car. Girls in grubby dresses cluster around him. Girls aged six or seven. The caption says 1931. I study each face carefully but I don't recognise Faith. These could be her neighbours, her classmates.

I must try to sleep, be ready to meet Edith in the morning. I will take a shower. What I really need is to soak in a hot bath, to let all this wash over me. I see it again, the image I have of Faith filling the zinc tub from the copper on the range. Frank, testing the water with his toe.

'Her twin? Stan was her twin?'

'She adored him,' says Edith. 'She told me that she refused to marry Frank until Stan was safe home from the war. Frank always resented Stan.'

I ask her about Stan's death, to see if she has the same story as Reg.

'What does it matter whether he jumped himself or fell; he were dead.'

'When was that?'

'I'd say about ten years before Stella died. My memory's not so good. She moved here to the bungalows in seventy-four, same as me. No, not as much as ten. I think he'd been dead five years when she moved here.'

I do the sums, think of Stella coming to see us the day men walked on the moon. That night we watched television into the small hours: Neil Armstrong and Buzz Aldrin bouncing around, leaving footprints that will stay for ever, no wind to rub them out. Stan lost his footing on the canal bank, that's why Stella came.

'Malcolm, my husband, he took Stella to see your mother in Chester. She was on her own then, you see, once Stan had gone.'

I ask Edith about Ezra and Freda but she's not as clear on them. It seems they died much earlier.

'There was talk about both brothers. Neither of them was right after being in the Trenches. Ezra was a melancholy type. They survived, in body that is, came back, folks said they were lucky, but they weren't the same. And Freda had never been right. She had a syndrome, what do they call it? Round face.'

'Down's Syndrome?'

'Maybe. She was born like that. Died not long after Stan lost his leg, I believe.'

There was no lover, simply a woman torn between loyalty to her husband and children, and her adored brother.

'You look very like her. She liked to keep up with what

you were doing. I remember you at her funeral, you were lost.'

I said I'd tried to find the grave yesterday but I couldn't, and I wondered if anyone had put a headstone up.

'She's buried with Stan,' says Edith. She reckoned she could find the plot, but not now, not with her legs this bad.

'She learned to live with it, I think,' says Edith. 'She was well thought of at church. She had a quiet life. There were times, towards the end, I would come in for a cup of tea and she would talk about Stan and what happened.' Stan's accident must have been around 1930, Edith thinks. When she heard, Stella was beside herself. She said she must go back to Bickersthorpe to look after him. Freda couldn't manage alone and Ezra was no use around the house. Stella would go to settle Stan back at home after the hospital; stock up the cupboards, get ahead with the washing. Frank made a fuss, which Stella thought was unreasonable in the circumstances. She was determined to go. Frank said: You'll be back here by Friday night or don't come back at all. She never took him seriously. She didn't want to upset the girls, Faith and Irene. She left them playing out in the yard, made like she was going to do the shopping. She took a bag of clean laundry and a pie she'd baked. She often wondered if Faith, with her sharp eyes, would have noticed that she walked away carrying bags which were already full. She wanted them to think she was going shopping. She regretted that, wondered if Faith might have felt differently if Stella had explained. She always kept in touch. She would knit for the girls; she tried to see them whenever she could. Sometimes Frank wouldn't let her see them. She thought it best not to try too hard. She thought that if she left him alone Frank would cool down, make it up, then they could all get back to a proper life. But things had been said that couldn't be gone back on. They had both gone too far and couldn't get back.

'Pride is a terrible thing,' says Edith. 'Stubborn pride. Stella and Frank both had more than their fair share.'

I move through the train to find a seat alone. I want to spread out. I need space for the stories I've gathered. I find an empty place with a table and put my bags on the other seats, hoping the train doesn't fill up. I take out the file of stuff I copied from Wilf Nowells and the book on Featherbridge. As the train speeds up, heading south, I feel the momentum of the last two days filling up inside me, ready to pour.

'Tickets please,' says the guard.

I fumble in my purse. It was in another lifetime that I stood on Kings Cross Station and bought this.

Scenes come rushing in. There is no order: what is real, what is imagined, what is hearsay?

I take the lid off the tea I have bought but the train is going so fast that I can't get it to my mouth without it spilling.

I stretch out and there you go again; fluttering inside me. I've got used to it now, I like it. Freda Kelsall, great-aunt Freda, was a Down's baby. You are one eighth Kelsall; another week and I will know.

I flick through the Featherbridge book again. I'm getting to know these pictures and the places they show. I think of Stella walking through these streets with her laden bags on the way to Bickersthorpe to care for Stan; Faith going to school past these shops; Frank drinking in these pubs.

I turn to the section called *Home*. Pictures of terraced housing, washing strung out in the yards and a girl in a work-stained apron, on her knees, scrubbing the front step. She lifts the cloth from the bucket of water, wrings it hard. Faith learning to survive, holding on to the routine of daily life. Faith filled the space left by Stella with cleaning, washing, errands, cooking, mending, knitting. Was this to keep Frank's anger at bay or was she always, in her mind, preparing for Stella's return? Faith took the ashes from the grate, swept and swabbed the hearth, laid a new fire; polished the wood until she could see her face, looked deep into the reflection, just in case Stella was there over her shoulder. If Stella were to come back, how proud she would be. There was nothing around the house that Faith could not do. As she grew, she learned more. I think of Frank counting out money from his wage packet; Faith buying bread, vegetables, meat once a week, offal. Frank liked tripe and sheep's brains. Irene was careless, would lose the change, add it up all wrong. Faith took over. She kept the money in a jar on the mantel, had to drag a stool over to climb up high enough to reach; she liked writing neat columns of figures: £, s, d. She wrote down what she spent, always checked her change. Faith shopping in Featherbridge on a Saturday would go first to Haslams Pork Butcher. Frank liked his bacon. Bacon, egg, fried bread, a pot of tea. 'A man can't work on an empty stomach,' he would say. Haslams with its fancy lettering over the door, wholesale and retail, the ranks of sausages and down the side of the window words that read like a poem:

Pork pies

Polony

Home fed Bacon

Sausages

Potted meats

Pure lard

Fresh Daily

Four rashers of best back and two ounces of lard, then, checking her change she would go on to Pike's Grocery Store because their loose tea was the cheapest, cheaper than the Co-op. Faith keeping herself busy so she wouldn't think about Stella walking away that time she played hopscotch in the yard. Faith stopped to wonder why the bags her mother carried were heavy. Stella did not turn, she did not wave as she disappeared round the corner. Faith washing Frank's salty work clothes, Faith ladling water from the copper, ready for her father at the end of the late shift. Frank lowering himself into the water, home from eight hours at the furnace. Frank soaking under the scum in the zinc tub; cooling down slowly, so he won't crack.

Mango and Raspberries

I left the studio early, came through the market and stocked up on fresh fruit and vegetables. I've bought flat bread from Sevgül. I ate badly in Yorkshire; Sandra's huge breakfasts and pub meals. You were moving again in the night, you woke me. I take it you're telling me you'd like something good to eat. I've bought all this for us, to detox, put us back on an even keel.

I unpack the bags on the kitchen table. See what I have: tomatoes, aubergines, peppers in three different colours, courgettes, red onions, garlic and dark capped mushrooms. Monique, the midwife will approve. I've done as she recommended and bought a fresh pineapple. I don't think it's quite ripe enough to eat. I have a soft juicy mango and fat, hairy raspberries ready for now.

I will make a meal from what I have: three peppers, red, yellow and green, I wash the dust from their shiny skins, slice them lengthways; firm courgettes, chopped into sticks; a red onion cut in half then in half again; tomatoes and cloves of garlic. I take the roasting tin and pour in olive oil, extra virgin. I haven't done this for ages. The chopping is calming, therapeutic. I'm still buzzing from my trip to Yorkshire. I've had a good day in the studio, got in touch with the work with those stories fresh in my head. I've been scribbling all day, ideas about how I might bring the new work together, make something of the connection to Frank. I've phoned Matt and discussed a piece he might make for me and agreed also that I will work at the furnace for one day at least. I want to know what it feels like. I've taken Frank's photograph to be copied. I can remember him now. I can see his face; the strong jaw, the dark eyes, the moustache which hides his mouth. I would recognise him now if he passed me in the street, fat chance.

I'm high on it, but tired, also. A strange, exhausting time. I hope Dom phones tonight, I really do. He feels far away; everything on the other side of Frank's photograph and one-legged Stan Kelsall feels far away. I feel as if I've spent the last two days in a Victorian melodrama. I called Dom's office a couple of times and left a message. It was late when I got back last night. There was a fax to say that Joe hasn't got a place at Cambridge. Not this year anyway, that's definite. *We're still considering other options,* is what it said. I winced at the 'we'. That's not the same 'we' he used on me.

I'm off alcohol but tonight I need a drink. I pour myself a glass of red wine.

When the phone rings I leap on it, surprised at how much I want it to be Dom.

'Mrs Barnes?' says a charming voice.

It's for Annie.

'Annie Barnes isn't living here.'

'Are you the occupant?'

'What are you selling?'

'Not selling anything, madam, but over the next few days . . .'

'I'm not interested.'

'No obligation. A free estimate . . .'

'I have to go, there's someone at the door.' I slam the phone back on its rest. There really is someone at the door; probably selling dusters.

'Dom?'

'I took a chance you'd be in. Sorry I didn't ring. I wanted to surprise you.' Also, I know, he didn't want to offer me the chance to give him the brush off. He needn't have worried. I have never been so glad to see anyone. I hug him, slide my arms around his lean, easy body.

'It's so good to see you,' I say. We stand in the hall, hugging. His hands feel kind and firm around my back, the bump is a little awkward between us.

'It's not been that long,' he says.

'Feels like a lifetime, feels like another lifetime.' I'm fizzing again, eager to tell him about Stan and the Kelsalls, Frank's photograph, but most of all I want to tell him about you, kicking inside me. There is so much to say that I say nothing, and then I remember.

'I'm sorry about Joe. How is he?'

'Angry one minute, philosophical the next.'

'What happens now?'

'I don't know,' he looks up, pulls away from me slightly. 'Why don't you tell me about Yorkshire first. Good trip?'

'Don't know if good is the right word.' I'm full of it, I feel it swirling around inside.

'What's that smell?' says Dom.

We hurry through to the kitchen. As I open the oven door there's a whoosh of smoke. The onions are turning black at the edges.

'Just in time,' I say, switching off the gas. I turn back to Dom and, for the first time in weeks, I look at him and I don't feel cross, simply pleased to see him.

'I've so much to tell you, I don't know where to start.' I want to tell him that I felt you moving, kicking or waving. He looks tired, strained. I don't want to create tension when he's only just arrived.

'Why don't you tell me about Joe. Want one?' I hold up the bottle of red wine.

'Please.'

'Let's go through,' I say, indicating the sitting room which I hardly ever use.

'Your vegetables. You were going to eat.'

'I can wait. They'll taste better cold.'

We settle on the sofa, side by side. This is rare. I think I would like more of this. Sitting on a sofa with someone I can feel easy with, given a chance. Nothing special, simply sitting on the sofa at the end of a long day, enjoying a glass of wine. A rare treat, for me.

'Tell me about Joe.'

He sips his wine. I can see he doesn't want to go over it again. I imagine that for the last two weeks it's all they've talked about. Joe hasn't got a place at Cambridge, there was nothing left for him in the Summer Pool. If he resits, gets his A, he will go next year. Joe wants to travel, to get away for a few months.

Dom and Tessa both think this would be a good thing, but for Tessa's father. Joe understands this, so he's not leaving town in a hurry. The most likely plan is that he will try to earn some money, work for his re-sit, keep an open mind on the travel, if and when. Nobody says it, but what they mean is, when Tessa's father has died.

'A year off might be good for him,' says Dom. 'So much pressure.' Dom also wonders if he shouldn't be urging his son to take what has come his way, which is three respectable grades and a place at Durham. None of them can quite let go of the results. What got to Dom in the end was Joe saying: I just want to know where I went wrong.

'Is getting a B going wrong?' I say. Which probably isn't helpful. It was supposed to be easy for Joe; it was Dom who had to slog and work against low expectations to get farther than anyone in his family had got before him. It was meant to be easy for Joe.

'I'm sorry, Dom, I'm so sorry. What about Durham, he still has a place?'

'He let it go. He's set on taking a year out now. We're adjusting to that.'

We, again. This is a we in which I'm not included.

I try not to mind.

'It'll work out,' he says. 'Where's this photograph?'

'It's not here, I've taken it to be copied. You'll have to wait.' I tell him what I have found out. I describe Frank with his workmates; the dispute and the rates for the job; angry Frank. I fill in the shadow.

'I have a story now, much more of a story than I've ever had.' I have somewhere to go when Faith won't talk. I tell him about the Kelsalls, a household of brothers and sisters. Stella thought she'd got away, started a new life with Frank. She was a parent to her brothers and sisters but not to her own children. I think of the Kelsalls and the Lilleys, their lives shaped, damaged, by war and work.

'What struck me,' I say, 'is that it's so, well, *ordinary*. It's what happened to families. Grim and sad, yes, but not a scandal, not a lover, just life. I mean, it seems so unnecessary that Faith has bottled this up. It's not the events so much as the bottling up.'

'Does she know all this?'

'I suppose she must, but maybe she doesn't.'

'She might not,' says Dom. 'She was a child. She was what, five or six you say, at a time when children were seen and not heard.' I see Annie's twins, looking at her through the glass, wondering why their mummy doesn't come to their outstretched hands. So intense, so baffling, so indelible these events to a child's eye. Faith watching Stella with her laden bags walking away from the house, not turning at the corner to wave. No explanation given. Hanging on for a lifetime to this moment of childhood terror. Now I know more, it doesn't feel as scary. It's easier to ask about something that you know happened than to stare into the dark folds of a curtain at night and have no idea what the silence is for.

'Are you going to tell her you've been there?'

'I don't know. I'll say something. I can't plan it. I'll wait until I'm there. Let's eat.'

In the kitchen I make a dressing for the roast vegetables. Dom pours more wine. We tear chunks of flat bread; and afterwards, mango and raspberries. We sit back, I look at him. He hasn't said if he has to go or rather, how long he can stay.

'I've saved the best until last,' I say.

'I couldn't eat another thing.'

'Not food,' I say. 'I've something else to tell you.'

Back in the sitting room we settle on the sofa again, I lean into him.

'She moved,' I say. 'I felt her.' I take his hand and place it on my belly.

'No regrets?' he says.

'No.'

He looks uncomfortable with his hand resting on me.

'Do you want this baby, Dom?'

He says nothing, looks defeated. I wish I hadn't said anything. I put up my hands, 'I know, I know, you didn't have a say in it.'

'No, I didn't,' he says.

'Would it have been different if you had? I mean, if I'd said, "Dom, I'd like a baby, give me one," would that have made a difference?'

'You never wanted children, you never talked about having children. It hasn't ever been something between us.'

'So you don't want this baby?'

'That's not what I'm saying.'

'What are you saying?'

He says nothing for a while, as if he's gathering his strength, trying to collect his thoughts, put them in the right order.

'Being a parent is something that felt worth doing. Being a parent felt like necessary work,' he says, running his hands through his hair. 'Now, I feel helpless. There's not much I can do for Joe. I can't make it right for him and at the same time, this baby, well, I don't know what to do. I'm sorry, this isn't making much sense.'

'Forget the baby, pretend it's not happening. Us. Without this baby. Where did you see it going?' I say.

'I've told you. I like what we have. If I thought anything, I thought you would tire of me.'

'So you hang in there with Tessa in case I don't work out?'

'There's no marriage, there's nothing with Tessa, apart from Joe. But each time I think about making it official, leaving the marriage, it feels like something I'd sooner postpone than get on with. Hurting her.'

'You'd rather live in a husk.'

'Some days it seems easier.'

He takes off his glasses, rubs his eyes, trying not to look at what comes next. What we don't want to say is this: How long would we have? If we set up home, cared for this child, how long would it be before we too lived in a husk? Is that what happens?

'I so want this baby, Dom, I do hope she's all right.' I think about great-aunt Freda.

'You'll have a shock if it's a he.'

'All I ask is that you will be a father to this baby in some way. I don't want her searching around in twenty years' time for evidence of who you were. I want her to know you from the start. That doesn't mean we rush off and play Happy Families. I can't see that, can you?'

'No. Not at the moment.'

I'm not thinking much beyond the test results. I'm taking this slowly. What I don't say but I've thought often is: Let's hope we don't have two troubling results in one month. If Joe has lost his place at Cambridge, let this baby be all right.

'Let's see what the test says. I hope she's all right, Dom.'

'Me too.'

After that, when we know what to expect, I'd like him to tell Tessa and Joe. They need to know. They need to know before the birth. Let's leave that for another time. I pour him more wine.

'Let's not fight it, Dom. We'll work round the obstacles. You'd think it would be easy wouldn't you?'

'What do you mean?'

'You and me sitting here, a baby on the way, why couldn't it always be like this?' We know it can't be. We're used to this; being together for a while, a semblance of a joint life, then moving off, being something else in a different life. Disjointed nuggets. Could we live with all the bits in between? Could we join it all up?

I sink into the side of him.

I put my hand on his thigh, content to feel his firm flesh through the cloth; a moment of deep affection. We say nothing, the press of his hand on my shoulder is reply enough. Then, from nowhere, an urgency. My breasts are on fire. His kiss is fierce, deep. My hand runs smoothly along his thigh, searching. I cup his balls. I'm wet for him. He's hard, big in my hands, and I want him inside me. Now. All of him.

White Noise 5

'Listen, Maddie, this is absolutely something you should be doing,' says Hal. 'If you really can't face it, I will call publicity and say you want to shift the date, is all. Not cancel.' Kathy with the tangerine hair at The MCA has arranged an interview with *Contemporary Art 4*. They'll give it six pages, full-colour.

'It's bad timing,' I say.

'It is. But these things are always an interruption.'

'All I can think of is getting the results.'

'I know. But you said yourself you can't ring the hospital until after one. You'd spend the morning wound up. What time is she coming?'

'Ten,' I say. 'I don't mind the interview, it's the timing.'

Tomorrow I will get the results of the test. I called the hospital a few days ago, which is when they should have been ready, but they said there was a back-log, something about not having a clear result, waiting a few more days. I don't like the sound of it, I'm more edgy about this than I was. I've been thinking too much about great-aunt Freda. I can call the hospital again tomorrow afternoon. The woman from *Contemporary Art 4*, Chrissie Deeds, said she wanted to do an 'in-depth', interview, going back over all my work as well as talking about the new glass pieces.

'She made it sound like she wanted to spend the day at the studio,' I say.

'If she's coming at ten, she'll be out of there by one,' says Hal. 'Get a cab to the studio, book the same cab to pick you up at twelve-thirty. Tell her before you start, you have another appointment.'

'My mind is elsewhere.'

'You'll do this with your eyes closed.'

'I'll do what I can.'

'Like I said, I'll make a call if I must but I think you're better going ahead.'

'All right.'

'Chrissie Deeds, you said?'

'Yes, what's she like? I've never met her,' I say.

'She'll do a good piece, she's a good critic, and she always recycles; she'll get something in one of the Sundays nearer the time. You know I wouldn't say this if I didn't think it mattered. I think you're better off spending the morning talking to Chrissie Deeds, rather than pacing around. It's a major article.'

'I'm going now, Hal, I need to get slides together to show her.'

'She'll love the glass, let the work speak for itself. And Maddie, good luck with the results. Phone me the minute you hear. I'll be over if you need me. I mean it.'

Chrissie Deeds arrives bang on time. She's small, skinny, dressed entirely in black, which I read as a bad omen. Her fragile legs rise from high platforms, as if to weigh her down; a micro skirt skims her thighs. Her skin is white, no make-up except for lipstick the colour of blood; her hair is a precise bob, dyed burgundy. She takes off her leather jacket, swings it round the back of a chair.

'A good space,' she says casting her eye round my studio, looking up at the half glass roof. She places a microphone on the table amongst the heaps of glass. It's almost as big as the tape-recorder.

'It will pick up anywhere,' she says indicating that we can walk around, talk in front of the work or sit and chat.

I make coffee for her, a herb tea for me and watch her as she jots down what she thinks of my studio on a pad of yellow paper.

'I'll sit here,' I say, joining her at the table.

She presses the record button. I see the tape move round, waiting to capture my words. I think of these words transferred to the pages of a magazine, tidied up, all the 'ums' and 'ers' taken out. I will think before I speak. I don't want to see anything on the page I wished I hadn't said. Also, if I take time to think, the tape will get used up. She will have blanks, white noise, the sound of me saying nothing.

'You started your career as a painter, and you were successful. Why stop?' she says, looking at me from beneath a silky fringe.

'Painting was what I studied at college. I had good teachers at school and on foundation, it was a natural progression. But even then I was interested in other ways of working, I always looked beyond painting. At eighteen you don't strike out.' This is the easy answer, the that's-what-it-was-like-then answer. She wants more.

'Did you become dissatisfied with painting?'

I wait. Let a few inches of tape slide by.

'With painting there is always the limit of the frame, of two dimensions. I want people to walk round the work, for it to have a real relationship to them, their body.'

'And photography,' she says. 'You painted the *Shadow* series in monochrome, and *Family Album,* I believe, comes from a photograph. Did you not consider photography?'

'I use a camera for research, to collect images,' I say, I don't want to get into the Faith photograph.

'Both those series of paintings seemed to be about something fleeting, something which the camera couldn't catch, so was that a dialogue with photography?'

'You could say that,' I say. It's time to be enigmatic. 'They are about trying to reconcile light and dark.' Faith's night-dark silence, my torch reaching towards the night sky. I almost say to her: Once, when I was a child, I stood in the garden with my brother's Pifco torch and pointed it at the sky. That's what making art is; shining a torch at the night sky, finding a way to make the light come back.

'Can you say more about your interest in shadows?' she says.

I would like to say, no, but it's too early in the interview to get rude.

'A shadow is a dark place which confirms the presence of something you can't see,' I say.

'Shadows in art have a lineage,' she says, and I sense her PhD surfacing. I let her talk about Pliny and the myth of the origin of painting, tracing a line around a shadow, the portrait made as a likeness for the lover who went away, the relationship between representation and loss.

'All art,' I say, 'well, for me, anyway, is about trying to get at something which is hard to reach.' Before she asks me what it is I'm reaching for I say: 'I like the idea that the shadow is a hole in the light. What's in the hole is up to you. You know where the holes are in your life. We could talk about that.' I regret it as soon as I've said it. She shuffles in her seat, pulls one side of her bob behind her ear.

'Mind if I smoke?' she says, reaching for her bag.

I do, but it seems antagonistic to say so.

I shrug, and get up to open the doors on to the walkway. She takes this as confirmation.

'Where were we,' she says, confidence restored with a fag in her hand. 'Oh, yes. There's a strong sense of narrative in your work: the figures in *Family Album*, *Shadows*, the absent tears in *The Uncried*.' She's done her homework. 'I get a sense of a cast of characters who we don't quite meet. I was wondering who they are?'

'Who do you want them to be?'

'Are they people in your own life?'

'Who they are is not the point,' I say. 'Like any artist I'm drawing on things which matter to me, but the literal source of this work is really not the point. If I pinned down the narrative, made it specific, that would limit the work. I leave a space for people to fill up with their own characters, their own imaginings.'

She gets up, walks over to the glass piece I mocked-up for photography, the tape absorbs the sound of her feet on the bare wooden floor, her exhalations of smoke.

'Tell me about the new work,' she says.

'It's a common experience, an ordinary one,' I say. 'Something gets broken, something which matters. In that moment, there are intense feelings. Turbulence. The work is about finding a form for the turbulence.'

'So for us, for the viewer,' she says, 'you're offering a space in which to release our own turbulence?'

I shrug.

'It's dramatic work,' she says.

'That's why I want to use the enclosed space,' I say. It's time

I gave her something. 'You could call it a dramatised space. Contradictory thoughts and feelings present at the same time. How it feels to recall the moment of breaking, or to glimpse how it might feel to put it back together.'

'So, your work is about simultaneity?'

'If you want to use that word,' I say. 'We often think one thing, do another, have conflicting thoughts at the same time: love, hate; create, destroy. If you say it or write it down you have to put it in a straight line. I want to make objects which hold the turbulence; each time you look at them you take things in, in a different order, or all at once.'

'So the ambiguity is not resolved but held in one place?' she says.

'It's about trying to hold on to opposing states at the same time. I mean, is the glass exploding or is it coming together? It can be both. It's up to you which way you read it.'

'I understand the glass you've used was mass-produced tableware?'

'The more commonplace the object the more experience it carries, the more likely it connects to real lives,' I say. 'Things have a social life, they live with people, become part of their lives. When those lives are gone, the things people owned are all we have to reconnect.'

'So it's about memory?' she says.

'Memories cluster around things. Ordinary things. An object recalled can release memories. Thoughts rush in.'

'It is stunning work. I have the feeling you're reluctant to give much away, about your own memories.'

'As I've said,' I try to keep the irritation from my tone, 'I hope people will be surprised, intrigued, will recognise enough to make their own connection.'

'So there's not a specific story to be recovered here?'

Not one you're getting your hands on, Chrissie.

'In the end,' I say, 'it doesn't matter how I explain the work. What matters is how others experience it. Your experience of it is worth more than my explanation.'

'Don't you think audiences want both?' she says. 'They will have their own response to your work, but they are curious about what goes on inside your head.'

'I'm not sure anyone would want to get inside my head,' I say.

'It has been said that your work is about giving a physical presence to silence, a kind of synaesthesia. Can you say more about that?'

I say nothing, let the tape spool on, collecting the silence, hoping this makes the point; but she looks at me directly, waiting, insistently, for words.

'Like what?'

'A specific silence or silence in general?' she says.

'Scratch the surface of most families and you find a tacit agreement, never to speak of something or other. The effort of keeping the silence has an effect on people, it can ripple through generations.'

'You're interested in the effect a silence has?' she says.

'If someone keeps quiet about something it starts to show, it can be distressing. You might say this work is about patterns of distress.'

'Isolde Maddox recently said you were a serious omission from the New Gen show. The MCA exhibition will put you in the running for the Contemporary Art Prize. Does it matter to you?'

'I could use the money. It's a lottery. We'll see.'

I've had enough.

'Look,' I say. 'I need to go soon. I have an appointment.'

'Just one more thing,' she says. 'I was wondering who you thought your work was for, who is your audience?'

I'd like to say that I make this work primarily for an audience of one.

Faith.

I hold up my signals, my patterns of distress.

Instead I tell her about a woman I once saw in an exhibition of mine, here at the studio gallery. She was elegant, well-heeled, in her late sixties, I would say. She looked out of place, like someone you would see at the Royal Academy Summer Exhibition, really there for the tea with friends afterwards, not someone who would make the effort to come to a warehouse in Hackney. She took her time, looked closely at the work. I noticed her eyes brimmed with tears. She sat down and cried, quietly. I wanted to ask her why, what was it she had seen? The hairs on the back of my neck stood up to think that, however briefly, however slightly, I had touched her life. From my solitude, I had reached into her solitude.

'It's like prisoners tapping on radiators,' I say. 'Sending messages to other cells.'

Holding His Breath

5

'Morning,' says Sevgül. 'Beautiful day. You back at college?'

'I'm off this term.'

'Of course. Lucky you girls these days, maternity leave and all that. How's it going, you look good.'

'I feel great,' I say. I feel as if I could fly, despite my heaviness. I am walking on air since the results.

'Christmas, isn't it?'

'January, end of January.'

'Big now, you sure it's not twins?'

'No, just the one, I've seen her.'

'They tell you it's a girl?'

'No, but I'm pretty certain,' I say. The hospital wouldn't tell me, even though they know. After I'd finished the interview with Chrissie Deeds, I took a cab home and phoned Dom. He offered to come over while I made the call. I said I didn't mind doing it on my own as long as I knew where he was; I wanted him to know as soon as I knew. I rang the hospital and, after all the waiting, she just said: no abnormalities. That was it. I couldn't believe it. I'd convinced myself that you were going to follow in your great-aunt Freda's footsteps. I said: I think my baby is a girl. There was a pause before she said that it was hospital policy not to disclose the gender. It annoys me to think they know for certain. I called Dom straight back, told him all was well. His relief was palpable even down the telephone. He cares, I thought, he cares about this baby.

'Girl or boy, what does it matter, you want a healthy baby,' says Sevgül. 'What are you after today?'

'Baklava,' I say.

'Help yourself.' She waves me over to the trays of newly baked pastries which sit in the window. I help myself to four pieces, picking up each one carefully with the tongs, laying them in a cardboard tray; each one oozes a clear honey.

'You stocking up?' She laughs. 'I'm only closing for two weeks.'

'I'd forgotten you were closing,' I say. 'When do you go?'

'End of the week,' she says. 'Two weeks. Customers forget us.'

'No we won't,' I say. 'We'll miss you.' Sevgül is off to Turkey for her nephew's wedding.

'I worry about what people do,' she says. 'People go somewhere else. We never close. They think we don't come back.'

'You won't give it a thought once you're there,' I say.

'Always thinking about the shop, customers,' she says. 'Who's all that for?' She points to the baklava.

I tell her that I'm going to try my hand at making glass. I'm going to do what my grandfather did, feel what it felt like to be him.

'Hard work, Maddie,' she says. 'You be careful, shouldn't be lifting things. Take a couple more. Have them on me.'

'You don't need to.' I take two more anyway, because I wonder who else might be in the workshop.

'Maddie, two weeks. You come back. You won't forget?'

'I won't.'

'Look at it this way,' says Matt. 'It doesn't matter how many books on sex you read, you don't know what it's like until you've done it.' It feels even hotter than when I was here before. It's one of those glowing September days, summer having a last fling. It doesn't matter that the doors and windows are wide open, what comes in is warm air.

'Think of it as a dance,' Matt says. 'This is how we choreograph it.' He talks me through the process, shows me the steps. I hold a blow-pipe, check its weight. It's heavy; Matt has shown me where to hold it to balance the weight evenly.

'Before you start,' says Matt. 'Walk up to the furnace. You need to feel the heat so it doesn't come as a shock.'

He walks over with me, slides back the door. It's unbearable. I feel as if it's taking off a layer of skin. I jump back.

'Don't panic,' says Matt. 'Try not to be afraid of the heat.'

'I'm not sure I can do this,' I say.

'It's up to you.'

I back away from the furnace, away from the fierce heat. I take a swig of water.

'All right,' I say. 'I'm ready.'

They all stop to watch me, Jim, Matt and Carol; I feel them at my back. I have the pipe balanced in my hands, ready to feed into the crucible. How easily and quickly Matt did this; it's all I can do to keep it steady, to steel myself to go back to the heat.

'Look for the pipe reflected in the glass,' Matt reminds me. I don't see, so much as feel, as I approach the furnace mouth. I feel it burn my hands, arms, face. I can't breathe. The air is too hot to breathe, it will singe the inside of my lungs. I take short, nervous breaths. I'm blinded by the glare. It's like staring at the sun, falling into the space behind my eyes. I pull back.

'Don't panic,' says Matt.

I think: The quicker I do this, the quicker I can move back. I go forward again, and I see it, the end of the pipe reflected in the molten glass, a pool of hot, sticky honey.

'Can you see it?'

'Yes. Yes.'

'Quickly.'

I skim the pipe into the pot.

'Don't forget to turn,' shouts Matt.

I turn the pipe, awkwardly, not smoothly, deftly like Matt. I remember what he said: touch down like an aeroplane landing then take off again, all the time turning. Three turns and out again, three full turns for a decent gather, he said. I feel Matt come up behind me, help me guide the pipe out. It's heavier now, with the sticky mass at its tip. He steadies me, takes some of the weight as we swing the pipe together on to the marver, the steel table. Sweat is pouring down my back, stinging my eyes, but I don't have a hand free to wipe my face.

'Keep moving,' he guides my hand as I roll the sticky hot gob, along the smooth steel surface.

'Ready?' he says. How would I know? He guides me to the chair. Relieved to sit down, all I can think of is to keep the pipe turning, however slowly, I keep it turning. How can I think of blowing and turning at the same time? It's like trying to pat your head while rubbing your stomach. The noise is getting to me, I can't concentrate with the click, click, click of the lehr, the roar of the gas and the awkward clanking of my pipe on the metal edge of the chair. How many times an hour did Frank do this? Frank would do this like breathing, without thinking.

'Lean back,' says Matt guiding the white plastic mouthpiece towards my lips.

'Blow.' I lean back, take the pipe in my mouth, and give it as much as I've got. A strong, hard blow; there's a tingle in my cheeks, my face might burst. Nothing. The glass hardly moves.

Matt guides me back to the heat, to the glory hole, to make the glass workable again.

Back at the chair he prepares me to blow. I fill my lungs.

'This time a steady blow, sustained,' he says. I've been practising my steady blow, breathing deep as if to plunge to the bottom of the ocean, filling up all the folds and fronds of my lungs. I let it out slowly, steadily, trying to control it, trying not to let the air fill my cheeks; I aim the pressure down the pipe so the air fills the glass. Don't breathe in, I say to myself, keep the breath going out and out. Matt holds and turns the pipe, so I can concentrate on the breath. It's the best I can do. I flop back, exhausted.

'Not bad, not bad,' says Matt.

I look down at a bubble of glass no bigger than an apple. Lopsided. It is not a perfect sphere.

Carol offers me a bottle of water.

'You were great,' she says.

'Yeah,' I say. 'Practice makes perfect. I don't know how you two do it.' I think how they work, no words just the rhythm of their bodies, perfect timing.

'Again?' says Matt.

'All right.'

I brace myself for the heat.

I take a cab home. Exhausted, burned, pleased with myself. I made several bubbles, the last one I pressed in on itself, shaped it to make a small bowl; they are cooling in the lehr. I will collect them tomorrow. I've talked to Matt about the big piece I want for the exhibition. It's beyond any skill I can achieve in the time. Matt says I can put some of the broken glass into the pot, melt it down into the batch. It will leave impurities in the finished piece but I don't mind. He's going to blow something near to the image I had in the dream; tear drop, pear drop. Sealed. He will let me make the first blow; it will hold my breath and yours, you in there, and Frank's. I sit in a cloud of my own stale heat. My arms ache.

I leave my salt-stained clothes where they fall, climb into the bath to ease my muscles. That first time at the chair I felt so clumsy, as if my arms were no use at all; but each time I tried again it became a little easier, my muscles remembered what to do. I think of Frank, apprentice boy, making piece after piece until the task was etched into his arms, no need to think, just follow the rhythm of doing, the fluency of his body. Frank must have been a strong man, physical, working all day at the furnace, a man who knew how to use his body, swinging the molten glass, filling it, shaping it with the power of his lungs. No time to talk on an eight-hour shift, six days a week. His body more fluent than any words from his mouth. I think of him as silent, a man of few words. The man in the photograph looks like a quiet man; he would have been good looking if he'd smiled. He was handsome; fine, strong features, deep, dark eyes and a mass of black hair.

I dunk my head under the water, rub shampoo to a lather.

When Frank had his bath at the end of a shift did he wash his hair? I see Frank rising from the tub, rubbing his clean skin briskly with a towel as the steam rises in the cold kitchen. He rubbed so hard that when Faith peeped to see if he was done, she wondered if he was trying to rub himself out. Trying not to be there at all so he wouldn't have to deal with two little girls. When his hair was dry he smoothed it with brilliantine, combed it back, sleek like wet ink on a page. I think of Frank as an angry man, his anger as dark as his hair. Since I found the photograph I've had the same dream, more than once. I wrote it down.

In the dream I feel as if I am Faith as a little girl. I am Faith waiting for Frank to finish his bath. There is a crack above me. A crack, a thump. Simultaneous lightning and thunder. The sky splits; a giant fork, a hairline crack in the night sky, zig-zagging above my head. An immense light. Then comes the feeling that the thunder is not thunder at all, but flesh on flesh. The sound of flesh being pressed into flesh, piston driven. Terrifying, yet a necessary release. I feel the presence of Frank, the man in the photograph. The dream ends in torrential rain; through the rain, the sound of Frank, sobbing.

I think of Frank as a sore tooth.

Frank's anger is like a toothache, entrapped rage; nerve pain trapped in a hard place. How can he make it go away and still exist?

Keep the tooth, remove the nerve.

Frank showed Faith how to remove the nerve, how to feel nothing.

Moth 5

The minicab slows, drops into a low gear as we turn down to Stonebank. It's four months since I was here. The balsam is high, almost finished; a dense, pink border all the way down the lane. I'm doing the trip in reverse this time; tomorrow I will go to Liverpool to discuss the layout in the gallery. I'm beginning to see it more clearly. I will tell Jude about the blown piece which I plan to make with Matt, and give her a list of the Bagshott's glass which I hope we can borrow from Featherbridge Museum.

'No,' I say. 'Not the Centre. The cottage, it's further down.'

'Mrs Armitage's?' he says.

'That's right.'

'Are you her daughter, from London?'

'Yes.' He's noticed the bump, it's almost impossible to hide it now. I'd hate the news to be round the village before I have time to tell Faith.

'You know my mother?'

'Church.'

He turns sharply and pulls up alongside Faith's cottage. The Virginia creeper, which sprawls up the front wall and round the garden side, is turning a reddish gold. The cottage is at its most welcoming at this time of year.

The driver takes my bags from the boot while I find money to pay him.

'She doesn't know, yet,' I say. We both look down at the bump. 'I've come specially to tell her. I'd be grateful if . . .'

'Not a word, wouldn't dream of it . . .' By which I take it he's off to tell his wife on his way back to the station.

I wait for a moment, not sure if Faith is in. I hope I've got the timing right and she's still up at the Centre. There is a key under a stone by the back door. I peer through the window. If she was here, she would have been out by now. I won't have long; she will have seen the car coming down the lane.

The stone is where it always is, a lump of millstone grit by the back door; beneath it, the single silver key. A beetle, which Edward understands better than he understands himself, scuttles out; it doesn't seem to know which way to go.

I let myself in. The anemones which I bought for Faith look exhausted, withered. I put them in the sink. Faith thinks flowers are frivolous, a waste of money.

I find the teapot, two cups. It's not tea I really want, I'm hot and thirsty, but I want tea ready for Faith. We will sit down, here at her kitchen table and, over a cup of tea, I will tell her that she is to become a grandmother for the third time. I must do that first; see how she takes it, see how that goes before I think of tackling anything else. I've brought the copy of Frank's photo. I've thought about all the things I could ask her. It's hard to know where to start, or whether I should start at all. The story of Frank, Stella, Stan, Freda, Ezra, grows in my mind. I have a story now, some of it based on things I've found out, but I've filled in episodes between. It could all be fantasy. If I do anything it will simply be to show her the picture, to ask if this is her father, my grandfather. I'd like to know for sure. I won't push her to talk about him, if she doesn't want to.

I set the table with cups and saucers, sugar bowl, milk jug. In the biscuit tin I find custard creams and Garibaldis which I arrange on a plate. The table looks welcoming. She will be pleased. I fill the kettle, set it on the hob and light the gas. Next, I find a jug. I let the tap run, the water is icy, it is good to drink because it comes from deep in the hills, a natural spring. I fill the jug with cool, clear water and set it on the table with a tumbler. I pour myself a glass and drink, slaking my thirst. I sit, content for a moment, as I listen to the hiss of the gas, the water rumbling to the boil. I look out of the window at the valley side. The tight broccoli heads of the trees are breaking up into patches of gold and red, in a couple of weeks a blaze of autumn colour and then nothing but bare branches. I think of Faith up here in the bleakness of winter. I think of you inside me; all you know is the darkness of your watery pouch and floating. I'd like to bring you here when you're earth-bound, to this solid rock, impervious to wind and rain. I think what a brave woman Faith is. She has come far, she is safe here. What right have I to disturb her? I might say nothing at all, keep the photograph to myself. I pour another tumbler full of water, it comes in a rush, filling the glass to the rim, above the rim. I watch the mound of water, held in by the skin of surface tension. The glass is brimming, one more drop and it will flood down the sides, flood the table. I lean forward, suck the water until the level falls and I can lift the glass to my mouth safely, without spilling a drop.

I hear Faith's footsteps on the path.

'Hello,' I call. 'In the kitchen.'

I won't stand up to greet her, I want to say something first to cushion the impact.

'Good journey?' she says.

'Good timing,' I say. 'Here.' I pour tea for both of us.

'I saw the car coming,' she says, her eyes fastening on me. Before I've time for the thought to form I know she has seen, realised. She recognises my changed shape, even with me sitting down.

'Madeleine,' she says, drawing up a chair.

'That's what I've come to tell you. I could have told you on the phone, but I wanted to be here. Thought it might be a bit of a shock.'

'You can say that again.'

'Here.' I pass her the sugar bowl.

'Whatever are you going to do?'

'I'm going to have it, of course.'

'You look far gone. When is it due?'

'Towards the end of January.'

'But who . . . I mean . . .'

'The father?' This is the tricky bit. She's never asked about my relationships. She might have the vague sense that there is someone, that there is a man, or men, in my life. She never asks.

'The father is a man I've known for some time.'

'Are you getting married, then?'

'No. He's already married.'

'This is beyond me,' she says. She fiddles with a strand of hair that has strayed from the back of her bun.

'How will you manage? And at your age. Isn't it risky at your age?'

'I'm only forty-one.'

'I don't know what to say. You've knocked the wind out of me.' She pulls a pin from her bun, tucks the stray hair back in, pushes the pin firmly back.

'You always were awkward, had to do everything different.'

'Have a biscuit,' I say.

'I couldn't eat a thing,' she says, then takes a custard cream and dunks it in her tea.

'I'll be all right,' I say. I can face the practicalities; it's in my genes. 'I really want this baby. I thought you'd be pleased.'

She looks baffled.

'It'll be hard work, you know,' she says, but the tone is softer. She has a look on her face which says she's torn between disapproval and genuine, pleased surprise.

'You can start knitting,' I say, pointing out the benefits. Wherever we live, with or without Dom, this baby will need clothes. Faith will be good at that. I tell her about Monique the midwife and how I'm eating lots of fresh fruit.

'Dom, did you say his name was?'

'Short for Dominic.'

'He'll see you right, won't he?'

'He'll be a father to this child. She will know who her father is.'

'She?'

'I'm sure she's a she.'

'They've not told you have they?'

'No, they wouldn't.'

'I should hope not. Well, I don't know what to say. You could knock me down with a feather.'

I can see her fidgeting, needing to do something. I see her look to the weather. She'll have a load in the washing machine if I don't stop her.

'Let's bake a cake,' I say. 'To celebrate.'

'I was wondering about doing a bit of washing.'

'No,' I say. 'Let's bake a cake.' I stand up to clear the tea things away and see the anemones, tired and limp on the draining board.

'Here, I bought you these.' She flashes a look that says: Waste of money.

'What shall I put them in?' I say. She goes through to the sitting room and brings back a glass vase, tinted green, with a fluted rim. I take it from her and, as I turn it over, I see J.M. Bagshott embossed in the base. I thought she had smashed it all.

'This is nice,' I say. 'Didn't we have this in Chester?' She says nothing, already in the cupboards checking for flour, caster sugar, jam. I won't push it. I fill the vase with water and arrange the tired anemones; floppy petals, red, purple, blue, at the centre of each, stamens like pins in a blue velvet hat. Prussian blue. I ease the fleshy pink stems into the water and hope they will drink in time to make a difference.

Baking is one chore which makes Faith seem more relaxed. The silence of baking is kinder, softer than the tense, starched silence of a washing day. It is light, fluffy like flour dust.

'Here,' I say. 'I'll do that.' This is what I always did as a child; only then, I would stand next to her on a chair, so that I could reach. I hold the sieve up high, letting in the air so the cake will rise, watching it fall into the mixing bowl. Faith stands next to me with another mixing bowl. She creams butter and sugar together with a wooden spoon. When I've finished sieving the flour I break eggs into a small bowl. She's not sure about this shared task. I can see that she wants to do it all by herself. I feel the oven getting warmer. I beat the eggs, then I grease the two halves of the cake tin. She takes the beaten eggs from me, adds them to the mixture. I smell the sugar, fat, eggs, blending together; an intimate smell. She folds in the flour. This was the bit I loved best as a child: watching it all come together, then her pouring the mixture into the cake tins. She would hand me the bowl and the wooden spoon. I would scrape my finger round the insides of the bowl, lick the spoon; the nearest I came to kissing her.

The smell of the cake baking fills the kitchen; air expanding, heat transforming the mixture into cake. I watch Faith as she clears things away and wonder if she is softening inside.

Glass becomes rigid when cooled but may be heated back to a liquid.

This is the easiest I've felt in Faith's company for a long time. She is pleased; underneath the disapproval and concern, she is pleased. She goes off to look through her file of knitting patterns.

We've always tiptoed around her because we didn't want to hurt her. I've got it now, I've got the story, part of it, enough of it. I'll keep the story; she can forget it.

There is a difference between letting go and keeping the lid on.

If only I could tell her, I've got it now. She can let go, put it down; soon there will be a new baby to hold.

I savour the smell of fat, sugar, eggs, flour, transforming themselves into sponge; sponge can never be cake mix again.

Not like glass.

'Why don't you go through, light the fire if you want to,' says Faith. Despite the sunny day, the evening here is chilly, an autumn chill on the air. I light the newspaper; the fire spits, fizzes as the logs catch. On the table between the two armchairs sits a pile of knitting patterns.

'I'll look for something new next time I go into town, but see what you think.' She's glad of a new commission; she's just finishing a cardigan for James.

'He'll need this soon for school,' says Faith. I watch her click away, think of all she has knitted, row after row. I want to say: Let's unravel this one, each tight row. Now perhaps, while she's safe behind her knitting.

'It's funny you know, being pregnant, your mind goes back,' I say for openers, warning her the past is on its way.

Is it my imagination or do the hands speed up?

'You like being a grandmother?' I say.

'Lovely boys,' says Faith. 'Bright like their father.'

'James and William think the world of you,' I say. We both look up at the photographs in gold-rimmed frames along Faith's sideboard.

'We didn't have that,' I say. She stiffens. 'A grandmother, I mean. With Grandma and Grandpa Armitage dying before we were born.'

I leave it, hoping she will stop knitting, say something. She says nothing. I can't stop now, I've started.

'I remember Grandma Lilley,' I say. 'Though we didn't see her much.'

She doesn't look up.

'I remembered something the other day,' I say, waiting, hoping she will say: Yes, what was that?

Her silence crackles, white noise, between us.

'I remember going to Bickersthorpe,' I say. She freezes at the mention of the name.

'I'll put the kettle on,' she says, laying down her knitting. She's on her way to the kitchen.

'Don't go,' I say, but she does. I hear the water filling up the kettle, hear her strike a match, the hiss of gas.

'Not for me,' I say, keeping the conversation going.

She doesn't come back. I follow her into the kitchen. She's wiping the work tops.

'Please, Mum,' I say. Her back goes stiff. 'I remembered the man with one leg who was there when we visited. I'd forgotten. I went back there.'

'Madeleine, please.'

I don't like the way this is going. I wonder about fetching the photo of Frank, something tangible, real, something for us to focus on instead of these words.

'I found a photograph of Frank,' I say. 'Someone who I think might be Frank.'

She spins round, looks at me. I don't like the look on her face. I go cold.

'You've done what?'

'I was doing research, into the glass, for my exhibition. I found a photograph. I think it's Frank.'

'It's none of your business.' There's something almost violent about her.

'I'm sorry,' I say, softening, moving towards her. I stumble on, try to explain. 'Whatever happened, it can't be worse than all the things I've imagined over the years. I just thought, you know . . . don't you want to talk about it?'

'Don't you speak to me like that, this has nothing to do with you. I'm going to bed now.'

I can't believe the look in her eyes. She's not melting, she's cold, brittle, cooled down too quickly. *Internal stresses will occur.* I don't like the way she is looking at me. If I were a Bagshott's fat-bellied jug, I swear she would pick me up, hurl me at the stern moor, scatter my particles down the valley until I dissolved in the stream.

I sit on my bed. Stunned. Too much, too quickly. I hear a noise that I don't like. I look up, there's a moth trapped in the lampshade, fluttering around the heat and blinding light of the bulb. What is it that the moth wants so much? Compelled, again and again it collides; no logic, no sense of direction, but an increase of wingbeats, a headlong rush. It drops, hard on the table, lies still for a moment. Dead, or stunned. Its wings merge with the grain of the wood. It struggles, rights itself. I open the window; it's free to leave but it doesn't go. It's up again, fluttering, battering. It doesn't understand: the glass is hot, the bulb will burn.

The source is sealed.

I wake early, wondering what to say to Faith, thinking that yesterday was a bad dream. It's a sunny morning, hot, though it rained in the night. Steam rises from the trees like a rainforest, releasing the burden of moisture back up into the atmosphere, liquid into air. *Neither a liquid nor a solid. Like a ghost.*

I smell bacon and eggs cooking. Faith is making a full breakfast. Is it for her, for me, for the baby? It's something she does well. I think of Faith cooking Frank's breakfast, up early for the early shift. Faith learned how to cook the perfect breakfast: rashers first in the pan, sizzling in lard and their own melted fat. She would tip the frying pan to make a pool of fat, ready for the egg. She would break the egg, carefully, into the pan. There is a moment, just as the white seals over the yolk, but before the yolk turns solid, that is the moment to ease the egg on to a plate.

As I come into the kitchen she lifts a rasher of bacon from the pan, its edge brown, crisp.

'I'm sorry,' I say. 'About last night. You don't want to talk about it, I know. It's just that I thought you ought to know.

The work I'm doing for the exhibition, I'm using the glass, the glass you broke. It was never thrown away. I saved it at Annie's house. I've remade it. I'd like you to see what I've done, but if you don't want to, that's all right. I wanted to tell you. That's what I've been working on. On the family history.'

I am at the furnace. I take my ill-formed bubble of glass back to the heat, to the glory hole, to soften it so I can form it again. *Each time you go back to the furnace you apply the greatest heat to the outside; it's cooler on the inside.*

I put my arm round her shoulder, something I've never done before but I don't want her to fall off, down the valley side, into the stream. I'll hold her, safely. Her back bristles, stiffens, she turns. Her eyes are colder than I've ever seen them.

Part Three

Waiting For Snow

It's a familiar smell but I can't quite place it. My head is thick with sleep, I need to work out how to sit up; how to move from beached-whale position to sitting upright. As I rehearse the movement in my head it dawns on me: turkey, roasting turkey. Hal is already up. I check the time, ten-thirty. He said he would wake me at ten if I hadn't made an appearance. He's taken pity on me.

'Merry Christmas,' says Hal the other side of my bedroom door. 'Can I come in?'

'Yes,' I say, still stuck on my side, my voice coated in sleep.

'Fresh orange juice and toast,' he says, clearing a space on the bedside table.

'Hal, thanks. I'm not sure I can.'

'Orange juice for baby, dear, not for you. Need a hand?' He heaps pillows behind me as I haul myself up.

'Merry Christmas,' he says again.

'Merry Christmas.' I take in, for the first time, his red apron trimmed with white fur.

'Where did you get that?'

'I told you, we do this properly or not at all,' he turns around so I can see the full effect. 'I'm right on schedule. Take your time, have your bath. I must go. I have to peel the baby Brussels.' He kisses my forehead and is gone.

'Hal,' I say, calling him back. His head peers round the door.

'Yeah?'

'Thanks so much.'

'The pleasure is all mine.'

The ultimate Bank Holiday; thank God for Hal. He arrived

late yesterday afternoon with a tree under one arm and the turkey under the other. Once we agreed to spend Christmas Day together he took it on as a project. He said we should do it properly. Or, rather, he would do it properly, since I was working flat out on the exhibition up until the twenty-second. He was glad of the opportunity.

'My mother, she was good on the presents,' he said. 'After Hanukkah she would buy us Christmas presents, but it was the food and decorations I wanted. She never would let us have a tree.'

'There's only the two of us, Hal,' I said as we unloaded his car.

He took over the kitchen.

'Two hours, I queued for this at Lidgate's,' he said, making room for the turkey in the fridge. 'I'm thinking: Why didn't I go to Marks & Spencers like the rest of the world? I tell you, if it weren't for those girls giving out mince pies along the queue, I would've been out of there.'

'You shouldn't have gone to so much trouble,' I said.

'Look, if baby's born tomorrow, we want it to know how things get done around here.' He has made two kinds of stuffing, traditional chestnut and lemon with parsley.

'It's fresh and tangy. You'll love it.'

He's brought a picnic hamper packed with bone-china plates and silver cutlery, inherited when his mother died. The crackers are from Harrods. He's set up the tree in the sitting room, dressed it head to foot in white and silver with a Star of David on top. There were more decorations in another box which he wouldn't let me see. He said he would fix them when I'd gone to bed.

I am relieved not to be in the bosom of my family.

My non-talking family.

Edward made it clear he thought it best if I stayed away, though of course, not in so many words. Nothing direct.

'Mother is coming to us for Christmas,' he said, way back in November. He's developed a new layer of pomposity in his tone. 'What are your plans?'

'Is that an invitation?' I said. I wouldn't have minded if he had given me a straightforward no.

'Nancy and I want a quiet family Christmas for the children,' was what he said. And there's no room in it for a pregnant cow who can't keep her mouth shut, I took that to mean.

We are not talking about it.

It.

I mean what I have done to Faith. Edward will not be drawn on the subject, he has written me off. Mad, bad, dangerous Maddie. It's for the best that I didn't go to Edward's. I don't want to be around his disapproval or Faith's chilly eyes.

After what happened at Stonebank I wrote to Faith, tried to explain that I hadn't meant to hurt her. In her reply she didn't even acknowledge the contents of my letter, she simply wrote, as she always does, of the latest events: Brian is having a new kitchen installed at Stonebank and James has settled well at school. Not the slightest reference to my visit or to what I said. I could see her sitting at her kitchen table writing it, occasionally looking up at the stone outcrop on the valley side. I've spoken to her on the phone; she is frosty, more distant than ever. There is no question of broaching the subject. There is only so much I can do, I must keep energy in reserve for the birth, a month to go. And there's the exhibition. I have sent both Edward and Faith an invitation to the private view. I put a note in Faith's saying I hoped she would come, but I could perfectly well understand that she might not want to. What more can I do, short of never having been born. This is me; this is what I was dealt; this is how I have dealt with it.

I spoke to her on her birthday, the twenty-first, shortest darkest day of the year. I thought about Stella pregnant with Faith, at the cold, dark end of the year, walking to Bagshott's to take Frank's hot dinner, heavy with Faith, Irene trailing along at her side. I wonder if Stella was happy, waiting for another baby to be born. I suppose she wouldn't have had time to sit and wonder. As I talked to Faith on her birthday it was difficult to believe that she had ever been a baby snuggling up to Stella's breast. It was a brief, clipped call.

'Happy birthday,' I said.

'Thank you for the gift.' I had sent a silk scarf.

'What are doing today?'

'The same as I always do.'

'Is Edward coming over?'

'No, he's coming tomorrow to collect me for Christmas. I expect you'll be having a quiet time,' she said. We're pretending that the reason I'm not coming to Edward's for Christmas is because of the baby even though there is a month to go.

'Well, happy birthday anyway,' I said.

'I have to go,' she said, something was boiling over in the kitchen.

Today, she will watch as William and James open their presents, Nancy will be busy in the kitchen. Faith will offer to help at every turn. This will make Nancy tense. I will call them later, if they don't call me.

Since Hal has squeezed this juice specially, I'd better drink it. It tastes good, fresh and clean. I lie back, see the sky through the roof window; a hard, bright blue winter sky. I swing my feet out of bed, rest a moment before standing. There's a tightness in the small of my back. I make my way to the window, open the curtains. There has been a heavy frost; the rooftops are coated in a crisp white frosting, the ground looks hard. As I stand there I notice clouds are coming in, grey clouds heavy with something; I hope it's snow. I would like everything to be covered in snow, for the world to go quiet, for me to stay folded inside for a while.

I think of Dom in Bristol. What kind of a Christmas will he have? Will they spend all day at the bedside in the hospice, or will they make some attempt at festivities back at the house? I am tempted to call him, a quick call on the new mobile phone, to wish him merry Christmas. I could, but I won't. I could open Dom's present but it's downstairs beneath the tree. Hal says presents must wait until after the feast.

'Shall I open it now?' I said, as Dom gave me the gold-wrapped box two days ago, on his way to Bristol.

'If you want to,' he said.

'I think I'll wait,' I said. 'Otherwise what will I have on Christmas Day?' I got the impression he wished I had opened it while he was there.

It's always been hard for me to give Dom presents. I have to give him something which he might have bought himself so Tessa won't remark. A book is what I usually buy. Or I don't buy him anything but plan a surprise, a day out or dinner somewhere we'd never normally go. This year, I've bought him a very practical present which I gave him early, a month ago in fact, so Tessa would really think he'd bought it himself. A mobile phone. I need to ring him when the baby comes. I need to have access to him. He still hasn't told Tessa. I don't know if it's because he hasn't tried, or because circumstances have prevented him; I'm trying to give him the benefit of the doubt. He bought me one, a mobile phone. It's come to this, I thought, buying each other hardware, the one cancels the other out. Then he dropped round with the surprise, wrapped up in gold paper. He stayed for something to eat but he didn't drink because he had the long drive to Bristol ahead of him. I was slouched on the sofa with my feet up. I could tell he was getting ready to go. He had that awkward look about him; torn between two lives, two sets of responsibilities. The baby moved.

'Look,' I said, lifting up my T-shirt. On the tight mound of my belly, smooth as an egg, there appeared a slight irregularity; a heel maybe, or a hand. No longer waving but trying to find its way out. Dom put his hand on the place, smiled as he felt the kick. I've been so horny, these last couple of weeks; big fecund creature, that I am, more animal than human sometimes, I think, all instinct and wanting. There was a moment last week at the studio when I almost went along the corridor to ask Patrick if he wouldn't mind. The light touch of Dom's hand on my skin and I was ready for him with a force that surprises me now when I think of it. Dom leaned down to kiss me. I was too big, too awkward to move suddenly, but I raised myself up to his kiss, reached to undo his jeans. I slid gently off the sofa, turned and knelt with my head in the soft cushion. He eased himself inside me with long tender strokes.

In the kitchen, Hal is checking his timetable which is taped to the wall by the cooker.

'Midday: potatoes to top of oven, baste turkey, uncork claret.'

'Are you sure there isn't anything I can do?' I say.

'Look after yourself and baby. Here,' he hands me a cassette of Christmas carols. 'Go have your bath, listen to these.'

'Can't I set the table or something?'

'All done. I've set it up in the room with the tree. You're

not to go in there,' he says. 'You're meant to be having a rest remember? Maddie, you've been working flat out. Go have your bath.'

'All right.'

'Before you go, got any of those little ramekin dishes? I need somewhere to put my chopped almonds.'

'I'm not sure,' I say. 'Try the cupboard next to the fridge.'

I turn both taps full on. I don't really want the ambient Christmas music, I hope Hal isn't offended. Hal is right, of course, I have worked so hard these last two months, every day at the studio, to be ready on time. It's all gone to Liverpool; Transart came to take it away, the day after Faith's birthday. Between us we packed the work, grouping the fragments of glass into small boxes, labelling them, then packing those boxes into larger wooden crates. The word F R A G I L E was stencilled on the side of each crate. This made me smile. It's already broken, I thought. When life starts up again in the new year, I will unpack it with the art handlers at The MCA. I am pleased with what I have done, I don't know what others will think, but it's the best I could do with the material in the time. I worked day after day, my fingers became hardened against the rough glass. Fine flakes of glass littered the studio floor, I wonder if some of them have sunk beneath my skin, seeped into my veins, even now maybe moving towards my heart.

I test the water with my hand. Too hot. I run more cold. The light is changing. The sky is grey now, the hard bright light was short-lived, there is very little daylight left. I ease myself into the water.

Something has shifted in me.

I have a story.

All right, it's full of holes and I'm not clear what is real, what is imagined. It is a myth, a myth of my making. I will offer my child this myth. I would rather have been given a half-formed myth than a deathly hush, the heavy drape of curtains drawn against the light.

I realise that I have forgotten to tie up my hair; too late, it's wet. I dunk my head under the water, lather up the shampoo.

I wish I could have gone away for Christmas. This time last

year I was in New York with Annie and Jack. Cold windswept streets, overheated bars and stores. I'm too fat to fly, too far gone. The good news is that Annie is coming in February. There was a note with her Christmas card. Her flight is booked. She's coming alone for ten days, her first time away from the twins. *I'm excited but scared too,* she wrote. *Don't be late, Maddie. I do hope you've had the baby by the time I come. I don't think they would let you go so far over. Anyway, that's what I'm counting on. Remember, it's all in the breathing.* She will see the exhibition when she visits her parents. I would love to talk to Annie right now, but they will be asleep. We will talk tonight, something to look forward to at the end of the day.

I remember once when Annie and I were about ten or eleven, it was near Christmas and I was sleeping over at her house. Annie's grandma was there for Christmas, her mum and dad were going to a dinner dance. Her mother wore a plum-coloured velvet dress with a matching bag. The bag was like a pouch, a silky cord with tassels pulled the pouch tight; a Dorothy Bag, was what Annie's grandmother called it. The next day Annie and I tried on her mother's shoes; we opened her wardrobe and touched the velvet dress. The Dorothy Bag was on her dressing table. We loosened the cord, watched the dark hole widening on to a crimson satin lining. Inside was a compact, a lipstick, a tortoiseshell comb and the smell of lavender. Last night I dreamed about a bag like that one. In the dream, I opened the bag, eased apart the tight neck, exposed the crimson lining; a tiny hand, then an arm emerged, waving. The skin was delicate, transparent, and I could see thread-fine veins, red and blue. Not yet, I said, not yet. I shouldn't have looked inside, I shouldn't have opened the bag. Not yet. I tucked the hand back inside the bag, carefully pulled the cord, closed the pouch tight.

I rub bath oil on my belly and wonder what it's like for you in there. It's getting tighter, there can't be much space for you now. A dark, red room; warm, wet space. Soft walls expanding to accommodate you. I think of you feeling your way, nudging the folds and crevices. There's a place where you can lay your head, the folds will yield, down you go along a tight tunnel with a light at the end of it. Out you'll come to a bright, dry place where you breathe air not water. I think of you upside-down, getting ready to push through the folds. Upside-down waiting to go from inside out.

I wrap myself in a warm towel, perch on the edge of the bath. I've done what Monique suggested, I eat fresh pineapple most days and drink raspberry-leaf tea. I'll try anything. Monique has gone to Mauritius for Christmas, to be with her family.

'Not seen my mother for five years,' she said.

'You will come back?' I said, at my last check-up before she went. I've come to believe in Monique. With Monique around I believe I can do this impossible task, without her, I'm not so sure.

'Don't you worry,' she said, palpating my belly, checking on your position, listening to your heartbeat through a funnel that was cold on my skin.

'Anyway even if I'm here you might not get me.' She keeps reminding me that there are others, she's part of a team. I've met Crystal and Jo, lovely women, but I want Monique.

'When are you back?' I asked again, though she's told me several times.

'Fifth of January and the first thing I'm going to do when I come on duty is call you,' she said, laughing.

'I'll be in Liverpool,' I said. I go up on the third; that's when we begin to install the exhibition. I gave her my mobile number.

'You take care, no lifting,' she said.

'There will be others to do that,' I said. I think of Monique at home in Mauritius, tropical hot, basking in the warmth of her family, not seen for five years. She's probably dreading coming back to grey London.

I try not to think of Faith's eyes as she turned on me in the kitchen at Stonebank. I try not to mind as I recall the chill that swept over me. As I stood there, watching her eyes fix and chill, I tried to think of her. Faith, who had had enough mother-love to know how to be a mother herself, but the heat was removed suddenly, she cooled too quickly. There is a cut-off point, internal stress, if you get too close. Faith, the child with the mother-heat removed too quickly. I tried to think what it must have been like to see your mother walking up the street with the bags already heavy when you thought she was going shopping. I tried to see it from her point of view which is why I reached out to hold her, to stop her falling down the steep valley side. I'm trying not to mind that she stiffened, wouldn't receive my touch, looked at me with those flawed, glass eyes.

'Hal, stop. I can't eat another thing.'

He lays a plate of his hand-made chocolate truffles on the low table in front of me. As he stands up he catches his head on one of the low-slung stars. When Hal finally let me in here, not only had he laid the table with a seasonal centrepiece from Wild At Heart and draped swags above the fireplace, he'd also hung silver-glitter stars from the ceiling on individual threads, dozens of them.

'I can tell you,' he said. 'It was much easier than tying up bits of broken glass.' Here and there a star is too low, we keep walking into them.

'Presents,' says Hal, going over to the tree, ducking to avoid the stars. He hands me a slim, flat rectangle.

'I know it doesn't look much, but I figured it's what you'll need, soon. Go ahead, open.'

I undo the white paper with golden cherubs flying all over it. Inside is a white envelope. Inside that, a token for a whole day at The Sanctuary.

'For after the baby and the exhibition. You need to be kind to your body.'

'Hal, if I could, I would get up and kiss you. Thank you so much. Marry me?'

'Please, Maddie, it would never work.'

'It would if you cooked for me like this every day.'

'The cooking would be the least of your worries married to me.' We laugh. Or, rather, I try not to, I don't have room enough inside me to laugh. I give him his present.

'Your turn,' I say.

'Let me guess,' he says, feeling the shirt-shaped parcel.

'Pretty obvious.'

'Well yes, but I don't know the colour do I?'

'Feeling the paper won't help you there.'

He opens it carefully, peeling back the Sellotape, not tearing the paper.

'Gorgeous,' he holds up the terracotta-pink shirt. 'Prada. Too extravagant, you shouldn't. Save your money for the baby.'

'You've kept me sane these last months. Thanks.'

He comes over, gives me a kiss on the cheek.

'You still have Dom's to open.'

I hesitate.

'He should be here,' I say.

'Did you two really exchange mobile phones?'

'I know, I know,' I say, holding up my hands. I do not want to talk about it.

Hal hands me the gold-wrapped box from under the tree.

'I'll save it,' I say. I want to open it later, alone. I will take it upstairs and open it before I go to sleep.

'Duty calls,' I say, trying to get up. 'I'm going to phone Edward, wish everyone, including Faith, a very Merry Christmas.' I need to do it now before I slump further into a stupor. As I haul myself up from the chair, the phone rings.

'Good,' I say. 'They've decided to ring me first.' I think seasonal thoughts: Peace on Earth, Goodwill to all men, including dear brother Edward.

'Hello, Merry Christmas,' I say, putting a smile into my voice.

'Maddie.'

'Dom?' The hesitant voice is not Edward, and I know before he says why he has rung.

'It's over,' he says, quietly. I can hardly hear him, the signal is patchy. 'He was peaceful, in his sleep.'

'I'm so sorry, Dom,' I say. 'How is everyone?' I can't bring myself to say, Tessa.

'Relieved, tired.' He says that Tessa is mainly relieved because she really didn't want him to go on living that way. But it's awkward, everything is shut down for Christmas and they all want to do something, to prepare for the funeral but they must wait until after Boxing Day. They are hoping to have the funeral on the third, the day I go up to Liverpool.

I wonder where Dom is on his mobile phone; detached, he could be anywhere.

'Where are you?'

'Out for a walk, down by the river,' he says.

I think of us in summer in Springfield Park.

There's a kind of grief I'd have to bear. It's the cutting off I dread.

I can't ask if he's told Tessa and Joe; there will always be a reason to postpone.

'When?' I say. 'When did it happen?'

'Last night.'

Of all the days in the year, to die on Christmas Eve, how sad. How sad for them all.

Aftershock 5

I sit in one of the deep window-seats looking out over the river. It is cold, grey, slightly foggy, I can barely see Birkenhead. I had hoped to go for a walk before the radio people come to interview me, but the fog is getting worse.

'All right?' says Jude appearing from nowhere. She must be taking a break from her meeting.

'I was thinking of going for a walk but it doesn't look good out there.'

'I'll be back in a minute,' she says on her way to talk to one of the art handlers.

The main gallery is buzzing with activity; they've done a great job. Three of them are working on the lighting today. There's a scaffolding tower on wheels with platforms at different levels; up and down they go patiently working along the lighting tracks, checking each unit, adjusting the angle of one, taking down those that aren't needed. The gallery has been transformed. I arrived a week ago to the smell of fresh paint; the decorators had painted the white walls dark blue, Prussian blue. Next, the art handlers put in place the three boxes they have made; we keep calling them boxes but they are each the size of a small room. Inside, I have hung my glass pieces, or rather they did the hanging, I directed. They have been patient with me in my lumbering state. They have lined or painted the walls inside the boxes to my specifications; all that remains to be done are the final adjustments to the lighting, to paint the lettering, fix up labels and text panels around the gallery. The outside of each box is also painted Prussian blue. A sign-writer is due later today to paint the titles on each one in silver-grey script.

Death of A Star.
Piece Work.
Aftershock.

Besides the three main new works there are two other pieces in here; a square block plinth holds the piece blown by Matt, and a table is laid with the loans from Featherbridge Museum.

There are two ways into this main gallery; if you come in one way what you see first is the plinth, also painted blue, on which sits the blown form, a large teardrop with surface irregularities. *Holding His Breath*, it is called. This teardrop sits, cushioned, on the folded apron I took from Stella. Viewed from the front it's simply an enigmatic object; make of it what you will. Round the back, I have used the plinth as a kind of information panel, giving facts about how glass was produced at Bagshott's when Frank was there, I have included a copy of the photograph of the Glassblowers Protection Society. So, I have both Frank and Stella in the exhibition. Also there are copies of the reports on the dispute, the filched glass and the girl who fell into the canal. On the third side of the plinth there is a picture of Matt blowing glass; on the fourth side I have listed the properties of glass from my earliest research.

Glass is a poor conductor of heat.
Glass may be transparent or opaque.
Glass is neither a solid nor a liquid; it is amorphous.
Glass becomes rigid when cooled but may be heated back to a liquid.
Glass must cool slowly from its molten state,
otherwise internal stresses occur. It might crack.
Glass has a memory. It remembers the actions performed on it.

If you come into the gallery through the other door, what you will see first is a table, spread with a linen cloth, set for four people using Bagshott's glass, borrowed from the Featherbridge Museum. It's the green-tinted range; sundae glasses in each place, a cake stand with embossed leaf pattern, sugar bowl, milk jug. The plinth and the table will be spotlit: work and home. In between are the three boxes, *Death of A Star, Piece Work, Aftershock*. I think of these now as dream boxes, desire boxes; somewhere beyond work or home.

In the two smaller galleries the walls are still white, hung with my earlier paintings.

In two days the exhibition will be open to the public. Perhaps no one will come. I've done what I can. I've more or less signed off now, it's up to the art handlers to have the gallery ready on time.

'It's fabulous,' says Jude. 'Are you all right to do the interview?'

'I'm as all right as I'll ever be,' I say. Kathy with the tangerine hair has fixed up an interview with local radio, they want to do a walk round the gallery, record something to go out tomorrow.

'Any news on the catalogue?' I say.

'It will be here by the opening, I am assured,' says Jude, teeth gritted. 'The printers shut down for two weeks over the holiday, it should have been here before they closed.'

'I'm going back to London as soon as I've done the interview,' I say. I need to catch up on things. I've got a check-up with Monique and I'm longing to see Dom. I've spoken to him once since the funeral. He sounds low.

'You'll be back for the press lunch on Friday?'

'Don't worry, I'll be here.' Jude looks anxious as if I might not come back. I'm travelling up first thing with Hal. We'll be here for the press lunch, then I get a break before the private view in the evening.

Jude squeezes my arm.

'Thanks, Maddie. It's stunning, it's going to attract a lot of attention.'

Maybe, but it's not the attention I was hoping for.

'Have you had lunch?' she says.

'I'm OK,' I say. 'I've got stuff to eat.'

'Kathy will be down soon, she'll look after you. I must go. See you on Friday.' She leans down, hugs me, kisses my cheek.

I move from the window-seat and squat with my back to the wall. I find this oddly comfortable, though I realise I must look clumsy; grotesque, perhaps, to the eyes of these young men. One of the art handlers, the one with dyed blond hair and black stubble, looks distinctly uneasy when I squat. He's looking at me now from atop the scaffolding tower, warily, as if I'm about to give birth, here in the gallery. I take out my packed lunch, like a school kid. I need my daily dose of pineapple. It's become an obsession. I buy one each evening on the way home, chop it up into cubes so I can munch on it all the next day. Today, I've brought the lot for my lunch. Meat tenderiser. Hal says I've gone too far with this, that whatever it is in the fruit that will soften my cervix will also rot my gums. I'm weighing it up: an easy birth versus losing my teeth. No contest, I munch away on my juicy cubes.

I've asked Kathy how local this local radio is. What I needed to know was: will it be heard in the suburbs of Manchester? Apparently it will. I asked because Faith is still at Edward's. She hasn't gone back to Stonebank after Christmas. She came down with flu on New Year's Day and has spent most of the last week in bed.

'I'm concerned,' said Edward, when I spoke to him last night. 'She doesn't seem to be getting any better.' He said her spirits were low, that she was not herself. I could hear the accusation in his voice. I think of Faith lying in her bed at Edward's and work hard not to let the old panic rise. I have hurt her so much that she might die, I think. I went through the old arguments with Edward; the loop that we go round and round. Even as I said my part I thought: Why bother?

'I didn't mean to hurt her,' I said.

'The basic flaw is your presumption that her life is hard, that she has this burden she needs to put down.'

'Something is wrong. Nobody who washes blankets the way Faith does is at ease.'

I remember the TV drama I watched in the B&B at Featherbridge; the dying father, the son who wouldn't come, wouldn't forgive. I've thought of going over to Edward's to sit at Faith's bedside, to beg for forgiveness. I think this is bordering on the melodramatic.

'Maddie have you got a minute?' says the boy with blond hair, down from the scaffolding. The sign-writer is here, wants to check exactly where the lettering should go. I press my back against the wall, it's easier that way for me to rise up to standing again.

'That's P-I-E-C-E, not P-E-A-C-E?' asks the sign-writer.

'Yes,' I say. If only.

It's also the title of the exhibition: *Piece Work*. We agree the height at which the letters should go. I look inside at the implied table setting, the bowls coming together or falling apart. For Faith, they are falling apart.

'And Aftershock – one word not two?'

'Yes.' The wave, the gathering water that needs to crash, to play itself out. Something starts small, a ripple, it grows. Great-uncle Stan, Stan Kelsall in a war he couldn't bear, came home, lost his concentration and his leg. Did the wave start to gather with the war, with the loss of the leg or even farther back, beyond my memory span? Stan made Stella's future, pulled her back from the future she'd made with Frank. She'd bettered herself; glassworks, a cut above the pit. Stella turned her back on the glassworks and her children, going to the shops with her bags already full, she made a future for Faith. Faith, curious about why her mother would go to the shops with the bags already full and not come back, busied away the awful questions, busied all thoughts from her mind. Even though she polished, scrubbed, washed, bleached, the questions weren't rubbed out, they didn't go away. Sometimes I think I inherited her questions as well as my own. A double dose of curiosity.

The sign-writer clearly doesn't want me hanging around watching him. I go back to the window-seat, think again about going for a walk by the river, but the fog is even worse. Also, when I took a walk down there this morning, I saw something that disturbed me. I went to get some air after our 'final arrangements' meeting, it was brighter then. I strolled along by the water's edge. A man appeared with a girl, his daughter I presumed. They were hurrying along the cobbled walkway by the smart new railings, past the signs which say: *Deep water, Strong Currents*. He was angry, she was distressed. He wore a smart winter coat. She was in school uniform. It was late for the start of school. Perhaps that was why he was angry, though it seemed out of proportion for such a small thing. I couldn't fathom it. He shouted at her. I couldn't hear for the wind and the slap of water but I could see the force of his words, as he stopped and turned on her; the body effort he put into the words: powerful, dark, adult rage raining down on a small girl. Her body shook, tears came. She didn't speak, but her body shrieked: Why? She stood before him, every cell of her being saying: Stop, what have I done? It was the way her shoulders hunched forward, the tension across her back, asking: Hug me, hold me, make it stop. He turned, said nothing, walked on, long, male strides propelled by rage. Does he not know how indelible his rage will be? Does he not know that she is standing on the edge of a bottomless pit. She stumbled, ran to keep up with him, the void getting closer, her feet on the edge. No pride now, only the desperation of survival. She reached for his hand, begged for it; the only way to stop falling into the darkness.

I will never know what really happened, inside that house at Featherbridge, the precise detail is beyond reach, though some of it is as close as Faith's memory. It might as well be as far off as the oldest, deadest star in the universe. An ordinary household, two little girls, a tired, angry, working man. I've looked at his photograph so many times. What kind of man was he? Sad, angry, defeated by his stubbornness, or was he cruel, violent?

I have a story, more of a story than I've ever had. The trouble with stories of real lives is that other people inhabit them and they have different versions. There is pain, sadness in the space between my version and Faith's silence. Nothing else will come of this. I have done too much already, I can do no more. I know that something has shifted inside me, something has eased, though other things make me uneasy. I will let go of the idea that Faith wants an easier life. She has the life she wants. *She's not asking for this.* Unconsoled or inconsolable? Me or Faith? Faith's cold eyes are the cost of her survival, this is how she learned to survive, this is as far as she can go, too quickly cooled. Any more might be the death of her, too much pressure on the inside.

'Say what you had for lunch,' suggests the producer holding

the microphone towards me. 'I need to check for sound.' He's so young, sixteen I would have said, though he must be older, he seems to know what to do. He's friendly but a bit frantic. They have to interview some pop star at Speke Airport, so they want me done, quick.

'Fresh pineapple,' I say.

'Can you say a bit more?'

'That's all I had. I wanted to go for a walk along the river but the weather was bad and . . .'

'Good, fine. OK let's start.'

This is for the arts slot on a local magazine programme. The presenter will ask me questions, she has a bright radio voice with a trace of a Liverpool accent; it sounds trendy, smart, but she looks homely in her old jeans and thick purple sweater.

She does her introductory spiel, a description of the gallery and the new work.

'We're standing here next to the one called *Piece Work,*' she says to the microphone, giving the sign-writer a wide berth.

I'm glad of the session I had with Chrissie Deeds. I have an answer now for most things that get thrown at me.

'It's a common experience, an ordinary one,' I say. 'Something gets broken, something which matters. There are intense feelings. Turbulence. I hope the work is about giving a shape to the turbulence, seeing something you wouldn't necessarily see but feel, I suppose.'

'These are very dramatic works, beautiful but quite unnerving at the same time,' she says. 'I understand that you've been here a week now, Maddie, painstakingly installing these fragments of broken glass. Don't you mind that in two months' time it will all be taken down again? It seems ephemeral for something so carefully made.' She looks genuinely distressed at the thought that the boxes will be dismantled.

'It's like putting on a drama, a performance. It can be restaged,' I say. 'What matters to me is that I made it. I've pictured these things in my head for a long time. Now they are out there.'

'I understand that this glass was possibly made by your grandfather and has been in your family for some time. Did you break it, can you tell us the story of how it was broken?'

I think of Faith in her fever, dozing under the duvet, listening to this. I might kill her.

'The details of my life, my family, aren't the point. It's not about my story,' I say, rather too hastily, too well-rehearsed.

'What do you hope visitors to the exhibition will experience?'

'I hope people will think about their own stories; their own moments of breakage, or repair.' I have explored and imagined the lives and events that accumulated around these things. I have done what I can, made something with what I was given. I think of Faith, who might be listening; perhaps I have made this work for an audience of one and that one person will never see what I have made. I am learning to live with this; the consolation, if there is one, is that I had the privilege of making it.

'Let's look at the piece called *Aftershock*.' She describes my cresting glass wave for the listeners. 'What can you tell us about this?'

'Things happen in families, all families, ordinary families. Someone decides to put the lid on it. It may be nothing. But putting the lid on has an effect. A pressure builds over generations. When does the wave break? When is it played out?' I now know the answer: probably never. All that happens is that as one wave crashes another is building up, other areas of turbulence, rumbling.

'Before we go,' says the presenter indicating that I should follow her, 'let's talk about this piece.' We stand before *Holding His Breath*, she reads facts about glass from my list. This liquid-solid stuff has shaped us all, three generations. It has brought out extremes: molten hot, brittle cold.

'And this, I believe, is your grandfather,' she points to Frank's photo.

'No,' I say. 'Turn that off. I mean I'm not talking about that on air. You'll have to cut that.'

Don't die, Faith, please don't die. *You're so destructive*.

'Oh, right. Well, I think we've got enough. Thanks.' They look at me warily as they pack up and prepare to meet the pop star. I'll be old news by the end of the week, if I even make it that far.

'I think that went all right,' says Kathy who has been hovering in the background. 'Great coverage.'

Covered. Exposed.

Making Waves 5

'He said he would try to be here, but it's awkward,' I shrug. It's difficult to explain how many obstacles Dom would have to cross to arrive in time to see Monique. 'He might not come.'

'It would be nice to meet him once, you know, if he's going to be at the birth,' she says.

'Have you time for a coffee?' I say, hoping Dom will make it before she leaves. She's busy, has a full case-load. I am one of many, though to me, at the moment, she is unique.

'A quick one,' she says.

I make coffee for her and a pot of raspberry-leaf tea for me. We sit at the kitchen table.

'Unusual, all these pots,' she surveys Annie's shelves.

'Not mine.'

'I don't know how you can drink that stuff,' she laughs as I pour my brew.

'I drink it because you recommended it,' I say.

'I recommend it, yes, but I don't know how you drink it, awful.'

'It's all right with a slice of lemon. Anyway, I'll try anything.'

'Nothing to worry about. Your blood pressure is fine, you're in good health. Baby's head is well down. Not long now. Have you got your bag packed?'

'Not yet.'

'Do it, Maddie. You'll get in a flap if you go into labour and haven't got what you need. You've got the list from the hospital?'

'Yes.'

'Take my advice: ear plugs. Most important things to pack are fresh nighties, your wash things and ear plugs.'

'Ear plugs?'

'It's noisy on the ward and you need your sleep more than anything.'

'I could ring him,' I say as Monique looks at her watch. I don't really want to. I want him to come of his own accord, I don't want to ring Dom on his mobile and beg him to come and meet Monique.

'I have to go, five minutes at the most,' she says. 'Is there anyone else who can be with you, at the birth? A friend, your mother?'

My mother.

I try to picture it: me labouring, heaving and howling, Faith mopping my brow, rubbing my back, urging me on.

'My mother's not well,' I say, as if that is all that stands in the way of her being there at my side. 'I have a friend who could be there.' Dear Hal, he said he would do it if that's what it took, but I think being around a labouring female would push our friendship to the limit. 'I could pace,' he said. I see me and Monique in the natural birthing room, me sprawled across the bean bag, the ambient sound of whale cries, and Hal in the corridor pacing, his stoop at its most pronounced.

'Don't worry. Whoever else turns up, you and me will be there,' she laughs. As Monique puts on her coat there's a ring on the doorbell.

'Just in time,' she says, ready to take her coat off again.

I go to let him in, relieved he's made it.

'Sign here, love,' the postman hands me a jiffy bag.

'Wrong man,' I say walking back into the kitchen. I put the package on the table.

'Sorry he's missed you,' I say. 'It really is quite difficult and . . .'

'You don't have to explain, I see all sorts in this job. Your situation is more common than you think, believe me. You're going to get some support from him aren't you?'

'Yes.' I think so, I hope so.

'Well, as long as he doesn't abandon you, he doesn't have to meet me.'

'I'm sure he would have come if he could,' I say, not sure of anything as regards Dom.

'Weekly from now on,' she reminds me. 'See you next week. Maybe he will come with you then?'

'I hope so.'

I sit at the kitchen table, rip open the package. It's from The Museum of Contemporary Art, special delivery; out slides the catalogue. The cover is pleasing, a smooth matt surface, a detail from *Aftershock* is wrapped around. On the front, superimposed over the image, is my name in silver-grey letters, matt also, or rather, not quite shiny, not brash like Hal's Christmas stars. *Madeleine Armitage* say the letters that seem a touch too big, too much a proclamation of me. Beneath my name, in smaller type, it says: *Piece Work*, an apt title, I think. I flick through quickly, to look at the colour plates. They look good. Twenty years of work, edited and presented in a run of images, as if it was that easy, as if that was how they were always meant to be. They've put a shape on something which I know was more random, more chaotic. Looking at it all now, the work seems almost to have nothing to do with me. Perhaps there is another Madeleine Armitage in the world who made those images. I'm not sure I'm ready to read the text. I turn to Jude's introduction: *Madeleine Armitage shapes silence. Her work over the last twenty years has been a study of the effects of the unsaid, the unsayable.*

I don't get any further, the telephone rings.

'Hello?'

'Is she still there?' It's Dom on the mobile.

'She's just gone. You missed her,' I try to keep the edge out of my voice.

'I'm sorry,' he says.

I won't ask why.

'I'll be there in ten minutes, I'm coming anyway,' he says.

'I'll put the kettle on.'

'I'm sorry,' says Dom, sitting in the chair vacated by Monique.

'Stop saying you're sorry.'

'She must think I'm some sort of shady character.'

'Well you are, aren't you?'

'Thanks.'

'She doesn't think anything. She's seen it all before, she says. Coffee?'

'I'll make it, you sit down.'

'I'm fine. Apparently the head is well down.'

'There's still over two weeks to the due date, though?' He's working out how much time he's got left to tell Tessa. An impossible pressure. He knows that, he doesn't need me to remind him, to turn the knife.

'How are things, how's Joe?' I want to know what's going on at home. I need to know. It's Tessa he tells me about first, even though it was Joe I asked after. Tessa is relieved. He says she's been grieving for her father all autumn, she's relieved, almost high on it. She's talking of handing in her notice, again.

'I think she might do it this time,' he says.

'And Joe?'

Joe has been working all hours at a brasserie in Camden Town. He's worked for three months but they've cut him down to weekends only now the Christmas rush is over. He's planning to go to Vietnam. Dom is uneasy; Joe says: Dad, it's country, not a war. Once his visa comes through, he's off. He'll be away until March then back to work for the resit. Dom's worried in case Joe won't ever go to university; he's had the taste of earning money.

'He can earn money babysitting his little sister,' I say. I regret it as soon as it's out. These days I can't help myself; if I think it, I seem to say it.

Dom's face goes still, he says nothing. He ignores what I've said.

I know why I have said it. I want him to confirm that he still hasn't told them. I could ask outright, but I think he ought to tell me. I know he hasn't told Tessa and Joe. First, it was Joe's results, and working out what he would do. We agreed, November he would tell them, before Christmas. 'November, it's a neutral time of year,' he said at the time. Then Tessa's father went into the hospice, and before you know it we're into December when all normal life ceases; out of neutral and into emotional top gear. Part of me knows it's only reasonable that he hasn't told them yet, that it's been genuinely difficult, that circumstances have prevented him. Dom can hardly sit down with his wife and son in the midst of all that's happened to them and say: Here's something else for you to contend with. Yet underneath all the reasonable explanations, I know that he's avoiding the moment. *There's a kind of grief I'd have to bear*. And haven't they all enough grief to bear?

He's trying to keep going as we have always done. He wants to keep the compartments watertight. He can't bear to hurt Tessa and Joe, can't go through the grief, but until they feel it, we'll all be stuck on the other side of it, waiting for it to happen. Not hurting Tessa and Joe hurts them anyway; hurts me, and soon our child. It's as if he's waiting for the perfect conditions to minimise the hurt. What does he expect: a perfect day when Tessa and Joe are brimming with happiness. Wouldn't telling them hurt even more on such a day? But he's here. He's not run away, yet. He talks about the baby. I want my child to know its father. The rest, I don't know. We'll see.

'Dom, I know, given what's happened, I know all the reasons, but I need to know: am I expecting too much, will you be there?'

He goes very quiet, there is a strained look again, a look that is becoming too familiar, too much part of him. I don't want to be the cause of it. There are more lines around his eyes, his skin is winter pale, almost grey. He's lost weight. He says nothing.

'Say if you can't. I need to know, either way. I need to prepare myself.'

'I want to be there,' he says.

'If you can't, Hal says he'll come,' I say this too quickly, trying to make him envious. I know why I've said it. If he thinks another man will be there, I hope, at some primitive level this will make him come. Ridiculous.

'I want to be there. I'm working on it,' he says.

How? I want to ask, but don't.

'I can't time it for when you have a chance to slip away.'

'I know, and you must call me, whatever time it starts.'

We both know that it's pointless to say any more. There's no point in fighting.

He picks up the exhibition catalogue.

'This is it?'

'It's only just arrived.'

He looks through it, carefully stopping at each section.

'I'd like to read it.'

'I'll get you a copy.'

'It's a marvellous achievement, Maddie,' he says, smiling, looking more relaxed.

'Shame you can't come to the opening,' I say.

'I know,' he says. We've already discussed this. It's not just home, it's work too. It's impossible for him to be there.

'You know I'll see the exhibition. I'll go up as soon as I can. We could have a night in a hotel.'

'You, me and the newborn?'

'Before the birth.'

'That's in two weeks,' I say. He's in denial.

'Anyway, you'll be busy talking to all the right people at the opening. My presence will be superfluous. It's the work I want to see, not the hangers-on.'

'Apparently there's interest from Berlin, there was a message yesterday when I got back from Liverpool. Hal was right, he's so excited.'

'That's great.'

'And his American collectors are in town.'

'You must be pleased.'

'I am at one level but there's still Faith.'

'How is she?'

'About the same. I'm going to call Edward tonight.'

If only Faith was all right. Making this work has brought me a kind of relief, but at what cost if it's hurt Faith?

He looks through the run of images.

'Seeing it all like this, you know, what strikes me is your discretion.'

'What do you mean?'

'There is a quiet intensity to these images, they don't scream at you, they don't obviously attack Faith or anyone. Isn't that in your head?'

'Maybe.'

'I was thinking about you and the glass; it's like forensic work. Memory, identity, who we are. The glass pieces are eloquent, moving. I think they will speak to many people.'

'Not to Faith.'

'Will you give her one of these?'

'I'd like to, but Edward thinks I should leave her alone.'

He flicks through to the sources section.

'I see they used it.'

'Yes.' We look at the reproduction of Faith and Irene, with their backs to the wall, a lifetime still to come. Faith with her scowl, her own difficult daughter not yet born.

'I'm trying to think how I would feel if Joe did . . .'

'Found the secret in your past?'

'Don't. What I mean is, I'm trying to think how I'd feel if Joe showed that much interest in me, I'd be flattered, I suppose, proud.'

'It's not the same. Faith feels attacked, invaded.'

'She is what she is,' he says and moves off into history professor mode, talks about the trauma of a war, how it takes time to work through it, how it needs to be shared out. Stan did what he could, went back to work in the pit, but he just wasn't the same. Stella did what she had to; went back to her damaged brother. Frank, angry Frank, could he have done otherwise? Faith did what she could, created a safe place in the ordinary routine of daily tasks. What else can we do but work with what we have at the time? Dom turns to the full-page spread of *Aftershock*. I tell him what I was thinking yesterday, how the wave is never played out; even as one dies down another is forming.

'Knowing what I know of Frank and Stella, it explains a lot, I don't know it all, but the fear is less.' The wave has played out some of its energy, but I'm still curious to know what kind of man Frank was.

'Are you worried about the opening?'

'I'm more worried about Faith and getting this baby out of me. It matters that I made this work. What people think of it can't take that away. Of course I'll mind if I get a bad review but I can't worry about it.'

'I have a feeling it will go well,' he says, flicking through the catalogue.

'You know I had that dream again,' I say. 'The one I've told you about before, the tooth dream.' I've had this dream for as long as I can remember. In the dream I have a loose tooth, I can feel it rocking in my gum, hanging on by a thread. I can't speak in case it falls out. I close my mouth, clamp my jaws, top teeth holding lower teeth in place, hoping the pressure of tooth on tooth will hold it in. Any moment, I think, it will fall, leave a wide, dark hole burrowing deep into my jaw. I will fall into my own jaw, disappear.

'Usually I wake up, relieved that all my teeth are in place. Last night it was different. It came out.'

'What, you've lost a tooth?'

'No, don't be daft. I mean in the dream. In the dream the tooth came out, I didn't fall in the hole and I didn't mind.'

I see Dom to the door, he's teaching this afternoon. He has to go.

'I'll be there if I can,' he says, before I can ask, which isn't quite good enough. I would like him to say with certainty that he will be there.

'We're creating another wave,' I say. He looks puzzled. 'With this baby, a new wave starts here.' We won't know how it gets played out. He says nothing, gives me an affectionate kiss on the mouth and opens the door. I watch him walk up the street and I think: With or without you, Dom, I will tell this child everything. The next time I see him, I could be holding our baby.

As he climbs in his car I wonder if the pressure of being caught between two families is too much to bear. Will he be like Stella, drawn back to the familiar? Or will he walk away from it all? You read about people who go out for a packet of cigarettes and never come back.

Don't be silly, Dom doesn't smoke.

A Private View

'You were great,' says Hal. 'Now, rest time. Come on.'

He ushers me out of the gallery, protective as a mother hen. We make our way up to the room next to Jude's office where I've dumped my stuff.

I've just done another interview, this time I was filmed. It's for *Weekend Review*, going out tomorrow night with Isolde Maddox, live in the studio, pronouncing on my fate. I hope they kept the camera to head and shoulders, I don't want to see my bulk filling the TV screen. I'm not needed now until the private view.

It is a relief to be in this bare room, the same room where we had the meeting back in May.

'Feet up, can I get you anything?' says Hal.

'Chips.'

'Chips?'

'I would love chips in newspaper with salt and vinegar.'

'Ugh.'

'Please, Hal, there must be a chippy round here somewhere.'

'I'll do what I can, all right.' And off he goes. I hang up the silk shirt which I will wear tonight. I thought I'd better make an effort. I drape it round the back of a chair, it's not as creased as I thought it would be. It's a beautiful dark blue, generously cut, it ripples around the bulge.

I sit down at the conference table, pull out another chair on which to rest my feet. When I think about that meeting back in May it might have been in another lifetime.

'Chippy schmippy,' says Hal, the smell of chips follows him through the door.

'That was quick.'

'These are from the café downstairs. Here, I found this.' He hands me today's *Guardian*. 'If you must.'

'Thanks, Hal, the plate is fine.'

'I'm off to Lime Street now to meet the Rosenbergs,' he says. The Americans. They are coming early because they need to be back in London this evening.

'You look the part,' I say. He's wearing the shirt I bought him for Christmas. 'It looks good.'

'Doesn't it just. Hey, what's with the gloomy face? Didn't I get you chips?'

'Yeah, thanks. It's just the thought of all those people coming this evening,' I say. And those who will not come.

'This is going to be a great success. Listen, it's a success already. Eat your chips. I've got to go. Bye.' He gives me a peck on the cheek. Lately Hal and I are more married than most married couples.

Success. Here, maybe, but utter failure as far as Faith is concerned. These chips are not bad, a bit on the thin side. I wanted real chips, thick cut. Faith was good at chips. I can see her now plunging the basket of chunky potato sticks into hot fat. They sizzled, fat bubbling up to the edge of the pan. At least she seems to be getting better, I haven't literally killed her. I spoke to Edward last night. He said she was improving, had been up all day and had eaten well.

'When is she going back to Stonebank?' I asked.

'There's snow up there at the moment.'

He didn't say a word about the exhibition, didn't even wish me good luck for the opening. Not a word.

'I'll be up in Liverpool again tomorrow for the private view,' I said to remind him. 'I could come over on Saturday, before I go back to London.'

'I don't want Mother to be disturbed.'

'I mean to visit, bring a bunch of grapes.' You'd think I was the mad axe man.

He didn't say a thing. That's what gets to me, he didn't say: Yes, all right if you must. Or: No, I'd rather you didn't. He just ignored my suggestion.

I'm hanging on to the fact that I have not literally killed her. She is coming back to life, to full health.

There's a knock at the door.

'Come in,' I say.

'Hope I'm not disturbing you,' it's Jude's secretary. 'This came for you.' She hands me a fax. It's from Annie. It's typed, letters as large as they can go: *Good Luck. See you soon. Can't wait. Much love, Annie*. It's over a year since I've actually seen Annie, which must be the longest time ever that we haven't physically met. She's the sister I never had. Let's say she's the sister I would have chosen if there were such a thing as choice in these matters. If Annie had been here, I wonder if I would have done things differently; Faith and the glass, I mean. I think about Annie and me walking to school; a railway track ran parallel to the road for part of the way. There was a high fence and a sign that read: TRESPASSERS WILL BE PROSECUTED. There was a loose plank in the fence and we would squeeze through and stand on the embankment, a steep slope down to the track. At first we thought it bold enough to have gone beyond the fence. We would crouch amongst the willow herb and brambles waiting for the express to pass. As our confidence grew we would go further down, closer to the line, still hiding in the weeds but close enough to see metal wheels on metal track, or a face at a carriage window. One day we stepped over the border of nettles and stood right at the edge of the track. Fifty yards on there was a tunnel; not very long, you could see the light at the other end. We walked along the track to the tunnel entrance, stared into the gloomy arch, blackened sandstone that smelled old and damp.

'Dare you,' I said to Annie.

'What?'

'It would only take a minute, we would soon be out the other side.'

She weighed this up.

'But we'd have to come back again.'

'What do you mean?'

'There might not be a loose board in the fence at the other side of the tunnel.'

I hadn't thought it through. I just knew we could do it, wanted so badly to do it, would have done it if I had been alone.

It scares me to think how wrong I was; the moment before I spoke, said the words in Faith's kitchen at Stonebank, I felt sure, confident that she would want to hear what I had to say. There was no one to pull me back, to tap me on my shoulder and say: Think again, there is no way out on the other side. I pushed Faith into a tunnel with no way out. I made her go in there; I hope she can get back.

'I shouldn't, but I will,' I say as I'm offered a glass of white wine by Kathy. I didn't recognise her at first, her hair is no longer tangerine; she has dyed it blue, the colour of the gallery walls. I don't like to ask why. We are standing in the foyer where drinks have been laid out. Ward Joffitt is wearing a suit.

'Ready for this?' he says, helping himself to red wine.

'I think so.' I must be nice to him. 'Thanks, for the catalogue. You've done a good job.' It won't hurt to be generous, I might never see him again.

'Thanks.'

'I thought if we stayed down here for the first half hour, you know, meet and greet. Would that be all right?' says Jude, looking chic in skin-tight black, head to toe. 'Do you need a chair?'

'I'm all right at the moment,' I say.

'Then we'll move up to the gallery for speeches after six. Where's Hal?' says Jude.

'He's gone to the station with the Rosenbergs.' I hope he's back soon. My nearest and dearest. There won't be many people who I know here tonight. Some of the team from college said they would try to make it, but Liverpool on a Friday evening is not easy for those unused to life outside of the M25. There will be people I worked with from the college here. Annie's mum and dad were going to come but he's down with the flu. I gave Dom an invitation and part of me still clings to the fantasy that he'll have found a way to do it, he'll walk through that door at any moment. Dream on.

People appear from nowhere, coming into the bright foyer from the dark. The security guard opens the front door, lets them in.

'Here we go,' says Jude.

As the applause dies down the hum of a hundred chattering

voices builds up again. The crowd breaks up as people go back down for a drink. No drinks in the gallery means they are torn between the booze and the art. Right now the booze is winning. I am pleased that eyes are off me for a while. I don't quite feel like me, it's as if I am looking down on someone who might be me.

'Maddie,' Hal puts a hand on my elbow. 'There's someone just arrived. I think you should come.'

'Must I?' Even as I say the words I see where he's pointing.

Faith. Edward.

She has on her best winter coat, navy wool with a belt, she has a white scarf at her neck, bundled up against the January cold.

A lurching sensation moves through my body, beyond my control. I am in a lift going down too quickly.

'Mum?' I say. The voice is not mine. From miles away I hear Hal's voice, at his most charming and attentive.

'Did no one take your coat,' he says. 'Would you like me to take it for you?'

'She insisted,' says Edward.

'No thank you. I'm fine,' Faith says to Hal.

We stand, stiff, awkward. I want to kiss her but daren't. It's not allowed. I daren't do anything. I'm standing at the mouth of the tunnel waiting for someone to tell me what the hell to do next. I think what Annie would do and a voice I don't recognise at all comes out of my mouth and says: 'I'm so glad you came. What a lovely surprise. Shall I show you round?'

'You look as if you need to sit down,' says Faith. She's right, of course, there is a dragging in the small of my back. I would like to lean against the wall, slide into a squat.

'Why don't you sit down,' she says again. 'I'll look round on my own.'

'I'll be over there,' I say, and make my way to the window-seat. I look out at the dark river. I've been caught, naked. Exposed. When I look back, I think, she won't be there. I have imagined this. It's the excitement. The drink. I shouldn't have had that second glass of wine.

When I do look, she is moving into the smaller galleries to look at the paintings. Now she's gone from view. I think of her looking closely at *Family Album*. Will she see her childhood self? Faith with her back to the door, never wanting to look behind, forward only. Stubborn little girl, her father's daughter. No difficult daughter of her own yet, no idea then that others might want to open the door.

She comes back into the main gallery to look at the new work, stops at the table laid with Bagshott's glass, deep in her thoughts. Her face gives nothing away. Does she feel like I do, as if in a dream, looking down on a version of herself? Her hand reaches out to one of the sundae glasses. She goes as if to put her finger on its rim, but stops short. She will have read the sign which says: PLEASE DO NOT TOUCH. I want to call out: It's all right, go on, touch it. She hesitates and for a second I think she will pick it up, hurl it at me. It's an ordinary, everyday object, a simple thing around which has gathered a story, scooped into its bowl, brimming up to the rim, an accumulation of memories too painful to be glimpsed in one moment. I'm afraid for her now; afraid of the rush of thoughts in her head; too much might tumble out too fast, thoughts swirling around these objects, images filling her head in no order, a chaotic deluge of things she thought were best forgotten.

Stan, Stella, Frank, Faith, Edward, me, the baby.

Lives separated by time and silence come together in the glass, held, for a moment, in one place. A place where we can look backwards and forwards. A present, a future, made out of the past, I hope. That is all I wanted to do. I didn't mean to hurt her.

What is she thinking? What does she know?

Frank the apprentice, waiting to marry Stella. Waiting for her brother to come home from the war. Stella is the woman Frank wants. He will wait. Stan back at work, not the same man. It's done in an instant, a leg spared in the war, lost in a lapse of attention. Frank finding the skill he's learned isn't wanted any more; machines can do what he can do, faster, cheaper. Angry Frank, wants to hold on to what he's worked for, waited for. *Things said, couldn't be gone back on. Pride is a terrible thing. Stubborn pride.* Faith learns to keep Frank's anger at bay. Takes his meals to the factory floor, fills the zinc tub on a Friday night, collects the glass to take to the canal when word goes out that the policeman will call. Angry Frank stops her. He's more than earned it. He filled his house with more glass than a family of three could ever need. Every day Faith set the table, then later she washed, polished, stacked it away. She never broke a single thing, not until, in another life, another place the telegram came to say that Stella was dead.

I watch Faith go in and out of each box in turn: *Death of A Star*, *Piece Work*, *Aftershock*. I try to read her face, she looks pinched, frightened. So much stored up, will she let it out, a drop, a slight oozing, or will it be a surge, a flood that will take us all with it? This is the moment before we drown.

I go to her.

'I'm sorry,' I say and try to hug her but my bulk gets in the way. She is awkward, not ready for this. *She's not asking for this.* She holds a hand up to me; it's not an aggressive gesture, not a reproach. I take it that she needs more time.

'I never meant to hurt you,' I say.

'You always did make too much of things, Madeleine,' she says, but the tone is not entirely harsh, more puzzled, as if to say: And it's beyond me why.

People are drifting back into the gallery, a final look at the exhibition before it closes. Jude is bringing a couple over to meet me. I nod to Hal, who all the time has kept a distance but also kept his eye on me; he goes to meet them.

'Is there somewhere we can go?' says Edward, who has been mute, baffled, throughout.

In the room by Jude's office, Faith sits down at the conference table.

'Can I get you anything, Mother?' asks Edward.

'I'd like a glass of water, I'm parched.'

She starts to talk, quietly, almost to herself. She won't look at me. She talks, staring out of the window at the dark river. Disjointed thoughts, that have been hidden for some time.

'She'd come on a Sunday. She brought things for us, clothes mainly, that she'd made. We weren't allowed to talk about her, not to him. He would stare into the fire. I learned to say nothing. I learned to do things for myself. It's the way I am.' She looks at me as she says this.

'Things change,' I say. 'You weren't on your own, you had Dad and us.'

'You get used to things. It's the way I am. I can't go over it all, not now. I've learned to live a certain way.'

'Look, I've had my say, down there in the work.'

'It's beautiful,' she says. It is the first time she has commented on my work directly. 'What I can't understand is why it mattered so much to you, it meant so much that you would make those things.'

'You're my mother,' I say. There are tears forming in her eyes, hot, molten tears. I want to ask her one more thing. If I don't ask now, I never will. If I do, the wave might crush us both, pound us to fragments.

'Frank,' I say, though it's not my voice. 'You don't have to say if you don't want to, but I imagine him as kind, hard-working, proud, stubborn. Is that how he was or have I got it wrong? Was he, well, cruel?'

She cries, an awful sound like a wounded animal, a baby lost from its mother, a gut-twisting cry.

'I'm sorry, I shouldn't have asked.' I go towards her.

'Both,' she says. 'He could be both. I don't want to talk about this again. Enough.' The sobs are loud, anguished, her face is wet, contorted. I see the door open slightly. Edward. I signal for him to move back into the corridor.

'Is she all right? What's going on?' His irritation is palpable.

'I think so.'

'Why have you done this?'

'You know why.'

'You'll make her ill again.'

'I don't think so. She's had a shock, but she's all right.'

'I hope so.'

'Stop this,' I say. 'Keep your voice down.'

I take the water from Edward and go back in, signalling that he should wait outside. I feel tears brimming in my eyes as I see her hunched into herself, howling. Who is the parent, who is the child? I am intently the parent of my mother at this moment, but also the bewildered, overwhelmed child.

I stand behind her, place the cup of water in front her. She takes a sip.

'Are you all right? Edward is here. Do you want to go home? Can I get you anything else?'

She says nothing for a while. Then the sobs subside.

'I would like to go now,' she says, and stands. She won't meet my eye. I go to hug her. I have to. I stand behind her, she can't see me but she must feel me there at her back. I lay my hands on her shoulders, a squeeze, a gentle touch to let her know I'm there. Not quite an embrace. She doesn't flinch, she doesn't stiffen but she doesn't slacken either. There is no reciprocation but neither is there the coldness of rejection. I think of the enormous effort this must be costing her, simply not to resist.

'Can I come in?' It's Hal, his worried face peeping round the door. I sit with my head on the table, sobbing, shaking.

'I think so,' I say between sobs.

'Have they gone?'

'She's gone back with Edward.'

'How was it?'

'I don't know, surreal. If you told me I'd imagined it, I'd believe you.'

'Here,' he fishes a handkerchief from his pocket, perfect pressed linen.

'Go ahead,' he says. 'It'll wash.'

'I'm sorry.'

'Jude's saying we should all go out to dinner. Are you up for that?'

'Oh God, I just want to sleep.'

He says he will talk to Jude. We're supposed to be staying at her house tonight. He will get the keys, take me there.

'Do you want anything, a drink?' he asks.

'No, thanks.'

He closes the door carefully as he goes.

The sound comes from inside me. Deep inside. I hear it through my body, a vibration rather than a sound in my ear. It is as if an elastic band has snapped. I feel a wetness, a warm gush between my legs.

Upside Down

The lights go on; I hear curtains being pulled back and a cheerful, encouraging voice. I open my eyes and see the nurse; a young woman with a tiny waist defined by a wide, black belt. She must be a different species entirely from me with my vast girth.

'How are you? Sleep all right?'

I nod.

She puts a thermometer under my tongue, winds fabric around my arm, fastens it tight, then squeezes the rubber ball.

'That's fine,' she says as she writes on the chart at the foot of my bed. 'Nothing yet?'

'I don't think so,' I say.

'Try to keep mobile, go for a walk, keep moving, that should get things started,' she smiles, moves to the next bed.

Nothing matters, not Faith, not Dom, not the exhibition.

I have one single task: to keep you alive, make sure you get out, safely.

My mouth is foul. I'm sticky under my arms and from between my legs comes the smell of old anchovies.

I would like to shower, wash my hair, clean my teeth.

Climbing Everest might be easier.

I get up, walk gingerly to the bathroom. There's a ring of scum round the tub from the last person. I'm not supposed to have a bath, risk of infection now the fluid has gone.

The shower is awkward, a gush of water which is too cold, then too hot. I fiddle until I've adjusted the temperature. It is an effort, a difficult, complex task; but once achieved, I stand beneath the flow, soak my hair, ease the ache in my back. I rub shampoo into my hair, soap under my arms. I'm careful between my legs. Nothing must go up there; I trust gravity and the flow of water will see to that.

I dry myself with the towel Monique reminded me to pack, then I put on clean knickers and my favourite T-shirt; the one with the steaming cup of coffee and the word r e g u l a r stretched across the bulge.

You've gone still. You haven't moved today. I know you're alive, I must believe that. If you don't come out today, they will get you out.

I climb back into my hospital bed and think about yesterday. I think I must have dreamt it, Faith turning up; it was one of my vivid dreams. Then I remember her tears. Real tears. How they must have stung, burned her eyes, her cheeks. Burning salt water, drained away for good, easing the pressure behind her eyes, a small space to relax in. I think of Faith, falling into bed in Edward's spare room, exhausted from illness, from the journey and the unfamiliar setting of The Museum of Contemporary Art, but most of all from the effort of her tears. She will have slept a deep sleep. She may have had dreams of things she'd rather not see, but she will wake, safe in Edward's house, refreshed, the stinging in her eyes will have eased.

I hope.

She was probably in bed, asleep as I made my journey back to London with Hal.

'For Chrissake, Maddie, there are hospitals in Liverpool,' Hal was not happy. I insisted.

'I need Monique,' I said. 'I want Dom.' If Hal wouldn't come with me, I would go alone.

I called Monique.

'Are you having contractions?' she said.

'Nothing, just leaking,' I said. Hal squirmed. Jude provided pads, which I had to keep changing. Monique said that if I was sure there were no contractions, and if I had someone with me, and if there was a train soon, then to go ahead.

'Better you're where you want to be than fretting in some strange place,' she said. I wanted to kiss her. She said I was to call her as the train approached London; if I was having contractions I was to get to the hospital and she would meet me there, otherwise to go home.

We were just past Rugby, less than an hour to London, when the train stopped in the middle of nowhere. There was no announcement. Hal was beside himself, I could see, though he tried not to show it. The only person we saw was the man who collects the rubbish, up and down the train with his black bin liner. He wore a badge that said: Brian.

'Excuse me, Brian,' said Hal. 'This woman is having a baby, can we know what is going on?'

'You'll have to ask the guard. I collect the rubbish.'

'Where is the guard?' I thought there was going to be a scene.

A voice came through the speakers: We apologise for the delay, this is due to trespassers on the line.

That's me, I thought: Trespasser On The Line. The line I drew without stopping, one continuous contour with a 2H pencil; the lines and lines of Faith's knitting, row upon neat row, unravelled by me; the line I painted around the shadow of Frank. Trespasser. I've broken through the line, filled in the texture, made volume where there was only line.

'Don't get hysterical,' said Hal.

'I have to call Dom,' I said.

'Go ahead.'

'I can't.'

'Want me to do it?'

'No, I'll do it. Can you get it for me?'

Hal reached up to the luggage rack, took down the bag with the phone. The train started to move again. It was nine o'clock and I thought of Dom sitting down to watch the news with Tessa. Why? I don't know if he sits down to watch the news with Tessa. He might be working late in his office at college. He might be anywhere.

What I got was the voice-mail. I said: It's happening. I'm on the train with Hal, we'll be in London in an hour.

At Euston station I felt the same, no pain, just the dampness between my legs. We took a taxi to the house. All the time I was listening for the mobile, willing Dom to find my message. I went straight to the answer machine at the house. Nothing.

'Call him again,' said Hal, I did. The voice-mail, again.

When Monique arrived she palpated my belly. She looked worried, didn't say anything for a while.

'You've felt nothing?' she asked again. 'No twinges, no back pain?'

'Nothing much.'

The leaking had stopped by then.

She felt again, round and round, pressing down on the top of the mound, then hands pressing in my groin.

'Now, don't panic,' she said. 'But I want to take you in.'

'There's something wrong isn't there?'

'No. But I think the baby may be in breech position.'

'Breech?'

She had a hand either side of my belly, pressed deep into my pelvis.

'I thought you said the head was well down.'

'Feels like a bottom to me. No fluid in there now, things feel different. I want the doctor to see you. If I'm wrong, you can come home, we'll give you another day to get going. Better take your bag, just in case.'

At the maternity unit they confirmed what Monique had suspected.

'Breech presentation,' said the doctor and sent me up here to the ante-natal ward.

Today, you haven't moved. I think this is because your pool is empty. There's nothing left for you to swim in, no room to move. I feel as if we've lost touch. I'm not getting your messages. These last few weeks I've grown used to our talk on the internal phone, pulsing along the underwater cable, sensational messages; your heel on my bowel, your hips in mine.

Have I said too much?

Did you swim the wrong way, up towards my voice? One more somersault; head first, down you go, it will be easier to swim out than to walk.

Monique says I mustn't worry: 'Relax, gravity will do most of it if you let it,' she said. She will be in later today. She will be at the birth, I think.

I will walk, pace, squat, do what I can to help gravity.

You won't turn now, will you? There's nothing left for you to swim in. Perhaps you have gone quiet as you work out how to reach with your foot, stretch your legs. I think about my dream of the hand waving from the velvet pouch and wonder now if it was a foot.

One small step. Step into the story, into your history.

Maybe I'm not meant to be a mother. I go cold, to think that after all this, I could lose you. I might never meet you, never find out who you are. I try to think what you might look like. If I saw you in a crowd would I know you? I know you as a pulsing eight-week blob and waving in your watery pouch with your camellia-bud hands bouncing off your nose. To think I might never see you, might never know you on dry land.

'Nothing doing still?' says the young nurse, cheerful. 'Come and get something to eat.'

The trolley is at the end of the ward. We slow-moving, lumbering creatures form a queue. We don't speak, all turned inwards, waiting. There is no space for conversation. I am hungry; I can still eat; I will keep up my strength.

The metal trolley has compartments, it's like queuing for school dinners. I would like treacle sponge and custard, but they don't have it. What they have is baked potato with cheese and salad, or lamb chop, which is mainly bone, with mash and peas.

'Baked potato, please,' I say.

As I reach to take the plate, someone tightens a hot metal belt around my middle. The shock, the pain is indescribable. I am caught, motionless. There is my outstretched arm, plate in my hand, stuck in mid-air, frozen in the moment of pain. Why am I holding a plate with a potato on it?

'Got a twinge?' says the woman serving the food.

Twinge?

Torture. It has come from nowhere.

'Shall I take that?' she says, reaching for the plate. 'You better sit down.' As she speaks the pain subsides; the relief, the lack of pain now, is so immense, I must have imagined it. I'm twice as hungry.

'I'll have some cheese on my potato,' I say, as if nothing had happened.

I take up my place with the other silent, lumbering women

at the table in the dayroom. I cut into the potato, mash the melting cheese and scoop a forkful towards my mouth. There it is again. I gasp, an audible gasp, drop the fork. The others look up. A woman in a candlewick dressing-gown says: 'Shall I get the nurse?'

'I need the toilet,' I say.

I sit down in the cubicle, the pain eases but I don't like what I see; a blackish green mud oozing from me.

From you.

The woman in candlewick must have called the nurse; a voice says: 'Are you all right in there?'

'No,' I say. 'Will it be all right? I think it's dead.' I tell her what I have seen.

'Straight down to the labour ward,' she says. 'Can you walk?'

'I think so. Is it dead?'

'No, no. Come on, don't fret,' she doesn't want to be the one to tell me. She wants me out of here.

As we leave the ante-natal ward, a familiar, lean figure strides along the corridor.

'Dom,' I say out loud.

'Who's that?' says the nurse.

'The father,' I say.

'She's going to the labour ward, you coming?'

'The anaesthetist is on his way,' says Monique.

The hot metal band around my middle burns hotter and tighter, there is no space between tugs. I could blow a globe of glass the size of the earth more easily than endure another second of this.

I howl.

'Come on, Maddie,' says Dom. He rubs my back but I can't bear to be touched.

'Don't. Don't.'

I could stand with my face at the furnace and not flinch.

Dom and Monique seem familiar enough, but they are somewhere else. It is an illusion that they are in the room with me.

'Hold on, Maddie, you'll feel easier with the epidural in,' she says. 'We need to get this baby born.'

* * *

What I feel is nothing. My legs are heavy. Nothing. I know they are there, and yet they might not be. They are of no use to me. As my body numbs, my mind comes back into the room. I can speak now, quite rational sentences.

'How did you manage . . . can you stay . . .' I say to Dom.

'Not now, it's all right,' he says.

'Time to push,' says Monique.

'I can't, I don't know how. When? I can't feel.'

'When I say push, you push.'

'I'll try.'

'Push.'

I give my brain the message, push, I say, go on, push, but I can't feel if it has been received. I do my best.

'Again.'

Again, I tell my brain what to do.

Monique looks up from between my legs to the monitor screen. She looks serious. She asks the student midwife to call the registrar.

'What's the matter, it's dead isn't it, why won't you tell me?'

'Calm down.'

'I've killed her.'

It's a fairground ride; the corridor whizzes past in a blur, the clang of metal and I'm in a lift, but I can't tell if I'm going up or down.

A room. A bright light. Strange people all wearing the same green; they have no mouths, only eyes. Some eyes I know. Monique's, Dom's. A pair of strange eyes is at my shoulder. Speaking close to my ear, tapping me with a rubber hammer. Can I feel that? No. Can I feel that, and that? No.

There is a cloth draped across me, a curtain that might open. At any moment the play will begin. On the other side of the curtain, a sensation across my belly, a tickle. Someone is rearranging my insides. A squelch that sounds as if a stone is being dragged out of mud.

A cry, hesitant at first.

'You were right,' says Dom. 'A girl.'

A hot, pink bundle, white waxy head; eyes tight shut. Legs tucked up like a frog.

The cry is strong, clear now.

Not a stranger or a blank. Her face is so utterly distinct. It is both new to me, and yet, at the same time, a face I have seen before. A face I know well.

I know you.

Stronger, more insistent, she asks: Where am I? What am I doing here in this dry, bright place? Who are you?

Monique brings her close to my face, eases her into my side, her mouth is reaching, eager to suck her way into the story.

'Just for a moment,' says Monique, 'then we must clean you up.'

She hands this hot, pink bundle to Dom.

'Please,' I say. I don't want to let her out of my sight. Ever.

'It's all right,' says Monique. 'She's quite safe, she's with her dad.'

As they wheel me away, I hold on to the sound.

A voice. A sound that is strong, clear, distinct.

Family Album

It was snapped in an instant, no thought to composition, a moment caught, not posed. The angle is slightly skewed.

The woman bends down, smiling at the little girl who wears a stripy sweater, all the colours of the rainbow. The girl has thrown off the matching hat, her head a mass of dark curls. She grins, proud of her antics, runs towards the woman's outstretched arms.

It's a bright day, but chilly; the older woman wears a thick sweater, a wool skirt, her hair is up in a bun. Neither the woman nor the toddler looks at the camera; their eyes are locked in each other's beam.

They are outside, in front of a stone cottage; the Virginia creeper is turning a reddish gold.

On the back it says: Stella, aged twenty months.

Stella will look at this photograph as she gets older, and all the other photographs taken since the day she was born. She will remember the older woman, her grandmother, as a kind person who knitted colourful sweaters, baked cakes and lived in a cottage by a bluebell wood.

In time Stella might be curious about the work her mother made; things to replace the missing photographs, the personal effects, the belongings, never handed on. Then again, she might not.

Acknowledgements

I would like to thank Tom Dearden for allowing me access to material in his archive and for sharing his knowledge of industrially produced pressed glass; Sara Bowler for sharing her knowledge of glass history and glassblowing; Steven Newell for talking me through the glassblowing process and for giving me access to his workshop. The mistakes are all mine.

The works of art in this book are fictitious but the work of several contemporary artists allowed me to imagine them, in particular: Caroline Broadhead, Howard Hodgkin, Anish Kapoor, Cornelia Parker, Deborah Thomas.

Warm thanks also to Amanda Dalton, Jane Kirwan, Anatol Orient, Victoria Pomery, Mary Stacey and Frankie Wynne for perceptive comments on various drafts; to Lisa Eveleigh for her commitment; to David, Jacob and Isabelle for their love and patience.